BOOKS BY GERALD KERSH

Sergeant Nelson of the Guards
The Dead Look On
The Horrible Dummy and Other Stories
Brain and Ten Fingers
Faces in a Dusty Picture
An Ape, a Dog and a Serpent
The Weak and the Strong
Neither Man Nor Dog
Clean, Bright and Slightly Oiled
I Got References
Night and the City
Sad Road to the Sea
Prelude to a Certain Midnight
The Song of the Flea
Men Are So Ardent
The Clock without Hands
The Thousand Deaths of Mr. Small
The Brazen Bull
Secret Masters
The Brighton Monster
Guttersnipe
Men without Bones and Other Stories

Gerald Kersh

FOWLERS END

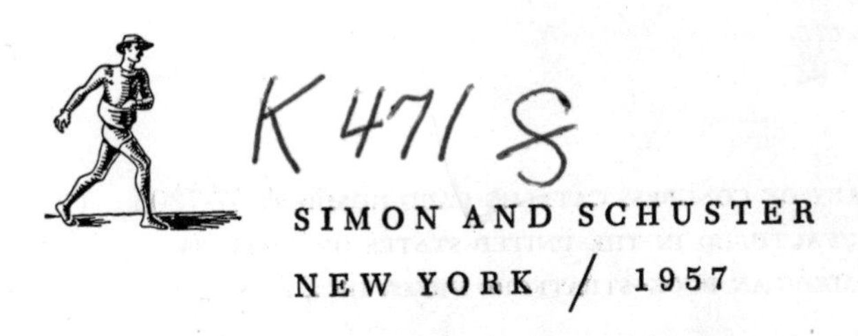

SIMON AND SCHUSTER
NEW YORK / 1957

PUBLISHED BY SIMON AND SCHUSTER, INC.
ROCKEFELLER CENTER, 630 FIFTH AVENUE
NEW YORK 20, N. Y.

FIRST PRINTING

LIBRARY OF CONGRESS CATALOG CARD NUMBER: 57-7305
MANUFACTURED IN THE UNITED STATES OF AMERICA
BY AMERICAN BOOK–STRATFORD PRESS, INC., N. Y.

Fowlers End is a place in (or, from another point of view, a spot on) modern London. It is a bustling, squalid, ramshackle community where bathtubs are considered effete, where the normal denizen would steal the milk out of his grandmother's tea.

To this wildly debased neighborhood (even the dogs look dishonest) comes Daniel Laverock, a strong, proud, awesomely ugly young man in search of employment. Thanks to his horrifying countenance, which conceals the softest of hearts, young Laverock wins a job as manager of a movie house called the Pantheon. It is a flea bag, a vile retreat for predatory children, a place where thugs relax between felonies. Its owner, Sam Yudenow, is a sort of philosopher. When one of his patrons tries to steal a light bulb from the ladies' lounge and is electrocuted Sam observes, "Well, that's show biz."

At first Laverock is dazzled by Sam—by his splendidly garbled speech, his flawless depravity, his complete emancipation from decent instincts. Sam is so perfectly, so irredeemably hateful that Laverock rather enjoys him. But not for long. Indeed, Laverock becomes a leader among the Sam-haters, a dedicated group that includes Copper Baldwin, the sardonic operator of the movie projector; Miss Noel, the bibulous lady who supplies piano accompaniment for the silent films; Kyra Costas, a fierce girl who is seduced by proxy; and Mr. Godbolt, a pious though thieving man who runs the general-goods store across the street from the movie.

The Get Yudenow movement hatches a series of plots and subplots, culminating in a sidewalk *Walpurgisnacht* too horrendous to describe here.

In short, *Fowlers End* is Hogarthian, Dickensian, *Beggar's Opera*ish—a book awaiting readers with a taste for characters and atmosphere as ripe as Liederkranz and writing as good as any they'll remember.

GLOSSARY OF COCKNEY RHYMING AND REVERSE SLANG, AND SOME COLLOQUIALISMS

Arf a tick: *Wait a bit*
Auntie Nelly: *Belly (Cockney rhyming slang)*
Bags of: *Plenty of; lots of*
Ball-of-Chalk: *Walk (Cockney rhyming slang)*
On the bash: *Dissolute life; primrose path; street-walking, etc.*
Bees-and-Honey: *Money (Cockney rhyming slang)*
Berk, or Berkeley Hunt: *Sucker; fool (Cockney rhyming slang)*
Billingsgate: *Gigantic wholesale fish market, traditional for violent invective*
Bob: *Shilling—silver coin worth about 14¢ currently, 25¢ in the 1930s*
Bobby: *Uniformed policeman;* see *"Bogies"*
Bog: *Lavatory*
Bogies: *Uniformed policemen; "bobbies"*
Bolo: *Off-angle; untidy*
Brassy: *Impudent; "fresh"*
Bread-and-Lard: *Hard (Cockney rhyming slang)*
Bucket-and-Pail: *Jail (Cockney rhyming slang)*
Bugger off: *Go away; scram*
Bullocked, or Bullock's Horned: *Pawned (Cockney rhyming slang)*
Bunce: *Perquisites; "gravy" or "schmalz"*
Busies: *Plainclothes policemen; detectives*
Cadge: *Borrow; promote; bum*
Carsey: *Lavatory*
Chancer: *One who "chances his arm"—i.e., a vain taker of impudent risks*
Charing Cross: *Horse (Cockney rhyming slang)*
China plate: *Mate (Cockney rhyming slang)*
Chit: *Bill; accounting; I.O.U.*

Chivvy, or Chevy Chase: *Face (Cockney rhyming slang)*
Cinema: *Moving-picture theater*
Cocko: *Buddy; male term of address*
Come the old soldier: *Be a chancer and malingerer at the same time; lie and shirk; "gold brick"*
Cop: *Grab; snatch; pilfer*
Cosh: *Blackjack*
Cruncheon: See *"Truncheon"*
Cuif: *Hair curl on or over a man's forehead*
Cuppa: *Cup of tea*

Daisies, or Daisy Roots: *Boots; shoes (Cockney rhyming slang)*
Damager: *Manager (Cockney reverse slang)*
Dekko: *Look; glance*
Ding-dong: *Song (Cockney rhyming slang)*
Doolally: *Balmy; crazy*
Do a flit: *Skip without paying room rent*
To do: *Flim-flam; con; cheat; frame; fight*
Drop o' short: *A short measure of spirits (Cockney slang)*
Duke-of-York: *Fork; hand (Cockney rhyming slang)*

Faggot: *Working man's rissole of chopped odds and ends*
Farthing: *Copper coin equal to ¼ British penny, currently worth ¼¢, ½¢ in 1930s*
Fascia: *Signboard above shop front*
Five-to-two: *Jew (Cockney rhyming slang)*
Flex: *Telephone cord*
A float: *Small change to transact day's business*
Flob your gob: *Vomit*
Flog: *Peddle; pawn; sell*
To fluff: *Catch on; get the idea*
F.L., or French letter: *Latex contraceptive*

Gaff: *Show; theater*
Gee up: *Encourage; egg on*
Get a wire on: *Receive an anonymous tip*
Graft: *Honest toil; i.e., a hard day's graft is a hard day's work*

Guinea: *Coin now out of circulation but still quoted in prices; equal to one pound, one shilling, or 21 shillings; worth $2.94 currently; $5.25 in 1930s*

Half crown: *Silver coin equal to two shillings, sixpence; worth 33¢ currently; 63¢ in 1930s*

Half-inch: *Pinch (Cockney rhyming slang)—i.e., filch; steal*

Hearts-of-oak: *Broke (Cockney rhyming slang)*

Heavens above: *Love (Cockney rhyming slang)*

Irish Rose: *Nose (Cockney rhyming slang)*

Jordan: *Chamberpot*

Johnny Horner: *Corner (Cockney rhyming slang)*

Johnny Rann: *Scran (Cockney rhyming slang)—i.e., food*

Joss paper: *Incense*

Jumper: *Sweater*

Keyster: *Suitcase; traveling bag*

Kip: *Bed; sleep—i.e., "cop a nip" is grab a nap*

Lark: *High jinks; frolic*

A lay: *Scheme; trick; plot*

Layabout: *Good-for-nothing; lazy bum*

Little Bo-Peep: *Sleep (Cockney rhyming slang)*

Loaf-of-Bread: *Head (Cockney rhyming slang)*

Lord-of-the-Manor: *Tanner (Cockney rhyming slang)—i.e., sixpence*

Love-in-a-Punt: *Beer (Cockney rhyming slang)*

To madam: *Hand out nonsense—i.e., "don't madam me" is "don't give me any stuff"*

Martin's-le-Grand: *Hand (Cockney rhyming slang)*

Mickey: *Spirit—i.e., "take the mickey out" is "cut down a peg"; "take the starch out"*

Milkman's horse: *Cross (Cockney rhyming slang)*

Mince pies: *Eyes (Cockney rhyming slang)*

Mincing machine: *Food chopper*

Mob-handed: *Rabble; in a mob*

Monkey-nuts: *Peanuts*

Multiple shops: *Chain stores—i.e., "Multiple chemists" is chain drugstores*

Nark: *Informer; stool pigeon*

Never-never: *Installment plan purchasing—i.e., "Never-never" can you finish paying*

Nicker: *Pounds sterling*—see *"Quid" and "Sovereign"*

Niff: *Odor*

Nipper: *Child*

Nip out: *Rush*

North-and-South: *Mouth (Cockney rhyming slang)*

Oliver Twist: *Fist (Cockney rhyming slang)*

Paisley Disaster: *Historic holocaust in movie theater where many children perished*

Take a pen'orth, or take a pennyworth: *Take a ride—i.e., go away; scram*

Pig's ear: *Beer (Cockney rhyming slang)*

Pong: *Unpleasant physical odor; "B.O."*

Put a sock in: *Stop; lay off; quit*

Pinch: *Pilfer; steal*

Plates-of-meat: *Feet (Cockney rhyming slang)*

Plong: *Sell stolen stuff; push "hot" goods*

Pope-of-Rome: *Home (Cockney rhyming slang)*

Poste Restante: *P.O. box*

Pot-and-Pan: *Man (Cockney rhyming slang)*

Potato crisps: *Potato chips*

Quid: *Pounds sterling—a pound being worth about $2.80 currently; $5 in the 1930s;* also see *"Nicker" and "Sovereign"*

Randy: *Round*

Raspberry tart: *Heart (Cockney rhyming slang)*

Rissole: *Rice-filled hamburger*

Rolling billows: *Pillows (Cockney rhyming slang)*

Rorty: *Quarrelsome; ferocious*

Rosie Lee: *Cup of tea (Cockney rhyming slang)*

Roundabouts: *Carousel; merry-go-round*

Scrounge: *Promote; borrow*

Shoot the Moon: *Skip without paying room rent*

Skilly: *Oatmeal and water; weak gruel*

Skiver: *Someone who avoids duty*
Skivvy: *Contemptuous term for domestic servant*
Skyrocket: *Pocket (Cockney rhyming slang)*
Smashing: *Wonderful; marvelous*
Snob: *Shoe mender; cobbler*
Sod: *Term of abuse*
Sovereign: *Gold coin withdrawn from circulation and worth a pound;* see *"Quid" and "Nicker"*
Smithfield: *Gigantic wholesale meat market and traditional source for reverse slang*
Spit-and-polish: *Immaculate dress (from military)*
Up the spout: *Up the flue; bankrupt*
Strike-me-dead: *Bread (Cockney rhyming slang)*
Stone: *Measure of weight, equals 14 lbs.*

Tanner: *Silver coin equal to ½ shilling; worth 7¢ currently; 12½¢ in 1930s*
Tea-leaf: *Thief (Cockney rhyming slang)*
Ting-a-ling: *Money; change*
Titfer, or Tit-for-Tat: *Hat (Cockney rhyming slang)*
Tosheroon: *Half-crown*
Tosser: *Any small coin*
Tram; tramcar: *Trolley*
Tramline: *Trolley tracks*
Try it on: *To con; gyp*
Turn: *Vaudeville act; vaudeville actors*
Twicer: *Double-crosser*
Twot: *Term of abuse for the female*
Truncheon: *Nightstick of British cop*

Uncle Ned: *Bed (Cockney rhyming slang)*
Upsy-down: *Upside down*

Variety: *Vaudeville*

Wallop: *Beer*
To wallop: *Sell under the counter; shove stolen stuff*
Weskit: *Waistcoat*
Wide: *Slick; smart; clever in illicit deals; derived from "wide awake"*

Wilkie Bard: *Card (Cockney rhyming slang)*
Woodbines: *Brand of cigarettes sold in packets of five*
Yet-to-be: *Free (Cockney rhyming slang)*
Yobs; Yobbos: *Boys (Cockney reverse slang)*

FOWLERS

END

1

SNORING FOR AIR while he sipped and gulped at himself, talking between hastily swallowed mouthfuls of himself, fidgeting with a little blue bottle and a red rubber nose-dropper, Mr. Yudenow said to me, "Who you are, what you are, I duddo. But I like your style, what I bead to say—the way you wet about applyig for this 'ere job. *Dish*ertive, *dish*ertive—if you get what I bead—*dish*-ertive is what we wat id show biz. Arf a tick, please—I got to take by drops."

He filled the dropper with some pale oily fluid, threw back his head and sniffed; became mauve in the face, gagged, choked; blew into a big silk handkerchief, and then continued, sighing with relief, "Wonderful stuff. It's deadly poison. But it loosens the head." He showed me the contents of his handkerchief, which might have been brains. "Confidentially, catarrh. Yes. I like the way you went about applying for this 'ere job. Millions of people would give their right 'and to manage one of Sam Yude-now's shows—the cream of the biz, the top of the milk! So?"

"Well," I said, "I saw your ad—"

"That's right, *ad*. Not advertisement. Ad. Like Biz, like Pix, like Lites. Good."

"I saw your ad, and it said at the end, 'Apply Sam Yudenow the Pantheon Fowlers End.' I thought to myself, there can't be many Sam Yudenows in the phone book, so I rang you at your private address."

"You said Joe told you to ring. What Joe? Big Joe or Little Joe?"

"Any Joe you like," I said. "Everybody's got some friend called Joe."

"I like imagination," said Sam Yudenow. "In show biz it's amperative. How much d'you weigh?"

"About fourteen stone seven, stripped."

"That's all right. You won't have time to strip. It's just about the right weight for a manager of the Pantheon. How d'you like the name Pantheon? I made it up."

"Greek?" I suggested.

"It's Greek for *kinema*. You can read an' write okay?"

"I think so."

"You need edyacation in show biz. You'd be surprised the idears you pick up reading. Only don't put on no airs. You'd be surprised what they'd do to you rahnd Fowlers End if you put on airs. When I first went into show biz I used to say 'please' 'ere and 'thank you' there—they soon knocked *that* out o' me. You got to adopt yourself, like me. Fowlers End ain't Park Lane—not quite. Me, when I'm in Buckingham Palace I talk like Buckingham Palace. But rahnd Fowlers End you got to talk like one o' the right yobbos. . . . Can you use your 'ands?"

"Box a little," I said.

"You won't need to—don't worry about that. They don't understand that stuff rahnd Fowlers End. If somebody gets rorty and buggers up the show, so come up be'ind 'im like a gentleman; put a stranglehold on 'is thvoat miv the left arm, pick 'im up by the arse from 'is trousers miv the right 'and, and chunk 'im into the Alley—one, two, three!—in peace and quiet. My last manager but two got punch-drunk, kind o' thing, and lost 'is nerve—tried to clean up the Fowlers End Health and Superman League miv a fire bucket, and *I* was the sufferer. Keep order, yes, but leave no marks. I want my managers should be diplomats. Look at Goldwyn, look at Katz. Odeons they started miv nickels, not knuckles, and you should live to see your children in such a nice position like they got. Remember, the Pantheon don't cater for royalty, and Fowlers End ain't Bond Street—not just yet it ain't.

"In the first place, everybody's unemployed—which is the opium of the people rahnd here. The rest, so they work in factories—which is the scum. Rahnd the corner is the Fowlers End Pipe Factory. They make gas pipes, water pipes—d'you foller? Well, all these loafers do, instead of making pipes, they make coshes: so they'll get a foot of gas pipe and fill it up with lead. One of them threatens you, don't call the police to give the show a bad name. This is a family theater. Warn him. If he 'its you to leave a mark, then the law's on your side. Put the left 'and rahnd his thvoat, the right 'and in the arse of his trousers, and chunk 'im out. And don't give 'im his money back. That is the opium of the working classes. Stand no nonsense if you want to be a showman. . . . Whereas, there's a mob kids from school, so there's a new idear they got. So they get a great big potato and stick it all over miv old razor blades; a bit of string they tie it onto, and right in the face they let you 'ave it. Discourage 'em. Threaten to tell their teacher. Lay one finger on 'em and the N.S.P.C.C. is after us for cruelty to children—and *I'm* the sufferer. . . . It's nothing; like a lion-tamer, just be cool and nobody'll 'urt you. Remember, this ain't the New Gallery in Regent Street, not already, almost. . . . You got a watch?"

"It's being mended," I said, having pawned it to get my last respectable suit from the cleaners. With the change I had bought two tenpenny cigars with gold labels, one of which I now offered to Mr. Yudenow, who, rolling it between his fingers and listening to it, said, "It creckles. That's the sign of a good cigar. That's another thing you should learn—you don't *taste* a good cigar; you *hear* it. . . . Zize saying—d'you foller me?—don't carry a good watch. Get two or three in Cherring Cross Road for a couple bob apiece—not to tell the time miv, but to give the babies to listen to when they start crying and buggering up the show. On a chain, better—I got sued once when some kid swallered one of my managers' watch. Miv celluloid, not glass—the little bastards bite —they cut their mouf, and *I'm* the sufferer. . . . You got diamond rings? Diamond rings you got?"

"Not many, I'm afraid."

"Take my advice, don't wear 'em. You cut somebody's face making peace and quiet, and *I'm* the sufferer. Anyway, it's a temptation. This ain't the Opera House, I think you ought to know. One of my managers flashed a ring once, and the yobbos from the pipe factory nearly took it off him. Would have done too, only his finger was too fat. They was 'alfway through the finger miv a 'acksaw blade when 'is screams roused the neighborhood . . . and I don't mind telling you it takes some screaming to rouse this 'ere neighborhood. Why, rahnd in Godbolt Alley—read about it in the papers?—they put up a new block of working men's flats miv barfrooms. A Greek barber called Pappas cut up his girl friend in the barf, and put the pieces in a crate. Didn't have the common savvy to gag her first. Nobody paid any attention. Little tiff, they thought. 'Come Up and Saw Me Sometime' they called 'im later. That's the class of people they are, rahnd Fowlers End. Give 'em a barf and that's all they know to do miv it. I don't mind warning you that, of all the people, these are the out-and-out opium.

"Thieves and drunkards. They'd steal the rings from under their mothers' eyes. The milk out of your tea they'd pinch. Last time I had the painters in, my worst enemies shouldn't go through what I went through with these stinkpots. Day and night I watched this 'ere show, and even so the lousebound lowlifes knocked off a five-gallon drum walnut varnish stain. Drunk it up, the swine. One old woman died from it. It only goes to show you what they are—a lot of rotters. The salt of the earth, mind you, only bad to the backbone. Turn your back five minutes and they strip the place to the bone. You got to keep on the toes of your feet. Only last week there was trouble in the laventry. A woman stands up on the wet seat to pinch the electric light bulb and electrocutes herself. That's show biz for you. You got to keep your eye out for things like that. It's not their fault. It's the capitalistic system—too soft with the bastards. Unions! The velvet 'and in the iron glove I'd give 'em, miv knobs on. So the way it is nowadays a carpenter won't pick up a paintbrush, an electrician won't pick up a gas pipe, a plasterer won't pick up a 'ammer. . . . And there's something else. Authority! Stand no nonsense from workmen. Give an order and it should be obeyed —one, two, three! If not, the left arm in the thvoat, the right 'and in the arse of the trousers, and 'Good day to you!' You'll get experience 'ere, I can tell you that. Believe me, I been in show biz twenty-five years, and you'd be surprised what a good showman can do miv a screwdriver and a bit of elbow grease in a place like this. 'Do It Yourself' is the motto by me. It comes natural after a bit. And always remember this: your audience is like yourself. Who's your best friend? Yourself. Who's your worst enemy? Yourself. Who've you got to blame always? Yourself. Treat them as such. What are they, after all? The salt of the earth, the toe-rags!

"I found this place a dump, and I turned it into a little paradise," said Sam Yudenow, with emotion. "The first pitcher I showed 'ere was called *The Covered Wagon.* Ever see it? I'd revive it if I could get a copy that wasn't all scratched up to bloody buggery—make a few streamers like LATEST!!!, THRILLING!!!!—and show it again. Remember? It's about the Pilgrim fathers, so they emigrate to America in a covered wagon. What do they see? A crap heap full o' cowboys and Indians. But are they downhearted? No! Miv a packet seeds and a shovel, up comes a gold mine in California. A proud hetirage. That's how I felt when I opened the Pantheon. I cried miv joy. That's how I want you should feel—like a covered wagon Friday and Saturday night miv the wild Indians. Peace and quiet in the wilds; the takings put away, all Sunday to yourself. The County Council, the bastards, they won't allow Sunday opening. . . . Yes, everyone in the biz knows Sam Yudenow, and there's men fifty years' experience in the trade would *pay* me to work for me. Only one thing I ask: if you got the idear in your 'ead that Fowlers End is Mayfair, get it out again. Because, confidentially between us, it's nothing of the kind.

"But come and look at the 'all."

There is a psychologists' variation of the game of hide-and-seek: someone conceals a small object in a large room, and you have to find it. You do this by linking arms with the other man and walking as it were casually round and round with him. As you get closer and closer to the concealed object the man who has hidden it, by subconscious muscular contraction, will tend to pull you away. You concentrate your search, therefore, where the pull-away is strongest. In a manner of speaking, this is how you find Fowlers End—by going northward, step by step, into the neighborhoods that most strongly repel you. The compass of your revulsion may flicker for a moment at the end of the Tottenham Court Road, especially on a rainy March morning. You know that to your right the Euston Road rolls away, filthy and desolate, blasted by the sulphurous grit that falls forever in a poisonous shower from the stations of Euston and St. Pancras. Take this road, and you find yourself in a hell of flop-houses, mephitic furnished apartments, French-letter shops, hopeless pubs, and sticky coffee shops. Here, turn where you like, there is an odor of desolation, of coming and going by night. On the left-hand side of this heartbreaking thoroughfare, the foxholes, rat traps, and labyrinthine ways of Somers Town beyond which the streets run like worm holes in a great chase northward again to Camden Town. But you know that if you cross the street you will wander forever in the no man's land that lies between here and the God-forgotten purlieus of Regent Square and the Gray's Inn Road.

Even so, since morbid curiosity encourages you to go on, you reason: *No. There is a catch in this somewhere. Here are rag-and-bone shops, junk shops, houses of penance for unmarried women. Something worth looking at.* So you go back. The left-hand branch of the crossroads leads past Warren Street toward the Marylebone Road in which there are clinics, blind blocks of flats, a Poor Law institution, a town hall, and whatnot. To your left, off the Marylebone Road, the Borough of Marylebone, full of whispering mews and streets of houses that were jerry-built in the eighteenth century and won't fall down—a place of mysterious back-doubles, redolent of drains and of human interest in general. *That won't do, either*, you say to yourself. *There is Hope here. The city is trying to nudge me away from my objective.* Say you don't go as far? You may turn into Albany Street, where the barracks are; and Albany Street leads to the monotonous Outer Circle of Regents Park, where a short walk will take you, again, to Camden Town.

At this you feel a slight repellent urge in your elbow, and know that you are "getting hotter." Why, then, since right-and-left and left-and-right both lead to Camden Town, so must the middle way, which is the Hampstead Road. Here the city becomes urgent in its discouragement. It says: *Don't waste your time—there's nothing here for you, nothing at all, nothing for anybody. I don't say it's bad, mind you. Only I put it to you that you ignore it. It leads to a kind of nowhere, in the long run. Come and have a look at the disused graveyard near Aybrook Street?* But now, having got the hang of this little game of reverse-compulsion, you go right on, straight ahead, past the hotels for men only, past the secondhand box-mattress shops, and the bituminous hole-in-the-wall where a man and his wife, black as demons, sell coal and coke by the pound, until you arrive at the tobacco factory at Mornington Crescent which used to be a Dream Factory because it was constructed in imitation of an ancient Egyptian temple. Here, two colossal plaster cats brood over the mouse-nibbled and rat-gnawed squares off Great College Street, which leads via the observation wards of the lunatic asylums back to Somers Town and Euston again. Between lies a hinterland of working men's colleges, railway clearing houses, infirmaries, the Working Women's Hospital, the Urino-Genital Hospital (better known as the Junior Sportsmen's Club), a group of secondhand florists who make up cheap wreaths and crosses, and—between cafés—secondhand clothes shops where old women who mutter behind their hands sell for beer money the night dresses their neighbors have saved to be buried in.

And this will never do, because it leads toward an awareness of life and death, may interest you in something. Even in the thrice-discarded detritus of the lowest of the low hereabout, the most discouraged imagination may find something to peck up and thrive on. On the other hand, behind the cigarette factory lurk those who wait in darkness—men who whistle after girls, and prowl Primrose Hill and Haverstock Hill in furtive groups. They believe that tobacco dust inflames the pudenda of the cigarette-makers, so that all they need do is shout, ''Ello, Betsy! Are yer bowels open?' to make an amorous overture. Here again the city tries to persuade you to stop. But if you know how to interpret a squeeze and translate the flicker of a muscle—having Fowlers End in mind—you will keep your eyes on the Cobden Statue and go ahead up Camden High Street toward the Camden Road, and so to Holloway, where the jail is; and past the allurements of this enclosed space through the perpetual twilight of the Seven Sisters Road, which takes you to Tottenham, where the only attraction is the Isolation Hospital for Infectious Diseases. Do not be led astray by this; go north to Edmonton and to Ponders End. Who Ponder was and how he ended, the merciful God knows. Once upon a time it was a quagmire; now it is a swamp, biding its time. Further yet, bearing northeast, lies a graveyard of broken boilers and rusty wheels called Slabsbridge, where creatures that once were men live in abandoned railway carriages. Between Slabsbridge and Uttermost there sprawls Fowlers Folly—someone of this name tried to build a tower there in 1790. He believed that the end of the world was at hand. Some vestige of the ruin remains. Only a mile farther on, where the ground, rising, is a little drier, is Fowlers End.

Here the city gives up the game.

This is it.

Fowlers End is a special kind of tundra that supports nothing gracious in the way of flora and fauna. Plant a cabbage here in this soured, embittered, dyspeptic, ulcerated soil, and up comes a kind of bleached shillelagh with spikes on its knob. Plant a family, a respectable working-class family, and in two generations it will turn out wolves. Fowlers End is barren of everything but weeds. Even the dogs are throwbacks to their yellow-eyed predatory ancestors that slunk in the trail of the sub-men and ate filth. There is a High Street about a hundred yards long, and the most woebegone railway terminal on the face of the earth where, with a dismal and sinister smashing and groaning of shunting locomotives, all that is most unserviceable in the way of rolling stock comes in with coal and sulphur, scrap iron and splintery timber, and goes away with the stuff they make in the Fowlers End factories.

As Sam Yudenow said, there is a steel-tube factory and a glass factory. There is a sulphuric-acid factory which looks like a Brobdingnagian assembly of alchemical apparatus out of a pulp writer's nightmare as it sprawls under a cloud of yellow and black that shudders and stings like a dying wasp between great hills of green-black and gray-mauve slag. When it rains—which it doesn't have to, because more water comes out of the ground than goes into it—some of the atmosphere comes down in a saturated solution, so that the hobnails in the soles and the iron crescents in the heels of the boots of the inhabitants are corroded in three days; and then, until they can raise the price of a re-studding job, they have nothing left to argue with but their hands and knees. The top of the War Memorial—the bronze sword of which was stolen and sold for scrap the night before it was unveiled—is already eroded, so that instead of looking like the ancient Roman gallows it resembles, rather, the old-fashioned English gibbet. Fowlers End got this monument by a bureaucratic error: only four Fowlers Enders died in the first World War, and one of these was shot for cowardice in the face of the enemy in 1916, so that, hard up for names to carve on its Roll of Honor, Fowlers End went over the Hertfordshire border three miles away and helped itself to fifty-six names out of the old graveyard at Ullage. Ever since then there has been bad blood between the people of these two places. Sometimes, generally on a Saturday night, the young men—women, too, and they are the worst of the lot—make up raiding parties and go out for mayhem and the breaking of windows. They always concentrate on the solar plexus, the seat of the soul, of each other's community—which is, of course, the local cinema. The men of Fowlers End have bankrupted five successive proprietors of the Ullage Hippodrome and sent several managers to the Bloodford Cottage Hospital with broken bones. As I was to learn shortly after I went to work in Fowlers End, the Ullage men were in arrears. They owed us two roughhouses and were biding their time.

Meanwhile the young bloods of Fowlers End were strutting, in their indescribably repulsive hangdog, drag-heeled way, in the High Street. And what a High Street it was, in my time! Except for a few clumps of rusty television antennae, I don't imagine that the place will have changed much unless some

German bomb, well placed for once, happened to fall nearby—in which case, good riddance to it! It wouldn't have taken much more than a five-hundred-pounder to make rubble of the entire High Street, which, when I last measured it when I stepped out of the Pantheon to clear my lungs with a whiff of comparatively healthful carbon monoxide and sulphuric acid after a Children's Matinée, measured exactly eighty-five long paces from Godbolts Corner to the end of the tram line where Fowlers End begins. And, bestially primitive as this cloaca of a street is, it must needs have two or three vermiform appendices, blind alleys! One of these was Godbolts, where the Pantheon stood. It was named after the real-estate magnate and general capitalist, a pious man who kept Godbolts Emporium on the other side of the street. He was a quick, hideously ugly little man, cold and viscous about the hands, with a gecko's knack of sticking to plane surfaces. Once, when I went into his shop to buy a handkerchief, Godbolt, telling me that he didn't have much call for that kind of thing nowadays but thought he had a few in stock, went to get one from a high shelf. It may have been the effect of the fog but I will swear I saw him run up the wall. He had a black-cotton fly of a wife who was always buzzing at him from a distance; she never came within less than five feet of him—for fear, presumably, that he might thrust out a glutinous green tongue and catch her. He was always watching her out of the corners of his horny-lidded, protuberant eyes. They lived, according to local report, on stale bread and margarine and tea, but I always thought that he found a source of nutriment in his mustache; otherwise, why should he be perpetually sucking it with such relish?

He owned the building in which the Pantheon was housed. It had been a church, once upon a time, built at considerable cost by the infatuated devotees of a demented tinker named John Nakedborn, who not only preached the Second Coming but more than hinted that he was It. It seems that he "married" the entire choir and then ran off to America; whereupon the sect broke up and the church stood empty until Sam Yudenow happened to pass that way. Always anxious, as he put it, "a good turn to do a feller," he was employing at that time for a pound a week a cross-eyed, clubfooted chauffeur who, sometimes, according to Sam Yudenow, "went two different diractions at once." He took his employer to Fowlers End under the impression that he was going to Chingford. There was no cinema at Fowlers End then; the nearest one was the ill-fated Hippodrome at Ullage.

Sam Yudenow, who was always intrigued by any vacant drill hall, barn or warehouse, however ratty, was fascinated by the naked, empty church: it had Gothic doors and windows and, instead of a spire, an onion-shaped dome. For the sake of that dome alone, if the building had been situated in the middle of Salisbury plain, Sam Yudenow would have been attracted to it. A dome like that who could resist? It was Class, it was Oriental, it was up-to-date. Besides, these were the days of the first cinema boom, when (if you believe the old-timers) all you had to do was find an old stable, paint it blue, call it the Majestic Picture Palace, paste up a forty-eight sheet saying *Opening Shortly*—and sell it for twenty thousand pounds.

Sam Yudenow said to his wife, "Lily—look! May you drop down dead this minute if this ain't the loveliest little site for a show you ever saw in your life! May you never live to see your children again!"

"You should live so sure," said she, looking at the place with horror.

"It's gudgeous!" cried Sam Yudenow. "Like . . . like . . . like an Indian tomb—artistic like an oil painting!" Then he sought out Mr. Godbolt and he said, "Uxcuse me, please. That place across the road, that ruin, it gives me the creeps. What is it? Why is it? What's the name o' this 'ere place? Where is it? How do I get out from 'ere? This 'ere place—*is* there such a place? I never *'eard* of it!"

"That's a church," said Mr. Godbolt.

"A church? *What* for a church? How *comes*, church? Who goes there, black men? What do you mean, church? What place *is* this, anyway?"

"This is Fowlers End, sir."

"What do you mean, Fowlers End? . . . A church, yet!"

"That's my property, sir."

"No jokes? Then I'm sorry for you," said Sam Yudenow.

"Is there anything I can do for you?" asked Mr. Godbolt from behind the counter.

"A pair braces I want. I want a pair braces. Green braces. A pair green braces I want."

"I'm sorry, sir, I have no braces in green," said Mr. Godbolt. "But I've got a lovely brace in a nice shade of mauve."

"I meant mauve. . . . 'Ow much you asking for these 'ere braces?"

"This superfine elastic brace is elevenpence ha'penny," said Mr. Godbolt.

"What, elevenpence ha'penny? What do you *mean,* elevenpence ha'penny for such braces? Miv the church thrown *in,* for elevenpence ha'penny?"

At this Mr. Godbolt looked hurt and said that this church, dome and all, was a very desirable property; to which Sam Yudenow replied, "So I dessay maybe God pays the rent praps?"

"Don't take His name in vain, if you don't mind," said Mr. Godbolt. "Fowlers End is expanding. The church would make a fine warehouse."

Sam Yudenow, who loved a play on words, said, "Warehouse for what wares where? What wares to house, and for why? Who for, warehouse? When, where? No jokes!"

Later that day he left Fowlers End, having taken a lease on the old church for ninety-nine years at eighty pounds a year. He managed to convey to Mr. Godbolt and his solicitor that he wanted to use the old church to store surplus cinema supplies.

But, loutish and obtuse as he may have been in almost every other respect, Sam Yudenow was a micrographer in contractual small print, and something of a master in the conveyancing of leases. He got away with a bargain, that day, but said to Mr. Godbolt on parting, "I'm temperamental—that's the ruination of me. What for did I *do* this, what for? Mr. Cobalt, you hyptonized me."

For a while Mr. Godbolt really believed that he had hypnotized Sam Yudenow and got the better of him. Accordingly, he conducted himself with all the condescension and magnanimity of a "good neighbor." To be a good neighbor you must feel, fundamentally, that while you are independent of the man next door, he had better not try to get along without you. The good neighbor is a kind of emotional pawnbroker, a usurer in everyday kindnesses who manages to sell you his undesirable proximity on the installment plan, and exacts a consultant's fee for every word of unsolicited advice. *Good fences make good neighbors*—nobody ever spoke a truer word. There never was a good neighbor who did not try to take some mean advantage of the newcomer to his neighborhood. It stands to reason: if your neighbor is socially your superior, you must live up to him and ruin yourself, or remain his inferior and abase yourself. Either way you must secretly hate him, belittle his success or magnify his failure. If he happens to be your equal, you will manage, if only by the weight of a snort, to tip the balance. He who has a neighbor has an enemy.

I hold no brief for Sam Yudenow, but it seems to me that Godbolt got exactly what he deserved. He and his wife rejoiced, at first, at what they thought was their victim's discomfiture. First of all, Sam Yudenow was bitten by a rat where the pulpit used to be. With ill-concealed glee, they commiserated and gave him a cup of tea. Then, when a green-and-orange truck came into the High Street and workmen started to put up ladders, they hugged themselves. Mrs. Godbolt winked at her husband with some of her several hundred eyes, while he treated himself to a double mouthful of mustache. Before long, however, Sam Yudenow was bellowing orders from the street while an army of lame, blind, and misanthropic scab laborers covered the dome with aluminum paint. Soon the whole front of the church was painted "Oriental Pink," and the door and window frames were brushed with orange and green. At night workmen labored by the light of naphtha flares. Then, on the decaying hoarding that advertised an adjacent quagmire as *A Desirable Factory Site,* appeared, in orange letters on a green ground, this slogan: CHEER UP! THE SUPER CINEMA IS COMING!

Mr. Godbolt went to Sam Yudenow and said, "I say. What's the idea, if I may ask?"

"What's what idea, what?"

"Super Cinema," said Mr. Godbolt.

"So? So what you want Sam Yudenow should open? A rabbidge hutch? A pig stile? Of course a Super Cinema, of course. What then? What you want I should edvertise? A flea-pit? Nothing but the best is good enough for Sam Yudenow."

"Now look here, I can't let these premises for a picture palace, sir."

"Read the lease."

"You said you wanted to store cinema accessories in these here premises."

"So? A few hundred seats? A couple projectors? A ticket machine? *Not* accessories? No? So if the County Council gives me a license to show a couple pictures Monday through Saturday, what's the matter, what? Read the lease, read!"

"I've been had," said Mr. Godbolt.

"The lease, read," said Sam Yudenow.

"I'll consult my solicitor, you swindler!"

"Consult your solicitor, but you can't consult me with your 'swindlers.' Read your lease; the lease, read."

So Mr. Godbolt went to see his solicitor in Edmonton, and they went over the lease clause by clause. It appeared that while the Said Samuel Yudenow had agreed not to conduct a Clay Pipe Burning Factory, a Brothel, a Tannery, a Soap Boiling Factory, a Public Slaughter House, or a Glue Boiling Factory on the Said Premises in the High Street—and much Fowlers End would have cared if he had conducted the whole lot singly or collectively—there was nothing in the lease about properly licensed places of public entertainment. The pebbled skin of Mr. Godbolt changed color, and his adhesive hands contracted, but he said nothing. Where a lion makes his kill and eats his fill, there must be pickings. A cinema must attract crowds. Where there are crowds there is a need for tobacco to smoke, sweets to suck, and tea to drink. Scuttling home, Mr. Godbolt conceived the idea of a café next door to Yudenow's cinema, the only other place of this kind being a hut near the end of the tram line where stewed tea and mysterious pies were sold to tram drivers, punch-drunk with the jolting and deafened with the clangor of the run between there and Ponders End. Mr. Godbolt had in mind a place with tables and chairs for the patrons of Yudenow's cinema. So he went to Jack Gutter, the Fowlers End butcher, and said, "Now those empty premises of yours, Mr. Gutter, just by the old church. Now what would you call a rental for them there little premises, Mr. Gutter, may I ask?"

Shuddering in the bitter draft, shivering in his grove of dangling tripes and dripping lights and calcified kidneys and purple livers—all gently swaying on their bloody hooks as it were by their own volition—the consumptive butcher poised his scarred red fists on the scarred red chopping block and said, "Well neow, Mr. Godbolt, that's not fur me to say."

"Not for you to say, Mr. Gutter? Why, that little shop's been on the market this past five year. Shop *and* upper part, I believe, Mr. Gutter. A matter of fifteen-and-six a week you were asking, wasn't you?"

"I *was*," said Gutter, playing with a pig's eyelids. He could make a pig's head appear to wink with one hand while with the other he slyly operated the muscles of its jaw so that it opened its mouth—what time he uttered, ventriloquially, an exact imitation of the squeal of the animal when it feels the knife go home. This trick amused the children and drew customers.

"Was?"

Gutter laughed in his frothy way and said, "Ah! But it's a peownd a week neow, Mr. Godbolt."

"Between neighbors, Mr. Gutter, I'll give you sixteen shillings."

"No, yeou won't, 'cause I let that thur shop and upper part this morning, Mr. Godbolt, fur a peownd a week on a twenty-yurr lease to Mr. Yudeneow. Bet he'll rush yeou half a creown extra, heh-heh-heh!"

Mr. Godbolt said, "Now I wonder, Mr. Gutter, what Mr. Yudenow would be wanting these here premises for?"

"Why," said Gutter, "that one's got some ideer of opening up just a little caffey like, it being handy fur his picture palace. Pity yeou didden call yesturdee." He split the pig's head with a cleaver, fondled the brains, and said, "Ah, Mr. Godbolt, if we knew what was inside *them*, we'd be as weise as this yur piggy, wouldn't we, Mr. Godbolt?"

"And what does Mr. Yudenow propose to do with the upper part, Mr. Gutter?"

"Ah! If I knew that I'd be as weise as Mr. Yudeneow," said Gutter.

Frustrated, Mr. Godbolt went home and said to his wife, "Mrs. Godbolt, Lord love me—"

"Keep your mouth clean in this house, Godbolt, or I'll scrub it with soap 'n' water!"

"I was saying, Mrs. Godbolt—you know that three-hundred-foot frontage lot where the signboard is? That factory site, so called? I've a good mind to buy it."

"You think yourself clever, don't you, Godbolt? Well, that man Yudenow has already bought it."

"What the devil!"

"Speak of the devil and he's sure to appear, Godbolt."

"He has. How much a foot did he pay?"

"Ten shillings."

"What is he going to do with it?" asked Mr. Godbolt.

"Something wicked, I dare say, just out of spite. Why, what were you going to do with it?"

"I don't know, Mrs. Godbolt. But with that man about, I thought it would be better to have it just in case."

"In case what of?"

"I don't know, I really don't know," said Mr. Godbolt. A little later, over his tea, he said, "And now, I dare say, I suppose we'd better get the shop painted up a bit." He added heavily, "Sometimes I don't know *what* to do."

His wife said, "Very likely. You don't, I dare say, Godbolt. But I know what *I'm* going to do."

When he saw his wife rubbing her front legs together over an inkpot, Mr. Godbolt knew that something was in the air. And when she got out a bit of notepaper, and squared her elbows, and licked a new pen-nib, he feared the worst.

As I was later to discover, this fear of his was not without justification.

I knew nothing of these goings-on when Sam Yudenow employed me as manager of the Fowlers End Pantheon.

"A little palace I made it of," he told me. "I want you should veneer it miv venerance—like . . . like . . . like a covered wagon miv Indians in the milderness. *Bing, bash, bosh*—another foreskin bites the dusk! Id*ills*, it's my id*ill*. Look north, look sarf, look east, even, and what 'ave you got? Mud, shit, snails, loafers—the salt o' the earth. Go west, young man, and you won't do it again in a 'urry, believe *me*! North is straight on but bearing right, then sharp left from the end o' the tram lines. West is in the other diraction, only kind o' sarf kind o' style, near Ullage. 'Ere, just 'ere is the . . . the . . . the osis in the desert. Corns on my 'ands they got, putting this place up—laryngitis I got giving 'em advice. It got me gruggy. . . . I want you should be prahd. Not too prahd to take your coat off and pick up a screwdriver. But prahd. Walk like you own the earth, so everybody should say, 'Aha! One o' Sam Yudenow's managers!' Be spotless, unmaculate you should be, so anybody should say, 'This gentleman will leave my laventry as he would wish to find it. One o' Yudenow's boys.' But I don't want you should be ashamed to put your 'ands in cold water, frinstance. Frinstance, the Ladies' gets stopped up, don't be afraid to roll up your sleeves and put your 'ands into 'em. A little bit soap, a little bit water, everything's gone and forgotten. For dead babies, inform the police. Anything," said Sam Yudenow earnestly, taking me by the arm, "anything so long you shouldn't think this is Buckingham Palace. A pioneer be, but leave no marks. Who knows? In this mud could be oil. Look!"

The inside of this deplorable cinema was decorated with what used to be called the "plastic effect"—in other words, wet plaster had been smeared about with a harrow that had palate knives for blades. The noisome dust of Fowlers End lay deep in the furrows. The walls were now gray-green, but still showed patches of emerald flecked with gold. Scarlet fire buckets hung from gilt brackets over radiators which might have been painted with smoke. The wall lights, which were enclosed in jazz-patterned boxes of orange-colored glass, contained incandescent gas mantles and painted electric bulbs which glimmered alternately with two different kinds of dimness.

From a peeling brass-plated rod fixed in the center of the roof hung a kind of orange-and-green dustbin made of glass lozenges. If there is such a thing as brown light, brown light leaked out of the top of this contraption, making a shapeless pattern which, when you looked at it, took away your will to live. Looking up as a quicksand closes over your head, you see such a light and such a pattern as the last bubble bursts.

"That," said Sam Yudenow, "that is my masterpiece, that. D'you foller me? It's *natural.* It's green, get me? And orange, d'you foller? Green and orange, they're natural colors, ain't they? Bugger the decorators, believe *me*—a thing is natural, it goes together like an orange. Look at a vose flahrs—ved voses, vi'let-colored vi'lets, yeller . . . yeller . . . yeller—"

"Buttercups?"

"Buttercups, cutterbups—yeller! Daisies, green stalks, mauve, schmauve . . . There's no such thing as decoration so long as it's natural. Not to forget but to remember this, when you get a lining brush an' a pot paint an' a bit paper to make a little 'Coming Shortly.' Use your 'magination. Nishertive, *nishertive!* Look at a vainbow. Any complaint from a vainbow? 'Ere, remember, you're like God. In the cupboard is plenty orange paint an' green paper—behave as such!

"Now I want you should see the genevator room." He took a key out of his waistcoat pocket and said solemnly, "Whereas—d'you foller me?—where*as* . . ." Sam Yudenow suddenly took a fancy to this word. "Whereas, in case o' fire, it is your sacred duty to test all the panic bolts so that the exits open outwards. Remember the Dundee Disaster! Three hundred children trampled to death by their mothers and fathers because some bastard shouted 'Fire!' an' the exits opened inwards. Not to forget this terrible thing! Burn me a few children to death, an' *I'm* the sufferer. Test them panic bolts every morning, but watch your fingers—they snap back like a rat trap. I slipped a few springs in 'em. It's a racket rahnd 'ere: some sod-pot pays his fivepence—they make a pool, the bastards, an' stake 'im—so 'e opens a side exit an' 'alf a dozen of 'em slip in. You see the position I'm in? Apart from taking the teef out o' my mouf, say an inspector comes in? Overcrowding I'm accused o'. Whereas I'm allowed six hundred seated an' twenty-nine standing, if they find one extra in the 'all, *I'm* the sufferer whereas. Get that pioneer's spirit, d'you foller me? If you see a few o' the salt o' the earth more than there should be, on the 'ole it would be better if you 'ung yourself. Six hundred twenty-nine sitting and standing is the capistry o' this 'ere show—fill it to such, no more! Whereas, no less. Six hundred twenty-nine audience is okay. Six hundred thirty is suicide. Six hundred twenty-eight I die o' starvation an' you're out of a job.

"Sometimes, Friday, Saturday, the Fowlers End Superman Association comes mob-handed to bust in, every one miv some tart from the acid factory miv a bottle fulsuric acid in 'er bag. 'Ere, use diplomacy. Let 'em in an' you're sunk. Lock the doors an' it's ten to one a fire breaks out. Argue miv 'em an' you'll go 'ome mivout a face. So jolly 'em along. Use, like they say in the Army, tictacs. Say, one at a time, 'There's a telephone call for you,' or something like that, like a gentleman—an' get 'em out into the alley. Then don't soil your 'ands on 'em. Knock their bloody blocks off but leave no mark. If one o' the gels threatens you miv a ginger-beer bottle full o' oil o' vitviol, kind o' shrug your shoulders like Ronald Colman an' turn away. The last one that threw vitviol over one o' *my* managers got seven years. So remember: Britons never never never . . . Zize saying, whereas everything else is open or shut as the case may be, this 'ere genevator room must always be locked, except."

This generator room of his must have been some kind of vestryroom in the days of the Nakedborners. In the middle of a dusty concrete floor stood a dilapidated old dynamo, weirdly illuminated by a double-jointed diffraction of sooty light that found its way in through a wonky stained-glass window. In one corner stood the Nakedborners' baptismal font, which looked like a *bidet* bristling with spikes. Goodness knows what sights that font had seen; now it contained a brown-ale bottle, a broken gollywog, and a stained pair of antediluvian corsets which, as I afterward learned, had been cut off a bloated matriarch who burst with emotion at *Ramona.*

"The brushes," said Sam Yudenow, pointing to the dynamo, "are kind o' groggy. I don't mind telling you the 'lectrician comes in 'ere in rubber galoshes to insulate 'imself when it's running. Sometime, to keep your 'and in, better rewind the core. Leave this 'ere door open and one o' the kids is dead certain to come in an' play miv the sparks just because they're blue. The salt o' the earth, mind you—but oh, what a lot o' shitpots! Last one tried that stopped the show, an' they didn't carry the poor little bastard out—I don't mind telling you, they chased 'im out in kind o' flakes miv a feather duster. Never mind that whereas. What I mean to say is, I mean to say—I don't want you should bring women in 'ere an' give 'em afterwards complimentary tickets. I want to be like a father to you, d'you foller? From women rahnd 'ere you get first of all a dose, an' afterwards bad public relations. Any woman that comes into one o' Sam Yudenow's shows should be treated like your sister—'ave nothing to do miv 'em! One o' my other managers 'ere, Booligan, so 'e used to bring women into the genevator room. Two 'e 'lectrocuted, an' one 'e got into trouble. What a ruffian! Everything 'e touched, so 'e got it into trouble and afterwards give it a complimentary ticket, that sexual regenerate. An' what a crook! Listen—you 'eard o' Jabez Balfour, you 'eard o' E. T. Hooley, you 'eard o' Bottomley? Booligan, miv the pretty cash, was the worst o' the lot. If 'e was short a few bob, all 'e did was write out a chit for torchlight batteries, an' 'elp 'imself. Miv Sam Yudenow you play that game once. Once bitten twice, irregardless! The usherettes I supply miv torches. Torches, yes; batteries, no! They can see in the dark rahnd 'ere, the layabouts. So never try that trick, young feller. Also, 'specially of an evening, the salt o' the earth stinks up the place, the miseries! Sam Yudenow begrudges nothing—there's an insect spray an' perfumed carbolic. Squirt 'em in the intervals, in particular the ulcerated legs. A spoonful essence to a pint water, an' squirt. But I want you should know it's checked, the essence. Attar o' carbolic, valuable. That Booligan, the hooligan, bought up a job-lot scent bottles an' flogged it eighteenpence an ounce to the girls. I found 'im out, an' I'm telling you so you shouldn't do it an' get into trouble.

"Temptations o' show biz! Oh, what a bastard 'e was, that bugger Booligan! Every girl 'e got into trouble. If 'e looked at a . . . a . . . a brick wall, so it would bulge. Even a nurse 'e got into trouble, that feller. 'E got *me* into trouble. Oh yes, that reminds me: so there's a jailbird—a welterweight; I backed 'im to beat Harry Mason for the championship but 'e gradually trampled somebody to death in some bar an' went to Dartmoor for life, only it turned out 'e was homicidal so they sent 'im to Broadmoor for a criminal lunatic an' gradually let 'im out. Booligan got 'is sister into trouble. This feller's name is Rooster. 'E's the salt o' the earth, right as rain; only one little fixed idear—so every manager o' the Pantheon got 'is sister into trouble. Goes about miv a meat chopper in 'is pocket, a sixpenny Woolworth's meat chopper. Pay no attention. Jolly 'im along, whereas. But leave no mark.

"Can you 'andle a typewriter?"

I said that I was not a touch-typist but that by diligence I had become fast and accurate enough with two fingers.

"That's the difference between a man and a girl," said Sam Yudenow. "My secretary takes both 'ands. You want balls to 'andle a machine. Zize saying, if you can 'andle a typewriter you can 'andle a ticket machine. The inside of an automatic ticket machine is just like a typewriter. A screwdriver an' gumption is what you need. I see somewhere in a book 'ow a machine is kind o' 'uman sort o' style. My Automaticket machine is sort o' 'uman kind o' style. To sin is divine: keep your eye peeled for 'er—she gets the squitters. Once, this ticket machine, pressed dahn for one eightpenny, farted out two hundred and fifty fivepennies.

An' 'ow d'you like that? Fivepenny tickets are yeller, eightpennies are blue. Emergency tickets, just in case, are white. Machine gets temperamental, lock the bitch up an' peel 'em off the roll.

"But you don't need to worry about that. Mrs. Edwards looks after the ticket machine. She's all right only she's got change-o'-life, so she's passionate. Every new moon—d'you foller me?—she gets convulsions. She goes doolally an' she gives. Tickets she gives away. That idear knock on the 'ead. Everything is looked after for you, as I dessay you begin to see. All you got to do is, put your 'ands in your pockets like a gentleman an' smoke—if possible, a cigar. Sam Yudenow wants all 'is managers should smoke cigars. One thing, only one thing you better 'ave: eyes in the back o' your 'ead. If you're not careful everything goes up in smoke.

"Take, frinstance, your chief projectionist, Mr. Blossom. Blossom is an artist; only a week 'eart 'e's got, asthma 'e's got, a chain smoker 'e is, an' all day long 'e drinks tea. No naked—uxcuse me! —flame is permitted in or near the projection room in case o' celluloid—in which case *I'm* the sufferer. But to Blossom turn a blind eye. Total disability pension because o' mustard gas an' shell shock. When 'e collapses, the rewinding boy will make in Morse S.O.S. on the buzzer. Nip upstairs, take over a few minutes. If Blossom's face goes blue, in a little box you'll find glass amplifiers—crush one under 'is nose so 'e'll 'ave 'ysterics and then right as rain. You've got that? . . . Good!

"Blossom comes cheap so I let 'im 'ave a gas ring for 'is tea in the projection room. Now I want you should remember, when the inspectors come, the coppers tip me the wink, if you foller me. Subdivisional Inspector Pin gives a tinkle from the station, an' 'e says, 'Glad to 'ear everything is perfectly all right.' As soon as you 'ear that, get the gas ring out of the projection room, an' snatch that cigarette out of Blossom's mouf. If necessary, swaller it. Then, rush dahnstairs an' count the Standing Room. If, as could 'appen, you got one-two over—the arm in the thvoat, the 'and in the arse of the trousers, an' 'Uxcuse me, please.' Remembering, mind you, no children in arms, an' leave no marks. . . . The kids 'ere are the worst o' the lot. Make a bruise an' the Society Prevention Cruelty to Animals 'as got you by the left tit; an' *I'm* the sufferer. Keep your eye open for old-age pensioners —they come in 'leven o'clock miv something to eat an' a primus stove, grab a seat in the aisle, an' stay all day. Give 'em two programs an' then chunk 'em out. . . . 'Andle paste?"

I asked, "What kind of paste?"

Sam Yudenow said, "What kind o' paste you think I mean? Joolry? *Paste!* Can you paste up a poster, a forty-eight sheet?"

"I've never tried," I said.

"Good, a new angle—that's show biz. It's like sticking up a double-crown, only more so. Get to leeward, or windward, or something, an' it pastes *itself* up. Like a dove! Sam Yudenow makes you or 'e breaks you. If in doubt, do it. 'Live an' learn' is my motto. . . . I would like you should wear a ved carnation sleeping an' waking. Grow a mustache. Elegance I want, elegance! If you don't need glasses, buy 'orn rims. Whatever 'appens, don't be like Booligan—you'll be surprised the enemies that man made in Fowlers End. I think I told you, Fowlers End ain't Park Lane? That's up to you. Do so.

"Check, check everything, all the time check! Oh, one little thing. I suppose you know we run variety turns 'ere? Yes, Sam Yudenow teaches you not only showmanship but stagecraft." He struggled for breath. "Waid a bibbib—I gorra take by dlobs." He took more drops while I waited a minute and, having wrapped up something like a star sapphire, said with a sigh, "Ah, that was lovely! Now wait a second an' I'll *show* you something."

2

SAM YUDENOW paused to slap himself on the forehead. I thought for a moment that some new, startling idea had occurred to him, but he said, "A flea. Bloody fleas—as soon as you chunk 'em out, the audience brings 'em back in again. Fleas you can't 'elp. I've tried fumigating the place miv sulphur once. All I killed was an old man—'e locked 'imself in the broom cupboard for the night so as to get in free of charge next day. It was Booligan's fault. And that's another thing I want you should remember: before you lock the show up at night, 'ave a good look rahnd. The people rahnd 'ere can 'ide in cracks, like bugs. They bring 'em in too, an' lice. Now once upon a time you could slip the sanitary inspector a couple quid an' a cigar, an' for all 'e cared you could 'ave snakes in the up'olstery. But now the capitalist system come in, you can't get the buggers to take dropsy any more.

"But the police rahnd 'ere is still a fine body o' men. Why, I bet you for a fi'-pun note I could get old Godbolt pinched for indecent exposure, the bloody little misery. I only wish 'e'd set foot in my 'all, that's all. I give 'im a couple complimentary tickets for my Grand Opening an' 'e tore 'em up an' 'e thvew 'em in ny face, the little stinker! Try an' make friends miv 'im. Be diplo-natic miv the old bastard. Offer 'im a cup tea, a bun. Try an' get im inside 'ere—that's all I ask. Then get 'old o' little May Geezle —you'll see 'er arahnd. Fourteen years old an' the most unnatural little 'ore in Fowlers End, an' that's saying something. Give 'er alf a dollar dahn an' promise 'er another 'alf dollar after the job. Get 'er to sit next to old Godbolt an' make 'er tear 'is face miv 'er fingernails an' scream 'rape!' Then chunk Godbolt out in the alley —the left arm rahnd the thvoat, the right 'and in the arse from the trousers—give 'im a bloody good 'iding, unbutton 'is trousers, an' give 'im in charge for indecent assault, the bloody hypocrite!"

Sam Yudenow smacked his lips and said wistfully, "I can just see that tart in court miv the paint scraped off 'er face. She looks like a proper little cherumb an' I don't advise you to 'ave any-thing to do miv 'er. She's got more claps than a football crowd. . . . No, you're new to show biz; better let me 'andle that *if* you can get Godbolt over 'ere, that little worm. A snake in the grass, that rat. Call Sam Yudenow your pal an' you can 'ave anything 'e's got from 'is wife to 'is toofbrush. But call Sam Yudenow a bastard, an' 'e's an out-an'-outer.

"Oh, yes. There's a little boy called Tommy. Every Friday give 'im a shilling. 'E chunks dead dogs an' so forth into Godbolt's shop. Only keep 'im up to the mark, because if there's one thing I can't stand it's idleness. 'E's a good boy though—got nishertive. One time when 'e run out o' dogs, 'e got a great big can o' scales an' guts from the fish shop, which was just as good if not better. When they shake out the coconut rugs an' what not, wait till the wind's blowing in Godbolt's diraction. 'Is wife, that bloody little misery, she's a 'undred times worse than what 'e is; she's always scrubbing the floor, the cow. Wait till she's finished scrubbing, an' then get some yobbo miv the muddiest boots you can find, an' send 'im over to Godbolt's to ask if 'e does watch repairing or something—use your 'magination. Give the bloke thruppence. . . . Or again, find a clean-looking girl. They exist, so find one. In the office you'll see a tube marked Hektograph Ink—undelible; it sticks like shit to a blanket. It never dries an' science 'asn't discovered what to do miv it once you get it on you. Give the girl a tanner, smear this Hektograph Ink all over 'er fingers, an' send 'er to Godbolt's she should look at piller slips. Or neckties.

"Yes, call Sam Yudenow a gentleman an' 'e's a prince; but call Sam Yudenow a pig an', oh Christ, what a bugger 'e can be! Don't you let Godbolt scare you, swelling up like a blubber. To some people Godbolt gives the creeps, 'e gives. Don't let it. Screw up your eyes to a gimblet like I do an' hyptonize 'im. I know 'is sort, believe *me*. Puntcher the bastard miv a look—a sharp look give Godbolt an' 'e's got a prick like a balloon. *Phut!*—the dirty schemer. Do unto others, but not Godbolt, that twicer! Love your neighbor as yourself, okay, but there's a limit, an' that limit is Godbolt. . . . What do I ask?" cried Sam Yudenow to the chandelier. "Little. To be loved for myself. Love Sam Yudenow an' it's the shirt off 'is back; 'ate Sam Yudenow an' vice versa. Better 'ate Godbolt."

"Why?" I asked. "What has Godbolt done to you?"

And now Sam Yudenow began to stutter and splutter, gesticulating like a semaphore. It was not, he finally explained, anything that Godbolt had done—not anything he'd *done*—but what he would do if he could. Done? What, Godbolt? To Sam Yudenow? He begged me not to make him laugh because he had a cracked lip. Envy, that was what was wrong with Godbolt, plain jealousy. And the cheek of the man was enough to give you the sick; so help Sam Yudenow, but the nerve of that hypocritical shrimp with the unsanitary mustache, it got you groggy! Just because Sam Yudenow had had the initiative to turn these lousy premises into a Pantheon, Godbolt had it in for him. There were, he assured me, certain people in the world like that—I'd be surprised. Why, if it hadn't been for Sam Yudenow, Godbolt would still have the church on his hands, a dosshouse for tramps, a restaurant for rats, a brother *cum* public lavatory for layabouts of all ages. Godbolt should be grateful; grateful Godbolt should be—instead of which all he did was lie awake at night with that bitch of a wife of his, inventing new ways and means to ruin poor old Sam Yudenow, bighearted Sammy who never did anybody a bad turn in his life, who never passed a blind beggar in the street without feeling sorry for him and thanking God that, if he had nothing else, at least he had his eyesight. And this too he would have given away already if it hadn't been for his wife and children.

Godbolt was trying to break Sam Yudenow's lease. So what if he *had* said verbally by word mouf that he intended to use the premises for a warehouse? A man had a right to change his mind, wasn't it? Anyway, a purely verbal agreement was not worth the paper it was written on. Besides, couldn't Godbolt read? Hymn books he could read, yes—if you gave that worm hymn books he'd pray you out of house and home. But if you showed that type hypocrite a businesslike lease he'd be so greedy for his quarter's rent money in advance that he'd lose his eyesight. He'd be in such a hurry to get good money out of you for a crappy old church that he'd sign anything. And complain afterwards! This kind of unsportsmanlike and ungentlemanly conduct, Sam Yudenow told me, gave him a pain in the left tit and, in general, shook his faith in his fellow men. Special leases he had printed yet, with typography of such delicacy that in places you needed a magnifying glass to read it, and so exquisitely drawn up that the Lord Chancellor himself couldn't find a loop hole.

But Godbolt had to come running, crying, "I've been robbed, I've been robbed!" Not once but a dozen times Sam Yudenow had, with the forbearance of a saint, patiently begged Godbolt to stop worrying him. And when at last he had, with all the delicacy in the world, warned the little rotter that if he didn't stop pestering him he, Sam Yudenow, would personally kick his arse from Godbolt's Corner to the tram stop, what did Godbolt do? Brought a summons out against him for uttering threats, or something. Actually, the shoe was on the other foot—it was Godbolt who had done all the threatening. Sam Yudenow politely, even piously, merely begged the Lord God Almighty to commit an unnatural offense against this pestilential man. And what did Godbolt do? Threatened to give him in charge for foul language and blasphemy! Anything to make trouble. And all the time Godbolt and his wife were writing anonymous letters to the police, to the inspectors, to the sanitary inspectors, to everybody you could think of, complaining. No, Fowlers End was not big enough to hold Sam Yudenow and the reptilian Godbolt. If that black beetle crossed my path I was, without fail, to stamp him flat, the same as a rattlesnake. If I was not too busy, while I was about it, I might tear out his liver and stuff it down his throat. . . . In the meantime I was to use my imagination and devise little bloodless ways of making his life a misery, such as: leaving newborn babies on his doorstep (you could get one for five bob in Fowlers End, blanket and basket thrown in, Sam Yudenow surmised); strewing the contents of his dustbin all over the pavement and ringing up the local authorities in a disguised voice; bribing methylated-spirits drinkers to defecate in his doorway; and breaking all his windows. . . .

"But don't do nothing beneath your dignity. Little Tommy's all right for the dirty work. Keep in miv that one. He's growing up to be a proper little Al Capone. Cross that little bastard an' it's better you should smear your arse miv honey an' stick it into a wasps' nest; it'd be soothing compared to crossing little Tommy. His own mother 'e 'alf killed miv a rusty stair rod when she tried to chastise 'im miv a copper stick for pinching 'er false teef an' selling 'em for eighteenpence to buy ginger beer for 'is girl. Yes, less than thirteen years old, an' a proper little womanizer 'e is already. An' 'is girl, she's another one—thirteen an' a half, an' already on the bash, already, at from sixpence a go an' upwards. She's already keeping 'im in cigarettes an' comics. 'E may 'ave 'is faults but 'e worships the ground I tread on.

"And while we're on these unpleasant topics I want you should keep an eye out for an Irishman called Darby O'Kelly O'Toole. 'E ought to be out in about three months now—'*e* won't get no time off for good behavior—and when 'e does get out, well, 'e's declared war on Sam Yudenow. An' that's another little thing I got against that sod Godbolt."

Now it appeared that this Darby O'Kelly O'Toole was distantly related to Mrs. Godbolt, the wayward son of some cousin by marriage—he came from the north. Even among the Liverpool Irish he was regarded as quite a lad. Egged on by the Godbolts, who put him up to it, Darby O'Kelly O'Toole applied to Sam Yudenow for a job as manager. "I got a manager." Darby O'Kelly O'Toole replied, easily, "That's all right, me boy, you won't have no blerdy manager for blerdy long. Where is he? Show me him, and you'll be needing a new manager in three minutes." A man called Left-Handed Hopkins was manager of the Pantheon at that time—sixteen stone of bone and muscle, and onetime heavyweight champion boxer of one of the Guards' Regiments. He had been a policeman in Greenock but had been dismissed from the Force for killing a docker. He lacked imagination, said Sam Yudenow, but was very good at keeping order. Before the three minutes were up Left-Handed Hopkins was running for the tram stop. He never came back.

"This Irisher give 'im a Liverpool Kiss. You know what it is, a Liverpool Kiss? Make a quick grab for the lapels o' the coat, an' pull somebody forward. At the same time bunt 'im in the face miv the top o' your 'ead an' kick 'im in the balls miv your knee. Naturally 'e falls forward. While 'e's falling, punch 'im in the jaw miv all your might so he gradually falls dahn senseless. Then, at your leisure, kick 'im in the 'ead. Naturally, I don't want *you* should do such things. . . . Well, the police was called an' they tell this O'Toole to go away he should stay away. But two days later so 'e comes back miv a mob ruffians from the fulsuric acid factory to smash the show up. I got a new manager by then. 'E used to fight by the name o' Kid Knuckles. So this O'Toole goes for 'im miv two razors an' cuts 'is face to shreds. For this, O'Toole got nine months—'e got a record for such carryings-on. The police 'ad to break three cruncheons on 'is 'ead and even then 'e fell dahn only because 'e slipped in the blood. . . . I was sorry for Kid Knuckles; but that's show biz. The show must go on! Well, they got the cuffs on this O'Toole an' took 'im away, but before 'e went 'e said, 'I'm coming back to murder you, you old bastard, and I'll burn your effing show down to the effing ground; eff me if I don't, you old effer!' And confidentially between us, there was something about that fellow I didn't like.

"Yes, I been unlucky in my managers. After that, there was Booligan, an' your worst enemies shouldn't 'ave 'alf a quarter the trouble that bugger got me into! But I think I'll be lucky miv you. If O'Toole comes in, act first! And don't be too gentlemanly miv 'im. 'E carries razors, 'e's got a criminal record. 'E did a feller in once in Glasgow only 'e got away miv it. There's a mallet in the cashier's box. You 'ave my permission to use it on O'Toole. You needn't worry if you kill that one. Be firm. Command respect. . . . Now I want you should see the stage an' the lighting system."

Now at the front of the hall there was a screen, on either side of which hung plush curtains, originally peach-colored but tinted by time and the atmosphere to the variegated shades of a black eye. Sam Yudenow explained that if I pulled the right string at the right time, these curtains would come together with the rush of a storm, covering the screen and thereby turning the Pantheon into a Palace of Variety. "Pull the wrong string," he said, "an' the 'ole bleeding lot is likely as not to come dahn an' smother you. An' then the bastards in the fi'penny seats will very likely come out miv a box matches an' set you alight just out of spite. So you want to watch out for that. Can you whistle through your teef? . . . No? You'll learn. Better, you see, because while you're 'andling the curtains miv the right 'and, an' the light switches miv the left up front, you ain't got much time to sign miv the buzzer back o' the 'all three quick buzzes for the spotlights. For the band to start, kick on the partition an' tip the wink to the piano leader. Whereas, you got to get your turns up on the stage at the same time. As long as you realize this ain't the opera 'ouse you'll be all right. . . . It'd be better if you could whistle through your teef. Better buy a dog whistle. In show biz it comes in 'andy.

"Yes," said Sam Yudenow, lighting a cigar, "not only is this Pantheon of mine the only show in Fowlers End, it's also the best. Work it out for yourself. For fi'pence, eightpence or tenpence from twelve o'clock in the morning till six o'clock in the evening I give the swine two full-length features, three shorts, and three first-class West End variety turns. From six to eleven or so, the same again, only after six, it's eightpence, a shilling, and one-and-thruppence. Do I poison the bastards? . . . With a five-piece orchestra yet in the evenings; in the afternoons, a lady pianist miv a degree from an academy already. Nothing but the best! Now miv musicians and variety turns you got to be a proper diplomat, I don't mind telling you. The bandsmen are an independent lot o' sods. They nearly all got daytime jobs and come in about six o'clock, so a kind of aristocracy they think themselves. Don't row miv 'em, whatever you do. If they get too big for their boots an' start asking for more money, be calm. Make miv a mysterious smile like this—" Sam Yudenow contorted his face in a grimace so frightful that my heart missed a beat— "an' say, 'Why, sure, certainly, ladies and gentlemen, I'll see what I can do for you. Don't you worry, ladies an' gentlemen, I'll speak to Mr. Yudenow about it this very minute.' Then give me a tinkle, that's all. What I do is, I got a amplifying gramophone, what they call a Panatrope; they make musicians unnecessary. A trade secret—my Panatrope's a dummy.

"Next morning I 'ave this 'ere Panatrope delivered an' put in a conspicuous place in the lobby. D'you foller? So the musicians come in, so you give a mysterious smile an' you say in a friendly tone o' voice, 'Lovely little machine,' you say, 'smashing invention. On this little record,' you say—I always send along a few dummy records—'on this 'ere little record I got Paul Whiteman, Jack Hylton I got, Caruso I got, the London Milharphonic Orchestra I got! An' at the turn miv a knob I could deafen 'alf Fowlers End,' you say. You know, nice an' diplomatic like Dr. Fu Manchu. 'An' people wonder why so many musicians are selling matches in the street.' That fixes those independent bastards for a little while. Because they all work kind o' locally, an' in the first place if they could get another part-time job in a show they wouldn't be able to get there from Fowlers End; an' in the second place even if they could, they'd 'ave to spend all their wages on tram fares; an' in the third place they'd miss the last tram 'ome. So they can't, an' that goes for the artists too.

"If you 'appen to get some specially nice-looking gel—say, for instance, a contortionist—give me a buzz an' say, 'Mr. Yudenow, come over quick, I got trouble in the genevator room.' Because, between you an' me, variety is a thing o' the past, so you'd be surprised what smashing turns you'll get out 'ere. People what earned fifty, sixty, seventy pound a week a few years ago come out 'ere for thirty bob for three days, an' glad of it. A double turn —that's two people—gets two pound ten."

I once knew an old boxer who, clumsily, picking the lint of airborne vocabularies off the fuzzy black wool of his mind, used to explain why he had failed to win the welterweight belt. It was, he said, because he had a super-brain; he was too quick. "Too busy" was what he said of himself in self-criticism, by which he meant one jump ahead of himself. Only some flatterer, when this battered little scrapper could still lay his hands on a fifty-pound note, had talked of his overactivity as "supersensitivity," and so forth—had a bit in the papers about it too, which was all that the much beaten man had to cling to in the gutter to which he gravitated after he could no longer be relied upon to carry a bucket at Blackfriars. It amounted to this: that Knockout Rugg lived in a dream world, in a mirror, fighting his own reflection. He countered too fast. Defending himself against an "inevitable punch" that his opponent never even thought of, he delivered to the ambient air what he liked to call his "sleeping draught"—and so awoke in the drafty dressing room. And, to his dying day, Knockout Rugg could not get it out of his head that he had been fouled. Even when his peculiarly aggressive tactics worked, and he walked up the aisle as the winner, his triumph was soured by a sense of grievance. "I dessay you saw what that yeller bastard was going to do to me in the tenth if I hadn't nailed him in the eighth?" he would say. So it was with Sam Yudenow. It seemed to me then that he despised Godbolt for not having anticipated him, and then hated him for trying to anticipate him.

"You don't believe, I dare say, what stinkpots a certain type people can be," Sam Yudenow said, leading me out into the High Street. "That toe-rag! The minute I turned my back, the reptile, what does he do? These 'ere premises next door 'e tries to buy up over my 'ead for a café miv a license to sell tobacco! Would you believe it? No. An insult, a bloody insult to my intelligence! Is Sam Yudenow a newborn baby in drapkins sucking 'is toes? Yesterday was I born? Anybody else, I'd put it dahn to 'is ignorance, but that twicer 'e *knew*—'e *knew*—where there's a cinema there's *got* to be a café. So he goes to Gutter the butcher miv a mysterious smile like a diplomat already, an' bribes an' corrupts 'im to get 'old o' these 'ere premises. 'E might 'ave known anybody in show biz miv enough sense to find 'is nose to pick it at once realizes that in a silent 'all a showman's nicest bit o' bunce comes out o' eatables. Miv talkies, monkey nuts an' potato crisps are a thing o' the past, but in a silent-picture palace they're 'alf show biz.

"Treat Sam Yudenow straight an' 'e's a die; treat 'im crooked an' better thvow a corkscrew into an electric fan. Yes, call me straight an' I'm a poker; otherwise I too can be a permanent wave. . . . But it only goes to show you the . . . the . . . the *mentality* of such hypocrites! So this Godbolt didn't know Sam Yudenow would be kind of a jump ahead, sort o'? I ask you—if you say to your grandmother miv a mysterious smile, 'Darling, let me teach you to suck eggs,' wouldn't she be right to give you the left arm in the thvoat an' the right 'and in the arse from the trousers? Naturally. But little did Godbolt know. . . . Two stones miv one bird I knocked dahn. I took the shop an' upper part. The shop I run as a kind o' 'igh-class snack place, sort o' style. Two rooms upstairs is dressing rooms for my variety turns. I wanted to put a bit of a beaver-board partition up in the genevator room, miv a curtain, so the artists could change an' nip out straight into the 'all. But Godbolt writes an anonymous letter an' the sanitary inspector says, 'Not enough laventries!' What, a laventry I should build for variety turns? A earthly paradise I make, 'ere, so laventries they should 'ave on top of it like Mayfair? Miv velvet seats praps, very likely? 'Don't make me laugh,' I says. 'I got a cracked lip.' So upstairs over my restaurant I got two lovely dressing rooms, one male, one female. No sexual intercourse.

"This way it's simple. Like this, all you got to do is show 'em in. Let 'em dress, let 'em make up to their 'eart's content—there's a looking glass in every room, and in the yard a lovely laventry. Comes five minutes before the hour nip out o' the 'all an' get 'em out. Then all they got to do is nip dahnstairs, nip into the front entrance, nip through my vestibule, nip up the back o' the 'all an' wait. This you should synchronize to the tick miv the end o' the second feature, which naturally comes on first. Sometimes, at the last minute, the variety turns get 'ysterical which one goes on last. Tell 'em you'll report 'em. Never mind who to—that one little word *report* is quite sufficient. Nip up front, whistle for lights, thvow switches, kick on the partition for the band, swish curtains —an' for Christ's sake pull the right string or you go up in flames an' *I'm* the sufferer—nip back, rush 'em on, rush 'em off, rush 'em out, rush 'em in. . . . A couple kicks on the partition, nip back, three buzzes, an' there you are—first feature, which naturally comes on last. In case of emergency, the show must go on. If necessary, borrow a lipstick, paint your nose ved—one-two-three—an' get up on my stage an' tell funny stovies. Or do paper-tearing—miv the Situations Vacant page *Daily Telegraph* you can tear out a doily, or a row dancing dolls, miv a running commentary. Remember Fowlers End ain't Buckingham Palace. If you tear paper, tell the doorman to shout from the back, 'Oi, Dad, don't tear up the tablecloth till I read the football results!'—an' there won't be a dry seat in the 'ouse. You'll see.

"An' always remember not to forget this: When in doubt, talk very slow; it makes up for not having nothing to say. Otherwise, when in doubt, talk very quick; it gives you time to think. But above all, when in doubt, shut up; then somebody else in doubt will talk and make a fool o' himself. If everything else fails, tread heavy on somebody's foot an' shout, 'Where you going, can't you?'

"Now look at the dressing rooms."

Sam Yudenow took out a large key and opened a side door adjacent to a mean little shop front—a deplorable, a repellent shop front made up of three gray panes of smeared glass rattling in Gothic frames. All the woodwork was painted in a singularly unsavory shade of blue. There is blue, and blue. Some kinds of blue remind you of babies' eyes, Mediterranean skies, sapphires, or flowers. Other blues suggest midnight and deep melancholy. But the blue of this place was of such a quality that, if you had seen it anywhere else, your first impulse would have been to call a doctor. It was something like the color of the lips of an asthmatic plumber dying of lead poisoning who has put himself out of his misery with cyanide. At every join in the woodwork there was a bubbly bluish-white froth of putty and poisonous paint expelled in a last gasp. The window frames on the floor above were of the same hue, only paler. Those of the second floor were gray streaked with orange. But on the fascia over the window was fixed a long glass plate, deeply engraved or countersunk with bold Roman letters in bright gold, which said: CAFÉ COSMOPOLITAN. Over the door, on a heavy wrought-iron bracket, hung a sign: RESTAURANT VITELLIUS. Yet on the lintel of the shop door some palsied hand had painted in pale orange, in small letters: *S. Yudenow Licensed to Sell Tobacco.* Behind the left-hand panel of the window I could see a plaster-of-paris ham, a celluloid bowl of wax fruit, and a pyramid of dummy cigarette packets half unstuck. The center panel was chaste, in the Japanese style—there was only a frying pan painted silver in which lay two slices of cardboard ham, a wooden tomato, a clay cutlet, and a lacquered red sausage. Over these goodies hung an appetizing vapor of cotton wool suspended on a bit of string nailed to the ceiling. The panel on the right was full of dummy chocolate bars and empty tobacco tins; but there was also a large gilded frame embossed Hotel Carlton-Waldoria, containing the menu of a special banquet given by the American Ambassador in honor of the Chinese statesman Li Hung Chang in 1897. Lower left, a photograph of a Greek wrestler autographed with a cross; a *Vanity Fair* caricature of Lord Palmerston; and an ostrich egg. Toward center, a printed card: COSTAS. LADIES AND GENTS TAILORS AND REPAIRS. APPLY WITHIN. Right, again, another card:

!!!BILL OF FARE!!!
!!SPECIAL THIS DAY!!

Eggs 1 Fried	3d!
" 1 Boiled	2½d!
" 2 Fried	5½d!
" 2 Boiled	5d!
Sausages 1	3d!
" 2	6d!
Fish	5d!
Chips	3d!
Fish & Chips	8d!
Egg & Chips	6d!

Meat Pie	3d!
" " & Chips	5½d!
Tea	1½d!
Coffee	2d!
Cocoa	2d!

Valet Service on Request
COME AGAIN!!!

And over all a burned-grease odor, as of Landru's kitchen.

Gesticulating with the key, Sam Yudenow said, "My café. Like the color, eh? It's blue. In show biz waste nothing. A bit paint 'ere, a bit paint there—never let 'em dry up. D'you foller? Miv a drop turpentine, the bottom o' one tin add to the bottom another, an' you'd be surprised the results! So long it's natural, it matches anything. I forget the indigredents o' this 'ere color, but look what a lovely shade blue it turned out to be! I was going to call it the Blue Café—a smashing title—only my old friend Hacker, 'e's a breaker. D'you foller?"

"A broker?" I asked.

"I said a *breaker*," said Sam Yudenow. "You 'eard of a ship breaker? A 'ouse breaker you 'eard of? So my friend Hacker's a general breaker. A breaker, not a broker. After a broker goes broke, then comes the breaker. My friend Hacker's a shop breaker, a restaurant breaker, a theater breaker, a ship breaker—a *breaker*, you know? Say a business is sold up, say: my friend Hacker's on the spot like a leopard miv a bid. Fixtures an' fittings, bars an' counters an' cupboards, signs an' shelves an' linoleum an' doorknobs—anything an' everything. Boarding an' beading, frames an' doors an' panels, sinks an' mantelpieces an' mirrors—whatever nobody wants my friend Hacker buys. Rags, bottles an' bones. 'You chunk it out, I pick it up'—that's my friend Hacker's motto; an' you'd be surprised!

"As I was saying, I was going to call this 'ere café the Blue Café only my friend 'ad this 'ere 'and-made Café Cosmopolitan fascia plus that there Vitellius sign thrown in. 'Chunk me in a mincing machine,' I says, 'an' it's a deal for thirty shillings.' In the end it was thirty-five bob, *plus* the ostrinch egg. . . . Mivout a mincing machine in a café you're a think o' the past. Rissoles —on the steam alone o' my rissoles they get fat rahnd Fowlers End. An' I dare say you wonder why I got two different signs 'anging outside my café? Go on, say it!"

I said, "I wonder why you have two different signs hanging outside your café, Mr. Yudenow. Well?"

He was delighted. "So you admit it got you asking questions, eh? It got you on the guess? You'd look twice at a place miv two signs, ain't it? You pause. You stop. Before you know where you are, you come in miv a mysterious smile an' say, 'Uxcuse me but whereas you got two different signs?' An' you go out miv a packet cigarettes or a rissole or a bar chocolate. Show biz . . . But you mustn't keep me 'ere chatting all day long. To the dressing rooms, for Christ's sake!"

As he opened the door, a girl looked out of the first-floor window. I caught a glimpse of a broad oval face, downy and juicy as an apricot, and one burning black eye surmounted by an eyebrow like a kitten's tail. Then she was gone.

"That's Costas' sister," said Sam Yudenow. "She's bad medicine. 'Ave nothing to do miv 'er. You know what these Greeks are, jealous, the uncivilized bastards. Only the other day, single'anded, Costas practically lynched half a dozen blokes for whistling at 'er. She'll make eyes at you. *She* won't mind your face—she never looks 'igher than anybody's fly. If Costas catches you so much as laying a finger on 'er, God 'elp you. So you better be careful. You never can tell. Some women like Victor McLaglen, some women like cripples. Not even you will be safe. Come on."

"Even I?" I said, following him. "I like that!"

"Don't get me wrong," said Sam Yudenow. "Personally I like your face. It's just the face for the job."

3

SINCE I AM of a timid and retiring disposition, I must admit that I am not displeased with my face. It enables me to pick and choose my company. If I do not like some importunate stranger I have only to look at him steadily; then he falters and edges away. If, on the other hand, I like the looks of somebody, it is necessary for me simply to say, "Nice weather we are having" to hold him, terrified. People are so surprised to find that I am an easygoing, even a gentle, soul that they tend to fall in love with me out of sheer relief. I am the kind of man who is glanced at quickly out of the corners of eyes. Men fear me and women are fascinated by me. "He must have been through hell," they say, with a thrill of sympathy or with a delicious tremor. "What a ruthless brute he must be!" Perhaps you remember the old heavyweight boxer, the Chopping Block, George Cook of Australia. It was almost impossible to knock him out; consciousness and unconsciousness were all the same to him. He used to be one of the barriers that had to be passed before anyone got to be a runner-up for the British Heavyweight Championship.

His sad, bewildered eyes glittered under heavy banks of scar tissue, and he had ears like a double portion of sweetbreads. Hundreds and hundreds of promising young heavyweights had hit him in the face with all their might. An old sportswriter told me once that George Cook must have taken, in the course of his career, at least fifteen thousand punches on the nose, which was not only flat and boneless but bent east and west in a lazy zigzag. He had the appearance of a man who, by supernatural toughness, has emerged alive from a concrete mixer. I look something like him; and I have never regretted the circumstances that made me so.

It happened in 1915 when I was a child. Airplanes were a novelty in those days, and I was fascinated by the German Gothas over London. They looked like a series of Ts floating in clear sky. For the first, and last, time in my life I was overwhelmed by a desire to fly. So I found a six-foot length of four-inch squaring and nailed to it two planks for wings, and a board for the tail. The propeller I cut out of the lid of a biscuit tin and fastened with one of my mother's hat pins. For armaments I carried a double-barreled cap pistol and a five-pound dumbbell which I proposed to drop on the gas works. For a helmet I borrowed my father's bowler hat and for goggles my mother's pince-nez. But when I straddled the thing, it wouldn't fly. Something was seriously wrong here. Then I remembered that airplanes had wheels. I took my sister's perambulator apart and fitted my machine with an undercarriage. It moved, then; but still it would not fly. So I took it to pieces, carried it up to the roof and reassembled it. As I calculated, all I needed was a good start. Shouting "Bang! Bang! Bang! I'm a German!" I took off. It seems that I described half a parabola on account of the steep slope of our roof, and went right over our garden fence into a neighbor's cucumber frame. I landed flat on my face. The dumbbell, which I was still firmly grasping, hit me on the nose. The wings folded and beat me about the ears, and my jaw was broken. "Never do a thing like that again," said my father; and I obeyed him. To this day I cannot look at a dumbbell without a sense of frustration, of grievance; and if, sometime, when things get too tough for me and I have a nervous breakdown and am found throwing dumbbells and crying "Bang! Bang! I'm a German," the psychiatrists will know exactly where to look for the first causes.

However, from the age of seven, after my face healed I looked not unlike that ancient pugilist Buckhorse, who, in his old age, having no face left to spoil, let anybody knock him down for a shilling. Later, when I filled out into a fine figure of a man, I improved and resembled old George Cook. My stature and physique I must have inherited. After the incident of the airplane I was not allowed to touch dumbbells, Indian clubs, hammers, nails, or wood; and I was followed every time I climbed the stairs.

They gave me an abacus to play with; I took a fancy to the red beads and swallowed them, and I felt so bad about the anxiety I had caused my family that I did not dare to say anything about it. For all I know they are in my system to this day, or else they were digestible beads. I looked in vain for their reappearance with a view to putting them back on the wires, but they never turned up.

I begged in vain for a bicycle. My father settled for a very low-built tricycle because it was impossible to fall off it. Even then my mother would not allow me to take it out of the playroom on the first floor. All the same, I rode it downstairs and through the front door, which was closed at the time. Carpenters had to be called to saw me out of the lower panel. As a result of this mishap I have an evil-looking scar which almost encircles my neck; this is always good for conversation—the politest woman in the world cannot help asking me how I came by it. I never tell the same story twice.

My beauty, again, was not enhanced by the Affair of the

Bicycle Pump. Needless to say, with my record, I was not allowed to let off fireworks on Guy Fawkes Day and dance around a bonfire with the other boys. So I decided to make a little firecracker for myself. Somewhere or other I picked up an old nickel-plated bicycle pump, which struck me as being the very thing for the casing; the next thing was to find something to put in it. Now my father used to own a duck gun and I remembered having seen a box of fifty cartridges in one of his drawers. I cut open these cartridges and emptied the whole fifty into the barrel of the pump, ramming the powder and the shot down hard with the piston. Then I made a fuse out of cotton string rolled in gunpowder, and attached it. With this firecracker I decided to surprise and delight the local police force on November the fifth. So I put it against an outside wall of the police station, set light to the fuse, and waited around the corner. The cracker was a success, only the wall came down and I was cut about the forehead with flying glass.

Everybody said it was anarchists. I kept my mouth shut about that one.

As if all this were not enough, I caught diphtheria (as they insisted) through eating pencils. I always was of a contemplative turn of mind. Even as a child, before committing myself to writing, I took a good mouthful of pencil. Most of my milk teeth had gone in the airplane crash, but I still had my molars, and made the most of them. The paint did not appeal to me much, but I enjoyed the savor of the cedarwood. I did not spit out the lead, having been politely brought up; I swallowed it. Lead, cedar splinters, paint, abacus beads—they all went the same way home. But eventually I contracted diphtheria. Considering this in the light of modern science, I believe I caught it from a gluttonous and feverish little boy who borrowed my pencil one drawing lesson and chewed all the goodness out of it. But our family doctor, a superannuated windbag who did not believe in microbes and diagnosed what ailed you by smelling your breath, swore that diphtheria was created by pencils. Anyway I caught it, and my throat seized up, so that they had to make an incision for me to breathe through. For a year or two after that I could not speak and when my voice came back it came in a sepulchral whisper which later mellowed into a throaty purr; so that now my voice has something of the quality and timbre of Tallulah Bankhead's, only it is deeper and more masculine. It is the kind of voice one associates with the most appalling depravity; it goes with the debauching of pious matrons, the buggering of young noblemen, the reciting of poetry with an ulterior motive, and seduction of convent-bred heiresses. In contrast with my face, it is really arresting.

But it was a long time, I assure you, before I was allowed to handle a pencil after that; and even then they coated my pencils with bitter aloes—the stuff they smear on leashes to discourage puppies from eating them. (Actually, when you get used to the stuff, bitter aloes isn't bad at all.) But in the meantime I was given crayons to write with, which, being made of wax, grew soft in my hot little hand, inviting me to roll and mold them into interesting and useful shapes. This suited me fine because I was never satisfied with the shape of a thing as it happened to be. Art begins that way.

I owe one of my "redeeming" features to an accident connected with this urge of mine to change the design of things.

Every boy must have a pocketknife. Not me. My mother would as soon have given me a vial of prussic acid, as a knife. So I decided to make one. . . . Looking back, sometimes, I feel that my life has been wasted. I ought to have been born before the dawn of civilization, I am so inventive and, once my curiosity is aroused (which doesn't take much doing), so completely devoid of fear. I might have got myself run over in the process, but I bet I would have invented the wheel; and although I should certainly have become a charred tribal demigod, I believe that I might have discovered fire. Lacking a knife, I say, I invented one. In those days, we used to play a silly game with pins. You take two pins and place them crosswise on a tramline. The tramcar rolls over the crossed pins and flattens them into the likeness of a pair of scissors. *Now what is a pair of scissors but two knives fastened with a screw?* I reasoned. *If two pins make two knives, one pin therefore will make one knife. An ineffectual brass knife, it is true; but a knife notwithstanding.* It was not bad for a child of my age, mind you. From pins I went on to nails; and I think I might have made something out of a tenpenny spike if I had not been caught, in the nick of time. The driver braked the tram to a standstill, its front wheels less than a yard from my fingers—other nails having been shaken off by the vibration, I was determined to hold this one down. "Promise me on your honor you will never do a thing like that again!" said my father. "If you do, all your fingers will be cut off and you will be sent to a home." I promised, and I kept my promise.

But my promise did not include trains. Not far from where we lived there was a railway line along which rushed the giant expresses of the South Western Railway, hurtling past at seventy or eighty miles an hour. We boys used to stand on the bridge and watch them as they passed—the idea being to catch in one swift glimpse the names of the huge locomotives and their serial numbers, which we solemnly entered in little notebooks. This was all very well, but when I said that I was going to make a knife, *I* made a *knife*. I found an iron bolt twelve inches long and nearly an inch thick. Knowing better now than to hold this down with my fingers under the Lord Wolseley, which was due to come through at 11:45 that Saturday morning, I fastened the bolt to the nearest rail with adhesive tape (which, God knows why, I soaked with iodine). As I calculated, the great Lord Wolseley and the countless steel wheels of all its carriages should do a real swordsmith's job for me and turn this bolt into a kind of machete. I had been reading the works of Major Charles Gilson at that time, and felt that this was all I needed to get me to the place where the elephants go to die. I crawled down the bank and waited. My calculations were almost accurate, but not quite. The Lord Wolseley passed dead on time, and its off-front wheel made a spearhead of the end of the bolt, but jibbed at its square head. This, caught in a flange, sent the sharpened bolt whirling away. The point hit me in the right cheek, half an inch away from the corner of my mouth, and came out at the other side. The result was that my poor mother had a nervous breakdown, and I healed with two fascinating dimples which, as a girl once told me, "illuminate" my face when I smile.

As if this were not enough, I lost the little finger of my left hand in the zoo. One of my aunts took me there to cheer me up while the wounds in my cheeks were healing. Slipping past the keeper, I tried to make a hyena laugh by tickling his lip. It is lucky for me the beast did not get the whole hand. . . . But it got me out of music lessons—my unhappy mother had conceived an idea that I might make a violinist, but nothing was further from my thoughts: I didn't know what I wanted to be, really, unless it might be an explorer.

Which is, in a way, exactly what I turned out to be. Only it didn't take me long to learn that you don't need to go to Africa for savagery, to Tahiti for the exotic, or to the moon for monsters. If I want the thunder of the galaxies or the interplanetary cold, I can find them in Beethoven and Sibelius. Just any old bit of ground is vantage point enough for me. I will do my extraterrestrial traveling when my time comes, not in a chromium-plated rocket but naked, out of a good old-fashioned wooden box six feet deep in my own familiar earth. And for this I am in no hurry at all. To put it tritely: Man is my Dark Continent, and his heart is my jungle. I actually like people in general, and enjoy being in company—any kind of company.

I get involved in it; I feel that it enriches me, generally. One reads of the love that casteth out all fear: I am inclined to believe that this kind of love is a sort of mysterious absorption of oneself in a state of sublime curiosity that lives on the frontier between conjecture and pure understanding. Fear is written in every heart, but seldom indelibly. Fear is a mere misprint which you need only recognize to correct.

Many a night have I spent in the rooms of my old friend John Sourbreast, who has a lease in perpetuity in Albany and two thousand pounds a year taxfree all to himself. I remember those nights with pleasure. That was not a sitting room; it was a set in a scene in which, if one were not perfectly comfortable, one ruined the act. There were the richly bound old books, the black walnut Bechstein grand piano licking itself like a contented cat in the firelight, the wonderful rug that came out of the palace of Abdul the Damned, the easy chairs by the fire, and tobacco and drinks ready to hand. Over the mantelpiece a painting by Sickert of the old Quadrant, seen in wintery slush with a fog coming down; in the foreground a man in a heavy overcoat splashing in the direction of the Café Royal to sit on red plush, drink something hot, and play dominoes. I always liked that picture—whatever the weather, you looked at it and said to the man in the overcoat, "Good for you!" And here we used to sit, talking of Life and Death, and Good and Evil. Sourbreast didn't seem to know which was which. In any case, he was uneasy about the whole damned lot.

Toward about two in the morning he would try me with the Fool's Mate of metaphysics: "Is God omnipotent?"

To this, for the sake of argument, I would reply, "Yes."

"Is God all-powerful?"

"Yes."

"But is God all good?"

"Yes."

"Yet you acknowledge the existence of evil?"

"Yes."

"Then how do you reconcile the existence of evil with the existence of an all-good and all-powerful God?"

Then I would counter, "Sourbreast, is it a good thing to torture a horse?"

"No!"

"Or a dog, or a cow?"

"Certainly not."

"But is it a good thing to die of diphtheria, smallpox, lockjaw, typhoid, et cetera?"

"No, it is not a good thing."

"Tonight we ate steak. Was it good steak?"

"Excellent."

"Yet, eating that filet, did it not occur to you that the steer was dragged in agony to the slaughterhouse, where it went down in a whole mess of blood and guts? That this steer was castrated to stay quiet and get fat for your table?"

"Stop it!"

"But the steak was good? It refreshed you, kept you going?"

"Well?"

"That's the way people are," I would say. "They wouldn't touch a dead cow with a barge pole, but oh, how they love her tripes! Without the butchers you'd starve, wouldn't you? Now tell me, is it good to be a butcher?"

Sourbreast would sigh and say, "They are a necessary evil."

"Hold hard there!" I'd say. "If a thing is necessary it can't be an evil. Evil is *unnecessary*. That is why it is evil. You observe, you are the sick calf, or horse, or dog, in the laboratory. You feel only your immediate discomfort. You can't say to yourself, 'Out of the misery of this base flesh may come a better life and longer hope for something higher up in the scale of evolution.' Which comes first, the man or the horse?"

Sourbreast always fenced then: "That depends on the man."

"Oh, I suppose you would have given preference to a lamb, just because you liked its looks, over a bloody butcher from the Midlands? Yet that butcher begot William Shakespeare. I like your presumption! It's like a mouse in a cathedral talking architecture."

At this point we generally had another drink, and then Sourbreast would say moodily, "You don't know the meaning of doubt."

My reply never failed to irritate him. It was, simply, "That's right."

"Yet anyone can see with half an eye that you've suffered like hell."

"In point of fact, I haven't," I would tell him. "Traumata are a lot of crap. Anybody who says he remembers a physical pain is a liar. You are not constructed to remember pain, or you'd never survive being born. *You remember only the fear of being hurt*. It is fright, not hurt, that destroys you."

So I told him, and so I believed—and so I still believe. Now, in perspective, I see my sentiments just as they were when I lived by instinct. I still believe that sensation is nothing but a spur on the heel of time rowelling the crotch of eternity. Pleasure and pain are neither here nor there; both are evil if you consecrate yourself to one or the other—if you do this, you fall in the scale of things; you sink under the surface of yourself. True happiness is to be found in a species of spiritual osmosis—in absorbing, and at the same time being absorbed. Be calm, hold on to the nucleus of yourself; let yourself be taken in by what surrounds you, and you will get back more than you have given, and so become stronger by having been thus involved. In the meantime, you will have given back some of your strength to its nameless source.

We are all part of a cosmic give-and-take. There is nothing to be afraid of—not even your own shadow, no matter what *danse macabre* it makes between guttering candles and the dying embers in the small hours when life runs down.

As for suffering, I am told that I have had my share of it. But it never took. Experience never taught me to be afraid. It taught me that a pain is a red light, a danger signal, something that warns you to be on your guard against what it presages. But the memory of pain suffered never dulled my desire to find out what lay beyond the pain, behind the red light. Why, good God, if there were any such thing as true remembrance of physical pain, there would be the end of adventure and high endeavor—which would be a great pity. Ninety-five per cent of the tales people tell about their sufferings are a kind of emotional sales talk. Take child-birth, for example, which is the commonest pain in the world and, while it lasts, one of the most acute: every woman talks about it but not one, not a single one, truly remembers it. Pain brings its own anodyne. One deep sleep, and all is forgiven. What they remember about it is the anticipation of it.

Fear is a kind of hate; they both smell alike. I should not be surprised if it turned out that many of the early Christian martyrs got no more than they asked for—hating and forgiving, and fearing and hoping all in quick succession. Whereas Daniel came alive out of the den of lions simply because he couldn't be bothered with them. By the same token, if you like, God destroys those who fear Him as surely as life destroys those who fear to live. Superficial observers believe that it is on account of my formidable appearance that I can walk unharmed, well dressed and talking like a gentleman, in places where the very policemen have to go in twos and threes. It isn't true. Apart from the fact that ill-disposed people, looking at me, ask themselves what the other fellow must have looked like when the fight was over, and respect me on sight as a dangerous kind of walking casualty, I think they get a spiritual feel of me.

Neither they nor their dogs curl a lip at me—well, hardly ever—because, my face notwithstanding, they know that I am of them, involved in them.

We are all breakables close-packed in one universal parcel.

Apropos of dogs: I was snapped at only once, and that was when I was ill with an undulant fever. Running away from bad dreams and lonely with an ineffable loneliness, I paused in a doorway to stroke a mongrel terrier. He warned me off, snarling. The dog was right: fear and disease give out a whiff of corruption which all healthy animals shy away from. The smell of fear, like pain, is one of nature's warning signals. *Danger—Keep Off!* it says. You must know yourself that, in school for instance, the least popular boy—the creep, the drip, the butt, the one who is most avoided—is the most fearful of you all. You feel that he carries with him a contamination of uneasiness. Whereas, though he may have all the vices in the world, you will follow the daredevil like a pack of hounds. No disrespect; it's only natural. . . .

"I admit," I said generously, "that I am no oil painting."

"Oh, you'd be surprised," said Sam Yudenow. "The year before last I and my wife, we went for a holiday to Belgium. I got a brother-in-law in the diamond trade. So they take me to the Weirtz Museum, an' believe me, a very nice class oil painter paints worse types than you. Don't you worry. You got the face for the *job.* Rudolph Valentino wouldn't last five minutes in Fowlers End—" He stopped abruptly and said, "Uxcuse me, what's your name?"

"Daniel Laverock," I said.

"Laverock," said Sam Yudenow, "Laverock—isn't that a kind of a cow?"

"No," I said, "that's a maverick. A laverock is Old English for skylark."

Sam Yudenow said, "I'm broad-minded. I don't care what your name is, personally. But Fowlers End ain't Old England an' they're sure to call you Laventry. Why not call yourself Carlton, or something?"

I said, "Call me what you like, so long as I get my wages. Oh yes, that reminds me—what *are* my wages?"

"You could go all over London," said Sam Yudenow, "an' not get a 'alf. There's men seventy, eighty years in show biz who'd *pay* me for your job, an' do my laundry an' darn my socks an' wash my back every Sunday morning. One o' my managers in Luton, '*e* got *less* than 'alf o' what you're getting, an' 'e used to cut my 'air every week. . . . You're not 'andy miv a pair scissors by any chance?"

"Not very. Seriously, how much?"

"It's a gentleman's life. It's a chance in a million. A lot o' people I know miv university edyacations would pay a premium to learn show biz from Sam Yudenow. An' 'ere you are, a beginner, an' I'm paying you wages like a prince. What more could you want?"

"How much was it you said?"

"I don't know why I should, but I like you. Speak any foreign languages?"

"French, Spanish, German."

"Forget 'em. Well, seeing it's you, Laventry, I'll make it forty-five shillings a week. That puts you in the upper brackets rahnd 'ere. Only don't tell anybody 'ow much I'm paying you—they'll *all* want a rise. If Mrs. Yudenow should ask, 'Confidentially, Mr. Carlton, 'ow much is Sam paying you?' I want you should keep a straight face an' take the Bible in your right 'and an' say, 'Mrs. Yudenow, I swear on this 'ere Book that I'm not getting a penny more than thirty-seven-and-six.' There's a Bible in the office, only the inside's been cut out to make a cigar box. Is your mother living?"

"Yes," I said.

"In that case, you can say also, 'I swear on my mother's grave.' If she ain't got one, it can't 'urt. Your father dead? 'E is? Then you can say, 'May I never shake 'ands miv my father again, Mrs. Yudenow!' But I want you should keep your fingers crossed at the same time because I never lie to Mrs. Yudenow. She always finds out. Where do you live?"

"My address," I said evasively, "is Poste Restante, Charing Cross."

"Give 'em notice. Why should you work for a West End landlord? Or if you got a long lease, sublet. I like my managers should be on top o' the job. So if you like, I can fix it up miv Costas you should 'ave a room 'ere an' breakfast for ten shillings a week." He cupped a hand over his ear and listened intently for a second. " 'Ear that chirpy noise? It's the critics rahnd the stove."

"Crickets?"

"I said critics, diddle I? Some people say they're lucky. When you got nothing else to do Sundays, trap 'em. Borrow a pisspot, an' put some crumbs at the bottom. They jump in an' eat themselves sick, the uncivilized little bastards, an' then they can't get out. When you got a pound or two of 'em, chunk 'em into Godbolt's. I dare say you're quick miv your 'ands. Catch fleas. Buy for a penny a tin pea-shooter. Get two bits cotton wool to plug it up. When you got a tubeful—an' you'd be surprised 'ow long those little buggers can live mivout food—go over to Godbolt's in the dead night, an' blow 'em thvough the keyhole. Only be sure to draw a deep breath *before* you blow. That bastard Booligan didn't an' for days 'e was complaining of a tickling in the thvoat. . . . Bedbugs, they're easy to catch. Fill up a paper cone; undo this cone an' drop the lot thvough Godbolt's letterbox. As I calculate, if only one in five gets into the woodwork, that's good enough. An' on no account drown rats. I got a wire 'Catch-'Em-Alive-O' trap in the cellar: its capacity is four. When it's full, take it to Godbolt's letterbox an' open the trap. Stir 'em up miv a sharp pencil an' in they go. There's a pencil sharpener in the office. Now . . ."

We climbed the dark stairs. There was a fine film of burned grease over everything.

"Now this," said Sam Yudenow, "is the ladies' dressing room." Sometimes, when the day is a gray waste in the middle of which I find myself lost, when I am alone among strangers and depressed, I think of that room. It was larger than the shop parlor. The shadow of an adjacent building kept it in perpetual twilight. Leaning out of the window to get away from it, you saw a blank wall. If you craned heavenward there was nothing but a cistern out of which came a strangled noise and a tangle of pipes wrapped in rags of sackcloth and sprinkled with dust and ashes. Below in a stone yard stood a dead plant in a tub of sour dirt, and a big dustbin. I am telling you that there was no escape. The room was cold and, at the same time, stuffy. Against the wall to the left of the door stood a washstand topped with a slab of mud-colored false marble on which was a jug of cold water in a big blue basin and an empty glass; at the lightest footstep, the jug and basin chattered like teeth. Below, icy white and gleaming, a chamberpot. The bed was of iron tubing covered with peeling brass: there was more comfort in the prospect of a grave than that of the bed at the end of a day—that pitiless, flat, naked bed with its skin-tight cotton counterpane. Instead of fire, the hearth contained crumpled red crepe paper. The mantelpiece bore two eighteen-pounder shell cases about which somebody had tied bows of pink sateen. Between them hung a yellow photograph of a man who looked like a hangman turned churchwarden: a dour, cruel old man in a billycock hat, clutching a black stick, resting one glazed-looking fist upon a book. Against the window stood a dressing table. There was an enamel pail and a small straw mat—nothing more except white wallpaper stamped with blue roses and marked in one place by a patch of dampness. Yet there was something else which I could not define: an atmosphere.

Women had used that room and somebody had cleaned up after them; but all the mottled soap in Fowlers End could not have scoured away an overhanging aroma of uneasiness, a taint of misery which clung there. I could distinguish a faint smell of mingled sixpenny perfumes and perspiration. In the crockery tray upon the dressing table lay two hairpins, one black, one "invisible." The woodwork bore the black marks of cigarette burns. Gloom had soaked into the fabric of the place. On the wall under the gas bracket somebody had written three words. They were written small, but the utter nakedness of the room made them conspicuous: *Out goes Pat.* The abandoned ones, the forgotten ones, the derelicts, the *Marie Celestes* of the theater had been dragged down this way by the undertow of time and change, leaving behind them nothing but a few cigarette marks, two pins, three words, and a desolation. . . .

Sam Yudenow said, "I don't know what your religion is but the way I look at it everything is a blessing in disguise. Variety's gone to rack and ruin, but like brothels it makes the town safe for respectable girls. Also for the likes of us. A variety turn *must* 'ave a wash at least once a week, 'specially if she's a contortionist; otherwise, the effects can be dangerous an' far reaching. Only before you 'ave a go miv one o' the ladies 'ere, better put down a sheet greaseproof paper on the coverlet. Costas guards 'is sister's virtue, an' quite right too. Booligan used to keep a roll of it. The men's dressing room is next door."

It was the same as the other room, only there was a lithograph of Garibaldi over the mantelpiece and more inscriptions on the walls. Also, I noticed an old-fashioned bidet. Sam Yudenow pointed to it with a laugh. "I got that in a job lot from my friend Hacker the breaker. For years, Mrs. Yudenow thought it was for pickling cucumbers in. Actually, if you sit on the floor you can use it for a kind o' table."

I asked, "And where's my room?"

"The way I look at it," said Sam Yudenow, "what more could

anybody ask for than the ladies' dressing room? Airy like a palace miv a cupboard that *locks*! During the day what do you want a room for, what? After the turns 'ave gone 'ome, Costas' sister tidies up, an' it's all yours. Don't worry, you'll be on the go like a gentleman from nine in the morning to 'alf past eleven at night. Ten bob a week miv a breakfast thvown in—what king could ask for more? For your other meals, ask Costas. 'E charges next to nothing. Don't worry, I'll fix it up miv Costas. My God, in a couple years you'll save money to buy me out! For you I'll be working. That's *la vie* for you. See? I talk French too, only in show biz the more you savvy the less you say. So all you got to do is, move in like a gentleman, you lucky bastard, an' live like a lord. From now on, you're God Almighty rahnd 'ere. When you say 'yes' it's yes, when you say 'no' it's no; your word is law—so long as you consult me first. . . . 'Ear that cveaking? That's Costas on the stairs. 'E listens. When Gveek meets Gveek, watch your step." Then Sam Yudenow, clearing his throat and winking at me, said in a loud, clear voice, "Five pounds ten a week, Mr. Carlton, take it or leave it!"

"Eh?"

He whispered, "In show biz always multiply by two what you earn, an' add ten per cent."

Costas was about five feet tall and a yard wide, built in the form of a cask, red-eyed and irritable, shaggy as a Highland steer, ominous and dark as the hour before a storm. An angry man—there was his story: a baffled Ajax, a frustrated Hector, an incarcerated Achilles. His face was of the color and texture of that worm-eaten willow wood which, because the softer parts of the grain have been worn out by water or otherwise eroded, has an appearance of antiquity and is, therefore, used by picture framers to set off thunderous and somber canvases. Easy stuff for time and tide to work on, nothing like as rugged as it looks; you can put a hundred years on it in half an hour with a handful of wet sand. I had *his* number—Costas didn't fool me for a moment. When Sam Yudenow introduced me, he grunted and tried to stare me out of countenance. Now I have remarkably pale-gray eyes and, being somewhat nearsighted, tend to thrust my head forward when observing something closely. I am motivated by nothing but friendly curiosity, I assure you; but the effect is frightening. A girl once told me that I look "like a lynx about to spring." Furthermore (perhaps because I am afraid of missing something) I hardly ever blink. The long stare having failed, Costas tried the hand grip. I will say this for him: he didn't wince, only he compressed his lips until his mouth looked like an old cicatrix. When at last we released each other, he said in remarkably precise English, "You pay strictly in advance, Mr. Laverock. *His* managers always leave suddenly."

Sam Yudenow said, "What I mean to say is, Costas, why worry; what for? We're all gentlemen 'ere. I'll personally deduct the rent from Mr. Carlton's wages." Then he said to me, "Would you mind waiting for me downstairs, Mr. Laventon?"

The acoustics of that decrepit house were remarkable. Also, Sam Yudenow's whisper had an extraordinarily penetrative quality—I learned later that he started life as a professional shouter for a fishmonger in Petticoat Lane—and anyway I have sensitive ears. I heard Yudenow say, "Don't worry. Every Friday regular I'll see you get your seven bob. Only if Laventon should happen to ask, make miv the mysterious—"

Costas did not bother to whisper. He said scornfully, "Okay, okay, okay."

"He's a gentleman," said Sam Yudenow, in that whisper of his which might have cut through a plank.

Costas replied, "You have had some bastards in your time, but this man is the king of the bastards. I like his face."

A door opened that separated the passage from the back of the café, and Costas' sister appeared. She looked at me and shrank back, cupping protective hands over her magnificent breasts. "How do you do," I said, bowing politely.

She said, "For Christ's sake, what next, I wonder!"—and went back into the café, slamming the door.

Then Costas and Yudenow came down. "You see?" said Sam Yudenow, looking at his watch. "I fixed it all up for you. An' now you got to meet Copper Baldwin. Be nice to Copper. Whatever 'e says, whatever 'e does, laugh it off. Because 'e's worth 'is weight in diamonds. A cinema circuit is like a machine—it won't run mivout a cog. An' if ever there was a cog, it is Copper Baldwin. Come!" As we went out he handed me the key of the front door. It weighed about half a pound. "I want you should hold this as a sacred trust," he said.

"That man Costas speaks pretty good English for a Cypriot tailor," I said.

Sam Yudenow, wide-eyed and openmouthed at the comment, replied, "What *then* should 'e speak? Bad English? 'E's an edyacated man. Why not? By Sam Katz in New York, before 'e'll let anybody wash out a toilet 'e's got to be a Doctor Philosophy! Sure, Costas is a politician. When 'e gives Cyprus back to Gveece, so 'e'll be in a very nice position. Only 'e done a couple murders. Well, live an' let live is my motto. One word from me an' they'd 'ang 'im up like a pig. Only don't let on you know about it or I wouldn't give tuppence for your life. Whereas in the meantime, if I tell 'im, 'e'll make you a Savile Row suit for three pounds *miv* secret pockets. . . . The way I look at it, who knows? Look at Russia. If the czar Russia 'ad said to Trotkin an' Lensky, 'Live an' let live,' he would be today in a very nice position. Whereas . . . In show biz, Laventon, one thing leads to another like . . . like . . . like the photo-electric cell.

"Live an' let live, keep your fingers crossed, an' keep your mouf shut. Was a time when Mussolini was a beggar, no bread to 'is feet, no boots to eat, no roof to 'is mouf. But your children should find 'emselves in such a nice position 'e's in now! Life is a covered wagon. It could be Costas might be a dictator yet—in which case a monopoly! There was a man, so this man 'elped some bloody dago when 'e 'ad no arse to 'is tvousers. Gradually, all of a sudden, this dago becomes dictator o' South America. So 'e says, 'Because you 'elped me out when I was already eating my boots an' sucking the nails like Charlie Chaplin in *The Gold Rush*, I 'ereby give you the monopoly o' green paint.' So this feller says, 'What do you mean, green paint? What for, green paint, what for?' So, miv a mysterious smile, this dictator says, 'Ah, *amigo*, but I 'ave made, uxcuse me, a law—everything should be painted green, or else!' My motto is live an' let live, because one never knows. Be international. So Costas shot a few Gveeks? So? You'd be surprised the way this class o' people breeds.

"Keep the ticket machine going, an' silence when you speak! An' remember never to forget—one never knows, an' you never can tell. An' above all, you better be nice to Copper Baldwin."

4

I DO NOT KNOW what I was expecting, but, when I first met him, Copper Baldwin disappointed me. Of course, it took only half an hour or so of Sam Yudenow to condition you for the monstrous, gear you for the abnormal—in general, to take you out of this world, as the saying goes. *Copper* Baldwin. It would not have surprised me if he had turned out to be a Yaqui Indian in war paint. Yet he looked ordinary enough. *Worth his weight in diamonds*: by Sam Yudenow's computation this should have meant that he was about the size of Primo Carnera and could tie his shoelaces while standing upright; but he was of average size and shape and coloring, a man of the crowd. His hair was of a dusty shade. There was nothing noticeable about his face, except that it drooped; every feature of it seemed to be set a little lower than it ought to have been. It was not exactly that his hairline was low; his forehead ended where the bridge of his nose might have been expected to start. Thus he seemed to have more eyelids than eyes, and his ears encroached upon the angles of his jaws. He had a long, melancholy nose and a long, deeply indented upper lip, a sad mouth, and a chin that sloped a shade too abruptly toward a large Adam's apple. He had a waxy, unhealthy skin, and was wearing a dungaree jacket, "Government Surplus" postman's trousers with red seams, and old tennis shoes. To pass the time away, he was trying to balance a screwdriver on the tip of his nose. Another screwdriver of the three-geared American pattern protruded from his breast pocket together with a tack hammer. From his right hip hung a holder containing one of those deadly looking tools with which a resourceful man can do almost anything—tear a house down or put it together again—a combined claw hammer, jemmy, tomahawk, lever and chisel.

"Copper," said Sam Yudenow, "I want you should meet Mr. Laventon, our new manager. Mr. Laventon, above all I want you should meet Copper Baldwin."

"What, another new damager?" said Copper Baldwin. "Well, for what we are about to receive the Lord make us truly thankful." And he looked me up and down. His eyes were the commonest-looking eyes in the world: "proletarian blue," as some high-brows call it, referring to that cheap dye with which workmen's overalls are colored; it washes pale but it never washes out. I guessed that he was about forty lean years old. His body drooped, as well as his face. It was not that he didn't stand upright—Copper Baldwin was, in fact, very straight in the back—only he was low-shouldered and long-bodied and conveyed the impression of having been poured downward instead of growing up. "Oh, well," he said in a fatalistic tone, "there's no 'arm trying him out. Pleased to meet you, Mr. Laventon."

"I don't mind what you call me," I said, "not a bit. Only, for the records, the name is Laverock."

As if Sam Yudenow were not there, Copper Baldwin said to me, "It's not so much that he's an ignorant bastard—which he is—but Yudenow lives in a world of his own. I forget the proper word for it, but it's the name of a disease. 'Foxy Sam' we call him and he's proud of it. Foxy. All a fox knows is the way from his 'ole to a chicken-run, and back again. That much, I grant you, Yudenow knows. Nothing much more. Don't mind him. Because he walks on two legs there's a law against shooting him and making a muff out of his skin. That's all *his* strength. Nothing but a fox, only he's got to have his chickens boiled. . . . All right, Mr. Yudenow—bugger off. Kind of scram. Go on."

To my surprise, Sam Yudenow chuckled. "Copper doesn't mean a word 'e says," he said. "Copper's a good boy, only no self-control. That means to say, Copper's a character. You'll love 'im, Laventon—you'll love 'im!"

"Go away," said Copper Baldwin. "Get out of my sight."

Still laughing, Sam Yudenow shook me by the hand. "Worth 'is weight in diamonds, I told you," he said. "So now you see what kind type man Sam Yudenow is—even in show biz unique! I'd like to see a Doctor Philosophy talking to Sam Katz like Copper talks to me. But of such are empires built—colosseums, too—that's me! God bless you, get stuck into the job an' remember never to forget to keep the fire buckets—"

"Go away," said Copper Baldwin.

"Your fire buckets full, to mivin one inch o' the rim. Two inches low in a fire bucket, an' *I'm* the sufferer. Ain't it, Copper?"

"Oh, for Christ's sake, take a pen'orth!" said Copper Baldwin. "Take a ball-o'-chalk!"

"Put your trust in Sam Yudenow an' keep your powder dry. Flea powder you'll find in a locker. Keep it under lock an' key, or the bastards rahnd 'ere will get 'old of it an' drilute it miv water, an' drink it up."

Copper Baldwin said, "For the last time, will you scram?"

"See you later," said Sam Yudenow. Then he climbed into an immense orange-and-green Renault limousine, and was driven away.

Copper Baldwin said to me, "Your name is Laverock, I take it. That bastard, he's got kind of a different sort of ears like a dog, or a rat, or something—not to insult them by mentioning Sam Yudenow in the same breath. Watch out for Yudenow, sonny—he's dead dangerous."

Colorful imagery was in vogue in those days; startling simile. I made a mental note of Copper Baldwin's tone of voice and manner of speaking, and decided that I would put it down as Sandwich Cutter's Knife. As a tailor grows accustomed to his own scissors and a barber to his own razors or a writer to his own pens, so that no one else can use them effectively, a sandwich cutter grows accustomed to his favorite knife. It begins as a common ham knife, one of a hundred thousand others out of the same factory. But something of the nature of the man who happens to take a fancy to it gets into the blade. The man gets the feel of the steel, and the steel works in sympathy with the man. Perhaps, by the power of idiosyncrasy, the knife undergoes a subtle molecular change and absorbs a little bit of the spirit in the hand that cherishes it—what do I know? Anyway, in the end you will see an old sandwich cutter carrying with him a knife which in anyone else's hand would be a mere encumbrance: it ripples, bends limply and, honed down to next to nothing, is as near flabby as steel can get. But let this old gray man take up this gray old knife, and a virtue seems to flow into it, so that it slices like a botanist's section cutter; grain, fat, or gristle, it knows them in the dark.

I thought of Copper Baldwin's tongue in this connection. He talked the lowest-down kind of Cockney I ever heard in my life—snorts, grunts, labials, glottal stops, rhyming slang and all—so that if he had been simply making conversation or passing the time of day, you would have had to listen twice before you caught the drift of him. But his tongue being unwrapped and wiped to carve, it became supple, sure, and accurate to the fraction of an ounce—and at the end, one little cut for overweight and good measure, always, almost but not quite, blunting itself against the fork of his perception. It is the perception that counts; never mind the dialect comedy—I will see myself damned before

I butcher Copper Baldwin to make a grammarian's holiday! Yes, he juggled his diphthongs and mewed his vowels and swallowed his consonants, used prepositions to end sentences with, negated his negatives and played pocket billiards with subject, predicate and object. But Copper Baldwin knew language and the meaning of it; tough as it might be he had got the grain of it, and knew how to whittle it into shape.

"What, dangerous? Who, Sam Yudenow?" I said. "I thought he was rather funny."

Copper Baldwin said, "If you want a 'ealthier bit of a laugh I'll tickle the soles of your feet for you. Like a Chinese nanny goat. Where d'you live?"

"Next door, in the dressing room with the cupboard that locks."

He looked at me out of one eye and then said, "How long have you been out?"

"Out of where?" I asked.

"I thought you'd been inside," said Copper Baldwin.

"Mr. Yudenow just showed me round."

"Listen," said Copper Baldwin. "One thing I don't like is madam. Don't madam me. I mean *inside*—bucket-and-pail."

"Oh, jail?" I said. "No, not just lately. Why do you ask?"

"Nothing," said Copper Baldwin, "only you're a funny one. You talk like a gentleman. Educated man?"

"It depends what you mean, Mr. Baldwin."

"They call me Copper. What d'you mean 'it depends'?"

"Well," I said, "I went to school."

"So did I, so did everybody. Ever pass a scholarship?"

"No. Did you?"

"Yes," said Copper Baldwin. "You don't mind me asking, what age did you leave school at?"

"Eighteen."

"I was twelve. What brings you 'ere?"

"Something to do, something to eat," I said.

"Is Laverock your real name? What's your first name?"

"Daniel, but they call me Dan."

"Why don't you join the Foreign Legion? Like they do in books when they go wrong?" he asked.

"Didn't have the fare to France," I said.

"You'd have been better off, you know. So it's 'earts-of-oak, is it?"

"Broke is the word, Copper."

"I'll lend you a quid till Friday," he said. "Later, we'll see . . ."

"I wouldn't think—" I began.

"Oh, yes, you would," said Copper Baldwin, "you would and you will." He fished out an old brass watch. "Twenty minutes to go. Come and 'ave a beer."

"It's only quarter to eleven," I said. "Are they open yet?"

He said, "Listen, for Copper Baldwin they'll open—" Then he stopped abruptly, shut his mouth with a click and moistened his lips. "See what I mean?" he said. "Who was I talking like?"

"Sam Yudenow?"

"Sam Smallpox—'e's catching," said Copper Baldwin, leading the way across the dismal High Street to the Load of Mischief.

"Is that why you said he was dangerous, Copper?"

"You wait and see."

Before we went into the pub, he took me to the urinal in the alley and pressed into my hand a ten-shilling note and four half-crowns, saying, "Put that in your skyrocket and order like a gentleman . . ." His voice died away, and he started, like a man coming out of a bad dream. "What am I talking about?" he said, spitting into the tarred gutter. "As you were! You do what you bloody well like, for Christ's sake! I'm buying the beer. You're a manager, see? And a gentleman in a very responsible position, see? And I'm sucking up to you, got me? Talk down to me—*you* know, treat me off'anded. Foller?"

"I said, "Damned if I follow, Copper. What's the idea?"

Copper Baldwin rubbed his forehead and said, "There I go

again, if you see what I mean. I'm warning you, Yudenow gets you groggy."

"That's another one of his expressions," I said.

"No, it isn't," said Copper Baldwin, "it's one o' mine. He picked it up off of me. That's the way it is wiv *'im*—he'll take away the very way you talk, and mess it about, and in the end you forget what's what. The simplest little thing Yudenow can make you uncertain of. And all the time innocent as a child, mind you! Talk white, and 'e'll turn it black; and when 'e lets you 'ave it back it's you that's led 'im astray. You wait and see. No, what I mean to say is, you take that quid and if Yudenow asks you do you want a few bob to tide you over, make wiv a mysterious—no, wait a minute! Tell him straight: 'Bollocks!' Only like a gentleman, d'you foll—Oh, for Christ's sake! Ever read about Dracula? Ever read about Svengali? Well, then . . ." He pulled himself together, shaking himself like a dog. "Don't let Yudenow lend you a penny, and pay cash for every crumb you eat up at the Greek's."

"Thanks," I said.

" 'Ave you read a lot of books?" Copper Baldwin asked.

"Quite a few," I said.

"I bet I've read more than what you 'ave," he said.

"Shouldn't be a bit surprised, Copper."

"I dessay you believe what you read. Well, don't. It's all a lot o' crap—every word, practically. One o' these days we'll 'ave a discussion. . . . Generally, I can size a bloke up one-two-three—I mean, generally I can size a bloke up. But I 'aven't got the size of you yet. Well, come on in."

So we went into the saloon bar of the Load of Mischief—a sad, damp place, close and cold at the same time. The landlord was a deaf old man, slow and heavy as lead. He wore green mittens, a balaclava helmet, and two knitted waistcoats. A paraffin heater burned behind the bar; but in the fireplace there was nothing but a quantity of crumpled red crepe paper, which, I gathered, was supposed to create an illusion of warmth. On the mantelpiece stood a shiny showcard depicting a lady in a tiara clinking glasses with a diplomat decorated with the Order of the Golden Fleece, and captioned CELEBRATE WITH CHAMPEX. There was also a shiny picture of a philosophical old gentleman with a churchwarden pipe, wearing a tasseled smoking cap, advertising CURLY MIXTURE —THE THINKER'S TOBACCO. Naturally, some joker had scratched out the TH and substituted ST. Similarly, there had been erasures and substitutions on the GOLD BRICK SHAG and the HUCKSTABLE TWIST showcards, and a very neat spoonerist job on the FRIAR TUCK ALE sign.

"The famous Cockney sense of humor," said Copper Baldwin, following my glance. "A scream, ain't it? You know—mix everything up. Instead o' saying 'a bottle o' gin' say 'a jottle o' bin.' If it turns out smutty, all the funnier. I don't think! . . . And there's some more of your famous Cockney humor for you. Simply say what isn't, that's all. G. K. Chesterton in 'is essay on Pickwick calls it 'fine irony' or something. 'E was another 'ysterical craphound. 'E was as bad as Dickens, if not worse. Fine Irony o' the Working Classes! All you've got to do is listen to the dirty sods enjoying themselves. Their idea o' fun is for an old woman to kick up her legs and show her dirty drawers, and scream 'Oops!' . . . Well, what's it to be? Love-in-a-punt?"

"What's that?"

"Pig's ear. Beer: f - - - ing-near-water. Or a drop o' short?"

"I'll have a beer," I said. "So you don't like Dickens?"

" 'E was phony to the backbone. So are they all, most of 'em. Liars, every last one of 'em practically. . . . Hoy, you! A Bass and a Scotch, you deaf bastard! . . . That's the only way to talk to the working classes—or the middle classes, or the upper classes, for that matter. The crook of the arm in the . . . I mean, treat 'em rough. Never argue, never give 'em a chance to think. Take 'em individually, one by one. I'll show you 'ow Saturday night. The public is muck; shovel it! Bloody rabble. Divide and conquer.

When in doubt, pick out the one with the loudest voice. Don't break your knuckles on 'im—the 'eel of your 'and under the tip of 'is nose, a swift poke in the Adam's apple, and let 'im welter.... Drink 'earty!"

"Sam Yudenow warned me—" I began.

"Yudenow! Pay no attention to 'im, I warn you. You've read 'ow they can concentrate a 'ole pig into a pill? That's Yudenow—a one-man Saturday-night crowd—the bloody Gadarene swine compressed. Just add water. That de'ydrated cesspool!"

He drank his whisky. My beer was, indeed, very flat. I ordered again, and then said, "So you've read Dickens, have you?"

"Every last word," said Copper Baldwin, "and did I enjoy 'im? Yes, I did. Like Mickey-bloody-Mouse. 'E ain't true, 'e ain't real. And don't give me all that stuff about 'aving met Dickensian characters. I know you 'ave, the same way you've met Gloria Swanson, or King George, or Jesus Christ in the Old Kent Road. Give the stinking rabble something easy to copy—that's all—and there you are: 'true to life,' as they say. 'Umbug! Crappy little sods like Dickens aren't true to life—life is true to Charles Dickens. And that goes for that poor bastard William Shakespeare, too—though I admit 'e done 'is best within 'is limitations. . . . And don't let the Frenchmen or the Russians fool you, either; you mark my words. They never wrote about anything they saw or knew. Zola got it all out of the newspapers; and those 'e 'ad to read with a magnifying glass. 'E was 'alf blind, like Kipling or Rider 'Aggard. You don't see anything with a microscope or a telescope."

"What do you see then?"

"Nothing. Did you ever see a church? No. Or a 'ouse? No. Or a man? No. Your poor bloody eyes are only made to take in a tiny little bit of anything at one time. You don't see a thing, cocko, you see a mess of blobs. The closer you get the less you see. The farther away you get the less you see. And when you get in range, what d'you see? Something in your imagination. And these poor stinkpots think they're writing about life. Why, Gorblimey, it would take all of 'em all their lives put together to write about one second! . . . And then some crackpot like Tolstoy, or somebody, sits down on his arse and writes about a million pages all about war—and you say 'Darling, isn't it marvelous?' Was 'e *in* that war? No. Was Zola in the Franco-Prussian War? Bet your life 'e wasn't—'e buggered off to Marseilles, and pieced that book of 'is together afterwards. But: 'Stark realism,' says you. Is anybody ever in a war? The answer is no. I know—I was in the last one from beginning to end."

"Get hurt?" I asked.

"Not a scratch," said Copper Baldwin impatiently. "Peace, so-called, is a bloody sight more dangerous. But did I see any war? No. I froze in the mud, I sweated in the dust, I washed when I could and went lousy when I couldn't; took orders from stinkpots that wasn't fit to run a cockle stall—it was the same as I'd always been used to. But as for seeing the war—Christ, nobody ever saw it, and whatever you read about it is a lot of eyewash, 'umbug, 'earsay, common bloody lies. Like when you read about somebody who 'knows 'is London,' or 'knows women,' or something. Why, not one man in a million could recognize 'imself if 'e met 'imself in the street—and people spend most o' their time looking at themselves, but seeing themselves in reverse, mind you. . . . No, it wouldn't matter what you read, it's all a fairy tale. A dream, get me? I say a dream, and if you believe otherwise, prove it. Time for just one more."

"A dream you wake up to," I suggested.

"I 'ave yet to be convinced that I am not fast asleep," said Copper Baldwin.

"But you were talking about Sam Yudenow," I said.

"We were talking about Charles Dickens. Now tell me something—why do you read a load of tripe like *Martin Chuzzlewit*? Why can't you put that crappy book down? Because you're interested in what 'appens to the 'ero? That twerp? No. Because you're interested in Pecksniff, the 'ypocrite, and Jonas, and Tigg, the bucket-shop keeper, and that dirty filthy drunken old stinking midwife, Sairey Gamp. You've got to see those bastards get what's coming to 'em. Ain't that so? Life is like that, too, son. The 'eroes, the 'eroes are fabricated. They read themselves up in books, or saw themselves on the stage. It's the villains that grip you, cocko—black bloody villainy, that's the salt of life, that's what keeps you guessing, that's what keeps you turning the pages! 'Ate pulls the strings that make you jump, my boy—'ate keeps you going. You know, you've got to be in at the death. Well, I've got to be in at the death of Sam Yudenow."

"You said he was dangerous."

"That's right. Look, there's millions unemployed, but I can always get a good job anywhere in the world, because there's nothing I can't do with these two Oliver Twists. I got a few quid put away. I could go to Canada, or anywhere in the world, and get a good living too. So why am I 'ere in Fowlers End, which is the sink of the bloody universe? 'Ave I got leprosy? No. Am I wanted by the police? No. Sam Yudenow's got me, that's what. You know what I mean? I'd never be able to rest in peace unless I got to the finish of 'im. 'Ate, it's the spice of life, sonny."

I said, "I don't know; I never managed to hate anybody, and I find life tasty enough."

He looked at me and shook his head. "Up to a point, a bellyful of warm milk and your thumb to suck is all you need to keep you 'appy. But as soon as you learn to crawl you want to get your teeth into something. You'll get weaned 'ere, my boy. Likewise, up to a point you're quite 'appy to listen to the tick-tick. But a little later you're miserable unless you can take it apart and see what makes it go."

"That doesn't mean to say that you have to hate the watch," I said.

"I know. Not necessarily. But what if it's a dead wrong watch, a deliberately wrong watch, if you can imagine such a thing, and the 'ole purpose of it is to make you miss your train?"

I said, "I'd keep it as a curiosity. And I'd be very interested to meet the man who designed it."

"If you found 'im," said Copper Baldwin, "you'd kind of meet the Devil, wouldn't you?"

"Maybe so. But in the meantime, as long as I knew how to tell the right time I wouldn't let it worry me."

"Okay. But what if that watchmaker made a practice of going about at night and altering the clocks all over the place so that they told the wrong time?"

"Depends what you mean by wrong time," I said. "If all the clocks tell the wrong time at the same time, that's the right time." I never can resist a bit of metaphysics. "At a certain hour on a certain day of the year, the Government says, 'Every clock and watch in the country must henceforward be an hour wrong.' And after that, if your watch isn't wrong it isn't right."

"All right, all right, all right! But what if every watch was *different*?" said Copper Baldwin.

"You'd still eat when you were hungry, if you had the price of a meal," I said. And, really, I am fundamentally as easygoing as all that.

"It's my fault," said Copper Baldwin bitterly. "I pick on the shittiest analogies. . . . Look, I see I'm going to 'ave an amusing time educating you. You're a treasure, that's what you are. Friction. You 'elp my wheels bite, and keep my works from rusting. What a pity this ain't Sunday! Wait, and I'll let you cut your teeth on my intellec'. You see, if I open my Norf-and-Souf at all these days, it's to talk to myself. But look 'ere. Do you believe in right and wrong? I mean to say, you know the difference, don't you? There's no time for definitions now, 'cause we got to open up the flea pit. Say, to go on with, your instinc' tells you to do what's right and undo what's wrong? All right. All right. And what if you can't undo what's wrong, but it starts undoing you? Well?"

"Well . . ." I said.

"That's War, ain't it? I mean, 'Oly War—Armageddon—Gawd versus the Devil in one f - - - ing fiery bundle. Ain't that so? D'you think Gawd don't 'ate the Devil? Assuming, o' course, they exist?"

Just to be annoying, I said, "I don't see why He should, Copper. But then I'm not a religious man like you."

"A *what* like *who*?" he shouted; then controlled himself and said with a sour smile, "I see I got a prize packet 'ere. When I've trained you to be my intellectual equal, it's going to be a proper bloody treat. I won't argue with you now; there's no time. Let's drop it. . . . But what the bloody 'ell did you mean by 'religious'? That's what I'd like to know."

"Too much hate," I said, with a passable imitation of Sam Yudenow's 'mysterious smile.' I was feeling cockily confident, extraordinarily cheerful. I slapped Copper Baldwin on the back; it was like slapping a tight-packed sack of pebbles. "Let's open up," I said with airy authority.

"I'll stick close for a week or two," said Copper Baldwin. "It'd be a shame to lose you just yet. Only remember what I said: if you want anything, come to me. Before going to Sam Yudenow for a few shillings, go to the carsey, lift up the seat, cut your throat, chuck yourself down the 'ole, and pull the plug."

"I'll do that," I said.

So we went back to the Pantheon, while Copper Baldwin said under his breath, "Religious, is it? We'll see about that, cocko!"

I had said it only to tease him, but I believe now that I was right, in a way.

Promiscuous haters get religion as promiscuous lovers get clap. It is a kind of occupational disease which they make a virtue of —you aren't a man until you've had it. The getting of religion by a hater is the sickly consummation of a masturbatory marriage: previously, he only flirted and fumbled himself in dark corners, but, having got religion, he is publicly himself to have and to hold, legally free to worry himself to death. Consider, for example, the sour sighs of such joyless acid-throwing, self-damnatory Holy Rollers as Dostoevski, Graham Greene, Tolstoy, Evelyn Waugh, and other self-digesters of all denominations, dutifully saving their own muck for orgies of mirror-pelting. Their hate got too strong for them, so that mere doubt became insipid. Hate is very lonely; nobody understands it. Love is never frustrated, but hate always is—it is never fulfilled, it wants always to be warmed and cosseted; but it has only its own bosom to fall back upon. So it goes mad; calls itself God, justifies itself, fears itself, adores itself; flagellates itself, licks itself into a shell of scar tissue, and forgives itself. Then, suspecting itself, it hires private detectives to catch itself being unfaithful to itself—and writes an indignant book about itself. Result? Literature.

In writing of myself I forgot to mention that I have a most extraordinary gift of repartee. I can always find the *mot juste*, the witty riposte, the devastating rejoinder—only it comes out ten or fifteen minutes too late. So now, on the very steps of the Pantheon, I said, "I mean to say, Copper, after all, if it's *reality* you're after, why read books? What do you want them for? You *are* reality—you're *living* it. Reading is a waste of time. So are pictures. So is talking. So is Yudenow; you can't see him, because your eyes distort and your brain's only a photographic plate that might be off-color. You know, Copper, light is only algebra, love and hate are only biochemistry, you and Yudenow are simply a couple of formulae—it's all mapped out and sewn up for you in red tape. Nice and easy, Copper—all you want is a label; paste it on and post yourself! You are all mixed up between naturalism and nature, and candor and truth—that's what you are, Copper. And you know what a 'realist' is? A destructive romantic, a sort of hen-pecked husband at a carnival who pays sixpence for the privilege of throwing little wooden balls at threepenny-worth of saucers. What is real is the good and the true and the beautiful—and that is a hunger and a love."

“ ’Ave you eaten yet this morning?”

“Why?”

“You should ’ave ’ad a sandwich,” said Copper Baldwin, with his sour smile. “ ’Unger, love, et cetera. A fat lot you know about that, I bet.”

If there had been time, I would have told Copper Baldwin that I knew a devil of a lot about all kinds of things. I might have said, for example, that, young as I was, hunger had already led me into crime, and thence to love; and that this love was leading me back to crime again; and that the whole mess had its germ in sheer stubborn pride. By “crime” I do not mean anything that would cast a man out from decent society. It depends, of course, what you mean by “decent society.” Decency, in society, is measured in strange ways. It is weighed in terms according to your capacity to foot the bill. Innocence goes in inverse proportion to need. If a tramp knocks a rich man down and takes his wallet, that is robbery with violence; if a rich man knocks a tramp down and takes his hat, that is an escapade.

It had happened two years before, when I was still in my twenty-second year and had already frittered away my tiny patrimony in a crackbrained money-making scheme that had been evolved in a Soho café by a man named Barron (or, as I put it, “lost my small fortune by untimely speculation”). I used to spend night after night in the cafés around Old Compton Street listening to all kinds of interesting conversation. Barron fascinated me. There was something godlike about the man’s tremendous scorn for the reading public—and for the writing public, and the arithmetic public too, for that matter. He could prove, conclusively, that everyone was a fool. According to him, he got a living out of the bigger bookshops in Charing Cross Road. The process was so simple that I wondered why everybody didn’t do it: all you did was walk in, go to the Latest Biographies shelves, pick up a twenty-five-shilling book, carry it without paying for it, of course, to the Books Bought Department on the second floor, and sell it for half a guinea. The booksellers hugged themselves at the thought of having cheated you, you hugged yourself at the thought of having cheated the booksellers, and everybody was happy.

Another trick of Barron's, which he confided to me, was equally simple and, by his irresistibly persuasive reasoning, highly moral. He would put on a pair of earrings and, carrying some cigar boxes under his arm, stand outside some newly opened shop, scratching his head and looking hopelessly bewildered. Eventually the shopkeeper would ask him if he could be of any assistance; whereupon Barron, simulating acute embarrassment, would say that he was looking for a man named Rose who used to live there—you know, *Mister* Rose, the connoisseur of fine cigars. He, Barron, was a seafaring man just back from Cuba and had smuggled past the Customs a matter of two hundred and fifty fine Coronas worth five shillings apiece, which Mr. Rose generally took off him for a fiver the lot. It was highly illegal, of course, and strictly hush-hush. But with no Mr. Rose, what the devil was he going to do with all these fine cigars? Would the gentleman like to try one and see? The gentleman would, and the gentleman did, and ended by beating the poor old seafaring man down to three pounds for five cigar boxes full of brown paper. (Why brown paper, God knows; somehow, Barron made it sound cleverer that way.) He was full of such tricks; as he talked of them in his haughty drawl they sounded, as it were, evangelic—he was a kind of practical missionary demonstrating that dishonesty does not pay. You do not have to cheat people, he told me; leave them alone and they will cheat themselves. . . .

But he had a legitimate scheme for making money, *real* money, he told me. What was the one thing a person borrowed that he invariably returned? A book. Why did he return this book to a library? Because there was always a crying need for something trashy to read. Start Circulating Libraries, said Barron, stocked with popular tripe, all in their dust jackets with celluloid covers; twopence per volume per week and no deposit! There was a fortune in that. Ninety per cent of the buying would be on credit, of course; that was easy; one had only to start a limited company with a registered office and embossed notepaper. Heavily embossed. Even the stationery could be got on credit, and the shelves, filing cabinets, et cetera. Unhappily, ready cash was needed for the rent of premises in populous areas—in the City, for example, where clerks and typists worked; and in the suburbs where, starved for love and adventure, they dreamed away their evenings over the claptrap of Rafael Sabatini and Jeffrey Farnol, and the musky goosh of Elinor Glyn and Ethel M. Dell. . . . As Barron calculated, such an investment would pay about ninety-five shillings in the pound—not fantastic, perhaps, but steady. All the proprietor would have to do would be ride from branch to branch and collect the takings in a heavy leather bag. You would need a safe, of course; but that was one thing you could always get on credit. Nobody ever ran away with a safe. . . .

The idea enchanted me. And so it came to pass, one bitter Saturday six months later, that I found myself faint with hunger in the British Museum with nothing in my pocket but a dirty handkerchief and that feeling of sick desperation in the heart that comes to a healthy young man when he has slept out of doors and had nothing to eat for seventy-two hours. It seems that Barron had met a helpless old lady in a Temperance Hotel near Russell Square. She had three hundred and fifty pounds in golden sovereigns saved up. Someone had told her that the surrender value of a golden pound was now twenty-five shillings. Did Barron know of an honest goldsmith? Now the value of a sovereign had risen almost overnight to twenty-eight and sixpence. Barron bought the old lady's hoard for twenty-five shillings apiece. When he opened the wash-leather bag he found three hundred and fifty of those lead disks with which tailors used to weight women's skirts. The old lady from the country, I may add, turned out to be an ex-girlfriend of Eddie Guerin's, a notorious character who sold the diamonds out of her front teeth to help him escape from Devil's Island and later, in France, was acquitted by an emotional jury on a charge of killing her mulatto lover by throwing him off the Eiffel Tower. But Barron, it transpired, was not a trickster at all; he was an unemployed shorthand writer out of Temple Bar who lived on the earnings of his mother, who had a little hand laundry in Paradise Street, Marylebone. That is how I lost the thousand pounds I inherited from my grandmother when I came of age. We did open the "main branch" of Laverock Libraries Limited, off High Holborn, and did, indeed, a brisk business. Fourteen hundred books were borrowed in the first day. Only ninety-seven were returned, and three of these were hopelessly stained with tea-and-cocoa rings.

I took this failure hard. The loss of the money did not move me very deeply; after all, I hadn't really seen it, and didn't know it, except to say hello and good-by to. But my pride was hurt. When I came home one day and told my mother that I was going to put my capital into a chain of Circulating Libraries, she said something like "I don't know anything at all about anything whatsoever, Daniel; but in the very nature of things, whatever you do of your own initiative must lead to disaster in the end. Your arguments are perfectly sound, I am sure. But for goodness gracious sake, don't, unless you are determined to bring my gray hairs in sorrow to the grave—which may be at any moment now. . . ." Then she went behind my back and called in my Uncle Hugh, who, when I told him what I intended to do, sniffed suspiciously at my breath and said in effect, "I am thirty-five years older than you, and therefore know better. I have spent thirty years in the City, and I can assure you that it won't work."

When I said, with some bitterness, "They laughed at Marconi, too," he replied, "And rightly so—the fellow got roundly swindled, and serves him right. You can take it from me, young man

—and, as a solicitor, I may claim to have some experience of human nature—nobody who gets a brand-new seven-and-six-penny book for twopence down and no deposit is ever going to return it." I told him that this was unthinkable because *Property of Laverock Libraries Limited* would be plainly marked in every volume with a rubber stamp. He laughed at that, and my poor mother, clutching at a word, kept saying, "Oh, Daniel, you must have a deposit!"

Then my Uncle Hugh said, "My advice to you, my boy, is this: Put that thousand pounds of yours into Fabricated Utilities and leave it there two years. Meanwhile, we'll get you a job with prospects. Otherwise, I can see you spending the night in jail for stealing apples off a barrow. This Mr. Barron of yours is evidently nothing but a petty adventurer." I cried out that he was nothing of the sort, and my mother said, "He may be a nice man, but!" I shouted that Barron was not a very nice man and there were to be no buts. Uncle Hugh said, "Oh, very well, Daniel, throw away your thousand pounds, and then, perhaps, you'll take my advice."

My mother cried, "Oh, Daniel, don't throw away your thousand pounds. Do take your Uncle Hugh's advice!"

"I will follow my instincts," I said. "They laughed at Sir Isaac Newton."

My uncle said, "And quite right, too, since the merest German Jew—one Einstein—has proved him wrong!"

"How do you know?" I asked.

"Figures prove it," said my Uncle Hugh. "There is a *law*, Daniel, a certain law."

After some thought, I said, "Look at the Middle Ages!" But my Uncle Hugh said that these were not the Middle Ages, and that this was the time to buy Fabricated Utilities at 1¼. My mother cried, "Buy Fabricated Utilities, Daniel, if only a few!" But I would not. In eighteen months, the Ordinary shares of Fabricated Utilities rose from 1¼ to 8¾, and I bitterly regretted never having listened to my Uncle Hugh's excellent advice. Everything was as he had foreseen it; and even my mother was right. I became an outcast, a wanderer. I became a Minority of One, with only myself to consider. Pride took hold of me. If I had gone to my Uncle Hugh and said, "All right, Uncle, you were right and I was wrong. Let's have that job," he would have taken me to lunch at Sweeting's and staked me to a couple of new suits; and my mother, writing off a pigheaded streak in me to the debit of my father's ancestors, would have thanked God that everything was for the best in this best of all possible worlds.

But I could not do it. It wasn't in me to go back with my tail between my legs. If my Uncle Hugh had only known it, I had given him the wherewithal to say, "I told you so," and with a vengeance. But I took good care that he should not know it. There is something humiliating, sometimes, in a display of penitence; and always something disgusting in a show of misery. It corrupts, it is indecent, it is bad for the soul.

Live or die your own way, I say.

To paraphrase Mark Twain: The next person who saves my life does so over my dead body. . . .

5

Because, after all is said and done, a man has his pride—or at least a certain decent habit of self-continence. But do you know what? The "harsh realities" that jostle him from point to point are matters for a healthy man to laugh off; he lives, at his fullest, in essentially imaginary noble quarrels, fierce triumphs, and saintly defeats.

Especially in the small hours, from the kind of people that like to spill their souls, I have heard a lot of talk about loneliness; and to deal plainly with you, I don't believe in it. There is no such thing as one person alone—this side Colney Hatch, where the lunatic asylum is. I went there once to pay a visit to a melancholiac, bringing him a harmless, nourishing, and beautiful bunch of grapes. An imbecile would have played with them. A maniac would have trampled on them. The melancholy madman did neither, but just looked at them without seeing. He had achieved—largely through wanting to escape—complete solitude, the last word in self-containment. You see, he was within himself, sold to himself. . . . Believe me, as long as a man knows that he is lonely, he is not alone; he is still fumbling the void for an imaginary companion, of no matter what sort.

It takes three to make a person—himself, a friend, and an enemy—even when he is in the self-imposed solitary confinement romantically known as Loneliness.

Most of your Great Lonely Souls, so-called, are nothing but stubborn babies crying to be picked up. And that is what I was, animated as I thought by manly pride. Manly pride? Frantic childishness refusing its supper in order to be coaxed and willfully hurting itself just a little for the sake of a lot of bandaging and cosseting; trying to make a virtue of an error, presuming on my childishness. A great sin, that: to wet your bed to water the seeds of guilt in your elders! I should have known better. Mine was something like the story of Little Trott, over whom I wept reading it in the *Children's Encyclopedia*. His mother having the presumption to suckle his newborn sister, Trott threw himself off a high-backed chair and bumped his head, whereupon he was taken back to the maternal bosom and to the paternal mustache discreetly redolent of toilet water. A swift slap in the jaw is what Little Trott wanted. So did I. To my horror, I got it self-administered.

Walking into the Pantheon, I felt that this was no time to treat Copper Baldwin with reminiscence (or what the critics call a flashback) but I knew what I thought I knew, and smiled at him —mysteriously. I was thinking about my pride, and it seemed to me that I was a hell of a fellow, and little he knew. Hunger, love, et cetera—I could show Copper a thing or two if I chose!

When the last of my valuables went up the spout, as the saying goes, and my landlady told me that, whereas she had all the faith in the world in my prospects, unless I let her have a little something on account there was a gentleman from Leicester in steady work who needed my room, I pressed my tie by putting it between two sheets of damp cardboard and sitting on it for two hours, and steamed my hat with the last of a pennyworth of gas;

said that I would return in due course to settle my little account and, every inch a gentleman, went my way down the windswept road of the night. Loneliness? I asked for it; it was romantic.

Mine was the pride of the eagle (that filthy bird which lives on mice and leavings) that brooked no company. Craggy was the word for my hauteur when I refused to have anything to do with other down-and-outs, when the Depression was going strong and if I had gone and sat on a bench on the Embankment where I belonged I might have got a cup of cocoa, a pie, a lecture, a couple of cigarettes, and a blessing. I tried it once, being parched and starved, but Pride stepped in the way. Cocoa, as a beverage, I detest; but I was cold and hungry, and no steam ever smelled more delicious. There was also a promising-looking oblong packet containing, as it had been whispered, a sandwich, five Woodbines, a piece of slab-cake, and a tract full of useful information about the Second Coming and Repent Ere It Is Too Late. Also, a bit of soap—to which I was particularly looking forward. But when it came to my turn I said to the lady with the packet, "No, no, thanks all the same—really, I couldn't dream . . ." Taken at my word, I went away empty—emptier, I believed, than any human vessel had ever been before—and walked away and away, drinking saliva until on the stroke of two I remembered that there is a little gate near the zoo through which the park keepers pass and the mysterious tradesmen who carry in the carcasses of horses they cut up for the hyenas. To this gate, twirling my cane in an elegant manner, I made my way hoping that if I were seen I might be mistaken for some gay young man-about-town seeing life.

This part of Regents Park borders on Primrose Hill. "The Scotchman's Zoo" they call it, because here is Monkey Hill where the baboons live and publicly perform certain acts which the local girls, peeping between their fingers, describe as disgusting. To this part of the Zoological Gardens are relegated the creatures that once were beasts—an old wild boar, undistinguishable, until it breaks wind, from the winter mud or the summer dust; one or two scabby dogs of the dhole or dingo variety, I forget which; a moth-eaten bison, a discouraged antelope, et cetera. You could look at them free any time the park was open; that is why this part of the place was called "The Scotchman's Zoo."

Well, as I had foreseen, the little gate was ajar, so I went into Regents Park and sat down, not far from the Lion House, to doze away the rest of the darkness on a bench, leaning on my cane—an elegant old malacca with an ivory knob which was still in my possession for three reasons: nobody would buy it, I could not give it away, and whenever I tried to lose it someone always brought it back to me. There was thunder in the air, and the great cats were restless. A lion roared first of all, and then a tiger; whereupon a leopard made a noise like a blunt saw going through plywood, and all the monkeys began to scream and chatter in terror, while my empty stomach grumbled in sympathy. Soon a man came by shoving a wheelbarrow.

"'Ow'd *you* git in?" he asked.

"Climbed over the railings," I said.

"You're not supposed to," he said.

I said, "Breath of air."

"'Ark at the lions. 'Ear 'em?"

"I thought I noticed something roaring."

"They smell blood, you know."

"Do they? What blood?" I asked.

The man was fragrant with breakfast bacon; I wished he would go away. But he lingered, and said, "'Orse blood. They'll be knocking orf an 'orse just about now, aginst feeding time. Bloody marvelous, that old 'orse."

"Bloody marvelous what old horse?"

"Charley, the old 'orse we keep in there. Just like a 'uman bean. You wouldn't think an 'orse could sink so low, would you? It's bloody marvelous!"

"So low as what?"

"You know a lion eats twenty-eight pounds of 'orse meat at a sitting? Well, every day, more or less, we slaughter an 'orse. Well, you know an 'orse 'ates the smell o' blood, specially 'orse blood? Well, old as they are, these 'ere old 'orses balk like 'ell at the slaughter 'ouse. Well, that's where old Charley comes in. Twenty-two years old, 'e is, and a bloody nuisance to 'imself, but 'e rubs along gettin' a livin' as a sort of a nark. Charley gives a kind of a whinny over 'is shoulder, as much as to say, 'It's all okay, chum, foller me and see.' Walks into the slaughter'ouse. Other 'orse calms down an' follers 'im in. Biff, bang, wallop! A 'umane killer right in the conk, and down 'e goes in all bloody directions like a carpenter's ruler. While Charley walks out the other side and 'as 'is breakfast. Marvelous!"

"Lucky horse," I said.

"In a 'uman bean, you'd think nothink of it. But in an 'orse it's bloody marvelous."

"It only goes to show."

"It do, don't it?" said this pestilential man, and hiccuped slightly. "My eldest gel married a farmer, and she sent me a flitch o' bacon from Wiltshire. I overate meself this morning."

"Too bad," I said.

"The Frenchies eat 'orse flesh. So do the Belgiums."

"They ought to be ashamed of themselves."

"And frogs. Snakes eat frogs too. Bloody marvelous!" He chuckled. "One o' these fine mornings, though, old Charley's goin' to git the surprise of 'is life. 'E'll walk in as usual, only this time the other 'orse'll be *in front* of 'im. I bet old Charley'll 'ave taught 'im 'is job, too. I'd like to see the expression on poor old Charley's face when they say, 'Wait a minute, Charley—' I bet '*e*'ll eat tough."

You have to be in just the right state of physical and mental balance not to be nauseated, or maddened, by the fundamentals —food and sex—and the whole cosmos, it seems, is generally in a conspiracy to rub you up the wrong way in these matters. If you hunger for physical love, the world is as full of full-blown female buttocks as a baby's pipe is of bubbles; you may look and yearn, but you may not touch. An invisible portcullis has been let fall between you and your desire. Come away, satiated with the embraces of some object of your affection, and (as if you have invented a new kind of man) all womankind will make tracks for you. Again: Eat your fill of your favorite food—eat *ad nauseam*—and wherever you turn you will encounter the sight or the smell of it, or hear some voluptuous talk of it, to turn your stomach. Fast, dream lustfully of how right your good mother was when, after you turned your nose up at fat mutton broth, she said, "You may be glad of it someday"—brood over the semolina you rejected, the custards you had to be bribed to eat, and so forth—and wherever you turn there is sure to be some malevolent spirit in the form of a park-keeper, or what not, talking food, food, food!

It is all very well for one of these martyrs you read about to go on a hunger strike. He has a cause; somewhere, somebody goes hungry with him out of sympathy; benevolent jailers coax him with steaming broth, et cetera. In any case, he knows perfectly well that a man, lying still, and upheld by his belief that the show must go on, can prolong his dying a couple of months on nothing but water. An Irishman out of the I.R.A. (it took him thirty years to eat himself to death in America on the strength of it) told me how he once went on a twenty-day hunger strike in prison. The first seven days, he said, were the worst; after which, the gnawing pain in the stomach having subsided, there was no discomfort but a feeling of lightness, of freedom from the flesh. Very likely. But mine was a one-man hunger strike, and I was full of an urgent desire to live. Furthermore, not yet having fully grown, all my tissues seemed to scratch and scream for nourishment. Yet again, I had no one to show off to.

And here, depression notwithstanding, was a world full of food, an atmosphere full of roars in anticipation of food, downtrodden minorities talking about Wiltshire bacon. . . . I walked to the lake in Regents Park with, I believe, some mad idea of stealing a duck. No doubt I was lightheaded with hunger; floating away from my body. All the ducks were gathered about an eccentric old lady in withered skirts who was throwing them bits of cake. I toyed with the idea of going up to her and saying, "Madame, I am Curator of Ducks. It is strictly forbidden to feed ducks with cake. A duck, as you know, has a special kind of digestive system. Cake is deadly poison to the duck. I am afraid I must confiscate that bag; and think yourself lucky!" But my nerve failed me.

I walked, with dignity, to a drinking fountain, washed my face, filled myself up with water, and walked, swinging that nuisance of a cane, into Baker Street. Where does one go from Baker Street? Why, to Orchard Street, and thence to Oxford Street. The restaurants were warming up. I hurried along, paused, and, for want of something better to do, asked a policeman if he could direct me to the British Museum. I pretended to speak little English; he held up the traffic while he pointed the way. So I walked eastward, window-shopping in the provision stores, until I reached Museum Street and so came to the museum, and sat for a while where the Easter Island monoliths are, wishing that I were a pigeon: a crop-filled, amorous, law-abiding pigeon, subject to no rules and protected by the state. Soon I went inside for another drink of water. A party of students was being conducted around the room on the ground floor where the Egyptian statues are. Now here you may find a certain glass case containing statuettes; look through it at a certain angle, and an empty granite sarcophagus twenty feet away is mysteriously filled with the image of the god Anubis, or it may be Thoth. It is a trick of reflection. Here was an inspiration—I might make a couple of shillings by pointing this out. Hanging on the fringes of the crowd, I hemmed and I hawed, and prepared my little speech; but nothing came out. The guide, who had been looking at me suspiciously, said, "Are you aware that this is a privately conducted party?"

I said, "Of course. I mean, no."

Then I went to the gallery, to look at that colossal mask of Rameses which hypnotizes with its blind eyes by virtue of sheer hugeness; it is just great enough, and small enough, for you to see in all its immensity from a distance of a few yards—if you get the right angle.

At this I stared and stared, until the stone eyes blinked and I had hypnotized the granite mask. But then I fell in spirals and awoke with a start. One of the attendants was tapping me gently on the shoulder and saying, "I'm sorry, sir, you're not supposed to sleep here, sir."

I said, "What do you mean, sleep? I was thinking."

"Ah, you want the library," he said.

In the lavatory, where I went for another drink of water, I saw my reflection in a mirror. These British Museum lavatory mirrors will impart to the best nourished and most carefully nurtured face a ghastly gray archaeological look. As I believe I have mentioned, I am no oil painting at the best of times; now I had a two-day beard. I hurried out and walked again. Now I might quite easily, without shame, have dropped in on any of four or five relatives, or one or two prosperous friends. It was lunchtime. It would be: *"Why, Daniel, my boy! How are you? Just in time for a bite. Have a chop, have a chicken, have a lobster!"—"No, no, not a morsel!"—"Come on, Dan, have a saddle-bag: twelve juicy oysters sewn up in a thick filet of steak and grilled until the bubbles come out at the seams?"—"Oh, well, just a corner, since you insist."—"Glass of burgundy?"—"Oh, no, really! Well, perhaps . . ."* It would have been like that, only pride held me back; they would have looked at the state of my chin and my shirt, and somebody would have said, "If only Daniel had listened to his Uncle Hugh!"

Rain was coming down in an uneasy, sporadic drizzle; evidently the weather was getting set to make a day of it, just out of spite. I wandered into Soho, where there were several men on the loose who owed me money or money's worth. But I could not bring myself to within the breadth of a street of where any of them might be found; I don't know why. At last I found myself —all roads led to food—in that market place between Berwick Street and Brewer Street. The city seemed to be bursting with a plethora of agonizingly appetizing food. The barrowmen were shouting, begging and pleading with passers-by to take the stuff away just for a few pence. The butcher's shop there had more meat than it knew what to do with; but I think that it was the smell of the cheesemonger's that tipped the balance. I put out my finger to stroke a beautiful round Dutch cheese, not much larger than a grapefruit; it had a waxy surface, which was so pleasant to the touch that I must have stood there for some moments in the attitude of that Philosopher with a skull, in the picture; until a black-browed man in a white coat came and stared me out of countenance. I went away toward the Café Royal, but here, too, the air was dense with the aromatic steam of food. So, via Shaftesbury Avenue, I arrived again at the market and stopped to look at a barrow-load of oblong tin cans under a sign which said:

BARGAIN! BARGAIN! BARGAIN!
TINNED HERRINGS IN
MUSTARD SAUCE!
per 2½d tin!

For some reason this twopence-halfpenny per tin drove me into a state of unreasoning anger. The triviality of the sum belittled the magnitude of my hunger; it mocked at my misery. "Twopenny-halfpenny" is a denigratory term, anyway: I have seen a Cockney woman sneering off all the "bitches" and "whores" her neighbor could lay her tongue to, but it took four policemen to hold her after she had been called "a tuppenny-ha'penny creature." What is more, the heartiness of the salesman was getting on my nerves. He kept shouting, "Ooo, they're delicious, mum! Ooo, they're scrumptious! Yum-yum! Ooo, won't yer old man give you a lovely cuddle if you bring 'im 'ome luscious 'errings in descruptious mustard sauce for 'is nice little tea! They're degorgeous, they're scruscious, they melt in the marf, they're degestible, all the way from 'Olland! Tuppence-ha'penny! Tuppence-ha'penny! *Tuppence-ha'penny!*" I wanted to kill that man, to tear him into little pieces. By way of a compromise, out of my great need, I decided to rob him. One of his innumerable tins of twopenny-halfpenny herring was balanced on the edge of the stall so that a touch might send it into the gutter. My plan was to brush it with my sleeve in passing and later, when nobody was looking, pick it up and carry it off. At present it seemed to me that the eyes of all the world were focused upon me.

The man went on, in a voice that went through and through me: "Delicious mustard sauce, mind you! Deluscious, degorgeous, degestible—it warms the cockles! Rub it on yer chest, rub it on yer feet—it cures ipsy-pipsy, pyorrhea, female ailments, lack of appetite, and the gout! Tuppence-ha'penny, gels! TUPPENCE-HA'PENNY!"

This was rather too much. Taking careful aim with my cuff, I brushed the balanced tin of herrings. It fell right back onto the stall. Believe me, anyone who tells you that hunger sharpens the senses ought to try it and see. But now my blood was up, and I was determined to get that tin of herrings and no other; so I picked it up boldly, scrutinized it with what I believed to be an air of mild amusement mixed with a certain disdain—all this with an eye on the salesman, whose detestable patter had attracted several customers. I took the tin by one corner, between thumb and forefinger; glancing left and right, convinced now that nobody was looking at me, I dropped it into my pocket and turned to go away—when I found myself staring at a silver-buttoned blue tunic which seemed vast as a night full of stars, and there stood the biggest policeman I had ever seen. From the boss of his helmet to the iron heels of his immense boots, he must have measured some six feet eight, and the expression of his face was such that I lost all hope. Drowning men are supposed, in a flash of recollection, to relive their pasts. (This, by the way, is untrue; I have nearly drowned twice, and I know.) I, in a prophetic flash, suffered the agonies of the future: I saw a shambling, shamefaced man, prematurely stooped, standing in a cemetery, weeping bitterly, while someone said in a penetrating whisper, "That is the ex-convict, Daniel Laverock. If only he had taken the advice of his Uncle Hugh, he would not have brought his mother's gray hairs in sorrow to the grave."

I said to the policeman, "Which is the way to the British Museum?"

The policeman's fist came up, clenched, from under the skirt of his tunic, and I stared at it, fascinated, for it was covered to the second joints of the fingers with black hair.

But then something remarkable happened. A girl took me by the arm and cried, in a high, clear voice, "Oh, *there* you are! Did you get the herrings?" And she slipped sixpence into my hand and pulled me toward the salesman. I looked back and caught one last glimpse of the policeman. His hairy fingers, uncurled, revealed what he had been about to let me have with that formidable fist—the price of a tin of herrings in mustard sauce, two pennies and a halfpenny. As in a dream, I took out my stolen herrings, held them up for all the world to see, and gave the sixpence to the salesman, saying in a feverish and hysterical way, "Delectable. Try delectable."

He said, "Well, strike me lucky, I never thought o' that one! Does it mean good to eat? . . . Oh, it do, do it? Gawd stone me for adultery!"

I said, "There is also deglutition."

"Well, bastardize me for a row o' pins! Take your tanner back —keep the 'errings—'elp yourself to a few tins more. . . . Come on, gels, they're delectable! They're deglutitious! All the way from

Amsterdam, and Amster*dam* sight better deglutition than you'll get in this delectable town! . . . 'Elp yourself, guv. . . . Ooo, de–"

I picked up three more tins, making four now, and offered the whole lot together with sixpence to the girl. "You see how easy it is—four tins of herrings to the good," I said, trying to be flippant. "Now let me show you how to crack a safe. All we need is nitroglycerine. If you have no nitroglycerine about you, dynamite will do. We'll try it out, as we say in the Underworld—a stick of dynamite, a gas ring, and a double boiler, and I can try out the soup in any stick." I must have been in that state of low fever when sensation really does float away, and reason is free to wander. I went on: "Better yet—let us get hold of the metal tops of soda-water siphons and make counterfeit half crowns. But first we must find a dentist who will lend us prepared gypsum for molds. The next step, of course, is to borrow a real half crown to copy. Thus, I get a stake, and get my face lifted, so that I can go back to my trade, which is the Confidence Trick. Get it, moll? . . . Everything would have been all right if my head hadn't got caught in the potato-peeling machine when I was working in the kitchen in Pentonville."

I expected her to burst out laughing. Instead, she said, "I suppose you know that all this leads nowhere? You know, you can't get out of life more than you put into it. You must give this up."

"Right-handed," I replied, holding up my mutilated left hand and talking in a tone of exaggerated bitterness. "Oh, yeah? And what did life give me? I was the best left-handed forger in the racket until my finger was bitten off by a shark."

You must understand that in the circles in which I had been used to moving we used to talk like that. We thought it was funny. No word was allowed to convey its proper meaning or was uttered without a certain note of irony. We went in for a kind of tonal double-talk—a manner of cowardly equivocation by expressions of face and voice. For example, we never said *love,* but *lerve;* and crime was not *crime,* but *cur-rye-um.* In any case, a mock-serious look followed, and a snigger, to indicate that whatever we said, right or wrong, we didn't mean a word of it. This is the way of the joker: the way of the comic-strip rabbit that mocks the hound from the mouth of a little hole, brave in the knowledge that behind him lies a complex of devious narrow tunnels, impassable to any creature bigger than himself. He always has some way of escape in the back doubles of the preposterous.

I expected her to laugh, but she was deadly serious. She said, "Why, you poor man—you stole because you were hungry."

Trying desperately hard to keep it up, I said, "Don't you believe it. Just to keep my hand in. I'm in training for a bank vault—starting small with a tin of herrings."

Then—it may have been hunger, or exhaustion, or shame, or all three—something caught me by the throat, and I choked.

She got me into a taxi in the nick of time; no sooner had the door slammed when I found myself sobbing thanks and gasping apologies, while she was stroking my head and calling me a poor fellow, and holding her handkerchief to my nose and saying, "There, there—blow!"

Pride had its fall indeed, that day.

A few minutes passed before the dimness was out of my eyes, so that I could see her clearly. Hers was a difficult face to categorize or describe. My first impression of it was that she had admired a very different sort of face in her childhood, and had spent a good deal of time trying to mold hers accordingly. Her expression was intended to be haughty, aloof, disinterested, *blasé*—the expression of the vamp, the *femme fatale*. But it didn't quite come off. From time to time, in her smooth pale cheeks, little dimpled imprints would appear and disappear, as if a ghostly conflict was going on there as Vanity locked horns with laughter. Her eyes, which were blue and extraordinarily large, were fixed in what she intended to be a deadly, hypnotic glare—which, however, ended up as a look of startled interest, of concentrated engrossment. It was her hair that fascinated me, just then.

Now how do you describe hair? Generally, in terms of minerals and vegetables—copper, ebony, gold, chestnut, silver, carrots, bronze, corn, and what not. Her hair resembled nothing so much as that Manzanita wood which the artistic photographers used to take pictures of from every angle, with grave reference to "Art Forms in Nature." Manzanita has since become the pride and joy of lamp designers, interior decorators, and other rabble. It has no color, but only form, suggestive of struggle against the elements. Sand-blasted, sun-struck, wind-beaten, fiber clings to writhing fiber, artfully tortuous, subtly stubborn. It seems to say, *Life, do what you will with me—twist me, turn me, freeze me, burn me—I know where I am going!* An inspired doodle, suggestive of something that has refused, point-blank, to live the easy way and has suffered accordingly—such is Manzanita, and that is what this girl's hair looked like. She had tried to cut it off at the nape of her neck, but it had clenched itself into a defiant knot there, seemingly of its own stubborn will.

"What is your name?" she asked.

"Laverock," I said.

"My name is June Whistler," she said.

"It's a very nice name. It's the sort of name you feel you ought to have heard somewhere before. Perhaps I have. Are you a film star?"

She said, "No. I work in the Office of the High Commissioner for Asia. When you have had something to eat and rested a little I want you to tell me all about yourself. Every word."

"A tall order," I said; and indeed it was, because, apart from the silly little fiasco of Laverock Libraries, Ltd., I had not a single interesting truth to tell about myself. And if you have a face like mine, you simply cannot say to a confiding female, "I got this way falling out of a window into a cucumber frame and afterward riding a tricycle down the stairs through a door." It would disappoint her. She would prefer not to believe you. It's frightening, when you pause to think to what an extent you live up to people and are being lived up to in your turn, how generally you fake yourself in blind obedience to somebody else's fantasy. The time comes when you wonder if you really are yourself and not a character that has been read about or seen in a movie. Whoever you are, you are the victim of somebody else's enchantment, doomed, like the people in the fairy tales, to go through life in an alien form—to hop as a toad, bray as an ass, or fly as a swan—until the kiss of true love honestly reciprocated releases you from your bondage and lets you be yourself.

"Yes," said June Whistler, "I can see that you must have lived a very full life—wild, terrible—"

"But—"

"No, you mustn't say a word until you've had a good meal."

She lived in one of those quiet crescents near Primrose Hill. "It's quite near the zoo," she said, as we got out of the taxi. "I can hear the lions at feeding time. Sometimes they roar in the morning, too. They were roaring this morning, you know."

"They were shooting a horse," I said. "Are you aware that a lion eats twenty-eight pounds of horse meat at a sitting?"

Luckily, she lived on the ground floor; I do not think I could have managed the stairs, I felt so weak.

"Make yourself comfortable," she said, "while I prepare some food. I'll make you a pork chop and some tea. Would you like some herrings first?"

"No," I said, "no, thanks—no herrings, not on any account, if you don't mind. I'll never touch another herring again as long as I live, I swear!"

And this vow I have kept. Since that notable day I have grown hardened to many gruesome sights and horrid odors, and have eaten food that would turn the stomach of a shark. But I cannot look upon a herring without nausea—especially a tinned herring in mustard sauce; and I cannot bring myself to pronounce the word *delicious.*

June Whistler's flat consisted of two small rooms, a kitchenette, and a bathroom. She was childishly proud of the fact that it was self-contained. She explained: "I *must* be alone. I must come and go as I please. If I want to bring men in I *must* be free to bring men in. I am answerable to nobody. My furniture is all my own, too. I hate the thought of using other people's furniture, don't you? I must feel free to put a cup or a glass down wherever I like, without wondering if I'll make a mark. And if you smoke I want you, please, to feel that you can drop your ashes wherever you like. I want you to feel absolutely at home."

Bloated with underdone pork chops—she told me that they were more nutritious that way—I was smoking one of her cigarettes and instinctively looking for an ash tray. I am punctilious in matters of tidiness and will go to extraordinary lengths to avoid making a mess of any sort. "I have a conscience about this kind of thing," I said, finding a little Japanese saucer. "It's anti-social to make extra work for your host—it robs him of his leisure, it robs him of his comfort." Whereupon, with my emphatic gesture, the long ash which I had been carefully balancing on the end of my cigarette fell onto the arm of the stuffed chair.

But she did not notice; she was gazing at me in her fascinated way, holding her cigarette in the center of her ardent little mouth and smoking it in short hard puffs, like someone who is determined at all costs to acquire the habit for the look of the thing. "What a remarkable character you are!" she cried, holding her cigarette at arm's length, little finger daintily cocked as she flicked ash onto her little Axminster rug. "What a remarkable mass of contradictions you must be! A hardened criminal—and yet you have a conscience about things like that. Why, I think that is absolutely fascinating!"

I had forgotten that I was supposed to be a pretty desperate character, and she had been so kind to me that I couldn't very well let her down now by confessing that I was nothing but a harmless fool; so I said, "Of course, that's only one aspect of it. There's another. All good burglars, murderers, et cetera, are necessarily very tidy people. Otherwise, don't you see, they would go about leaving clues. Many a good man has gone to the gallows on account of a stray bit of cigarette ash. A fingerprint here, the stub of a certain kind of cheroot there, a triangle of cloth carelessly torn from your trousers and left on a nail somewhere else—you'd be surprised how it all adds up. You think your shoes are clean, perhaps. But they're not, you know. Scotland Yard would put a microscope on those shoes and tell exactly where you've been and at what time this past week."

"I didn't think of that. You must tell me everything—you must let me study you from every angle. I like you. You give me all sorts of ideas." She blushed very red, and added hastily, "I mean . . . I don't mean . . ."

"Simple common or garden ideas?" I suggested.

"Do you read much?" she asked abruptly.

"A little. Why?"

"Because one of these days I am going to write a novel," she said, with an aggressive hitch of the chin.

"What about?" I asked.

She bared her small white teeth now and talked through them, while her eyes flashed. "I want to write about Life: Life in the raw, Life as it is lived in the depths, the uttermost depths! Do you hear?"

"And the heights?"

"Those too. I know all about those. But the depths, yes, the depths!" She hurled her cigarette end into the fireplace and took out another. When I rose to offer her a light, she waved me back with an imperious gesture and said, "Sit down. I suppose you understand that to me you are nothing but raw material?"

"I thought you came to the rescue out of sheer kindness of heart," I said.

"Oh, no," said June Whistler in a matter-of-fact way, "I'm not kindhearted at all, really. I used to be awfully softhearted, but I'm not any longer. The creative artist must be hard, *hard*! No mercy, no pity. Cold, impersonal, clear-minded. Like a surgeon. Like a zoologist. Like a vivisector with a knife. Understand?" She smiled kindly, and encouragingly.

The chops were settling now—I must have had the digestion of a crocodile in those days—and I found it hard to keep my eyes open. It was very pleasant to lounge there and listen to her talk. The fact that I had heard it all before in the Soho Cafés made the atmosphere so much the more homely. I hated to think that in a little while good manners would compel me to take my leave and go out again into the inhospitable streets.

"I want to help you, Laverock," she said. "Will you let me help you? Please? Will you teach me things? I want to know *your* world. Will you let me help you?"

"You have helped me enough already, Miss Whistler," I said drowsily, "and I am very grateful to you."

Her mood had changed now. She was pleading like an anxious child. "You don't have to be grateful. I didn't do anything. But if you are grateful, if you want to be grateful, you can show your gratitude by letting me help you. Now won't you, please?"

I said, "Well, if you have any hot water, I'd be very grateful if you would let me have a good wash—"

She was out of her chair and into the bathroom in half a second. I heard the splash of water and the thunderous hollow bang of a gas heater, and then she was back, saying, "Yes, of course, a good hot bath. Are you verminous?'

"No."

"I have some verbena bath salts. Would you like that?"

"No, thank you. A bath is more than I'd bargained for. I'm ashamed to give you so much trouble."

Instinct warned me that I was letting myself in for something here; but the lure of that hot bath was too strong for me. I rose abruptly, intending to say, "Thanks again, and good evening," but found myself walking straight into the bathroom. I climbed into the tub, scraped myself from head to foot and lay back to soak.

From the living room came a familiar brushing-and-clanging noise. I had heard it many times before in my mother's house.

The bohemian June Whistler was busy with dustpan and hand broom, sweeping up the ashes.

Then I fell asleep until the water grew cold.

June Whistler was sitting on a little sofa in a vampirish attitude. I noticed that she had changed her simple dress and put on a most peculiar garment of bright brocade. It had an immensely high Borgia collar and was cut very low and square at the neck. The skirt was long at the back and short in front, and the sleeves, which were wide, stopped at her elbows. She was also wearing high-heeled slippers and a collar of pearls as big as marbles, with earrings to match.

"And where do you think you are going?" she asked languidly, after I had thanked her for the bath.

The question took all the refreshment out of me and left me tired again, because I hadn't the faintest idea where I was going. I could only say, "I really must, I'm afraid."

She waved imperiously. "You will drink a glass of wine with me. It is in the kitchen. Bring it!"

And there, indeed, was a bottle of three-shilling port. She must have run to the grocer's and bought it while I was in the bath. In the accents of Du Barry, she said, "There is a corkscrew in the tin opener. In the drawer, next to the tea strainer. Fetch it."

I obeyed.

"Set out glasses. There are two behind the teapot. Fill them. . . . Now, my friend, let us drink. . . ."

I took a tentative sip. My father, who might have been something of a *bon vivant* if his conscience had let him, had taught me a little about wines and their characters. As I swallowed the stuff there came into my mind, clear as a photograph, a projection of the old man's face. I could see it twitch and grow rigid; and I could see him trying to disguise the disgusted pulsation of his poor harassed nostrils as he twirled the glass in his long nervous fingers, what time his worried eyes looked left and right for a surreptitious flowerpot. But June Whistler emptied her glass in two gulps and said, with a peculiar cachinnation that began as a gasp and ended as a giggle, "It's a very special wine. It comes all the way from Portugal." Then, humor and candor getting the better of her, she made an amendment: "It says Oporto on the label, but it can't be any good really, I suppose. Would you like to kiss me?"

"Well, yes," I said. "Naturally. Who wouldn't?" I was unaccountably confused and embarrassed. "If I had met you at a party, say, or in any other circumstances, why, you'd have to keep me away with your fingernails. But as it is, I don't know why, I'm what they call inhibited. I don't suppose I make myself clear, but it's like a shady sort of way of paying for a meal, and a bath, and a good turn."

She was silent, then, for about half a minute, when she lifted a shoulder in a practiced shrug, doggedly lit (all on one side) another cigarette, and said, in a strange and lonely little voice, "Drink, and pour more wine." And her eyes, filling with tears, became larger and took on a vague, wavering underwater look.

So I drank my wine, replenished the glasses, and drank again. "I didn't mean to offend you," I said, overtaken by remorse. ". . . I'd better not drink any more of this excellent old wine or I'll fall asleep."

She said, "Yes, of course. You must have some sleep. Go to bed at once!"

All the reasoning part of my mind, now, was packed away in wool. I said, "Oh, all right," and went obediently and dispassionately into the bathroom, closed the door to undress, because I have a delicacy about such things, and then went to bed.

June came in and asked, "Are you quite all right?"

"Quite, thanks. Would you mind telling me something? Where did you get that gown?"

"I made it myself out of a pair of old French curtains. I didn't use a pattern either. I make all my own clothes, except shoes and stockings, and I never use patterns. I despise patterns, don't you?"

"Oh, very much. . . . But where are you going to sleep?"

You have seen the sickly smile on the face of the fool who, on a double-dare, breaks the ice on the lake to take a plunge on Christmas Day? Such was June Whistler's expression as, unhooking her brocades, she said, "I'm going to sleep with you." Then the light was out, and she was climbing into bed with me.

"Have you enough room?" I asked.

In a loud, clear, but tremulous voice, she replied, "Oh, yes, thank you. Have you?" Then, talking tensely through her teeth again. "The depths! I want to explore the depths! . . . Why don't you say something?"

"Well, what, for example?" I asked stupidly.

This floored her. In that tone of ill-concealed anxiety in which a frugal housewife asks you if you are quite certain that you wouldn't like another helping of pie, when she knows there is no more in the kitchen, June Whistler said, "Would you like to crush me in your arms and bite me?"

"Good Lord, no!" I said.

"Quite sure?"

I said, "Madam, you are good enough to eat, but you look so much better in one piece."

"You're perfectly welcome, you know," she said.

"I'd rather not bite anybody just now, if you don't mind," said I.

Then she began to talk, but I was too tired to hear more than a snatch or two of what she said: ". . . of people have asked me to marry them, but . . ." and: ". . . have experienced in order to live a full life . . ."

The last thing I remember, that night, is the normal, earnest voice of June Whistler saying, "You may not believe me, Laverock, but I have never done anything like this before in all my life!"

I awoke late next morning and reached for my clothes. They were not there. Only my hat and cane lay on the chest of drawers.

Overcome with a nameless panic, I draped myself in a sheet and went into the living room. There was no trace of dust or ashes. The place had been swept. I opened the bathroom door. The tub had been scrubbed, and a fresh towel hung on the rail. To this towel was attached, with a hairpin, a message scrawled in eyebrow pencil on a piece of toilet paper: DON'T GO AWAY! RETURNING SOON! JUNE WHISTLER.

Go away in a sheet, with a hat and a silver-headed malacca? I took the liberty of opening the bedroom cupboard. There I saw something like an amateur theatrical costumer's collection of eccentric garments, but no clothes of mine. I waited. One o'clock was striking from St. Mark's when June Whistler came in, brisk and businesslike, carrying two large paper parcels. "My clothes!" I cried. "For God's sake, my clothes. My shoes, at least."

Now she was airy and nonchalant. She said, "Well, really, you know, the condition of your suit was deplorable. So I emptied the pockets and took it to be cleaned. I hope you don't mind. I really am determined to help you, Laverock."

"But what if I do mind?" I asked helplessly.

"Oh, I couldn't help noticing one or two pawn tickets: GENT'S SUIT 18/ and 1 PR. GENT'S SHOES 6/6. You know? So I got them out. I put your shirt in the wash. I bought you a new one, and a pair of socks. It will never do for us to look scruffy, will it?"

"Us? What us?" I asked.

"You said you'd let me help you, you know. Teach me, show me things. You promised." Her eyes began to fill with tears again.

I cried, "But you *have* helped me, haven't you?"

She folded her hands, smiled like La Gioconda, and said, "Really, it's time for a showdown. I'm awfully good at working things out, actually, you know. I have ever so much presence of mind, honestly. And I'm quick to pick things up. Don't you see, I've made my mind up to *help* you? . . . Only you must show me the ropes."

It occurred to me, in a shocking flash of reflection, then, that June Whistler, believing me to be a desperate criminal, had taken it into her head to become my accomplice, coadjutor, or moll. I have never been more shocked in all my life; but it was necessary for me to do some quick thinking, so I said, "No. I am so sorry, Miss Whistler, but I have been thinking it over ever since you tore me out of the clutches of the police. I used to say to myself, 'Only mugs work.' Now I know different. You don't know what you did to me. From now on, I want to go straight!"

Then this unpredictable young woman said, "All right, Laverock, let's go straight. Will you let me help you go straight? . . . Really, after all, you know, you can't get more out of life than you put into it. I'm so glad!"

"Oughtn't you to be at the office?" I asked.

She said, "Oh, yes. But I rang up and told the office manageress that I couldn't come because it was my nasty pain time."

I said, "You know that is not true."

She sighed, like someone relieved of a great burden, and said,

"Laverock, let's help each other never to lie, but always to go straight, because you cannot take out of life more than you put into it."

"Meanwhile," I said, with a sinking of the heart, "I owe you some money."

Now she was the wanton Serpent of the Nile, chucking pearls into vinegar. "Never mind," she said loftily.

But I did mind. It is a quirk of my character—so long as I owe any man money, I am that man's slave. Especially if he happens to be a woman, as Sam Yudenow would say. (Damn that man! He is pervasive, even in restrospect!) I was oppressed by a terrible weight of obligation.

Since I could not bring myself to become an enemy of society, the least I could do, I felt, was give my benefactress the pleasure of reforming me—which she proceeded to do with such firm belief in my dark past that I must have been made of stone to disenchant her and such hope for my bright future that I couldn't help falling in love with her.

But this was none of Copper Baldwin's business, and so I kept my mouth shut.

6

As we went into the lobby of the Pantheon—that dreary, odorous tepidarium which Sam Yudenow insisted upon as a "vestibule"—Copper Baldwin muttered to me, "Remember. Scowl and growl. As far as possible, keep your trap shut. Look 'em straight in the eye, the mongrels. Fix 'em. Anybody asks you a favor, growl and scowl. Give them the big ha-ha and turn away."

"Aha!" I said. "I begin to see where Sam Yudenow is dangerous. You caught him, Copper! So help me, you caught him and you can't sweat him out!"

Copper Baldwin said, "Kind of put a sock in it."

But the beer had gone to my head, and I was full of pleasant desperation. I said, "What *is* Sam Yudenow? Why is Sam *Yudenow*? *Who* is Sam Yudenow? *You are Sam Yudenow*!" Then I burst out laughing.

But with admirable self-control Copper Baldwin said, "All right, all right, Mr. Laverock. Just remember what I told you. That's all. I'm telling you for your own good. Stare the sods out of countenance, and don't give 'em so much as a smile. I'm warning you. . . . Now 'ere's Mrs. Edwards. I 'ave only one word to say about 'er. Beware! A female Judas Iscariot, you mark my words. Take no bloody nonsense from 'er, therefore. In my opinion she's in the pay of that bleeder Godbolt. If 'er bowels gush out one of these days I shouldn't be a bit surprised. They practically do, every afternoon in the cash box, anyway. I'm warning you, son, this show is as full of narks as a tinker's bitch is of worms, and every last one of 'em would half-inch the sugar out of a diabetic's pee. Mrs. Edwards, 'ere she comes—a bloody little conniver, a proper old malingerer. . . . For Christ's sake, don't let *'er* come the old Change of Life with you. She'll try it every time, she'll try it every time. She can throw a hot flush or a cold sweat at the drop of a hat, the cow!

"Oh, yes, and it's no use offering to sack the old bag, or any other member of the staff for that matter, because it won't work. This place, don't you see, is just about the end of everything. Only Sam Smallpox 'as got the power to fire anybody; and when 'e does they won't go. There's nowhere else to go. You see, once you're 'ere, 'e 'as a 'old on you. But by this same token, you got a 'old on 'im. If you get me, there's just about a limit to 'ow low a bastard can sink, and this is just about it. See what I mean?

"Everywhere else in the world this proverb applies: *Brute force and ignorance will get you nowhere*. Everywhere else; not 'ere. Use it—"

"Miv a mysterious smile?" I asked.

"I didn't say that, did I? Now you look 'ere, cocko—I'll stand by you because I'm bloody starved for intellectual conversation. All I ask is, mark my words."

Now Mrs. Edwards had got into the cashier's box and was testing the ticket machine. She was a wretched little sycophantic woman who looked like some succulent mauve flower on the verge of seeding, and who filled the vestibule with a nauseous smell of rotten vegetation—as of chrysanthemums that have died before their time because their water has not been changed. She sat on an air cushion which she punctiliously blew up; and somehow I felt that the whole place was impregnated with the exhalation of this air cushion when she had let it expire last night.

Copper Baldwin spoke to her brutally: "Mrs. Edwards, this is our new manager, Mr. Laverock. Look at 'im, and ask yourself is this the kind of person will come the old soldier with. Well?"

"Oh, I'm sure!" said Mrs. Edwards, with a simper.

Obedient to Copper Baldwin's admonition, I said nothing; but being (as I have said) short-sighted, I leaned forward to get a good look at her; whereupon she cringed and said, "I'm sure everything is going to be different now!"

Employing the toughest expression that came into my mind, I said with great deliberation, "Sister, you spat a bootful."

"Now," said Copper Baldwin briskly, "Mr. Laverock wants to give the staff the once-over. So round the scum up, Mrs. Edwards. That's what Mr. Laverock wants you to do; ain't it, Mr. Laverock?"

"Round me up this scum," I growled; and Mrs. Edwards darted away into the dimness of the cinema.

"Well, so far so good," said Copper Baldwin. "Oh, Jesus, 'ere comes the relief pianist! Now look, son, don't be—you know what I mean?—" His tone could not be described as tender; only the loathing in it was tempered with commiseration. "She plays mornings till when the band comes in—and oh gorblimey, what a band! The Speckled Band. No, straight, if you think you got a bloody Berlin Philharmonic Orchestra 'ere, unthink. But this girl, Miss Noel, she *can* play. 'Er weakness? Drink. Red Lizzie payday; otherwise methylated spirits. Sometimes she 'as to be carried in, shaking like a leaf. And does she pong!"

"She smells bad?" I asked.

"Yes, she pongs. The trumpeter's feet are bad enough, but poor old Noel. . . . Case in point: she was so full of meth once that when she lit a cigarette in the orchestra, her breath exploded and blew 'er against the barrier and gave 'er concussion. But still she played on, because once she finds keys under 'er fingers . . . Well, occasionally you 'ave to carry 'er out. Dead musical! Only do me a favor: don't take the mickey out of 'er—leave 'er be, poor bitch. She's a lady, if you don't get to leeward of 'er."

I said, "Oh, class conscious, are you?"

He began, indignantly, "Listen, before the cradle marks were off your arse—"

But then Miss Noel came in walking as it were on feather beds; a deplorable figure of a woman, bloated about the abdomen and with attenuated limbs dressed in a long fuzzy gray garment, so that she reminded me of half a bird-eating spider. About her face there was a sort of heartbreaking dignity. She was trying to control her mouth, but the muscles of her chapped lips were broken loose like the snap of an old purse and wouldn't stay closed. Her poor purple eyelids had not the strength to raise or lower themselves; they hung askew over her cloudy gray eyes, like broken blinds in the windows of a condemned house.

I said, "Miss Noel, I believe? I am glad to make your acquaintance. Mr. Baldwin tells me that you are an accomplished pianist."

Miss Noel looked at me twice before she saw me, and then, focusing her eyes with a tremendous effort, said, "It must be my vision that is deceiving me, I dare say. Oh, please, tell me that it is not my ears. Pay no attention to me. I am not very well, and for the moment—tell him not to laugh at me, Baldwin—for the moment, sir, I thought I was being addressed by a gentleman. Baldwin, don't let him make fun of me!"

"Get me?" said Copper Baldwin, picking up one of her wretched hands, between finger and thumb, by the loose skin on the back of it, somewhat as one picks up a diseased cat by the scruff of the neck. "Get me? And yet, you know, she can make that pianner talk, once she gets 'er Duke-o'-Yorks on it. . . . Can't you, now, old gel?"

She whimpered, "Really . . . Sometimes I don't know what to do, I simply don't know *what* to do . . ."

"If you don't mind waiting a moment, I will tell you what to do," I said, and went next door to the café. Costas' sister was behind the urn. I put down a shilling and said, "If you please, Miss Costas, a cup of strong tea and a ham sandwich."

Her eyes, in any light, had the curious phosphorescent quality of a dog's eyes in the dark. She served me without a word and gave me my change. She spoke only when I was carrying my order to the door, saying, "People aren't allowed to take the crockery out. My brother won't allow it."

I said, "And quite right too, Miss Costas. The things people lose that way!"

"I want those back."

"Eventually," I said, carrying the tea and the sandwich back into the vestibule. "Here," I said to Miss Noel, "you eat this nice sandwich all up, and drink up this nice cup of tea. . . . There now, there, there!"

"Well, Gawd stuff me gently!" Copper Baldwin muttered, as she obediently ate and drank. "Gawd stone me over the 'urdles! Stone my aunt Fanny up Fetter Lane and f - - k me for pins and needles! No, stone me definitely blind!"

I said, "And now, Miss Noel, if you will, let us hear you play."

She came out of some rickety dream, blinking about her, not remembering where she was, and asked, like an obliging debutante, "Schubert, perhaps?"

"By all means," I agreed.

"Delighted."

Copper Baldwin said, "Now this is something I have *not* seen before!"

Then a little yellow light went on over the upright piano, and Miss Noel began to play "None but the Lonely Heart." Now, out of the darkness from which everyone came, and into which, in the Pantheon, everyone seemed naturally to recede, came a man with only two teeth—incisors, and both of them black—making a sort of goulash out of red shag, cigarette paper, and spittle.

"Mr. Blossom," said Copper Baldwin, "this is Mr. Laverock, the new manager. You won't get away with any of your attacks with this 'ere gentleman, and so I fairly warn you. Will 'e, Mr. Laverock?"

"No attacks!" I said.

Mr. Blossom whimpered and said, "Can I help my heart, sir?"

"You had better," I said, deep in my throat.

"That's right," said Copper Baldwin, "that's *'is* motto: 'You can break your mother's 'eart, but you can't break mine.' Eh, Mr. Laverock? No malingering, no skylarking—eh, Mr. Laverock?"

"I will stand for anything but that," I said. But I could not take my attention away from that cigarette of Mr. Blossom's, which was in some horrid state between form and utter disintegration. He had got it stuck down, somewhat (I imagine) in the shape of one of those *mahorka* cigarettes which Creatures That Once Were Men used forever to be rolling in the more sordid Russian novelettes. Naturally, I offered him a light. Inattentive in striking the match, I touched the flame to the open box—and twenty matches went off with a *whoof* in a pillar of fire and a cloud of smoke. Then it was as if Mr. Blossom had been struck by some death ray; he became rigid and blue, and ceased to breathe. But before I could apologize, Copper Baldwin said, with a nod and a smile, as if he had been waiting for this very thing to happen, "Get me? Mr. Laverock is a man of few words. This is Mr. Laverock's way of showing you by direct demonstration exactly what's going to 'appen if you keep on smoking in the projection room. So watch out, cocko. 'Ere comes the New Era round 'ere. And Mr. Laverock says, better get rid of that gas ring, otherwise. Eh, Mr. Laverock?"

I said, "Above all, no gas rings in the projection room." I added, in a flash of inspiration, "Otherwise, *you* will be the sufferer!"

Having caught his breath, Mr. Blossom said, "I used to work the Magic Lantern for the Reverend Sturgeon—"

"Mr. Laverock knows all about that. Don't you, Mr. Laverock?

And Mr. Laverock will 'ave you know," said Copper Baldwin, with deadly sarcasm, "that there is a certain difference between pious glass slides of the 'Oly Land and nitro-cellulose film which, at a touch, will blow us all to bleeding buggery. Eh, Mr. Laverock?"

"Definitely to bleeding buggery," I said.

Copper Baldwin said, "Look at this gentleman. Do you think for one moment *this* one will stand for any of your shenanigans? Mr. Laverock told me to tell you next time 'e ketches you smoking or making tea in the projection room—or 'aving a 'eart attack—it's a fire bucket o' cold water right in the face, the crook o' the arm in the—"

In a voice that was half a snarl Mr. Blossom said, "Norn 'it me!" throwing up an arm to ward off an imaginary blow. "You touch me at your peril, and I've got a doctor's certificate to prove it. I'll have an attack, you see!"

"An attack," I repeated. "Oh, yes, that's right, you'll have an attack."

Although I meant nothing by this, something in the very expressionlessness of my tone seemed to terrify him. He cried, "I've got a doctor's certificate!"

Copper Baldwin muttered, "You'll get a bloody death certificate if you don't mind out."

"I've got heart disease, and asthma, and I've suffered with mastoids. I'll tell Mr. Yudenow!"

"He knows already—" I began.

But the mention of Yudenow's name seemed to infuriate Copper Baldwin, who snarled, "Put a sock in it, you little chancer. This 'ere Mr. Laverock doesn't give a flying tossorf on a galloping kangaroo if you got mastoids, 'emorrhoids, damaroids—pyorrhea, diarrhea, or gonorrhea—do what 'e says. You can break your bloody mother's 'eart, you skiver, but you can't break 'is. That right, Mr. Laverock?"

"You take the words out of my mouth."

"Mastoids. I got a scar behind my ear to prove it," said Mr. Blossom, trying to show me a hole in his skull—which, in my shortsighted way, being an obliging sort of man, I leaned forward to scrutinize out of politeness. But Copper Baldwin caught me by the arm and pulled me back, saying, " 'Old it, Mr. Laverock. Don't kill the bastard just yet. You've warned 'im once. Don't be too 'asty."

Now Mr. Blossom turned to a boy who had been watching all this with infinite delight. He was a swaggering, round-shouldered, pugnacious boy of fifteen or so with obstinacy in every wiry hair of his gingerish head. Where other boys' hair grows upward, his grew forward; it seemed to stay stuck to his scalp against its will, like coconut fiber in a door mat. He smelled strongly of what I thought, then, was nail varnish but was soon to recognize as amyl acetate and acetone, which he had been using in the rewinding room to mend a reel of damaged film. He was always breaking film. There was an impetuousness about him; something in him that chafed at the slowness of our groaning old rewinding machine. Besides, as I was later to learn, he wanted to develop his arms at all costs.

He said to me, "Do 'im, guv!"

Mr. Blossom said to him, "Johnny Headlong, I call you to witness!"

Johnny Headlong said to me, with a nod and a wink, "I'm the Three Wise Monkeys."

"And this is another one o' Mr. Yudenow's finds," said Copper Baldwin, "Johnny Headlong. Fugitive from a reformatory school. ... This is Mr. Laverock. Remember, you, Johnny Headlong, Mr. Laverock has only got to say one word and—"

"I was framed," said Johnny Headlong.

I felt patriarchal now, drugged irresponsible with an overdose of responsibility. "And what did you have for breakfast, Headlong?"

"Fried bread."

Copper Baldwin said to him, "You address Mr. Laverock as *sir*. Look at this gentleman, you. Is this the kind you talk bolo to?"

The boy looked at me, summing me up; he was not quite sure. I gave him fourpence and said, "Go next door and buy yourself a pie—a *meat* pie. Be back immediately," I added very severely, "and don't get crumbs all over the place."

Johnny Headlong took the money without a word and swaggered out. Copper Baldwin whispered to me, "You should 'ave 'ad a sandwich. The marvel is, you got no back answers from Johnny. You must 'ave kind o' hypnotized 'im. Svengali. Now, better go down to the orchestra, and tell *'er* to stop playing whatever it is, because we open in a minute. And mark my words, never give these sods any money. It corrupts 'em through and through. 'E should 'ave been back by now with that pie. But no. Not the likes o' *that*. Coconut cakes—I bet you a tanner, 'e'll blow the 'ole lot on coconut cakes. They'll flog their bread for circuses every time, the working-bloody-classes. I mean to say, if they can get four coconut cakes for a penny each, which are sweet but will give 'em a bellyache, why should they buy nourishment? . . ."

At this moment Johnny Headlong came back breathless. Drawing himself up, he took out of a trousers pocket a little torpedo-shaped cigar with a great red-and-gold band, which I recognized as a Flora-Flora, widely advertised as a bargain at fivepence apiece. With infinite condescension he handed it to me and said, "Put this in your mouf and smoke it. You'll enjoy it. That's all right—you and me'll get along together, I think. Go on, smoke it."

I lit it, anyway; it tasted of acetone. As if some alarm clock had gone off in her head, Miss Noel started to play a military march with tremendous force, just as the first customers of the day began to creep in.

"Look at 'em, just look at 'em," said Copper Baldwin. "You or me, or anybody, you 'ear a nice quick march and you fall into step. You can't 'elp it, can you? But these poor sods—well, *look* at

’em! . . . This is what we pay taxes for. This is what they call the proletariat. You know, there are *three* classes in society: one that produces but does not accumulate; one that accumulates but does not produce; and the majority, which is good for nothing. Vermin, in other words. Mussolini is right—give the bastards a shirt to wear that won’t show the dirt, and a marching song, and they’re ’appy. And the Russians are right, too—a bit more forced labor is what the workers need, the despicable buggers; pick-and-shovel drill till they drop in their tracks, the mummified corpse of Lenin to cross ’emselves in front of, ‘Kiss my arse, comrade,’ for a chunk o’ black bread, and for relaxation some film o’ some skivvy with piggy eyes set a foot apart and long gums and short teeth, grinning from ear to bloody ear, driving a tractor. For a bit o’ spice, let ’er be seven months gone and carrying it ’igh. Art? Cover ’er fat face with sweat, and stand ’er against the ’anging branch of a tree loaded with apples ripe to be plucked and covered with raindrops.

“They’d go for it ’ere, too, the contemptible sods, given a bloody good ’iding and a starvation diet. Which they’ll get, which they’ll get! The working classes are a lot o’ filthy parasites. Look at ’em, Gawd strike me lucky, look at ’em come! Look at old Lazarus-Raised-from-the-Dead spending ’is old-age-pension money—my ’ard-earned taxes—to see Greta Garbo in *Wild Orchids*. Are you aware that beer would be a penny a pint, cigarettes twenty for twopence, and bread and meat *pi* times the logarithms of Sweet Fanny Adams—if it wasn’t for the likes of this?”

Then he stepped aside and stopped a little woman who was carrying in her arms a thirteen-year-old boy wrapped in a shawl, and said, “Now then, Missis—you put ’im down, will you? Gawd suffering blimey, Mr. Laverock! Keep your eye on this one. What they won’t do for a free ticket! Parasites, malingerers, skivers, scroungers. Down with the bloody working classes!” he shouted. “Down with the King, down with the Queen, up the Bolsheviks, labor camps and castor oil for ever! If it comes to breeding, oh,

Jesus, give me fruit flies every time! . . . Come on, you stinkpots, it's your money we want, it's your money we want!"

A rebellious old man, hobbling in a network of gray veins that stood out like vines on a sapped jungle tree, growled, "And it's my money you'll get, you cheeky little bugger!"

Copper Baldwin yelled at him: "That's about enough of that! I don't mind telling you, Mr. Laverock's got his eye on *you,* and if you're not bloody careful 'e'll bar you. And you can go to Ullage for your Greta Garbo. Now then."

"I never said nothing," the old man said.

"Well, don't say it again. What, I wish I 'ad you in Russia. Euthanasia you'd get, not Greta Garbo. Where's your bloody economic value, you and your Greta Garbo? Answer me that! Believe me, you wouldn't last five minutes with me in Italy, you bleeding ulcer on the body politic. Greta Garbo, I ask you!"

The old man shook with impotent rage, and it seemed that his veins swelled, but he said nothing. He wanted to see Greta Garbo in *Wild Orchids.*

" 'Ow old are you?" asked Copper Baldwin.

Itching to get into the cinema, the old man said, "Seventy-two."

Copper Baldwin said, "By rights, your expectation of life is fifty-two years, you layabout. In the Ideal State, gorblimey, I'd 'ave 'ad you in a lethal chamber twenty years ago. No shame, no social sense. Look at yourself. Three square meals a day for seventy-two years, and what 'as the state got to show for you? Greta Garbo in *Wild Orchids.* Oh, you bloody vampire, you!" Then he whispered to me, "Give 'im a complimentary ticket."

"Complimentary ticket for this gentleman, Mrs. Edwards," I said. She tore one off a roll and gave it to the old man, who didn't know what to do with it. There was something like a game of draughts at the box office with his pennies until, at last, he took back his money and shambled into the hall muttering, ". . . Too old a bird to be caught wiv chaff. . . . They gives you fourpence, and they takes a shilling. . . . Jews are the ruination—Jews and the underground railways."

"Why underground railways?" I asked, thinking aloud.

Copper Baldwin said, "Why not? You've got a lot to learn, son, about the bloody proletariat. Call a meeting, give everybody a cup o' cocoa and a bun, and say, 'The trouble with the world today is 'orses,' and you'll get results. Oh, Christ, 'ow I 'ate the working classes!"

"And the ruling classes?" I asked.

"That's what I mean," said Copper Baldwin, "the iron 'eel o' the working classes (so-called) on the neck o' civilization and individual liberty. Cancer in the family—working classes. Strength goes to support weakness. 'Ealth kills itself for disease. There's your benevolent-bloody-state."

"Copper," I said, "to which class do you belong?"

He replied, "No class. I wear no man's collar, son. My mother was a finder o' the pure. My grandfather—"

Then Mrs. Maybrick, the grisly beldam who was called "Chief Usherette" came to the vestibule very agitated and said, "I'm sorry, sir, but young Dilly is making trouble. Would you kindly reprimand him, or eject him, sir?"

Copper Baldwin said, "You don't want to be afraid of Dilly. All pastry and coconut. Don't eject 'im, son. Chuck 'im out, in plain English."

"He got in without a ticket," said Mrs. Maybrick. "Oh, I knew, I knew, but when I asked him he told me to go and something myself. If you want him out of here, he said, you and who else can something well come and fetch him. He keeps whistling."

I said, "Actually, shouldn't there be a doorman for this kind of thing?"

Mockingly, Copper Baldwin said, "*Actually*, yes, but . . ." Then he went on to explain that Sam Yudenow staffed his cinemas—which were where he found them, in the unlikeliest places—with the leavings, the droppings, of the population. Recently, he told me, Yudenow had haggled with Hacker the Breaker over a set of jazz-patterned glass panels which, if you put a revolving electric light behind them, could turn a flea pit into a super cinema at the snap of a switch. Four pounds the lot. Only Sam Yudenow had managed to get Hacker the Breaker to include, in this deal, a uniform—bankrupt stock from High Life Film Studios out at Acton—which had been designed for the man who played the Duke of Wellington in one of their productions. The producer had taken it into his head that the Iron Duke was six and a half feet tall. Stopping me short when I protested that Wellington was a skinny little fellow, considerably under the average height, Copper Baldwin said, "Yes, I know; he was half-arsed. So was Nelson. But look at Nelson's Column. What d'you expect? Suckers, suckers for their own tit. I mean to say, it stands to reason. 'You must 'ave faith in your own product,' they say. But I ask you, son, 'ow does that work out? Like this: Develop an appetite for your own crap. That's all. Sell yourself on your own trailers. Believe me, the best producer or exhibitor is the proto-bloody-type of 'is own best customer. 'Istory is bunk; the Duke o' Wellington stood six foot six; and Bob's your uncle. . . . But as I was saying, it ain't worth Yudenow's while to fit a uniform to a man—it's cheaper to fit a man to a uniform. The Turners Green 'Ippodrome, which is a quiet 'ouse, 'as got Napoleon. Procrustean, bloody procrustean! . . . Meanwhile, chuck that Dilly out."

So, uncomfortably aware of the beating of my heart, I followed Mrs. Maybrick down the dark aisle. The offensive Dilly had made himself comfortable in the middle part of the hall. Tapping him on the shoulder, I said, "Excuse me, may I see your ticket stub?" Then Dilly made the kind of sucking, squeaking noise old ladies make when they call cats and said, in a mincing voice, "Oh, stop it, Horace dar-ling!" So I had to throw him out.

I invited him to step into the aisle and be thrown out like a gentleman. He would not. He made a circle of the thumb and the forefinger of his left hand into which he inserted the first two fingers of his right, while, with tongue and lips, he made a loud noise. From all over the hall people began to complain. I got into the row behind him and took his throat in the crook of my arm, dragging him into the aisle. His trousers held as I lifted him off the ground. Not knowing what to do with him then, I carried him into the vestibule, where Copper Baldwin was waiting.

"Like this?" I asked.

Copper Baldwin's mouth twitched a little, but his stomach heaved with laughter. He said, "Better let him down."

Dilly sprawled on the floor, gasping. I picked him up and shook him. "You know," I said to him, "you're supposed to pay for your ticket, and not to whistle. . . . Mrs. Edwards, please give this gentleman a complimentary ticket." But young Dilly blinked at me and, easing his neck by a series of gyrations, went quietly out into the street.

Copper Baldwin said, "All right. The arse o' the trousers is good psychology."

"Sam Yudenow told me—"

"Don't be silly, *I* told Sam *Yudenow*! Read your Von Clausewitz, read your Falkenhayn. Go for the weak spot. Not more than three in five round Fowlers End 'ave got an arse to their trousers. Remember that. Those three are scar tissue, if you like. Say you've 'ad your appendix out and it's just sewn up, and I make a feint at you. Where will your guard drop to? Your belly. That's 'ow it is 'ere, with the arse o' the trousers. But remember, everybody in Fowlers End wears a muffler, and there's a vulnerable point, son. Go for that choker and twist it. Whatever the bastards breathe, they can't do without it for long. In the 'ot weather, 'it 'em in the kidneys. They're ain't a 'ole pair o' kidneys in Fowlers End. But you shouldn't 'ave offered young Dilly a complimentary. . . . But wait about a bit. The turns should be turning up about now."

He took from Mrs. Edwards a fragment of paper upon which

were listed our "Live Bookings" for the next three days. At the top of this list stood the name of:

Johnny Mayflower, Trick Skater

But this was crossed out in blue pencil, and close beneath it was written, in violet ink:

Canceled—pawned skates; substitute

Johnny Lambsbreath, the Man Who Made the Prince of Wales Laugh

Copper Baldwin said, "That was Edward VII, when 'e was Prince of Wales. Oh, the poor bastard! Now this next one, Sam Yudenow will turn up for . . ." He put his thumb on:

Eena, Oriental Contortionist

"Oh, 'e loves 'em, 'e loves 'em, them Oriental contortionists! And last, but not least, the Double Turn . . ."

Hanky and Panky, Eccentric Dancers

"Don't worry, son. Show 'em where they dress, and et cetera. One o' these days we must 'ave a real intellectual conversation, but in the meantime better let me give you a few wrinkles in applied psychology. Just be calm, look everybody straight in the face, and say nothing. Look at it this way: if you do 'em a good turn, they think you want something out of 'em; if you don't do 'em a good turn, they think you already done 'em a bad 'un. You can't lay down law, bylaw, formula, rule, or regulation. Do nothing, but do it at the right moment. There's the royal road, son, when the last comes to the last. But if you've got to do something *positive,* follow your intuition; and then do it as if your life depended on it. Which it will, son. See what I mean?"

I thought it polite to say "I see what you mean."

But I did not see what he meant, for the time being. He continued: "Gawd give me fruit flies! 'Ere's where the 'uman element's always got you bolloxed. Destiny depends on the individual. Lenin, Mussolini, me—too many of us. The trouble with the world today is, a bloody sight too many chromosomes flying about all over the place. Spermatozoa, et cetera, swarms of 'em, in every yob in Fowlers End. And to every tart that'll come into the generator room with you, ova. It makes you think, don't it? Gawd give me fruit flies! I'd ration their eggs, I would!"

I said, "Can't very well, can you?"

Copper Baldwin said, "No, I know. But I would if I could."

"Be God Almighty?" I asked.

"Why," said he, "what does young Dilly, for example, want with spermatozoa? Are you aware—I'm not pretending to give you the right figures—that in about ninety years from now that layabout Dilly will have devoured about a quarter of the earth's surface, or something like that, 'im and 'is spermato-bloody-zoa? A quick X ray right in the testicles, and sterilize the buggers."

"And what business had *your* mother with an ovum?" I asked provocatively.

"You wait and see. You'd laugh if you knew," said Copper Baldwin. "Now that I come to think of it, if you imagine you've seen the end-all of everything—talking o' variety turns—wait till you meet Billy Bax the Agent. Wickedness. It works by kind o' centripetal force. It rushes in on itself and makes an 'ard lump. With the possible exception o' 'Acker the Breaker, Billy Bax the Agent is about the only man in the world Sam Yudenow looks up to."

"How's that?"

"Because Billy Bax the Agent is a bit lower than 'imself, so 'e looks up to 'im. Wrong end o' the telescope, get me? The cosmos upsy-down. . . . Meanwhile, better ring Sam Yudenow—I daresay 'e already give you the office—about the Chinese contortionist. You know the signals? The password is *generator room*—do you fluff?"

I said, "I fluff, Copper."

The manager's office was a kind of cubicle between the rewinding room and the ice-cream machine. It was furnished with the skimmings of some of Hacker the Breaker's job lots—a boule table, an Elizabethan ash tray left over from a bankrupt production about Sir Walter Raleigh, a chaise longue of the Second Empire, one of the earliest Japanese imitations of an old American typewriter that had as many keys as a calculating machine, and a telephone upon which Sam Yudenow had evidently been trying out some silver paint so that it had a flaky and leprous look about it. I got Sam Yudenow's number and told him that there was trouble in the generator room.

He replied, cryptically, "More tvouble again? Who miv, this time?"

I said, "Contortionist."

He sounded brisk, businesslike; one could recognize that he was talking for the benefit of a third party. The tone of his voice was such that I could not tell whether he was admonishing me, or giving me a secret signal, or making a burlesque. He said, "Mr. Daniels! Whereas you are raw to this business, Sam Yudenow wants you should work your way up thvough its bottom. You should understand, Rome wasn't built mivout tvouble in the genevator room. A vose by any other name would smell. But what's the billing?"

I said, as quietly as possible, "Chinese contortionist, name of Eena."

Then he said, with asperity—I could almost see him flapping about with his free hand—"Take a scvewdriver. Are you there?"

"Yes, I'm here."

"That's not what I asked. Are you *there?* . . . Right. Praps I'll look in, in an hour or two. I'm making allowances, mind you, because you're new. But . . . when I was your age, the scvewdrivers wasn't even insulated yet. Genevator rooms! What, again, is the nature of the tvouble?"

Losing patience, I said, "Eena, the Chinese contortionist."

"'Ow many you got in the house?"

"A matter of a hundred or so," I said.

"I'm ruined," said Sam Yudenow. Then, in a very meaning voice, "I'll get along as soon as I can, about the genevator room. See that everything is in order, but do nothing until I come. Any tvouble yet?"

"Chucked out a fellow called Dilly," I said.

He replied, "Then you've as good as signed my death warrant. . . . You can't turn your back five minutes. Hang up the receiver, Laventry. Do you vealize that all this chatter is costing me a bill? A thing you should vealize. If possible be like Shakespeare—no speeches—a word of one syllabub. One-two-thvee, and every picture tells a story. I'll be right over. So what are you sitting there talking for? Count *tukheses*—uxcuse the expression, I mean arse holes—you should know what you got in every seat. Why ain't you downstairs? Answer me."

"Because I am talking to you upstairs," I said.

"You go down and leave that genevator room to me."

I rang off. By the time I got downstairs the extension phone in the box office was ringing. Mrs. Edward said, "Mr. Yudenow on the phone—urgent."

I shouted into the mouthpiece, "Well?"

"Where are you?"

"In the lobby."

"Vestibule! Good-by."

Some more people were coming in. The ticket machine went wrong: it made a noise like a hacking cough which gradually muffled itself until it became mute; whereupon Copper Baldwin discovered that, one of the tickets having got bent, some scores of others, blindly following it, had made what he called a "raffle" just under the slit where they were supposed to come out. The grinding urge of the powerful machinery had reduced these tickets to shreds, which we had to sweep up and put into a bag to satisfy Inland Revenue on entertainments tax.

Meanwhile there slunk into the Pantheon a middle-aged man of indeterminable race. He was about five feet tall, and of the color of an old penny—repellent in his expression, which was at once abject and arrogant, ingratiating and sullen. The whites of his eyes were brown, and his lips were a crusty purple. He was buttoned to the neck in a sad old velvet-collared coat and wore a bowler hat. He had no teeth.

"What can I do for you?" I asked.

He put down the Gladstone bag he was carrying (I thought he was going to try to sell me a fire extinguisher) and, thrusting a skinny hand under his clothes, started as it seemed to pick at himself as you do when your skin is peeling after scarlet fever. He had the same rapt expression. He paused for an instant to lift his hat and scratch his glabrous head with one finger before he offered me his card. It read:

EENA, THE CHINESE CONTORTIONIST
FACIAL CONTORTIONS
WORLD-WIDE IMPERSONATIONS

"How do you do?" I said.

"I walked all the way from Brixton," said Eena, the Contortionist, in anything but a Chinese accent. "Anywhere I can cop a kip for half an hour?"

Copper Baldwin said, "You can lie down in the gents' dressing room for 'alf an hour if you like, Mr. Laverock says. I take it you *are* male and not female?"

Eena said, "I got a wife and six children. Can I sub ten bob?"

"Mr. Laverock will let you 'ave two tosheroons, if you like. . . .

You are prepared to let this artiste 'ave two 'alf crowns on account, ain't you, Mr. Laverock?" I observed that Copper Baldwin seemed to be enjoying himself. He patted Eena on the shoulder and said to Mrs. Edwards, "Five shillings advance for Eena, Mr. Laverock says. Mr. Laverock will sign the chit." Then, to Eena, the Contortionist: "Mr. Laverock says, where's your note from Billy Bax?" He took the soiled slip of paper which Eena scratched out of himself and handed it to me. I gave it to Mrs. Edwards, who put it on a spike.

The feel of a few shillings in his hand worked wonders with Eena. He said, in the manner of a temperamental star, "O' course, I shall want a consultation with your musical director. I got my music with me. I'll need to give him his cues. When I say 'Dracula' I want a bit o' Grieg, and a green spot on my face. Et cetera. And when I cover the whole of my nose with my lower lip—"

"You go upstairs and 'ave a nice rest, and tell it to Mr. Yudenow," said Copper Baldwin. "Eh, Mr. Laverock?"

"There is a blue light in the generator room," I said. "He's impressionable, Mr. Eena. You never can tell where it might lead."

"Well, I'll pull a few faces for him, if you like," said Eena.

Copper Baldwin said, "That's right. You cover your nose with your lip."

"I can touch my forrid with my tongue," said Eena.

I said, "By all means."

So I showed him to the gentlemen's dressing room, where he immediately unpacked his suitcase. His wardrobe consisted of a little girl's party dress with frilly bloomers, a wig of blond corkscrew curls, silver-buckled shoes, and a Dracula cloak.

When I got back into the hall, Copper Baldwin said to me, "I think you kind o' bring me luck. I 'aven't laughed so much since Father died."

"Tell me, Copper, what does Sam Yudenow *do* with his contortionists and what not?"

"If you want my candid opinion, cocko—nothing."

"Tell me something else, Copper. Where did you get all your education?" I asked.

He said, "It come natural to me. I told you, my mother was a finder o' the pure."

"And what's that?"

"Pure, son, is dog's dung. It's best 'and-picked, and in the better quarters o' the town, or round the posh kennels."

"What do they use it for? Growing flowers?" I asked.

"Gawd, no! Pure is death to flowers. But it's the only thing you can possibly treat Russia leather with. Dog's dung and no other dung's got some chemical principle in it that makes Russia leather supple and fragrant. The best sort was worth a few pence a pound, and it 'ad to be picked by 'and so you knew what you was getting. None o' your biscuit-fed pure would do, nor your bone-eating pure. The real meat-fed stuff with body in it. . . . Didn't you know that? It's still in use, but Gawd knows who collects it. My father was a finder in the sewers. But I'll tell you all about that some other time, one o' these days. . . . The old woman put a bit by, and when she got too rheumatic to bend, she opened a little general shop back o' the Polygon. Well, there was the garret going empty, so she lets it to some old geezer that was writing a book. Don't ask me what book. We called 'im Old Maunder. 'E 'ad thousands o' books of 'is own, but 'e was writing another 'un. 'Alf a crown a week rent Old Maunder paid—earned it addressing envelopes. I used to go up, when my old man wasn't about, and bring 'im a bit o' cake, or something, from my old woman, and sweep up a bit. My old woman covered up for 'im; 'e never paid no rent for the last few months, and my old man would never 'ave stood for that. (My old man lost 'is nerve when 'e was attacked by rats in the sewer by Lambeth and didn't do much.) So this Old Maunder used to tell me stories—the Glory that was This, and the Grandeur that was That, and so on—and I soaked it up.

"'Abit-forming. My old woman dies, and I know what's going to 'appen to Old Maunder then, and to all 'is books, sick as 'e was. That's what made me cry, when they buried the old woman. Not 'er. She was as good to me as she knew 'ow to be, which wasn't very; but we all got to go sometime. I could see poor Old Maunder out in the street, and 'is books . . . Well, anyway, I sold papers, I run errands for a few pence, which I give my old man. But every Sunday I got up five o'clock in the morning and walked out to 'Ighgate, where the fat man they called Jolly Rhino 'ad his pub and 'playing fields.' Also, roundabouts and swings and coconut shies, and all that. Champions was bred there, yes. But 'undreds was ruined. One o' Jolly's big attractions was the 'Junior Events'—which meant to say, two twelve-year-old boys fought it to a finish wiv gloves in a ring. The winner got 'alf a crown and 'is dinner, apart from praps a few tips—what they called 'ring money'—chucked into the ring if 'e was 'specially good. Loser take nothing, and a bloody good 'iding. Unless 'e was 'specially game, in which case 'e got 'is dinner and 'is fare 'ome—because you can believe me, 'e'd be in no condition to walk.

"After that, a football match. Then 'ome. I never lost a fight. They used to call me 'The Little Eel,' I was so slippery, and I'd go 'ome and give my old man 'alf a crown, and tell 'em, 'Old Maunder's rent.' Generally, my old man give me a bloody good 'iding for being out late or, if I 'appened to 'ave a black eye, for fighting. Because the more the bastard lost 'is nerve, the more ferocious 'e'd get. Typical. But in between times, I'd sneak up to sweep out Old Maunder's place, and 'e'd tell me about the abdication o' Diocletian, and Shelley, and all that. I thought it was worth it, but now I doubt it.

"One day I got a job with a furniture mover, to 'elp 'im take a van down to Cardiff. I always 'ad a light 'and wiv 'orses. Like 'orses?"

I said, "I can take them or leave them alone, Copper."

"Leave 'em alone. I admire 'em, mind you, for one thing—they don't like people. But I despise 'em, on the other 'and, because they're subservient to man. Madness is catching. All 'orses are mad. As I was saying, my old man made me take this carrier's job to Cardiff. Ever been to Cardiff? No? Congratulations. It was a special load, see, that couldn't go by railway or canal—a bit to be picked up 'ere, a bit to be dropped off there. Well, it was three weeks before I got back, and there was no more Old Maunder. It seems 'e caught pneumonia in my absence, and died. The parish buried 'im. My old man got all 'is books and stuff onto a cart and sold the 'ole bloody lot in the Farringdon Road for thirty bob. What Old Maunder was writing, Gawd alone knows, because 'e never finished it, but there was enough of it to stuff a sofa, and the rag-and-bone man gave eighteen pence for it. That's when I 'ad my one real bundle with my old man. 'E weighed fourteen stone, but it was beer fat, and 'e was yellow. Never touched *me*, but I cut 'is face open, and closed 'is eyes, and bloodied 'is nose—crying like a babby all the time, mind you, just out o' temper. Then I left the 'ouse and got a job as plumber's mate. . . . You wanted to know 'ow I got my education? Now you know."

"I thought you told me," I said, "that you won a scholarship."

Copper Baldwin said, "So I did—could 'ave gone to grammar school. Would 'ave, too, if my old woman 'ad 'ad her way. But she was too sick with a growth in the inside, plus rheumatism, to fight my old man; '*e* wouldn't 'ear of it. Gave me a tanning wiv 'is belt for daring to presume to go and pass scholarships when my own father couldn't read or write. I got the scar to this day, on my 'ip, where the buckle cut in . . . and there was my poor old woman crying with rage, too much in pain to take a frying pan to 'im, poor old girl. . . ."

"And what happened to your father, in the end?" I asked.

"What 'appened to *your* father, in the end," said Copper Baldwin. "Died. . . . Blimey, 'ark at Miss Noel play! Crossing 'er 'ands, I bet you. But wait, she'll tail off—ginger 'erself up with a dose o' Red Liz and go on till she unwinds. Poor cow. I think you made a proper conquest there, son."

And he would not say anything more until Sam Yudenow arrived, half an hour later, saying, "Tvouble in the genevator room already? And this Eena?"

Copper Baldwin said, "Eena'll be in the generator room in five minutes—won't she, Mr. Laverock?"

I said, "Oh, definitely."

So Sam Yudenow went into the generator room carrying, for the look of the thing, an insulated screwdriver, while Copper Baldwin went next door and roused Eena out of a deep sleep. The Chinese Contortionist put on his Little Nell dress, but covered himself in his Dracula cloak, and came down. As they hurried past me, I heard Copper Baldwin saying, in his most affable voice, ". . . Yes, touch your forehead with your tongue, by all means, and cover your Irish Rose with your lip. And you say you can dislocate your jaws? Do that, and I'll stand you a quart. . . ."

Then they disappeared in the dark. If my life had depended on it, I could not have kept away from the door of the generator room. Copper Baldwin came out and whispered to me, "One good 'eart attack ought to finish that twicer. . . . D'you 'ear anything?"

I could hear nothing; only I had a sense of quiet tumult in the vestibule, which I ran to investigate. There stood a hornet of a woman hunched in a mink coat and wearing a lot of precious stones. She must have been pretty, in her day; but she had the appearance of the victim of an acid-throwing outrage—if you can imagine corrosive acid thrown from the inside outward. She said to me, "You're the new one, I suppose, are you? I am Mrs. Yudenow. Where's my husband? . . . Don't bother to lie. I heard every word on the extension. Give me the key to the generator room!"

I gave her my keys. She knew exactly where to go. More customers were coming in, but "To 'ell wiv 'em!" said Copper Baldwin. "This is an education." Mrs. Yudenow got the right key—she knew the feel of it in the dark—twisted it, flung open the door, burst in, and began, "So, at last—" Then she let out such a scream, so high and sustained that it was later alleged that the factory hands of the locality went to dinner. She fell back in my arms unconscious. Sam Yudenow got her by the legs and said, "Give Mrs. Yudenow a lift out into the fresh air, Laventry. Copper, get a glass cold water—a glass cold water get."

For "fresh air" we carried her to the office and put her on the chaise longue. The Chinese Contortionist, who had followed close behind us, took off his wig and fanned her with it. She awoke with a sneeze.

Sam Yudenow said, "Dolly, what's the matter, what? Tell Sammy, Doll, what did somebody do to us?"

"That face! Oh, that face!" cried Mrs. Yudenow.

"What? Mr. Eena?" said Sam Yudenow. "A new attraction. A face is only skin deep. But this one, Dolly, is made of India rubber. I got a use for 'im. Cashier, praps. . . . Eena, make again miv the ears. . . . Can you imagine, thvough a box-office window, such a face, for example? . . . But what d'you come here for, Dolly, notmivstanding? You wanted something? Only speak!"

Copper Baldwin said to me, "Get what I mean, Dan? You can't win. Begin to get what I mean?"

7

LATER, I SAID to Copper Baldwin, "Look here, Copper; I get what you mean all right about Sam Yudenow. But I don't see why I should be expected to share your hate for him. He makes me laugh, like Sairey Gamp, and Montague Tigg, and—"

"No literature, please," said Copper Baldwin. "Like I began to tell you, I was born and bred and brought up among these characters that your friend Charles Dickens never saw except with a police inspector at each elbow. 'You can't tell me nothing about bringing up children,' the old girl says to the welfare worker. 'I've 'ad thirteen and buried ten.' Lovely, eh? You like population, don't you? As I gather from your attitude, Mr. Laverock, one of 'em might write a sonnet, or something. Okay, let 'em breed. But you feed 'em—I won't. According to you, that filthy old greasy midwife is 'charming,' just because 'er front teeth 'ave rotted away and she says, 'Put the bottle on the mankleshelf and let me put my lips to it when I am so dispoged.' Instead of 'disposed.' But I was dragged into the bloody world by Sairey

Gamp, and me and my sister were the only two that lived, out of eight. Lovely, tell your mum!

"And by the same token, you and the rest of 'em shove down your kids' throats the charm of the Eatanswill election, in the *Pickwick Papers.* Charming. The voters was bribed and dragged to the polls blind-drunk. And the journalism was scurrilous. But that was good old English, so it was delightful, wasn't it? Old Mr. Pickwick could get drunk as a tinker's bitch on cold punch and chucked into the pound in a wheelbarrow. But that was character, wasn't it? Whereas, Charles Dickens goes to America—'e was disappointed, you know, in a Mississippi investment on which 'e expected the Yanks to pay twenty-five hundred per cent—and when they didn't was disgusted because they run personalities in a newspaper, drank cocktail before dinner, and rigged an Eatanswill election. 'Umbug, bloody 'umbug! And so are you.

"But you cry your eyes out because Edgar Allan-bloody-Poe was dragged drunk to the polls in Baltimore. . . . Look—did you ever 'ear of an empire getting great on Mr. Pickwick and the Cheeryble Brothers? I mean, the spirit of innocent benevolence? Your friend Charles Dickens's city merchants? Did you, bloody hell! You make me tired. Old Pickwick, I'll lay you nine to two, was selling Indian opium to China. So don't give me this stuff about Sam Yudenow amusing you. It's literature and lies, son—fiction. Just because Sam Yudenow is such a bloody out-and-outer, and you've read too many books, you see what you call a character. You'll live and learn, son, believe me."

I asked, "What's the nature of a character, Copper?"

"Something dirty in a picturesque kind o' way," he said, after a moment's pause. "A madman for 'is own benefit. That's a character. And always remember, son, there's no such thing as a young character or a middle-classer that does a regular 'ard day's graft and pays off on the furniture. A character is a parasite. I don't say 'e doesn't put as much work into being what 'e is as somebody else might put into doing what 'e does. A character is a kind o' clown. First 'e makes you laugh, and in the process feels your pockets. Sam Yudenow's one."

I said, "I don't mind if he feels *my* pockets so long as he makes me laugh."

"Very likely," said Copper Baldwin dryly. "Because, after all, what 'ave you got o' your own inside 'em? . . . 'Ello, what's this? Not that I blame 'im, but there's a geezer staring at us. Look of a gentleman—man with big boots. Know 'im?"

The Pantheon was closed for the night, and the only light burning was a sickly one under a yellow-and-green shade in the vestibule. The Film Renters On-the-Dot Delivery Service, which picked up old cans of film and delivered fresh ones the night before change day, was late as usual. As Sam Yudenow was eventually to tell me, On-the-Dot worked "on stvictly Amevican lines"—that is to say, the manager smoked a cigar. For a consideration, On-the-Dot would deliver not only films but other perishables, from Aldgate Pump to Southend-on-Sea. For example: one October evening they tossed into my vestibule a box of fireworks and a case of butter. Sam Yudenow had his eye on the delivery boy, with a view to making some kind of manager of him—that boy could throw an oblong steel trunk containing twenty cans of film sixteen feet, so that it landed on one of its corners with such force that it made a hole in the floor. And he was never out more than three inches.

So we stood back while the man in big boots who looked like a gentleman came clumping into the vestibule, muddy to the knees with the hopeless, useless, clayey mire of the neighborhood. There were splotches of this same mud all over him and a great smear of it on his lip, where he had wiped his nose with his finger, which he managed to wear like a guardee mustache. On him, it had a calculated, cosmetic appearance. Yes, indeed, there was no mistaking this newcomer for anything but a gentleman. It was not that his breeches had been cut to fit, or his boots made to measure—he was dressed in old army surplus stuff. It was, simply, that nobody but a born gentleman could have turned up in this strange place, mediocre in every line and filthy from head to foot, with such an air of owning it.

God knows how they have—not what it takes but what it lacks—to do it! By rights, I am supposed to be something of a gentleman myself (or so my poor mother used to insist) but I could never file myself blunt and blatant enough to fit the wards of the lock that opens the door to the gentry. It has always struck me that there is something swinishly unfair about the aristocratic attitude.

Now the humblest workman has it. Turnabout is fair play, I dare say; but still I don't like it. Top or bottom, it implies a *drôit de seigneur*, to which I will not submit.

This man with big boots bellowed, "I say, look here, my car's broken down—and where the hell *am* I?"

I looked at him closely—which means to say that the tip of my nose was less than a foot distant from the tip of his—and saw a face such as is generally described as "attractive." It was shaped somewhat like a dancing-master's fiddle: broad at the temples, curving in at the cheeks, and swelling out a little at the jaws. There were even two symmetrical creased dimples something like *f* holes in the belly of this kit-face, which had the appearance of having been stained to a weather-beaten look. Only, where the finger board should have been, hung a most atrocious tie with which I was miserably familiar—the tie of the Old Valetudinarians, which may be worn only by those who were at school at Snellgrove-in-the-Vale. This tie cannot be mistaken for any other: the background is flowerpot red, and it has diagonal stripes of emerald green, buff, black, sky blue, orange, and gray.

I recognized the man at once then—he had been a prefect when I was in the fifth form at Snellgrove—and quite a figure he cut, as I remembered. He used to lash about with an ash plant, wore his hat at a distinctive angle, and had the right to put his left hand in his trousers pocket. I used to admire him tremendously; he was a leader in games, surreptitiously gambled for money, and was the son of a magnate. It was he who introduced to the seniors the practice of parting the hair neither at one side nor in the middle, but two inches off dead-center. He used to have six pairs of flannel trousers and a staring way of looking that took the heart out of younger boys. It all came back to me in a rush. His father was involved in the building of medium-priced houses somewhere south of the Midlands, but something went wrong and he took to drink—breakfasted off brandy, fell into a log fire, and died of burns. His mother turned up for the last sports, and nobody had ever seen a more truly bred gentlewoman. It was the first time I had ever seen a woman with pale blue hair. I heard my mother telling my father that she used to be a *vendeuse* in *haute couture*—"a shopgirl." Then our hero swaggered off with his flannels and his dimples, and it was generally supposed that he could have done no less than make a fortune.

I said, "I beg your pardon, but isn't your name Cruikback?"

"Yes, it is," he said, in his old frank way. "And upon my word, aren't you young Laverock? What the devil are *you* doing in this hole?"

"Well, what are *you*?" I asked.

Who was it that wrote of "the pathos of distance"? There is a profundity in this abstruse expression—which means nothing more than that distance lends enchantment. (How the poor poets must wrack their brains to design new dresses for old clichés!) If I had been called upon, ten minutes earlier, to describe Jack Cruikback, I would have called back into memory a man about seven feet tall, muscled like a water buffalo, and altogether enviable—cool, ruthless, indomitable, good at mathematics—a giant, a gentleman, and a scholar. But now I saw before me someone miraculously shrunk to a miserable five feet ten—he couldn't have grown much since that last cricket match—a good two inches shorter than I, and slender rather than lean. The *f* holes in his face were more pronounced, and so was the bridge of his nose. He still parted his black hair the same way, though; but the big, slightly curved cuif on the right-hand side of his head somehow conveyed the impression of an ebonite chin rest. Much as I hate the overdone metaphor, he had an air of having overstrung himself; and for the first time I noticed that he had prominent little ears, like pegs. But his fingers were still long and sinewy, with prominent veins, such as we used to regard as proof of manhood, and he wore the same carnelian signet ring that he had flaunted at school: the seal engraved with half-obliterated heads of stags and lions and bears and pigs-in-triplicate, with bars and bends and crowns galore. It was whispered, when I was in the Fifth Form, that he was a lineal descendant of Richard Crookback, otherwise known as King Richard III, and therefore entitled to the throne of England. Only, Cruikback's illustrious ancestor, he said, was ousted by the murderous machinations of a certain Harry Tidder—offspring of a flighty French floosie named Katherine and a penniless Welsh squire, who had the nerve to call himself Tudor. . . . And so, he would say, his father had come down to being a mere builder.

At this (how vividly it all came back!) a nervous man in the Sixth Form suddenly went into a species of hysterics and said, "That's nothing. My name is Cohen, and I don't mind telling you that if a Cohen had had a crooked back he jolly well wouldn't have been allowed to serve at the altar!" Cruikback said loftily, "You haven't got the common savvy to understand, execrable Jew!" They fought it out with fists. By some system of bobbing and weaving, ducking and feinting, crouching and jabbing, Cohen bloodied our hero's nose and knocked him down. Cruikback explained, later, that in the first place he had been brought up to fight with the long straight left like a gentleman, and that in the second place his foot had slipped on the dry, polished grass in Lower Meadow, where the fight came off. And we all believed him—he was wonderfully plausible, in his didactic way—he had as many "of courses" as a society columnist. It was Cohen who slunk away, while Cruikback flaunted his reddened handkerchief like a pennant; and when, having had his bleeding stanched by a key put down his back, he offered his long, aristocratic hand and said with all the condescension in the world, "Now then, Cohen, you've had your lesson. Take your medicine like a soldier, and let bygones be bygones," and poor Cohen shook that hand, we all cheered although Cohen was unmarked.

But still I felt young and worshipful in his presence, foolishly tongue-tied, so that Copper Baldwin answered for me: "Mr. Laverock is the boss 'ere, mister."

Cruikback gave him a long, cold, blue-gray stare; slightly bloodshot, astounded, incredulous. Then, completely ignoring Copper Baldwin, he said to me, "What? Who, me? What am *I* doing here? Doing where, old thing? Don't even know where I am!—" this, with a gush of confidence, free and easy, man-to-man—"What an enormous great fellow you've grown into! Lord, but it all seems about five hundred years ago, though, doesn't it? In point of actual fact, Laverock, where is this? . . . Fowlers End, you say? Oh, God! Now I *am* in for it! I live near St. John's Wood, and my blasted car has gone squiffy, and I don't seem to see anything like a garage round here. . . . Lord, Laverock, what a long time it's been! Remember the time I thrashed that Jew-boy down in Long Meadow? But you were in the Lower Fifth then—"

"Where's this car o' yourn?" asked Copper Baldwin.

"If you can call it a car," said Cruikback to me. "I left it a mile or so down the road, between here and Ullage."

"What on earth were you doing there?" I asked.

"Oh," said Cruikback, "I'm a surveyor now, you know."

"And what the 'ell is there to survey round Ullage?" asked Copper Baldwin.

Cruikback did not look at him—he winced at him—and said, "Oh, things go on, you know. They expand, Laverock, you know. I suppose you know that the working classes have bred beyond all statistical correlation? Or don't you? You always were a literary kind of bloke. Well—but I'm not here to tell tales out of school. Had the surprise of my life when I saw you here."

"Statistical correlation to what?" asked Copper Baldwin.

"*You'll* understand what I mean, Laverock," said Cruikback. "Statistics of overcrowding, and all the evils that go with it—such as incest, you know—are correlated with overpopulation in a given area. London wasn't built to house ten million, you know. . . ." When Cruikback started to talk like this, he had what they call a "silver tongue"—he could make something new and warm and personal out of the deadliest truism, or make a remark about the weather sound like a new advance in meteorology. Our doddering old headmaster, a Doctor of Divinity, had more than once voiced a hope that Cruikback might go into the Church, or Parliament—he imparted such a warmth, such a resonance, such an air of newness to the twaddling platitude. . . . You *must* know, Laverock, old thing, that no city was originally built to house ten million? Let alone your heavy industry? And here, don't you see, is where your statistical correlation comes in—I mean, of course, the statistical correlation between your expanding city population, *plus* your expanding heavy industry, *plus,* of course, rising land values in your outlying suburbs. Well, that's what I'm out here for, of course."

"Depending on that city's economic value," said Copper Baldwin.

"That's right!" cried Cruikback, as if Copper Baldwin had let fall a veritable trip hammer of ratiocination, hitting some knotty problem in just the right spot and breaking it open; his eyes sparkled as if they were reflecting newly bared veins of pure bright thought. "Perfectly right. These things work, of course, in a ratio. . . . I beg your pardon, I'm afraid I didn't catch your name?"

"Baldwin."

"Oh, yes, Mr. Baldwin. My name's Cruikback—spelled with a *u* and an *i*, of course. How d'you do? . . . I say, I don't suppose it's possible, Laverock, to get a drink in this hell-hole at this Godforsaken hour, is it? Is there some sort of bottle you keep for visiting royalty, and so forth?"

One always felt called upon to cut a dash in the presence of Cruikback, so that I was embarrassed and could only say, "The pubs are shut, I'm afraid, old thing."

"Then don't give it a second thought, Laverock!" cried Cruikback, with manly magnanimity.

But Copper Baldwin said, "I got a drop o' gin, if you don't mind gin, sir."

"*Mind* it? I adore it!" Cruikback's eyes sparkled again. Copper Baldwin got his tool bag and took out half a bottle of gin. In the cashier's box there was a twopenny tumbler in which Mrs. Edwards used to keep her teeth during the day. He rinsed this in the ladies' lavatory and poured Cruikback a heavy drink. To me he offered the bottle, saying, "Have a go."

And at this, inexplicably, my feelings were hurt. I went next door to the café, bought a threepenny ginger beer, and walked away with the bottle and the glass before Costas could stop me. Then I accepted Copper Baldwin's gin, which I discreetly diluted. Cruikback downed his at a gulp. I could not help saying, "I hope Mrs. Edwards took her teeth out of that glass before you knocked that back, old thing." And I explained, half hoping for some nauseous reaction—because there came into my mind a memory of a playing field ten long years ago:

. . . I had spent my last pennies on a bottle of some gassy yellow stuff called Lime-O, of which I had taken my first voluptuous mouthful, when Cruikback appeared in a straw boater and a blazer. "Let's have a sip of that," he said. ". . . Oh, you've been sucking at it, have you? Got a clean handkerchief?" I had, and was proud of it. Cruikback wiped the neck of the bottle with it most scrupulously before he drank. He returned me the bottle, empty. "All gas," he said. "Muck up your stomach. Keep away from it, young thingummy. It rots the constitution." He judiciously examined the handkerchief, then pocketed it, saying, "I'll let you have this back properly laundered." But he never did.

Now, looking at me gravely, he said, "Oh, but that's perfectly all right, you know. Glass can't carry germs, and alcohol, of course, is a disinfectant. Internal and external. There's a distinct statistical correlation between the use of alcohol in surgery and certain kinds of infection. Look up your Decker. Read your—but what am I going to do about this confounded car of mine?" He appealed, now, to Copper Baldwin. "You've got the savvy, the common savvy," he said.

To my disgust, Copper Baldwin seemed flattered by this. "Ring nearest garage and get you a tow," he said briskly.

"Right you are!" cried Cruikback. "Only I've been in the wilds all day. Cash me a check, and let's get going."

"Can't, I'm afraid," I said, wishing that I were more pleased with his company. But as Cruikback went on and on drinking us up I felt as I had felt that afternoon when the Lime-O disappeared, and my handkerchief after it. And Copper Baldwin's attitude distressed me. Now, purged of character, he was the Acting Unpaid Lance-Corporal sucking up to his immediate superior, for the sake of a stripe of tape.

"Let's have another bit of that gin," said Cruikback, "and give the matter thought. Oh, but I say—look here, a man's credit's good, surely?"

"Not rahnd Fowlers End," said Copper Baldwin.

"No, naturally not," said Cruikback, with some irritation. "Stranger here. I mean, with you, Laverock. I'm good for a quid or two, I suppose, until tomorrow or the day after?"

Before I could reply, Copper Baldwin came bustling in to save me embarrassment: "There's a couple o' quid in the petty cash, I think, Mr. Laverock. I'll get it." Then he darted into the cashier's box and sank out of sight on his haunches. He came out a few seconds later and gave me two crumpled pound notes, which I passed to Cruikback, who handled them and said, "They're horribly warm and clammy, aren't they though?" He yawned. "Well, never mind. Thanks, anyway, young Laverock. Oh, Lord! Look. It's hellishly late, and I've got to be back on the job by half-past six. It occurs to me: is it *worth* getting up to town and back again tonight? To say nothing, of course, of the delay mucking about with garages and what not? Could you give me a chair or something to sit on, Laverock? I don't need a great deal of sleep, of course."

I could only say, "Take my bed, Cruikback, old thing."

"Don't be such a confounded young ass!" he said severely. "Take your bed? What the hell do you take me for? No, there *is* a limit! What bed, anyway?"

"I have a room over the café next door," I said. "You can have it for a few hours if you like."

Cruikback was astonished. "No! You aren't going to tell me you actually *live* in this hole? But you always were a strange little fellow, weren't you? Look, Baldwin, do you mind terribly if I take just another wee sip?"

"Carry on, sir."

"Gordon's Dry," said Cruikback, scrutinizing the label. "I'll return it with interest, of course. . . . So you live here, do you, Laverock? Over a café, too. Poor old fellow, you must have a hell of a time with cockroaches, of course? Black beetles and what not? Bugs and all that? Smell of stale cooking, et cetera, et cetera? Poor old Laverock! I wouldn't deprive you of your bed for anything in the world. However—"

He took another "sip"—I counted five distinct up-and-down

movements of his Adam's apple—until I said, "Leave another man a bit, old thing."

Cruikback wagged an admonitory finger at me. "*Not* to be a drunkard! But you always were a little guzzle-gut, you know, young Laverock. Many's the time I've stopped you making yourself ill with all sorts of bottled stuff. Oh, well, look here—if you really want me to, I think I *will* have a nap over this café of yours, Laverock. What?"

"What about the jam-jar, sir?" asked Copper Baldwin. "I mean, the car."

"Oh, that. It can wait till morning. Nobody's likely to pinch it, and it belongs to the company, anyway, and is insured for more than it's worth, you can bet your life, of course. Personally, I'm too whacked to do anything more—exhausted."

"How about your instruments?" I asked.

"What d'you mean?"

"Surveying instruments—theodolites, or whatever you call them—and what not," I said.

"Oh, oh those," said Cruikback. "Come, now, young Laverock—you don't imagine I'd leave my instruments in an unattended car in these parts, do you? They're locked away, of course." He sniffed. "I think I'm catching a beastly cold. I say, Laverock, do you happen to have a clean handkerchief on you?"

He could see that I had: it was sticking out of my breast pocket in a neat triangle. "Oh, good show," he said, without waiting for a reply, and snatched it away. "Of course, I'll let you have it back properly laundered. Share and share alike was always our unofficial motto, Baldwin; at Snellgrove, of course. Eh, Laverock?"

I said, "I noticed the 'share and share,' but I can't say I saw the 'alike.'" The gin was biting. "As I remember, it was: big boy eat little boy; strong boy bully weak boy; and dog eat dog, Cruikback."

He replied, "*Whatever* you do, don't get the wrong attitude, Laverock! What was our real motto? '*Per Ardua ad Astra*,' wasn't it? Meaning what? 'By Toil to the Stars.' Now it has been worked out by statistical correlation that if everybody shared alike, the world would be bankrupt in less than seventy-two hours. Whereas, on the other hand, I ask you—see for yourself, Laverock, see for yourself!—the more *ardua* they put into the thing, the less they see of the *astra*. Eh?"

"So help me," I said to Copper Baldwin, "the man's been listening to Sam—"

Copper Baldwin said, "Shush! Let 'im talk."

"There must be integration," said Cruikback.

"That's right," said Copper Baldwin. "I mean to say, it's a law o' nature, ain't it, sir?"

"Yes. '*All for One and One for All*' is romantic. Good enough for the Three Musketeers," said Cruikback. "Work it out in its statistical correlation, and what have you got?" He was at a loss for words, so he cantered off in another direction: "The code of the racketeer is what you have there, old thing. And while the code of share and share alike is a *bloody* good thing to cut your milk teeth on, Laverock, the end result is what we call—"

"Fascism and the corporate state?" I said.

"Communism," said Copper Baldwin.

"What we call *Anarchy*!" cried Cruikback, clapping us both on the shoulder. "I'm glad you agree. Now let's take '*Per Ardua ad Astra*.' 'By Toil to the Stars?' Right. But by *whose* toil, eh? And to what stars?"

He made a rhetorical pause, of which I took advantage to say, "Define, Cruikback, *define*!"

"Say I have a washerwoman," he began.

"Say you haven't," said I, with a hard look at my handkerchief, which he was waving.

Unabashed, Cruikback said, "Not a bad point, old fellow. Not a bad point at all. Thanks, old thing. Let's put it *your* way. I'm quite agreeable: say I *haven't* got a washerwoman. Hypothetically, of course."

With all the irony I could put into my voice, I said, "That you haven't got a washerwoman goes without saying, let's say. Skip the hypothesis and come down to the 'of course.' "

"I'm afraid you're getting over my head," said my old hero. "You'd better get some sleep. Sleep it off, old man, and take a good dose of salts the very min*yute* you wake up. Pump ship and dredge off the bilge. Preferably in hot water, naturally, you know. Piping, of course. And by the bye, where *is* this famous bed of yours?"

"Next door," I said.

"Then lead me to it. Meanwhile think things over. D'you take me, Laverock? Nothing'll lead a man closer to nowhere than an uncorrelated muddle without integration—better get that straight from the start, young Laverock. Take me?"

"I don't know what the hell you're talking about," I said.

Cruikback said, with agonized patience, "Naturally not, not now; not right at this minute. Sleep on it. I'm just about used up. Where was it you said your bed was?"

Reluctant to let go a point, I persisted: "Washerwomen aside —say you haven't got a handkerchief?"

"I'm afraid I don't quite get the drift," said Cruikback. "But do, please, cut out the metaphysics and get some rest, my dear Laverock! I absolutely must be out of here by six. Call me. You will, of course, won't you?"

"And what kind of a car is it?" asked Copper Baldwin. "Yours, I mean, sir."

Cruikback stared at him. "A Daimler, of course," he said.

"Right," said Copper Baldwin. "But remember, you ain't supposed to kip over the Greek's. Mr. Laverock is a gentleman in a very important position, sir."

"I quite understand," said Cruikback. "See he gets some rest, and don't let him drink too much. Is that quite clear? Very well then. A Daimler Saloon—got that? Now beddy-bye."

"Take my key, Copper, and see the gentleman to bed," I said. "Only keep it discreet. You understand, Cruikback, my position?"

"It's okay," said Copper Baldwin. "The gaff is shut for the night and the Greeks 'ave gone to Uncle Ned."

"He means to bed," I said to Cruikback, disliking the apologetic tone of my voice.

"To Bopeep on their rolling billows," said Copper Baldwin, with a certain relish. "Where their loaves o' bread repose."

"I mustn't be called a *minute* later than a quarter to six," said Cruikback. Struck as by an afterthought, he added, "I'm grateful to you, you know, of course. Naturally, I'll prove it. Oh, don't imagine I mean with dirty money—nothing of the sort. Only I might make millionaires of you two. *Verb sap*. You can rest in peace tonight, Laverock; old Cruikback is looking after you, as per usual. Pleasant dreams!"

"What do you mean, 'millionaires,' for God's sake?" I asked.

Cool as a half-commission man, confident as a young fellow whose father is a broker who comes home redolent of B-and-B and Corona-Coronas, Cruikback said, "Of course, you know I've taken your hospitality, Laverock?"

"Oh, don't be silly," I said.

"Pardon me, young Laverock. You too, Baldwin. I'll be as silly as I choose. I confess I don't quite like your attitude, Laverock. But if I say I can put you in the way of making a million—*verb sap*! Oh, very well, say I exaggerate: call it four hundred thousand, and not a million. All right? Then I mean it, you know. Laverock, have I ever broken my word? Look me in the eyes and call me a liar."

"Of course you aren't, old thing," I said, in a dribble of sentiment.

"You wait and see," said he darkly. "As it happens, I am in possession of information."

"All correct, sir. Come on now," said Copper Baldwin, and then he saw Cruikback to bed—to my bed.

When Copper Baldwin returned, I said, "Look, Copper, you can't go lending people two pounds out of the petty cash that I'm responsible for."

"I know I can't," he said. "Because Smallpox sees to it that there's never more than three 'alf crowns in the petty cash; and that under lock 'n key. I loaned the gentleman that couple o' nicker out o' my own pocket."

"But you handed the money to me, and I handed it to him," I said, very agitated. "Therefore, I'm responsible for it to you!"

"Think no more of it," said Copper Baldwin. "It was out of my *own* pocket. All warm and clammy. Take it easy, cocko."

I would have argued the point, only the deliveryman threw a case of film cans into the vestibule at that moment. It missed my foot by about two inches. In one of my rare—perhaps all too rare—bursts of temper, I picked up the box of returns and threw it right back at him, shouting, "Damn your eyes! Henceforward bring this stuff in like a civilized human being!"

There was some consolation to be got out of the blank astonishment on the man's face as the big steel box flew over his shoulder into the empty street; and, if I had been in a mood to appreciate it, something gratifying in the way he said, "Well, Gord blind O'Riley! Sam Yudenow don't 'alf pick 'em!"

But I never felt more cold, lonely, and frustrated than when I lay down, at last, in the office. For the first time in my life I had a feeling that I was being abused and was indignant without being able to define the reason for my feeling—which is unhealthy.

And my temper was not improved when, at six o'clock in the morning, somewhat puckered about the *f* holes in his fiddle face, Cruikback breathed in my face as only those do who have stale breath, and said, "Sorry, but that gin, or whatever it was, made me a bit icky. I didn't know where the bog was, but luckily there seems to be a jordan under the bed. I used that—I suppose you don't mind terribly, of course. . . . But what a little sinner you are, Laverock! Whatever did she see in you? Appeal of the brute, what?"

"What the hell are you talking about?" I asked.

He said, "Must have been about three or three-thirty. That gel from this café of yours popped into bed with me. Thought I was you, I imagine. Well, Old Valetudinarians stick together; you *told* me to be discreet, didn't you? So I didn't say a word. We you-knowed *cinq fois*. Then she slipped away like a wraith. *Up the Vale!* What a hot little bitch—I *beg* pardon, young Laverock—what an affectionate lady! But (a word to the wise) you'd better watch out. Bad for the stamina. It's proved by science that a man has only a certain number of eggs. And I'm a married man—"

"Oh, please go away, Cruikback!" I cried.

"I'm on my way, old thing," said Cruikback. "Back in a few days."

He was gone several minutes before my slow, groping wit dredged up out of my silted consciousness the horrid significance of what he had done to me. Preoccupied at first with the jordan, or chamber pot, which he had used in my name, I could think of nothing else—I am morbidly sensitive about such things.

Only a little later it occurred to me that I had by proxy taken into my bed and seduced the sister of my landlord, the Cypriot dynamiter Costas.

8

Now I felt that everything had happened to me. In retrospect, the agony of a silly young man put to shame is a laughing matter—and rightly so, because the shame, the exaggerated shame, of your self-conscious boy has in it a certain idiotic pomposity. He has too high a regard for himself, and for his mistakes and his pimples, and his enthusiasms, which are a sort of pimplous eruption of the spirit.

But, oh, my dear reader, think back to the time when you used to blush and didn't know how to stop it—call back to memory that awful anguish which was yours after your voice broke, when it seemed to you that you were the focal center of a million eyes and nostrils, to every one of which you gave a separate, sharp offense!

I say: I was growing up, at an awkward age, and especially prone to self-examination. I hated Cruikback now with a deadly hatred. We had, I believed, spoiled the purity of Kyra Costas. This, no doubt, was a dreadful thing; Costas was a killer, and I was a man of honor. But over and above this—having reconciled myself to the role of rapist—above all, I say, clung the thought of appearing in Kyra's eyes as the loose-gutted fellow who used the chamber pot.

It may be silly, but this was on my mind. I will say it again: I have a prejudice against using these articles of bedroom crockery ever since I went through the cucumber frame. I do not mind carrying a pot for someone else but hate the thought of that someone's carrying a pot for me: let the psychiatrists make what they will of this.

So I went upstairs, seething with hate for Cruikback, and discovered that he had indeed used that chamber pot—from every body orifice, as Zola says—and I thanked God that he had, at least, aimed straight. Once a Valetudinarian, always a Valetudinarian.

The thing to do was to get rid of this vessel. I thought for a long time, as it seemed, and then decided to put it on Godbolt's doorstep. But the house was already alive. From below, I heard a bass baritone singing in a quavering, yearning tone some such tune as the Byzantine nuns must have played on a three-holed flute. A hot gust of the fumes of stale cooking fat came upstairs. I heard a woman's footsteps clattering in backless hard-heeled slippers.

Panic took hold of me. I opened the window and put the pot on the sill. Then Kyra came in without knocking. No doubt about it, she was a beautiful girl in a duck-legged, satchel-arsed, Cypriot way—heavy-lidded, heavy-haired, each breast looking as if it weighed seven pounds and was crouching, palpitating, on a marble slab waiting for a weighing machine.

Kyra said, "Well?"

Sweating heavily, I said, "I'm afraid I have no explanation to offer."

"I should think not," she said very slowly, wrinkling her nose and dilating her nostrils.

I said to her, "I would offer to kiss you, darling, only I have not yet brushed my teeth."

"Oh, you would, would you?" she said. "At the best of times this room stinks, but now—" She went to the window and saw what I had discreetly placed outside.

There was an appalling silence and then—I kick myself whenever I remember it—I said the first thing that came into my mind: "It must have been burglars . . ."

To my surprise, Kyra began to laugh. "Oh, come on, now," she said, "you don't smell sour. *You* didn't flob your gob last night. Gi' me a kiss."

"Let me explain—" I began.

"Tell it to the Marines," said Kyra. "Do you like breasts?"

I said, "Oh yes, very much, but—"

"So do I. I can't imagine myself without 'em."

"About last night—" I began.

"I thought of you," she said. "What's your name? Laverock? I think it's a darling name—it sounds like it ought to smell like a bunch of flowers. . . . Do you kiss wet or dry?"

A sort of obfuscation, a blankness, came over me. Goodness knows what might have happened, only a heavy voice from downstairs bellowed, "Kyra! Kyra kyralina!"

As she advanced to kiss me good-by, I instinctively retreated. My behind touched the handle of the chamber pot. I was aware of its teeter-totter on the edge as Kyra squeezed me; and then I heard a most appalling crash. It had gone through the skylight into the kitchen.

Then I was alone, thinking that if only I had a pistol I would hold it at arm's length and shoot myself in the face somewhere near the nose. This way, I reasoned, no coroner could call it suicide but only accidental death. After all, who shoots himself in the nose? But I did not have a pistol; and, touching the matter of noses, Cruikback had my last handkerchief.

Hitherto, give or take enough folly to last an average neurotic about sixty-five years, my life had been devoid of serious complications. Now I was in a nightmarish maze. Intellectually speaking, it was as if I had cast my line into a fog without keeping my thumb on the reel. Then I knew fear, blank idiot fear, and tried to grapple with it. It would not be departing very far from the truth if I said that at that moment I went into a kind of delirium—a half-sane man's delirium, which is nothing but fact in mutiny. Probably the crash of the skylight set it up in a misprinted bar. More likely it was a sense of frustration and injustice at having the name without the game. All the mistakes of my misspent little life came down to irritate me like so many grains of pepper—only I did not dare to sneeze, because Cruikback had my handkerchief.

I went downstairs, determined to have it out with somebody. The first one I met was Kyra, who was washing the urn which, I believe, was used indiscriminately for tea, coffee, and cocoa. I had a speech in mind; but when she looked at me I forgot every word of it.

She said, "My brother would like a word with you."

This suited me perfectly. I was ready to break him across my knee. Costas appeared then and led me to the kitchen. Pointing to the scattered result of what had exploded on the floor, he asked, "Are you responsible for this?"

I said, "No, sir, no. No, I am not responsible for this! And I will thank you, henceforward, *not* to put your Midday Special to cool where I cannot see it. It is enough, God damn it, that I have to put up with the smell of your cooking from a distance. If you are not careful I will inform the Ministry of Health—I am a personal friend—and they will close you down in a pig's whisper. The public analyst is my cousin. Now then! Well?"

It did not occur to me until later that I was already beginning to talk like Sam Yudenow—in this short space of time he must have got into me by osmosis.

I added, "And get that skylight repaired. Also clear up this mess. One of the yobbos gets a bit of glass in his faggot, Mr. Costas, and he rips his esophagus all the way down. Study anatomy. Man has a hemorrhage. Who's the sufferer? Worst of all—I daresay you know what they are like round here—it passes through his system and makes a gash coming out. In which case, as a man of your perspicacity will no doubt appreciate, that fellow Godbolt will unquestionably bribe him to swear to an unnatural offense. Therefore, Mr. Costas, be advised by me: don't put it back; simply sweep it up and throw it out." Marveling at myself, I heard myself continuing: "You come from a sunny, peaceful country. It would surprise you to know what they are like in this locality. All they have to hope for, all they have to look forward to, is a lump of glass in their food. Then come lawyers and a settlement out of court. And who suffers? I leave it to your imagination. So don't let it happen again, will you, Mr. Costas?"

I was expecting some terrible outburst—indeed, I had been talking in that frightened way which is commonly known as "in fun," which is the coward's way out—but, to my astonishment, Costas, winnowed of ferocity, said, "Very well, sir."

He took up a stiff bass broom, paused, and said, "Are you a relative of Mr. Yudenow's?"

"Certainly not," I said.

Then, from the doorway, came a voice which I seemed to have heard all my life, crying, "Miv a bass bvoom? Is everybody stark staring? A bass bvoom, I want you should understand, is like hundveds of little spvings. They scatter. Take, better, a piece of tin and scvape. Two pieces o' tin, like a steam shovel in Amevica. One feeds the other. Economics. Then on to a reliable newspaper, and save it for the boys for Godbolt's shop. Afterwards, hot water, a squeegee, and perfumed carbolic. It's not Mr. Laveridge's fault; he's new to show biz. So whereas, I got a new idea."

It was that man again—shaven like a bridegroom, with a nose dropper in one hand and a cigar in the other. This cigar, as I later learned, was his "waving cigar"—it was made of wood and lit up at the tip when he pressed the other end. It was eight inches long, an inch in diameter, and bore a wide red-and-gold label with what most reliable witnesses would have sworn to be the imprint of Corona-Corona—only on examination it said, Croona-Croona. His pockets were full of gadgets of a similar nature. He was the pioneer of bubble gum in England: pretending to eat something during a conference, he would simulate a hiccup and then, to everybody's horror and disgust, blow through moist lips something about the size and color of a pig's bladder, suck it back, and say, with an air of quiet resignation, "Pay no attention, boys—it's internal."

Now he tried it on me. It started with a bubble that grew and grew; what time, seemingly unaware of it, he switched his wooden cigar on and off and contemplated the ceiling. It was somewhat more than I could bear. I got up to go. This horrid membrane was immediately sucked back where it came from like the cloaca of a duck, while he said, "It's because o' worry about my staff—and my business. What's going to happen to me, what? Everybody's wiring for sound, Laventry. Mayerowitz is wiring up the Crystal Palace, Luton. Connolly's wiring up, Rappaport is wiring up, MacDougall is wiring up. It's a cvaze, Lavender, but what am I supposed to do? Wire up? Before Sam Yudenow wires up *he'll* be wired up—to an electric chair he'll be wired up. McGoogan is wiring up. Everybody's wiring up. So what for should I wire up? Give me liberty or God forbid! Forty, sixty per cent of the gross for the sound system? Over your dead body! Now you're a man of education, culture. You can't help your looks, but even so God made you, or somebody, if you get what I mean. And you got nishertive. You're a learned man. Believe me, Laveridge, the public don't want sound—the public wants reality."

"No, it doesn't," I said. "Is the stage reality?"

Staring at me as if I had just sprung out of the floor, Sam Yudenow cried, "If it ain't reality, what *then* is it?"

"Does Othello really smother Desdemona every night?" I asked.

He replied impatiently, "O'Thello—miv an Irishman, anything can happen. Look at Booligan. Wait till you see O'Toole. Miv 'im, if she was only smothered to death she'd thank her lucky stars. But how comes O'Thello? Whatever you do, don't change the subject. We got to face reality. In this life, what comes first? Eating. Now I'm asking you, as man to man, is there any fun sitting through a program mivout eating something? I'm asking you again, candidly, is it possible to eat mivout sound? No. I lay awake at night—me, also, I'm a thinker—and it works out like this: all talkies have done for show biz is put up the price of monkey nuts and chocolates, so now they're sold without shells. Hacker the Breaker offered me a cargo monkey nuts ready salted—they got a bit spoiled miv sea water. Don't worry, I got an idea about that, too: 'Marine Peanuts.' But round Fowlers End they ain't educated up to this kind thing. They're lovely, mind you—soft as butter, melt in the mouth. I'll try 'em out elsewhere. To cut a long story short, I want you should be a pioneer in Fowlers End. Remember *The Covered Wagon*—only no firearms. . . . By the way, did you remember like I told you? You know, the crook o' the arm in the thvoat and the right hand in the arse o' the trousers?"

"When I chucked Dilly out," I said. "I had to carry him—he had no arse to his trousers."

"A nice way to begin!" said Sam Yudenow. "Dilly he's got to chuck out! I'm ruined. He's right-hand man in the Ullage mob. Take arsenic, but miv Dilly be diplomatic. But what was I saying? Ah, the question of nushment. Napoleon could see the way things were going in advance, so he went there first, and when they arrived he said, 'Hello.' The new tvend calls for soft food during talkies. Now it's like this: I just bought from Hacker the Breaker three still frames, a genuine carpet, and half a gross Exit signs in red; only he made me take a load army surplus dehydvated cabbage. Marvelous stuff, the very thing! It seems they take a cabbage and they take the water out of it. What's left? Cabbage. Put a couple spoonfuls in boiling water and there you are, seven pounds delicious cabbage. Now I'm coming right to the point. Have you eaten bubble-and-squeak?"

I had. If you are very young and desperately hungry you can eat it practically without nausea. In Soho, in the small hours, the café proprietors used to give it away—this being a benevolent way of cleaning their kitchens. It is made as follows: Procure left-over potatoes. Add to them anything you like which, somehow, always happens to be yesterday's cabbage. Take a heavy instrument—any heavy instrument—and beat this mixture without mercy until it is quite flat. Put the resultant cake into a pan which you are heating to burn off coagulations of old fat. Fry until you can no longer see through a blue haze. Then give it to a passer-by. He will, most likely, hurl it into the street, thus saving you the cost of an extra garbage bin. When cold, a portion of bubble-and-squeak can be thrown a great distance, like a discus, and has been known to inflict grievous bodily harm—for which purpose it is better than brickbats or bottles because, if charged, the thrower can always plead: "I was only offering him a midnight snack." Bubble-and-squeak has been known by various nicknames, such as "poor man's leavings," and "lump-in-the-stomach," and "constipation tart." I did not dare to tell Sam Yudenow that I could write a brochure about bubble-and-squeak and its various uses—I felt that if I did so, he would tell me where to find the pencil and put me to work at once.

So I said, "I don't know. I'm not sure."

"Bubble-and-squeak," said he, "is the best thing for the working classes, the bloody loafers. Listen: I know a man, Meyer the Buyer, so on account of bankruptcy he went to South America.

Nobody's enemy but his own: put all your assets in your wife's name, by all means, but if so don't be caught miv your hand down the knickers of a Welsh servant girl. Notmivstanding. Meyer the Buyer went to South America miv a cargo of surgical boots. Well, the black men there eat bubble-and-squeak from their mother's bveasts, and at the age of fifteen they can put a grand piano on their back and run up to the top of Mount Everest. Miv a raw onion for dessert naturally and as much water as they want to drink. . . . Now in show biz we always try a project out in the provinces. Lavenheim, new as you are, I want to give you a chance to make good. Call me 'pal.' "

I said, "Pal."

"That's the way I like to hear a man talking!" he cried, with enthusiasm. "Call me 'pal' and I'm your pal. But call Sam Yudenow a bastard—don't do it!—and oh, believe me, it's like the Indian proverb! 'Who gets a toe-rag by the tail can't dismount.' Thank you, Daniels. All night I was thinking. Miv any product the main thing is a good title. My bubble-and-squeak turns out bright green. It seems like the contractor to the War Office—Hacker the Breaker's second cousin—so he discovered that this dehydvated cabbage is kind of white. Well, so this contractor's son is studying for a dentist, and he gives this advice: 'Put in a little bit copper sulphate. That's what makes tinned peas green.' A fool to himself, Hacker the Breaker's second cousin—generous to a fault. He shoves in a couple sacksful. And believe me, Laveroff, many a good man now living on the fat o' the land off of total disability would at this very moment be pushing up poppies. Or at best the Unknown Warrior. . . . Now, you know what a hamburger is, I dare say?"

"As I understand it," I said, "a hamburger is a sort of rissole between two halves of an artificially inflated bun."

"Genuinely inflated," said Sam Yudenow. "Now, what do you say to a lovely bubble-and-squeak in a roll? Don't interrupt, please, I'm coming to the title." He drew a deep breath, slapped me on the back, and shouted, "*Greenburger!*" and looked eagerly up at me. "Say something."

I said, "I'd have to be pretty hungry before I ate one of those."

"I knew you'd get my point," said Sam Yudenow. "I tried it on my chauffeur, and his belly came up like a football. So say we charge twopence apiece? I even got the subtitle for you: 'A Good Blowout for Twopence.' "

I said flippantly, "Why not put a penn'orth of the muck into a paper bag, with printed instructions, and sell it for sixpence?"

Sam Yudenow paused, thunderstruck, but quickly said, "This I thought of too, but first . . . you got to learn to swim before you can float. I want Costas should make up a few dozen Greenburgers, we should give 'em away for one penny apiece Friday and Saturday. Look at Woolworth, look at Henry Ford. Only here's the secret: first let the mixture swell, then dry it out golden bvown. Underdo that mixture, and the salt o' the earth washes it down miv a glass o' ginger pop; it swells in his stummick and he bursts, and I'm the sufferer. The most filling penn'orth they've ever seen. Contains copper salts for anemia. And why am I taking you into my confidence like this? Because you got an honest face. I want to leave a few sacks o' dehydrated cabbage miv you to keep in the genevator room. Deal it out two pounds at a time. Scales you won't need; put it this way—an old film can filled flat to the brim, call it two pounds. In show biz, a showman shouldn't be ashamed to take a tray round his neck and go up and down the aisles shouting, 'Oh, Lovely Greenburgers!'—et cetera. Or, 'Sizzling Hot!' Never mind what's sizzling hot. You sell the sizzle. And believe me, son, I won't forget you. This is Sam Yudenow's reply to the talkies. In your spare time, write up a nice little piece and send it to the *Daily Film Renter* or the *Times*; and if it comes out buy me six copies and write out a chit." Then he was busy with his chauffeur, the cross-eyed, clubfooted man who was loaded like a Turkish porter with a mountain of small sacks. Beating him with his hat, Sam Yudenow was driving him toward the generator room.

I shouted after him, "Hey! I must go into town this afternoon to get my luggage."

"And confidentially," said this unforgettable character, "regard your wages as raised by ten bob a week as from next January. Only don't tell a soul. Stick by Sam and Sam will stick by you."

"I say, I must take an hour or two off to get my things."

"Naturally. Get 'em. Dock yourself two hours—no, come on, what's a couple hours between friends?—take your time, dock yourself four hours and make me out a chit in triplicate. Don't blame me, blame the capitalist system. They're responsible for so much taxation in this country. You'd be surprised. . . . *Greenburgers*! Ah!"

He was full of the glory and the dream. He went on, with that silly kind of smile on his face which is most often seen curling the mouths and lifting the eyebrows of spiritualists, Christian Scientists, clergymen accused of hatchet murders, and other ecstatics. "My boy, miv a good lawyer anything can be done. But the law of nature you can't get away from. And what is the law of nature? Nothing is ever wasted—don't chunk it into the dustbin until it's hopeless. But while there's life, there's hope. When in doubt, put it on a shelf. Let me tell you a little story. My father was in the provision business—fish—and he was strong as a lion. Believe me, like Golliwog—" I suppose he meant Goliath—"In those days round Billingsgate Market, believe me, you had to be. Blame the law of nature. Well, so one day he lifted up sixteen stone of haddock and got a hernia. He won the bet, but he had to go and buy himself a tvuss.

"So. In Billingsgate, six in the morning, you can buy anything —a watch and chain, picture postcards, anything. Well, so my poor father goes in for a brandy, and much to his surprise he sees his poor inside coming out. So, naturally, he is taken aback. Then comes in a loafer, one of the salt o' the earth, what they called him Tommy Tea-Leaf. Miv education this Tommy could have been respectable—he was so dead clever he could take the shirt off your back while he was talking to you, and you'd never know it. But he didn't know how to apply what the Lord gave him, so he simply went around pinching things mivout discrimination. This particular morning—Tommy always came straight to Billingsgate to flog what he'd knocked off the night before—so he turns up at this pub miv a marble statue of a Roman king, a complete set of the 'Complete Works of William Makepeace Thackeray,' and a tvuss still warm. He'd got it off a girl at the Alhambra, who'd had one too many, in the open street, pretending to dance the polka miv her.

"My father bought the whole lot for five bob. The 'Complete Works of William Makepeace Thackeray' was worth that much in itself, for wrapping up fish—there was a shortage paper at the time. The statue was classy—solid marble—we touched it up miv a bit paint here and there and it was lifelike. The tvuss fitted like a glove, and my poor father wore it twenty years. Wait a minute! So years and years later he passes away. I kept that tvuss. Believe me, anything can come in handy. Years pass. I make my first deal for my first show. I agree to put a hundred and twenty pounds down. I don't have a hundred and twenty pounds. Naturally, I was occupied in my mind, uncomfortable. I went away thinking, and just as I stepped off the curb—like Ejilah in the Bible—I sneezed, coughed, hiccuped, and farted all at the same time, and ruptured myself. So I took my father's tvuss from the wall, and there you are. And I wore it twenty years until horsehair came out of the pad. Waste not, want not. So let it be with Greenburgers. . . . And as for that little suggestion of mine about putting the stuff into little bags—think it over, Lavender, think it over. Always remember never to forget it takes two to make an idea—be advised byme, I've had hundreds of 'em. Me and Hacker the Breaker.

"Just to give you an example, during the war, so there turns up a Belgian refugee miv a formula for boot polish, and as luck would have it, his name happened to be Spiton. Now I'm a busy man, Laveridge, and I can't stand here all day long chattering. The long and the short of it is me and Hacker the Breaker got the formula for a fi'-pun note, miv the man's name thrown in. This was *my* anspiration, because the indigredients of this polish came dear. But the name Spiton was worth its weight in gold: 'Spit-and-Polish'—'Spiton Polish.'

"Do you begin to follow me? Alas, because I was ruptured, I couldn't fight in the trenches—besides which, in case you didn't notice, I got catarrh—otherwise, believe me, I'd have been only too delighted. But some of my best friends were millingtary men. Moishe the Goniff got a govmint subdizzy he should open a cap factory, to give you one example. But Hacker the Breaker's brother-in-law, Harry the Go-Between, what dealt in hides and corned beef—he would have got a knighthood only there was a sabotage, and they got mixed up—from him I got a little secret: *Miv boot polish, the thing to do is apply sparingly, but use a lot of spit.* Therefore, my 'Spiton Polish' we produced for twice the price in a half-size tin, miv instructions to use saliva on a rag. In big letters, in red: WARNING! ON ACCOUNT OF DOUBLE STRENGTH OF THIS POLISH, USE SPARINGLY! SAVE FOR VICTORY! And it went like hot cakes. Unfortunately, because of the cost of the indigredients, we had to leave out wax, et cetera, so it dried up to a little nut covered miv green fuzz. Get what I mean, kind o' style? Whereas, if the working classes had been ejucated then like they are now, so they should have imagination, we might have sold them empty tins miv instructions purely and simply to spit and apply elbow grease. It's spit and elbow grease that polishes. Boot polish is a lot of eyewash. So what, for example, is to prevent you trade-marking a name like Elbow, cutting up a bar cheap castile soap wrapped up miv a man in a beard? ELBOW GREASE—APPLY SPARINGLY—4D PER CAKE. You're laughing. Go on, laugh. Laugh! They laughed at Einstein, they laughed at Epstein, and even at Weinstein they laughed—and you and I should both be in *his* position! So I got ideals—what's so bloody funny? You take all the shine off a thing, Laventry. You ain't got no Covered Wagon in you. . . . *Greenburgers!* Does that word sing a song in your heart? It don't? Then see a doctor; a doctor see, a telescope he should put to your chest. A lonely giant I turned out to be. . . . As for my idea of putting Greenburgers in a paper bag for fourpence, don't try and pinch that, Lavender—I changed my stragety. A little box, miv a celluloid window. Believe me, nowadays nobody buys anything in a bag. It looks cheap. You were right to correct me; but we could add 'Spices,' separate, in a scvew of paper—*wax* paper—pure wax paper. Blue or green?"

"Pink," I said.

"White, for purity. Miv the same printing job you can stamp the spices wrapper miv pale blue lilies. On the front, a motherly woman in an apron miv a dish in one hand and a ladle in the other. Fourpence? What are you talking about? *Seven*pence! . . . There's a woman does charring for my wife. Give her a bit rag she should blow her nose and a matchstick—if necessary, a hairpin—she should get the wax out from her ears; lend her a comb—the kind you can boil afterwards—and put her on a bib; goose her so she laughs—she's very ticklish—and get a quick picture. Make a cutout. Get two, three layabouts to smell a fried sausage. Get a cameraman to shoot the expressions on their faces—hold the sausage on a string just above their heads, so their eyes roll—then *click*! Make a montage—cut a block! The camera never lies, and what does it cost? Nothing. Can you wonder, with ideas like this, I can't sleep?"

"No," I said.

Then Copper Baldwin appeared with an expression for which I can find no other words but melancholy satisfaction on his long face. From some vantage point—he had the strange gift of being able to merge into his surroundings, thereby cloaking imself in invisibility—he must have overheard the whole conversation, because he said, "As if I ain't got trouble enough already with the plumbing!" He winked at me and jerked his head. "Perfumed lady to see you, Mr. Laverock."

My heart did not know what to do with itself: it leapt up, sank down, and described orbits. Perfumed lady: I thought of my mother, who used lilac, and of June Whistler, who, if she could not find an appropriate perfume in one of the multiple chemists' shops, exuded it by effort of will.

"*What* perfume I didn't say," said Copper Baldwin. "She's waiting for you down in the orchestra." Sam Yudenow being now out of earshot, he whispered, "Miss Noel. It would appear that she got blotto and slept under the drums." He cleared his throat and went on in a haughty, superior kind of tone: "You've read your Russians, I dare say? You can't repent unless you've sinned. Right? I mean, a child's repentance ain't worth a fart in a colander. Whereas . . . Well, anyway, the Russians 'ad something there. If you've got any conscience at all, the worse you sin, the better you repent. The deeper the repentance, the firmer the purpose of amendment—so up you go: by which token my father ought to be well established in 'Eaven by now. What I mean to say is, Miss Noel is down in the orchestra with the 'orrors. Between you and me, Dan, she kind o' defiled herself. Do me a favor, as manager o' this gaff, and go down and talk to 'er. I rely on shock effect. Nothing personal, you know; only you might kind o' shame the poor bitch, if you get what I mean. It's all right, I'll clean up. Do be a pal, kind o' talk to 'er, and I'll get a pot o' strong tea. Will you please?"

"Of course I will," I said.

"She is sort o' fragrant," said Copper Baldwin. And so she was, with a fragrance that I can only describe as something like meat boiled in spirits. She did not smell of herself but of an aftermath —a predigested smell, and she was sitting in some mess of her own creating as far away from the piano as she could possibly get, crying her poor heart out. It touched my heart. I did not know how to address her, so, on that wheezy old piano, with my nine fingers, I attempted to play the *Moonlight Sonata*—whereupon, as if I had stretched her like an accordion, she became a person in one piece. Then Copper Baldwin, whose timing was perfect and who must in any case have been looking at the whole operation and listening to it from a distance, came down with his tea. He took one look and one sniff and left me alone with Miss Noel.

Poor lady, she wept, while she wiped her nose on whatever came to hand and apologized for weeping.

I said, "Oh, come now, Miss Noel, please don't cry. I give you my word, there's nothing to cry about. What's the matter? You've taken to drink? Oh, please, I beg you, don't let it distress you. Put it this way: in distressing yourself you distress me."

"Not for the world!" she cried.

"Well, say for example that we do. Let's just say. Can't you see where it leads? It makes a trail of evil. Get me? You must go your way down, and if I have any love for you, or any loyalty to you, what can I do but follow you, trusting in God? Oh, my dear Miss Noel," I said, "look at yourself. Can you imagine the taste of a rotten stomach, a bloated liver, and I don't know how many yards of intestines packed with corruption—all this translated into what I can only call an effluvium? Oh, my dear Miss Noel, please stop to consider!" I played a few chords of Schubert. "You are worthy of so many higher things. You have no right to go to the devil the way you are going," I said. "Now look here, I will stand by you."

She cried, so bitterly that I was sorry I had spoken; but presently, taking a double handful of air less than a foot in front of her nose, she seemed to catch hold of some vagrant bit of herself. Then she spoke like a conscious woman.

She said, in the most woebegone voice I have ever heard,

" 'Stay with me, Beauty, for the light is dying—my dog and I are old, too old for roving'—what am I talking about?"

I said, "My dear Miss Noel, it seems to me that you are talking sense out of place. That means to say, making no sense. You are in the Pantheon, Fowlers End, and must conduct yourself accordingly. As your manager, it is my duty to see that you do so. And by God, so you shall! . . . Now look here, my dear, I have only nine and a half fingers, and rusty at that, but while Copper Baldwin brings us a cup of tea I will play you a sort of rendering of something I remember while you tell me about yourself and why you condescend to go under yourself. Speaking for myself," I said, "I am, Miss Noel, a protagonist of good old freedom, and I loathe and despise anybody who wants to strangle freedom, in the state or in the individual. Now listen to me—what are you, Miss Noel, but a kind of state? There is a sort of tyrant dictating to you at the present moment. Isn't that so? He makes you do what you don't want to do. Aren't I right? Yet you obey him. You do, every minute, against your better judgment, don't you?"

She said, "Yes."

"Why?" I asked.

"Would you do me a very great favor?"

"If I can, Miss Noel."

"Then will you please go away?"

"Why?" I asked.

"I made messes and I smell. I'm filthy."

Always the one for a bit of metaphysical discussion, I said, "Meaning: if I go away there will be no mess, et cetera? That my absence will cleanse you? No. The muck, such as it is, will still be here. *You'll* still be here, double dirty. You'll make a whole rigmarole in your poor head about what you think I saw and multiply the dirt like the grains of wheat on the chessboard—swamp yourself with it. Come now, Miss Noel; what you have inadvertently dropped on the floor is nothing in itself. Everybody's full of it. It's only a matter of keeping it in its place and putting it where it belongs. Somebody told me once that dirt is only misplaced matter. Be that as it may, in general; in this particular case, if that's all that's on your mind, it's nothing Copper Baldwin can't shift with a bucket of water and a mop. The real significance of it is what it left behind when it came out—I mean, shame."

"I am ashamed," said Miss Noel, crying.

"Always have been," I suggested.

"They made me," she said, between two sobs. "Oh, please tell me, what am I going to do?"

There being no more time for dissertation, and she being in such distress, I said, "Have a good wash, change your clothes, and play the piano. There's nothing like a wash and a change and a little quiet music to clarify the intellect."

"I haven't got another dress."

I said, feeling like one of those characters you read about in books, "Then you shall have another dress. . . . Copper, a word with you." I took him aside and said, "Since you seem to be so lousy and free with your bloody money to all the Cruikbacks and what not, lend me another couple of quid. On my honor, you'll get it back."

Without argument he gave me two pound notes, and then said dryly, "Anything else this morning?"

I said, "Get hold of some boiling water and fill up the hand basin in the ladies' toilet. I'll be back in a couple of minutes."

Then I walked across the street to Godbolt's, memorizing my order, which, in my haste, I blurted out in a breathless rush: "One gentleman's handkerchief, one lady's handkerchief, one lady's jumper, one skirt, one pair lady's knickers, one pair stockings, one comb, one cake scented soap."

Mr. Godbolt looked at me curiously—he was yet to discover that I was Sam Yudenow's new manager—while he made a hunchback of himself in his obsequiousness. "We have a very nice quality gent's handkerchief at sixpence—"

"One of those, please—"

"And a very nice lady's handkerchief at two shillings a dozen."

"Could I have sixpennyworth?"

"I could do you three for sevenpence," he said.

"The way that works out, one of the handkerchiefs out of the dozen is free of charge," I said.

He simpered, "That's right."

"May I have that one?"

He was not the sort of man who appreciates a good, subtle joke. But he tittered in a nervous way and started to pull out shallow, square boxes tied up with green ribbon, saying, "Guaranteed to be one hundred per cent."

I said, "Oh, all right, do me three for sevenpence. Now what about the underwear?"

"I can do you a very nice knicker for one-and-eleven-three."

"Do me one," I said.

"Would the lady like a lovely shade of vyoo-rose?"

"You haven't anything in brown?"

"Not in brown, sir, but I can do you a beautiful knicker in navy blue. What size, if I may ask?"

"Say, a lady about five feet two, with wind." I drew him a diagram in the air. "And make it vieux-rose." He was unused to this way of doing business and could not stop his sales talk: "Guaranteed one hundred per cent genuine art silk. I have another very superior knicker that will last you a lifetime, in blue serge, with a cotton washable knicker lining at three-and-eleven—"

"Congratulations. But I'll have the first one you mentioned."

"The medium size has plenty of give in it. It fits small and large alike."

"The very thing. What about a jumper of the same nature?"

"I have a very popular line of jumper at four-and-elevenpence-farthing, in royal blue, peach, vyoo-rose, black—"

"Black. And do me a skirt, also black, if you will." He did me one at nine-and-elevenpence-three-farthings, which is draper's language for ten shillings; and a pair of guaranteed one hundred per cent genuine artificial silk stockings, flesh color. When I told him that I had seen flesh that color when somebody I knew upset boiling water on her foot, he shook his head with hypocritical regret and started to quote one of the Psalms, breaking off in the middle of the fourth line to ask whether the lady wouldn't like a suit of combinations. And that struck me as being a good idea, the weather being what it was.

"Better give me a suit of combinations," I said.

"I have a lovely comm, knee length, at six-and-three." Here, Godbolt looked left and right, and left again, lowering his voice. "And the French opera comm with genuine blue shoulder straps at eight-and-four—"

"The common or garden, and make it snappy," I said.

"As for the soap," said Godbolt, "we have an arrangement with Mr. Laylock the chemist. He sells no underwear, I sell no drugs, tee-hee! That will be twenty-four-and-threepence."

Having the money safe in his hand, he said, "A gay young sprig, I dare say? Showering your wealth, in a manner of speaking, on the Strange Woman of the Scriptures? Oh, however you may have sinned—and I read it in your face—settle down, settle down!"

"Who with?" I asked.

"Oh, I have lived a decent life, but I know the world. Why are you buying these undergarments for the lady except, as they say, to 'try them on' her? Get married. Will that be all? Could I interest you in a satinette tie? Oh, be warned! Laylock's shop is on the left, and don't forget to say Mr. Godbolt sent you. I thank you, sir, and a very good day to you."

Laylock the Chemist, whose establishment was no more than twenty yards away, was a shop to which its proprietor had transferred his ancestor's sign, LAYLOCK—CHYMIST—ESTAB. 1824. His window was filled with a great cardboard advertisement for tangerine-colored lipstick. Above this, on the left, was stuck a gelatin transfer which said, *Dr. Bissell's Cachets for Feminine Disorders.* This was in blue. In red, to the right of it, was stuck another sign saying, *Male Weakness? Take Street's Striped Pills No. 74! Say: "Seventy-Four!"*

Laylock was a secretive tall man, dressed all in black; I remembered him, years later, when I saw Boris Karloff playing the dope fiend in *Smart Money.* The whole place reeked of cough drops and scented soap gone bad. All over the place, ersatz violet waged a running battle with paregoric; and there was, on the side, a pincer movement, a secret collaboration between a stopped-up drain and the miasma of the street. Someone had tried to attack all this with carbolic, traces of which, sprinkled from a punctured tin can, were visible on the bare floor. Looking at Mr. Laylock the pharmacist, I was impressed by the scrubbed complexion of his hands. He must have washed them every hour or so. But they did not convey an impression of cleanliness; they put into my mind an idea that he had just scoured and pared them after burying something in the cellar.

And it was: Oh, was it a cake of soap I wanted, then? No, really now, only one? He could do me a golden gift-wrapped box of six. No? One only? Then right I was—here was a silver-wrapped box of three . . .

"One!" I cried.

"Have two?"

"One."

"Glycerin soap, baby soap, or disinfectant?" asked Laycock.

"I'd better have one of each," I said.

"Yes, yes," he said comfortingly. "I'll do you the three for ninepence."

"And while you're about it, do me a bottle of eau de cologne."

"Genuine *7211*, full half-pint, eightpence?"

"That'll do."

"Let me do you a sponge now, sir. I've got a real honeycomb. . . . No? Well then, a lovely loofah, only tenpence; worth three-

and-six, only you don't have much call for them round here. In fact, the last one I sold, a boy ate it. You're a stranger here, I see. The standards aren't high, sir. Oh, let me do you a loofah for tenpence. Ninepence?"

"Oh, all right, a loofah. Also a comb—"

"A Wave-Comb?" he asked, producing a coarse comb with bent teeth. "Guaranteed to give a lovely wave? Sixpence?"

At this I revolted, and shouted, "And how the bloody hell do you work that one out?"

He said, "Thou shalt not take the name of the Lord thy God in vain. A fine comb, perhaps? Could do you one for sevenpence."

"All right. Do me, at the same time, a sixpenny nail file."

"Oh, I couldn't do that, sir—they run threepence, fivepence, sevenpence—"

"Fivepence. And a bottle of aspirin tablets—"

"Ten, twenty-five, fifty, one hundred—"

"Ten."

"Will that be all, sir? I thank you, sir. . . . Stranger here, sir? Delightful place, sir, but overcrowded, overpopulated. A nice douche can, sir? For purely hygienic purposes—or something in the rubber-goods line? We all have our own faith, and personally I am very strict. The climate hereabout is inclement. I can do you a line of rubber goods in the finest latex at three for six-pence in a tin box, on the understanding that you undertake to use them only to keep your money in, the way sailors do. . . . No? Well, they *do* say in Fowlers End that it *is* like shaking hands with gloves on. . . ."

I paid him, picked up my parcels, and ran across the street. Sam Yudenow was still communing with his soul, I suppose, and brooding in his eyrie over the concept of the Greenburger. Down in the orchestra poor Miss Noel had the shakes. She had been drinking methylated spirits. Knowing it to be a fact that if you give a methylated-spirits drinker a glass of water the morning after, he will get mad drunk again, I got her some milk and made her drink it, while Copper Baldwin stood by and watched with wonderment thinly disguised as scorn. I said, "Now, there —there, now then, drink it all up. I want you to play for me when you feel better. Don't we, Copper? . . . Copper, for Christ's sake, did you put that hot water in the basin, in the ladies' toilet? Then lend a hand while we get her there. You swabbed up, I see. Come on then—lend a hand with Miss Noel."

"What to do?"

"Get her washed and changed," I said. "She's offensive. She's offensive to you, and me, and herself." I added, "And who will be the sufferer? Everybody will say I did it. I don't mind telling you, I'll see myself damned before I let this sort of thing go on every night. Into the ladies' toilet with her, before Sam Yudenow comes down!"

So we got her there. She did not take much undressing, since she was wearing only a vile old slip and what they used to call a "jumper suit" of knitted wool.

"They'll do for Godbolt's doorstep," said Copper Baldwin, pushing them aside with a squeegee. "Come on now, pull yourself together like the gentleman says, Miss Noel. Mr. Laverock wants you to play for him, Miss Noel, and 'e's a gentleman in a very important position. Come on now, Miss Noel. The gentleman's accustomed to better be'avior than this, you know. . . ." Meanwhile I washed her with a loofah.

At a certain point she said, "I'll do the rest. Please go outside for a moment."

And so we did, but not before Copper Baldwin had picked up the bottle of eau de cologne and put it in his pocket.

"You mug, she'd drink it," he told me, with his eye to a crack in the door. ". . . It's all right, chum. I'm looking for a purpose. Yes, she's washing all right. We'll sprinkle 'er with this stuff afterwards. . . . Gawd stone me blind if she ain't washing 'er 'air! Now this is something I 'ave not seen. . . ." He imparted to this commentary a quality of breathless excitement, like one of the better sports commentators. "Now she's drying it—now she's combing it—now the comb's bust! . . . No, it ain't—yes, it 'as—no, it ain't; it got through! . . . Wait a minute, the insides of 'er arms are wet. She's groggy, but she's dryin' 'em—and oh, my, does she look bruised! Yes, sir, she must 'ave 'it 'erself in the shoulder with the piano. . . . Now, what's the first thing she goes for? 'Er combinations! She never 'ad none before. . . . Drawers coming up! Oh, nicely, nicely! A bit low in the knees but lovely, tell your mum! Stockings now. . . . Oh, pity, pity—no garters? Ah, good gel, very good gel—rolled 'er tops—that's right, twist 'em. Good, good. Now it's the lipstick—steady now, stea-dy—that's right! Jumper, skirt—it nearly fits. Comb again. Pat, pat, pat with the old towel, and it's the old sweet song: 'Johnny, I 'Ardly Knew You!' . . . And now she's picking 'er nails with that little file. . . ." There were tears in his eyes now as he said to me, " 'Ow did you do that, Dan?"

"Not I," I said.

Then Miss Noel came out of the lavatory, looking drunker than ever, but in a different way. Copper Baldwin sprinkled her with the stuff Laylock called eau de cologne and said to me, "You ought to got 'er a toothbrush, some face powder, and a bit o' glycerin-and-rosewater for 'er 'ands—"

I was going to explain that I had intended to buy a mouthwash but had felt certain qualms about getting close enough to her to observe whether she had any teeth, when Sam Yudenow came down humming a tune. "Look at Rockfellow, look at Armour, look at Corned Beef! Out of oil alone, you'd be surprised—" he began. Then he saw Miss Noel, and said, "The lady's face is familiar, pardon the familiarity. Could the name be Noel?"

Miss Noel said, "That is my name."

Ebullient and confidential, but at the same time abstracted, Yudenow said, "My pianist's sister? No doubt. Pleased to meet you. Believe me, Miss What's-a-name, blood will tell. Vice versa, murder will out, and love will have its way. Blood will tell. It told. That your sister had unfluential relatives, I knew. So I took her into my bosom. Good enough? Good enough. Out of the hands of the police I have kept her—didn't we, Copper? Nourishment I gave her—didn't we, Lavendrop? Right. Especially in good families is always a black. Sheep, I mean. There is a science about it, miv which there is, if you will uxcuse me, bed-wetting, et cetera, et cetera. . . . So, you come to get your sister. And quite right too. A man's got a heart, so I took her out of the gutter. And believe me, Miss, rahnd 'ere you know why they got reinforced tires on the busses? The gutters. Acid. It'll eat you away to the bone. . . . She had some terrible misfortune maybe? A disappointment? Don't worry, she'll be in, in a little while. Whereas, in the meantime, I ought to tell you, there's a little bill owing. I'm sorry to say your sister lost control. There's a cleaning bill. All in all, it amounts to—look, I'll leave it to you. I'm like a father rahnd 'ere, Miss Noodle; ask anybody, miv the soluntary exception of Godbolt. Ah, many is the time your poor old sister has helped me out miv Godbolt, specially on the Saturday morning after payday. Believe me, she was worth her weight in dead cats. Once I paid her fine, five shillings, 'drunk and incapable,' and for the stumminck pump half a guinea. But I'm like that, I'm a funny feller. Be done by as you do, Miss. Sam Yudenow asks no reward —he leaves it up to you—" He stopped abruptly, looked at her with more attention, and said, "Now you're crying I recognize you. You are Miss Noel. But all dolled up?"

I think that out of one of the blind alleys in his labyrinthine mind emerged some ghostly idea that Miss Noel had come into money. It is a fact that, newly washed and dressed, even in Godbolt's slops, she had the air of a lady. In what this air consists, nobody knows. To describe it would be to describe recognition, which involves something to which our vocabularies are not fitted. If you could describe, in so many words, what you recognize in an expression or a manner, you could write a definitive work on diagnostics—which hasn't been done yet, and never will be done. Because language is allusive, in its highest forms. You can no more describe a human condition than you can define, say, the contradistinction between the odors of roses and onions.

One can only make images and trust to one's neighbors' senses. For example: in Soho there used to be a most degraded drunkard of a girl. She was only twenty-three, but it was impossible to think of her as anything but forty-odd. Her manners and her uncleanliness revolted the lowest whores in Old Compton Street. There was nothing she would not do for a drink. And yet she was accorded a certain respect because she was a "lady." By the same token I know a filthy little criminal who once beat up his father and robbed him of his monthly pension money to buy dope; who lived on the immoral earnings of a factory girl; but, although he was the merest apology for a man, not much over five feet tall, hollow-chested and racked by a bad cough, commanded a certain respect even in places as tough as the Dive because he was a "gentleman."

Yet again, I know a rough-and-tumble, foul-mouthed woman from Cumberland who can outdrink the fish she sells and fight all comers. Provided she kept her voice down, I would take her anywhere: there is something about her that causes people in general to defer to her as a "lady." It must be something in the blood, something in the spirit.

So it was now, with Miss Noel. She had regained a certain fortitude of the ego, an attitude which Copper Baldwin had sensed all along, but which Sam Yudenow—with a shock of surprise—had only just got the hang of. Yes, snuffling where he belonged, he had picked up the trail of human dignity.

If I had had the sense I might have known what that meant: that whenever animal smells man, comes fear.

Now it must be remembered that poor Sam Yudenow, our boss, was not cruel any more than a pig is cruel. Cruelty involves at least a little forethought; and Yudenow could not think, except as a pig thinks, in terms of appetite. He could not scheme:

he could only sniff with his brain along a track to the trough. Poor wretch! He lacked a certain sense of value that is necessary to pure pity.

Yudenow was incapable of love or hate. He was blind appetite. He was mindless—which passes as single-mindedness and makes executives—and whatever he may ever have had in the way of morality must have been something thin and flimsy like one of those joss papers our mothers used to let smolder to smother sickroom odors. It was a smoke screen between himself and his shame.

Yudenow was a controlled panic of self-preservation on two uncertain legs; abject slave to a mad desire for what beasts know as blind survival.

A comical beast, I thought, but asked myself, "Why prolong mere living for its own sake?" The question answered itself: "Because a beast is blind." In Yudenow's case, he was animated by nothing but a terror of Nothing, a horror of ceasing to be; by a hopeless desire to evade consequence and issue, parry cause and duck effect. But he had—and you can read it in the faces of defeated fighters, doglike to the verge of tears in the outer offices—the hope-against-hope that, by fiddling and scraping against all the odds in the world, his ringcraft might outmaneuver the inevitable.

And do you know what? There is the Spirit of Man in this—good, bad, or indifferent, a certain heroism.

So, while I soon learned to hate Sam Yudenow, I couldn't find it in my heart to betray him—though it did not take me long to decide that, if he ever said one offensive word to me I would knock his head off.

Only he never said that word in time for me to act on my decision.

9

IT MUST HAVE BEEN about then that the sharp points of experience began to puncture the overblown inner tube of youthful enthusiasm. There is life for you: you go to sleep a child and wake up an apology for a man or a woman.

It was then, I am sure—pitying myself in retrospect—that I really started to know my place in the world, and who was who—to realize that what I had hitherto seen in a mirror was not myself, nor even anyone I had ever seen, but only the projection of a shadow.

I don't believe them when they say that wisdom is something gently acquired. It may come gradually over your head, but it hits in a flash and with a shock. Such wisdom as you have strikes like lightning, and you are none the happier for it—if you are wise. I can liken it only to a sudden and agonizing eructation of perceptiveness, upon whose sad wind your years of innocence are belched away, leaving a bitterness which it takes all the years of your maturity to purge you of—if you are lucky.

Do not ask of me a definition or an explanation of how it came to pass; but I got wise, in this moment, when Sam Yudenow caressed Miss Noel's newly washed hand. It was a curious gesture. There was nothing sexual in it: you have seen the last couple of strokes of a barber stropping a hollow-ground razor? Imagine that. He was taking a little more sharpness out of her hide. But although I somehow sensed that there was nothing but bad luck for Miss Noel in this gesture, there was nothing I could say. It takes a less introspective fool than I to find a cause for direct action in the smile on the face of the tiger. Besides, it seemed to gratify her, so that she appeared to gain at least an inch in height; and when Sam Yudenow said, "Mmm! Such nice perfume!" ten years fell off her.

God knows how obtuse a man can become. Perhaps Sam Yudenow was still delirious with his Greenburger, or something. He seemed in an instant to forget what he had just said, and went on: "Believe me, Miss, I've done what I could for your sister. Didn't I, Copper? Whereas, however, she's incorruptible—she won't even help herself. A pail I put down for her; out of the gutter I've picked her. But what's the use, Miss? It's a . . . a—" he made a twisting movement with his hands as one who works a lever "—a vice. I deliberately paid her less, for her own sake, and then she drank up a pint shellac the minute my back was turned, so Copper Baldwin had to make a stomach pump from a carbolic spray in reverse. Could a father do more? Miss, more a father couldn't do. Believe me, for scented disinfectant alone she cost me a pretty penny, miv her wind in the bells! . . . So if, perhaps, there might be a small bill . . ." He started like a man who has been dreaming of falling from a great height and sighed with pleasure at finding himself safe and sound on the pillows of his adjustable consciousness. "Uxcuse me, I was thinking of Booligan," he said. "Miss Noel, you may confidently expect a rise in salary as soon as talkies go out. Meanwhile, keep on the job meanwhile. Believe me, it does me good to recognize you only by the tears in your eyes!"

I saw Copper Baldwin calculating the distance between his left hand and Sam Yudenow's chin. Indeed, I believe that if he had struck and missed I would have gone for Yudenow myself in my close, shortsighted way; only Miss Noel said, "The piano is somewhat out of tune, Mr. Yudenow."

He said, "Copper, take a scvewdriver and tune it. Nothing but the best is good enough for the Pantheon—eh, Daniels?"

It was impossible not to laugh. I said, "You mean a corkscrew."

"A thing miv a handle," said Yudenow impatiently. "Borrow it from the pub. . . . And while you're about it, in the genevator room you'll find a pair of bellows. Give those piano wires a good dusting. For Sam Yudenow's musicians, Miss Noel, nothing is too good. Remember that, Laveridge, and Sam Yudenow will remember you miv love and gratitude. Only no false pride, please! You take the bellows to the piano; you see here and there missing a few wires—take off your jacket, roll up your sleeves, and put 'em back. There's a roll wire in the genevator room. The tone depends on the way it's stretched. Here a wire, there a wire; it's a question of tension. Okay? Okay. I thank you one and all. Uxcuse me, please, I got to take my drops. Let the show go on, which is the Ten Commandments of the biz. The Eleventh, I already told you: a capacity house, or there'll be a wave of unemployment rahnd 'ere. Enough chatting—you think I got nothing bigger on my mind? Get on the job!"

"I've got to go to town to get my things, you know," I said.

"What do you mean, 'town'? What town? Things? What sort of things? . . . Oh, yes, I remember, Laventry—go right ahead, don't hesitate for one moment to dock yourself up to four hours, and to hell miv the expense. I'll gladly give you a lift. Which way are you going?"

"Toward Regents Park," I said.

"I like your conversation—there's never a dull moment—and I'll gladly give you a lift in the opposite direction. . . . What, you don't want to go in the opposite direction? Why not? . . . Oh, your things. What a pity. Good-by now."

When he was gone, Copper Baldwin said, with something curiously resembling pride, "And *now* do you begin to see what I mean? I tell you, Danny-boy, that one's a sort of a genius. . . . By the way, what's your definition of a man o' genius?" When I said that I didn't have one, he said, "Nor me, neither. But as I see it, a genius is a 'uman being evolved from Sam Yudenow. Ain't 'e a bastard? An' does 'e still make you laugh? You wasn't laughing much a couple o' minutes ago, unless my eyes deceived me."

"Not until he talked about tuning a piano with a screwdriver," I said.

"Then you said, 'You mean corkscrew,' " said Copper Baldwin, with a sour smile.

" 'A thing miv a handle, borrow it from the pub,' " I said. Then my sense of the ridiculous got the better of me and I burst out laughing.

Copper Baldwin laughed too, and then said, "Can't 'elp loving that man, can you? Grows on you, don't 'e? 'Abit-forming, ain't 'e? But lousy to the backbone, wouldn't you say? Evil! 'Owever, so long as 'e makes you laugh, 'e's got you by the balls, ain't 'e? Well, so long as you begin to get what I mean when I call 'im dangerous. But you mark my words—"

He was interrupted by a burst of music from the orchestra pit. Miss Noel was down there playing her poor scrambled heart out —playing the most extraordinary music I ever heard. I have since heard the wild, picturesque, and sometimes terrifying ravings of a literate drunkard in delirium. They consist, generally, in a kaleidoscopic review of broken memories. Such was Miss Noel's playing now. Those medleys, which are always so popular with that rabble of half-listeners and stuffs the ears of the spirit with pure noise, are edited jumbles of whole tunes. She was not making a medley but a most fantastic delirious mishmash of half-remembered and partially distorted bars and phrases from all the classical compositions in the world—everything she had ever heard seemed to be passing through some mixing machine in her head and coming out in foam at her fingertips. It is indescribable. She remembered, for example, that Handel wrote the tune later known as "Yes, We Have No Bananas," played a recognizable fragment of it, staggered back, somehow, to Scarlatti, tripped over him, picked herself up out of a kennel in which trickled some dregs of Mozart—only to lurch, wildly groping, into the arms of the surly Brahms, who shoved her back into the hairy hands of the impatient Beethoven, through which her bruised soul slipped, after a brief contact, onto the nervous knees of Berlioz, who kicked her over to Liszt. Imagine all this played in an empty hall on a piano with a wooden frame, so long untuned that every note sounded like some other note—some hiccuping, husky, whisky-voiced note, still beloved but rendered only half recognizable by dissipation and neglect.

"I played that for you," she said to me when she had finished. "It was one of my little compositions, or improvisations."

"Thank you, Miss Noel. And could you play it again for me, do you think?"

"Oh, yes, Mr. Laverock. For you. Only will you talk to me a little bit every day? It isn't that you have anything to say to me, only could I just hear the sound of your voice?"

"Of course I will, Miss Noel, but I must go now."

"But you'll come back?"

"Only if you promise not to have anything to drink, and to eat the poached eggs Copper Baldwin is going to get you."

"I do promise."

So, at last, I got away and, having caught a variety of trams and busses, arrived at three o'clock in the afternoon at June Whistler's flat near the zoo.

It is odd, wherever you live or have known ever so little relief, you leave a little bit of yourself, and, returning, try to take it back to yourself. But having grown into an entity of its own, it repels you. June Whistler's flat, which, a few days before, had opened its arms to me, didn't seem to want me. Yet some little living piece of the grateful, well-meaning fellow named Daniel Laverock was lost there, running around the walls. I do believe in haunted houses. Whoever lives in June Whistler's flat now, some portion of my ghost will continue to haunt those rooms; and if there are "thought forms," I see one materializing in the shape of a spaniel made of mist with an uplifted paw, begging pardon. . . .

June Whistler was there in a flowered apron of outlandish design. It had a bib such as no one had ever thought of before, and a flounce, and it was sewn out of linen patterned with blue tulips and trimmed with mauve upholstery braid. She had put on a pair of orange slippers with yellow pompons, and it was evident that she had been crying.

Now, although my heart went out to her, I felt the constraint of a stranger; and, I believe, she felt the same about me, because of the way she said, "Oh, hello."

I did not know, then, as I know now that people, like houses, may be taken over by spirits and inhabited by ghosts when they feel they are deserted and empty. You may be possessed, in spite of yourself, by the shadow of a dream. June Whistler was silently weeping in the grip of Elinor Glyn and bleeding internally in the talons of Theda Bara. Romance had got inside her—that secret poisoner.

Being young and very foolish, I did not stop to reason that the nature of a person should not be judged by the outward and visible signs but by the inward and spiritual trends of romanticism. I did not pause to consider the difference between the romantic whose fantasy is of biting the full-blooded and the romantic whose dream is of giving blood to the empty. Perhaps I was overtired, perhaps Fowlers End had already got caught in the jaw by some hook dragging in the muddier part of my perception—I only know that I observed, with painful clarity and ill-concealed distaste, a red-eyed girl preposterously dressed, from whose presence I wanted to escape as soon as possible.

"Hello," I said. "What's the idea of the fancy dress?"

"Oh, it's just an old apron."

"Sorry, June, I never noticed it before. Mind you don't hurt yourself with it, because I seem to see a needle hanging out of the hem."

"You have such wonderful eyes; is that all you see?"

"Why, what's the matter?" I asked, alarmed by her tone.

"Nothing," she said; and her eyes filled with tears.

Now this "nothing," said with that deliberate nonchalance, irritated me. I said, "What do you mean, nothing? There must be something."

"Very well, darling," said she, with appalling calm, "if you say there must be something, there's something. Although I must say, really, that to stay away days and nights and then come back in a stinking temper, criticizing, is really rather much!"

" 'Rather much,' " I said, imitating her intonation. "That's a new one. Did you pick that one up from some girl, all sophisticated in beads, at the Ministry? Or did you read it in *Peg's Paper*?" I was getting worked up now into a fine irony. "You know, darling, the owner of the cotton mill makes the heroine drunk on brandy; she resists his advances, so he drugs her with morphine, chloroforms her, hits her with a lead pipe, binds her hand and foot, and has her carried in a curtained limousine to a perfumed bedroom. Do you follow me? Then he produces a large glass syringe full of an oily liquid—sulphuric acid, of course—and an Australian stock whip, and a charcoal brazier in which branding irons are glowing. He will give her the whole works—unless. The heroine says, 'No, really, this is rather much!' "

June Whistler said, "I can get along very well, darling, without any of your bloody sarcasm. Where have you been?"

"Oh, getting a job. And what have you been doing, darling?"

Her blood was up now; and while, in affectation, she might use strong language as she might cock her little finger lifting a tea-cup, her real self did not take kindly to it. She was going to call me a bastard, but there was a hair-trigger reaction between the beginning and the middle of the epithet, so that she said, "Oh, you barling! If you must know, it being a half day off, I have been making meringues. Not that you care, but I burned my finger. No, really, one of these days I'll end it all—" and thereupon she burst into a terrible passion of weeping. "I wanted to make meringues for *you*!" she cried, between sobs. "I followed the book. There must have been something wrong with the eggs. The meringues turned out liquid. Lemon meringues!"

Now my heart was touched, and I felt that nothing I might ever do could make up for my brutality. Kissing her burned finger, I said, hastily improvising, "Why, darling, you probably got the wrong recipe and made soup. A gourmet's soup, what they call '*Soupe à la meringue.*' "

"You're only trying to comfort me . . . but I'd like to see you beating up the whites with a fork!"

"Wait a minute," I said, and ran to the nearest baker's shop, where I bought a shilling's worth of lemon meringues, which I cunningly concealed under my coat.

"Forgot to send a telegram," I told June Whistler when I returned. "Now you sit down, sweetheart, and let me look at this '*Soupe à la meringue.*' "

I went into the kitchen. God knows the girl had tried, because the oven was almost red-hot still. The baking dish was full of a kind of frothy, lumpy glue, which I poured into the sink. Then I wiped the dish, put in the meringues which I had bought, slid it back into the oven and shouted, "I see nothing to cry about here!"

She came running to look. "Well," said she, with shining eyes, running a hand through that manzanita-wood hair, "I really *must* be neurotic. Forgive me if I was impatient. Really, you must give meringues time to come up. And there must be absorption, because I made four and now there's six. Really, darling, you'll never know what a relief this is. Now we can have tea."

We did, and I was compelled to eat four of those baker's meringues. Of what they were made I do not know, but I am sure they did me no good. In the course of tea June Whistler questioned me about my new job.

"I am about to become an executive in show biz," I told her.

She said, "Oh, Dan darling, I'm so happy I could cry. Dan, you really do love me, don't you?"

"Why do you ask?" I said evasively.

"Then we could get married, couldn't we?"

"Why," I said, "we've had hundreds of conversations about it in a general way, and you've always led me to suppose that you disapproved of that sordid convention."

"I used to think so, but really, darling, the bedrock of society is the happy home. No, really, theoretically I used to be all in favor of state support for children. But when you come to think of it, isn't that like putting childhood into a great big orphanage? And when you come to think of it, what *for*? Don't you honestly think that a loving family unit makes for a pronounced individual?"

I said, "Well, yes, but as for my marrying you, that would have to be much later."

"Very much later?"

"Not for years, perhaps."

"Oh," she said, and her eyes grew wet. "Do you really like my apron?"

Glad to change the subject, I said, "I think it's charming, only you ought to take it in. You don't mind my saying so, but it looks like one of those maternity robes. You know what I mean—those shepherd's smock arrangements they sell to women eight months gone. I'm not criticizing, only that's my opinion."

She said, "Yes, I know. I made it like that on purpose. Really, you know, I'm awfully frugal. I hate waste. I can put a couple of tucks in it now and simply let them out again later on. As a matter of fact, there's a lot of tucks in it already. At a moment's notice, with a penknife I can let this out to forty inches bust and forty-eight inches waist."

"It's a good idea," I said, anxious to please her, "but what's it for?"

"It's awfully unhygienic to constrict a foetus," she said. "I'm going to give up girdles, too. As a matter of fact, darling, I'm going to have a baby—a little baby."

Literature is full of descriptions of shock and dismay: read them, make a composite of them, and you will arrive at some idea of how I felt when she said this. I have no words to describe my sensation: I can only tell you that I upset a cup of hot tea over my chest, bit my tongue, trod on my own foot, and inhaled a morsel of meringue which sent me into an ecstasy of coughing, recovering from which I put a lighted cigarette into my mouth the wrong way round. "You're going to have a baby?" I asked at last.

"A *little* baby, just for you and me. If it's a boy, I'm going to call him Eric. But if it's a girl, I shall call her Greta. Don't worry too much, darling. I'll have to give up my job, of course, but I've got two pounds ten a week of my own, and seven hundred pounds saved up for a rainy day. What was the name of that school you went to? Snellgrove-in-the-Vale? We'll send him there. But if it's a girl, I want her to have a degree in economics. Don't you think Eric Laverock is a fine name for a boy? Doesn't it sound like the sort of man that climbs Mount Everest and gets knighted—Sir Eric Laverock? And if you're going to be in the cinema business, you could go with him with a camera. And really—I was talking to somebody in the office—these travel pictures make millions. . . . But if it's a girl—don't you think Greta Laverock is a good name?—first she must win scholarships, don't you think? Then she must go to the London School of Economics. I will teach her etiquette, and how to dress. You see, I want her to be a power behind the throne. You know, it isn't prime ministers that run this country but their wives?"

"I wasn't prepared to look so far ahead," I said, with a heavy heart. "And when do you expect to have this child?"

"Our little baby? Well, really, you know you can't say to within a day. Do you know the signs of the zodiac?"

"No, I'm sorry to say I don't—except one or two," I said.

"Well," she said triumphantly, "as I've worked it out on my little calendar, Eric should be born under the sign of Sagittarius, the Archer." A new thought struck her: "We could call him Sagittarius—or what do you think? Too much of a mouthful? I know! Archer Laverock!"

"They would simply call him Archie in the end," I said gloomily.

Meanwhile the beasts of the zodiac were roaring and whinnying and bleating in my ears, like the zoo on that ill-omened dawn when they butchered the horse. This accursed zodiac spun in my mind as a roulette wheel spins when your last chip is on the table: lions, goats, fishes, twins, bulls, rams, all ran into a sickening blur. Then a number came up, so to speak: the sign of Sagittarius. I shouted, "Wait a minute! Did you say Sagittarius?"

"The Archer," said June Whistler. "I looked it up in the office. It means that Eric will be a leader of men. Headstrong, perhaps, but better than a Pisces."

"But my dear," I said, "I've just remembered—the sign of Sagittarius covers the month of November."

"Yes, I know."

"This is only March," I said.

"I know, darling. I'm at least five days gone. Isn't it wonderful?"

A well-known hangman once told me that men reprieved at the foot of the gallows have a tendency to fall into a deep sleep.

This is exactly what I did; and when I awoke about half an hour later, there was June Whistler looking gravid, with her feet up, baby wool and crochet hook in hand, murmuring to herself, "Knit one, slip one, knit two together," and consulting the Directions Supplement in a magazine called *Little Mother*.

"I think pink is a sissy color," she said, "so I'm using white wool. I think it's a good omen. I read it up. Belisarius was the greatest general that ever lived, darling, and the greatest archer of his time; and his name means 'White Prince.' . . . Oh, I used to think that it would be nice to be a man, but one thing you will never know—the feel of a little baby beating under your heart."

"You've got something there," I said, picking up my suitcase. "And now I must be on the job. I'll see you Sunday."

"Do you see any big blue veins in my breast?"

"I can't say that I do."

"It says in the book that the labia turn mauve and get tumid. Am I mauve?"

"Normal," I said.

"Tumid?"

"Not particularly."

"What *is* tumid? Because if it means frightened, I'm not, you know."

Before I left to visit my mother, who lived at Turners Green, June Whistler said, "If it's a girl I'll call her Labia."

What was the use of arguing?

Turners Green is a middle-class, respectably established kind of Fowlers End; only it is situated in a westerly direction near a creek by the River Brent, the official name of which is Nobbut Creek but which the local youth calls "F.L." Junction, because of what gets washed up there. Goodness knows from where these flaccid tubes of latex drift, or what wicked current carries them; but the fact remains. When young, I believed that they had something to do with aqueous animals—like, say, cuttlefish bones—and started to collect them. It was a terrible moment when, in my innocence, I brought the whole three hundred into the sitting room in a boot box when my mother had visitors for tea. She put them in the dustbin with the fire tongs, and when I reported to her that the dustman had said, "These quiet ones are always the worst" and asked her what he meant, she boxed my ears.

"If only your father were alive!" she cried. I knew that if that kindly, ineffectual man had been around he would have gone into his study to stifle his laughter under a green cushion, and then, having had his laugh out, said something like this: "Dan, my boy, never touch one of those things again. Otherwise you will come out in blotches and your head will fall off."

There was a time, though, when Turners Green was very genteel—that is to say, inaccessible to the common herd—one of those outlying suburbs where people like ourselves made cliques and wouldn't talk to anyone but ourselves. We used to have a variety of nods and smiles—big ones for the vicar and his wife, medium-sized ones for the tradesmen, and the merest smidgeons of smiles cut off in that central cleft of the upper lip (by means of which zoologists associate men with fishes) for the working classes. There really was a Green there, too; and it was quite a Green when I was about three feet high—full of shrubberies and fraught with mystery. I never quite got over my astonishment at the fact that, when I was eighteen, I measured its periphery in one hundred and three strides, and the trees were dwarfed. It is bordered by a graveled path and used to be presided over by an old man with a badge and a drooping mustache who was notable for his hatred of children. His name was Marsh. Marsh by name, Marsh by nature. Whenever he saw one of us he would double misshapen, earthy fists like prize Idaho potatoes and shout in the most debased kind of Hampshire accent, "Git orf my grass, or I'll tan that arse orf that!" There is a gasworks in the vicinity (I wonder how I failed, accidentally, to set light to it) and, over all, the gentle thunder of the railway, to which I used to listen before I fell asleep. I still love that exciting clash of shunting and the desolate wail of whistles in the night.

We lived on what they called the Bridge, close to All Souls Church. The psychiatrists will say that there must be something wrong with me but, although my life there in my infancy was a chapter of accidents, I cannot think of the place without affection. There comes back into memory that smell of peace and quiet that seemed to come over the world between the wars, when we were too young to prophesy. . . . At the foot of the street was the Broadway, in which there was a cinema where Tarzan of the Apes was to be seen; and a progressive furniture shop that went in for hire-purchase. God knows how, but an American had found his way there and opened a dry-cleaning shop with a steam pressing machine—made by Braithwaite, he told me, and weighing nearly a ton. Every evening at sunset he would walk into the middle of the street, take a little Union Jack out of his pocket, blow his nose into it, and return. Nobody paid the slightest attention to him. We all thought that it must be, quite simply, a patterned handkerchief.

I always had a catching at the throat when I went home. True, everything and everybody were smaller and shabbier; but I could not forget my delight in the places where I used to spend my pocket money, fourpence, on a copy of the *Magnet Library* and a chocolate-coated marshmallow bar. Let it be said to my credit on the Everlasting Plane that I always saved a penny to give away. Then I would go and lie on my stomach on the Green, reading the misadventures of Billy Bunter and voluptuously eating the marshmallow bar. Then I would go home, pilfer whatever I could find in the larder—half a dozen apples, bread and butter, pie, cake, cold potatoes, or anything like that—and go away to work up an appetite for tea, still reading Billy Bunter.

And there was a meal I always loved: my father kindly and dignified, my mother busy and solicitous, and Raymond the servant proud of me because of my appetite, which was voracious. . . .

After tea, plethoric with all that I could consume, I sometimes walked to the public library, which was situated on the other side of the Green until the Germans bombed it under the false impression that it was Whitehall, and get myself, if I were lucky, a bound volume of *Chums* or *The Boys' Own Paper.*

After Snellgrove-in-the-Vale, this was bliss. Indeed, I was happy there—everybody loved me, I loved everybody; nobody pestered me, I troubled nobody. Why, sometimes I was so delighted at the realization of my happiness that my eyes filled with tears and I gave my marshmallow money—twopence—to a beggar in the street. For we had a beggar; he pretended to sell bootlaces, and said he had lost his legs in the Boer War. Apart from having my hair cut, they were good times.

I remembered, as I made my way there, with what ineffable glee I used to greet my father when he came up to me with his hands behind his back, looking severely juridical. I knew what was coming. Up would come one of his fists, clenched in a threatening gesture. Then it would open and I would see on his palm a shilling. He was treating me to the cinema. . . .

Such recollections as these bring into my mind an image. It is of a shabby-genteel man in a pub, who has a red nose; starting off with observations on the state of the weather, the government, and the world at large, he works his way to the present state of his finances, and the better days he has seen. In the end you buy him a pint of beer. Your memory, when it gets around to the child that was father of the boy, is just such a maudlin liar, on the bum for buckshee tears—for which, from time to time, you have a craving when the ducts are dry and there is nothing to cry about. As for my youth, considering it carefully, I wouldn't have it over again for any consideration. Dr. Faustus was all wet; neither by divine nor diabolical agency can you have your cake and eat it. Youth is a dream, middle age a forlorn hope, and old age a nostalgia with a pervasive flavor of newly turned earth. Turn your back for five minutes and nothing can ever be the same again.

My mother was psychic—that is to say, she lived in a state of permanent premonition, so she was right at least half the time. If the sky became black and raindrops as big as shillings started to come down and there was a rumbling overhead, she had a premonition of a thunderstorm. If, at bedtime, my father's thermometer said zero, she would say, "I don't know what it is, but something seems to tell me there will be a frost tonight." No disrespect to her memory—she had a good heart—only I state the innocent fact. She had taken to telling her own fortune with the cards and was always forewarned of coming events. Today, as it happened, there were crumpets for tea, and she said, with delight, "Oh, Daniel, I dreamt of you last night, so I told Simmons to deliver half a dozen extra. Something seemed to tell me you were coming, and I know what a sweet tooth you have, so I made some meringues. . . . Your Uncle Hugh will be here at any moment. He said he'd drop in."

Here a rationalist might have broken down the dreams, omens, et cetera, by reminding her that if there was one dish Uncle Hugh liked better than crumpets it was meringues. But I could not hurt her feelings. I stroked the cat. My mother said, "Be careful, son—something seems to tell me she's going to have kittens." Since the cat's belly was almost touching the floor I said that I shouldn't be surprised. But the subject of pregnancy had become distasteful to me, and the appalling thought came into my mind: *And what if the Costas girl should prove to be pregnant, with the other one five days gone?* But I said, "I came to tell you, Mother, that I've gone into show biz."

"I thought you looked tired, poor dear. Shall I give you a little brandy?"

"No, really, thanks. I'm all right."

"It's so long since I've seen you. A thimbleful won't hurt you with your tea," she said, and filled a liqueur glass. "I keep it in case of illness."

"Right you are," I said, and took a sip.

"Oh, dear, you're not going to turn into a drunkard, are you? I had such a terrible dream . . ."

But then Uncle Hugh was driven up in his great Lanchester limousine. She loved that, the dear old lady—she could see in her mind's eye a cautious movement of lace curtains up and down the street and a glitter of envious neighborly eyes. But before he came in she whispered to me, "I've had such dreams about you, dear. I've been so worried. I've put aside a little money for you. Three hundred pounds—out of my dividends. I don't need it. It's for you, my boy—*only you mustn't tell your Uncle Hugh!*"

"Thank you," I said, pressing her hand. "You save it. I don't want it. But thank you very much." I had to blow my nose to get the tears of gratitude out of my eyes before I could put on an air of dignity for Uncle Hugh's sake.

In those days, which were still the days of Barron, I regarded Uncle Hugh as the prototype of the bourgeois; only his stomach was not protuberant, and he did not wear a white waistcoat and a silk hat. True, he smoked cigars, but not very big cigars; and I can put my hand in the fire and swear that he pinned to himself or ringed himself with no diamonds. About this kind of thing, so long ago, one's attitude was: *Aha, a capitalist who wears no white waistcoats and no diamonds! O-ho! A bourgeois who keeps no mistresses and smokes no cigars with the bands on! Double-beware!* But now I see Uncle Hugh as a good, earnest kind of fellow. A bourgeois, yes, but none the worse for it. I have known—God forgive me!—an earl's son who went about in navvy's moleskins strapped under the knee and hobnailed boots in order to hammer home the fact that he was associated with the working class. While I admired him no end, I felt that somewhere, somehow, something was lacking in those moleskin trousers. Give him a road to lay, give him a ditch to dig—and look for him in the public library.

Now I know that there was, about Uncle Hugh, a permanence and an intransigence. But I did not know it then. I hated every word he said but would defend to the death his right to say it—two minutes after my speech for the defense. Uncle Hugh was necessary—necessary to be held up and forgotten, written off. Such are the joys of youth.

He was a pouter pigeon of a man dressed in gray, with an iridescent tie and a didactic air that set my nerves on end. My mother assured me that Uncle Hugh knew everything: therefore, I hated him. Uncle Hugh was always right: therefore, it was incumbent on me to be in the opposition. He did me no harm; only I had to hate him. Now that I know him for what he was, I am overwhelmed with a great regret that we had not come together and become friends. If it gives peace to his soul, let it be said that I like him in restrospect.

I know that he liked me and would have given me the last pound out of his pocket. Only he would have wanted to know what for, and, perhaps, offered advice which I could not swallow. Even when you put on a front for Uncle Hugh, you knew—or thought you knew—that he would see through it. He had some sharp instrument up his sleeve to puncture you with, just when you were at the most comfortable stage of self-inflation.

Now he came in, abominably clean and distressingly crisp, *ha-ha*-ing in his black overcoat, and blowing. Weather was good for Uncle Hugh. He could see Charles Dickens in a fog or Charles Kingsley in a bitter northeaster. Impervious was the word for Uncle Hugh. If you punched him in the jaw his reaction would be to find a cold bandage for your hand.

He said, in a voice which in those days I likened to a foghorn, "Well, damme, if it isn't little Danny! Give me your hand, m' boy—grip it, shake it! Well now, educated the working classes yet with Circulating Libraries? Delighted to see you. Made your fortune, no doubt? Lend me three million and I'll guarantee you four and a half per cent."

"Daniel is in show business," my mother interposed, with a certain dignity.

Then Uncle Hugh became interested, dropped his badinage, got keen. "And I'm delighted to hear it," said he, "because I can tell you without reservation that the fortunes of the future will be got out of talking pictures. There, for once, my young friend, you made a wise move. We are agreed now, aren't we, that that wheeze of yours about libraries was a folly? No shame to you, no blame to you, m' boy—I've done worse myself in my time. On my word, when I didn't know better I pinned my faith, like that kids' game, blindfold, with the donkey's tail. Know better now, though. Live and learn, eh? You don't live unless you learn, and vice versa. Who's your firm?"

"I am at present," I said stiffly, "manager of the Pantheon at Fowlers End. It is a silent, but we run variety. We are a conservative house and will not wire for sound. Sound is not here to stay—I have it on the best authority."

Uncle Hugh said, "Look here, m' boy, it's all very well in times like these for a man to make an honest living the best way he can. But whichever way you take it, Dan, there is always tomorrow. You can take it from me that the only way to live (not counting the present) is in the future. Silent, did you say? Give it away. And variety, I think you said? A corpse."

"Oh, advise him, advise him!" my mother cried. "Oh, Daniel, Daniel, listen to your Uncle Hugh!"

If there is one thing I cannot take, it is good advice from those who know best: it brings out the mule in me. And of all the advisers on God's green earth the last one I might regard would be Uncle Hugh. So I set my teeth and said nothing. It was, I suppose, that I didn't like his manner. You could have lit a fire under me then, and I wouldn't have budged, just out of perverse spite, while he went on, "No, Dan, while all experience is necessary, give it up. I give silent pictures just under a year. I think I can tell you with confidence that the electricians are taking over, and the patent holders. Look, for example, at Western Electric, and the other boys with the sound systems. No, young fellow, the photoelectric cell has it because, to tell you the truth, the public wants reality. What are you showing?"

Very stiffly I told him my running-sheet. He laughed in his borborygmic City way and said, "And look—Morton Downey is pulling in the fortunes with *Home Towners.* There never has been a success on earth like Al Jolson in *The Singing Fool.* 'Climb Upon My Knee, Sonny Boy'—give you my word, Dan, it brought tears to *my* eyes. . . . No, don't interrupt—"

"Don't interrupt," said my mother.

"What you boys don't see is the future; only the present. I'm no artist, as you know, and I don't pretend to be a fortuneteller. But your silent days are over. There's a new era developing. I give your show under a year."

Inexpressibly irritated, I said, "Oh, so *you* give it such-and-such a time. You *give* it, do you? Much obliged. Now let me tell you—"

"Oh, don't, don't!" said my mother, beginning to weep.

If Uncle Hugh had, at this point, broken a plate over my head, there might have been a certain catharsis, and we might have come to terms. Only he chuckled in his good-natured way; and this I found intolerable. He said, "I have certain contacts. It's time you grew up—"

"Oh, no, Hugh, no!" my mother cried, putting the little finger of her right hand in her mouth and clutching her cheek with the other four.

Uncle Hugh was beginning, as the saying goes, to have about as much of this as he was prepared to take. He took out his big gold watch, flicked it open, closed one eye—drawing a bead on it rather than consulting it—snapped it shut, pocketed it, and said, "I will give you about six months."

I said, "I have no faith in your time machines, sir, nor in your power to give me a month here or there."

Then his good humor got the better of him and he said, "Oh, look here, Daniel. We all have our little Wars of Independence. All right, m' boy, follow your star. Only mind that it isn't a falling star. But if it is, come to me."

Without saying anything I vowed that I would see him in hell first, and doubly so because he looked so calm and affable, and said, "Sow your wild Circulating Libraries."

With this I decided to declare the vendetta against Uncle Hugh. And all of a sudden I felt a nostalgia for Yudenow and the Pantheon, and for Fowlers End, which Copper Baldwin described as "the arse hole of the universe." The mud had become my home, and I wanted to go back to it. Meanwhile, whatever anybody said, right or wrong, I would say the opposite and fight for it too.

When I got up to go, Uncle Hugh came with me, saying, "Where was it you said you were going? Fowlers End, did you say? Why then, m'lad, take the Lanchester. Don't argue now; take the limousine. I've got to talk to your mother. The chauffeur will whisk you there and get back in good time to pick me up. And look here, old boy—do believe me—silent pictures are dead. So are live variety turns. The sound systems, Dan, the sound systems have control of the future. I happen to know. Come to grief, if you must, my dear fellow, but for God's sake do it in a businesslike way, and like a gentleman. Meanwhile (between ourselves) if you need anything, bless you, come to me and I'll fix you up." Then he said to his chauffeur, "Oh, Pearce, take Mr. Laverock to Fowlers End and come right back!"

Before I could think of anything to say, Uncle Hugh, holding up a folded bit of white paper, said, "A hole in your pocket? Or are you chucking it away?"

My pockets were always full of papers, so I took it automatically, shook hands with him mechanically, and got into his car. His chauffeur, who wore bottle-green livery, covered my knees with a rug and took my suitcase in front. We were well on our way north when it occurred to me to wonder what paper I might have dropped.

It was a twenty-pound note, folded small. Emotion overcame me. I got my money's worth out of Godbolt's miserable handkerchief before I got back to the Pantheon at nightfall.

The great Lanchester pulled up close behind Sam Yudenow's Renault. Uncle Hugh's chauffeur unwrapped me and carried my suitcase into the vestibule. I knew that I was being watched and overheard, so I drew myself up and said, "Thank you. Better go home now."

Then, when the Lanchester withdrew its nose from the butt of Yudenow's car and swung away with a gentlemanly growl of disgust, Yudenow came out from behind a curtain with his hands clasped behind him and said, "All the time I knew you were a gentleman in disguise. Meanwhile this won't butter the baby's drawers. Copper's having trouble miv the genevator room and Dilly is back miv a pal. Valor is the better part of discretion, and I got trouble miv my nostrils. Behind the curtain I had to watch operations from—and oh my Christ, do they need a dusting! Come in, quick. In the case of Dilly and his pal, for God's sake, be diplomatic. Put your arms rahnd their necks like a brother—a long-lost brother—then bang their heads together with all your might. After which, a grip of the hand under the ears, run them out of the show as fast as my legs will carry you, and into the rain miv 'em. What are you waiting for?"

They came quietly enough. I had them out of the place in thirty seconds. Dilly's friend must have been respectable, for I found a ready-made tie and a celluloid collar afterward.

Having seen them off the premises, I looked at and inhaled the desolation of Fowlers End. As usual a corrosive rain was falling; but now something had gone wrong with the sulphuric-acid factory, the smoke of whose chimneys was green. "By any chance, did you bring back any more of those cigars?" Sam Yudenow asked, and when I said that I had forgotten, he said, "A fine way to get on in show biz!" Two young women had a fingernail fight over a young fellow I would not have given you twopence for, using language which I wish I might print. Copper Baldwin came from the generator room and said, "Okay, Yudenow. This is straight, and I'm telling you. You don't get a new genny, I'm warning you, there's going to be another bloody Paisley Disaster in this gaff!"

"Why should you talk like that?" asked Sam Yudenow. "I'm only human. Disasters come from God. You're only saying it to upset me. . . . Aha!"—for young Johnny Headlong was in with a tray slung round his neck, fitted with soggy oval objects, each of which seemed to emit the concentrated odor of a fifth-rate boarding house on a humid night in August. You go into the passage and it strikes you—"Aha! Greenburgers—the first batch. Have one?"

Copper Baldwin said, "For Christ's sake, talk sense. Have one! Look at young Johnny—brought up on skilly an' 'e goes black in the face at the smell."

"Believe me, Copper, there is no more filling twopenn'orth in town," said Yudenow. "If so, name it and I'll give you a fi'-pun note!"

"You mean that?"

"Are you making me out to be a twicer?"

"Well then, try 'alf a pound o' raw rice and a pint of 'ot water."

Yudenow said, "Don't be silly. Take one, Copper—to please *me!*"

Dreamily, Copper Baldwin said to the ceiling, "Ever sleep in a fivepenny kip rahnd Seven Dials, in the season when they're chucking out spoiled cabbages in the garden? The down-and-outs can cook their own grub, if they got any, on the stove. So there's bad fat—you know, stale lard what's been used twenty-five times for sausages, and bloaters, and bits o' bacon, and kippers, and warmed-up chops somebody found in a swill bin before the pigman came to collect, and kept all day in 'is trousers pocket. To stay their stomachs, this *lumpenproletariat* 'as been at the spoiled cabbage, raw, and saved the rest for frying. Arterwards, when they lean back and decide among themselves whether they should withdraw from India, or somethink, there comes what they call the wind session. They make a pool: sixpence for the one that can fart the loudest, while they all light up pipes and cigarettes made of dog ends three times rerolled and dry their wet toe rags and boots. . . . Well, that's what this Greenburger smells like. Take it away!"

"I'm saying, '*Please*, Copper!' You don't know what this means to me." Yudenow had already pressed one into my hand. "See? Mr. Laveridge has got one. Try a taster."

Copper Baldwin took one, sniffed at it, and said, "Filling is right. One niff, and I don't think I'll ever eat again as long as I live. Why don't you eat one, Yudenow?"

"Because the effect of these nourishing Greenburgers is, I wouldn't be able to eat my supper and my wife don't like me to eat out. . . . What about you, Mr. Lavendorf? Eat up!" His manner was almost obsequious, but he tried to make it offhand as he asked, "The car miv the shofar—whose is it?"

"Oh, the Lanchester, you mean?" I said. "Oh, that belongs to one of my uncles."

"What does he do?" asked Sam Yudenow. "Because, believe me, a motorcar of that description they don't give away for twenty-five coupons out of packets cigarettes."

"He is in the City," I said.

To change the subject, I put my Greenburger into his gesticulating right hand, took out the twenty-pound note, and said, "That reminds me. Got change for a twenty?"

He had the day's takings in one of those locked leather bags—such as bank messengers carry—chained to his wrist, but he said, "Tomorrow."

On a sudden impulse, I asked him, "Mr. Yudenow, what made you leave the fish business?"

He said, "Confidentially between us, believe me, there's no future in fish. But in show biz, for an ambitious man, there's a future, romance. Look at Hyman Melville. If he'd stayed in fish, he'd still be pushing a barrow and shouting his bloody guts out. Whereas, he goes into show biz and makes *Moby Dick* miv John Barrymoor; and you should be in such a nice position he's in now!"

"For Christ's sake, shut up and let me close down!" shouted Copper Baldwin.

"Did I say something?" asked Sam Yudenow. But as he hurried out, he called over his shoulder, "Get those curtains brushed, Copper—there has been malingering here. Good night all."

Then Copper Baldwin and I closed the Pantheon and put up the bars.

"Now, before we go to Uncle Ned," said Copper Baldwin, "let's 'ave something to take away the taste of them Greenburgers," and he produced half a bottle of gin and a paper bag—the latter with an apologetic air. "I got a sweet tooth. I never 'ad enough sweet stuff when I was a nipper, and sometimes I get a craving. . . ." He offered me the bottle and then, with infinite care, took out of the paper bag three large meringues. Thereupon, uncontrollably, I laughed as I had not laughed for what seemed to me a donkey's age. The reverberations of that laugh went flapping and echoing in the empty hall until the whole of that squalid interior seemed to shake with the nameless enjoyment of some dimly understood joke and to laugh with me just for the sake of laughing, like a factory girl on a bank holiday.

I have never felt more pleasantly relaxed than I did in that few moments. It is for this kind of thing that your Faustuses are prepared to sell their gray old souls; only for convenience' sake the dramatists call it youth.

10

There was no use talking: much as I hated to admit it, Uncle Hugh was right. "Live" variety and silent films were in the dumps, and the electricians and the renters, and the distributors and the bankers were taking over. The ones I pitied most were the old music-hall stars who had been idols in their day—whose names are still bywords among those who are old enough to remember them—who had rushed from music hall to theater and from theater to music hall without wiping off their make-up, putting on five or six acts a night. They earned up to a hundred pounds a week (which, at the turn of the century, was a fortune) and cast it to the hangers-on. Always, in their minds, was the memory of what they had suffered before what they called "Luck" had got them out of the gutter. In their heyday nobody had to ask them twice for a pound to tide him over. But when times changed, it was terrible to see the empty despair of entertainers whom everybody had known compelled to repeat their names two or three times—what time they showed cuttings from newspapers long since dead, or absorbed—to a new generation of agents and managers of such places as the Pantheon.

Leo Dryden, the man who sang "Don't Go Down in the Mine, Daddy" and lorded it around Leicester Square in his time, came to sing his old songs on our sad little stage—but that which had made him a kind of Al Jolson in the 1890s raised nothing but derisive laughs in Fowlers End in my time. The old comedians were laughed at, too. But for the wrong reasons. The laughter of the mob is a terrifying thing. If it is aroused, say, by Charlie Chaplin as a comedian, well and good. But if the mob laughs at Charlie Chaplin for being a comedian, why, then you hear the howl and see the bared teeth and the curled lip; and you perceive the cruelty that is fundamental to most mirth.

Comedians, above all men, are sensitive to laughter. Look at poor old T. E. Dunville, the king of clowns in the days of the music halls. When variety was at its very last gasp, somebody had the idea of resuscitating him, and he went on at the Stoll Theater in St. Martin's Lane with his old routine. He sang, in his machine-gun style, a song that had convulsed the nation:

> *Every time he moved his pants went*
> *Poppety-poppety-pop . . .*

—which had to do with a man in a ready-made suit which had shrunk in the rain. And the audience laughed. But there was a derisive quality in their laughter, and comedians are not to be laughed at. So T. E. Dunville left the theater with dignity, and drowned himself in the Thames.

I had the handling of such stars, who were trying in their old age to ward off the ineluctable falling leaves of the calendar. . . . I had a dignified old gentleman, in all that was left of a magnificent overcoat with an astrakhan collar, who had been famous for his impersonations of Sir Henry Irving. He insisted on buying me a cigar with his last sixpence to soften me for a loan of five shillings for something to eat. They laughed at him. When

I went into the men's dressing room and saw him crying into his hands, I took out one of Uncle Hugh's pounds and gave it to him, saying, "My dear sir, we are enthusiastic! This is a bonus. Congratulations!" Then he cheered up and seemed to put on weight, and went away in high spirits.

Again, gallant in her old age, came one of those corseted and curved ladies like Maidie Scott, who used to sing "I'm One of the Ruins That Cromwell Knocked About a Bit." Thirty years before, with a thirty-eight-inch bust, twenty-inch waist, and forty-four-inch hips—sixteen-and-a-half-inch calf, twenty-four-inch thigh—a royal duke stood her a nebuchadnezzar of Veuve Cliquot champagne. Now she was a huge, haggard matron; and when she came on, wearing a stuffed chicken on her head and singing:

You don't know Mary like I do,
Said the naughty little bird on Mary's hat . . .

they laughed again, but in the wrong places, the yobbos. I gave her a bonus, too. . . .

Yet, with the business manifestly gone to the dogs, there were innumerable able-bodied men and women struggling to get into it. Thank God for this, for such is the spirit of man: he must give his lifeblood to the dying.

Once the agent Billy Bax (Sam Yudenow left the bookings to him) sent me a double-turn, Franky and Johnnie. The female half of this team turned up with the agent's slip. She was a pretty young woman, not more than twenty-five years old, but already showing signs of want and wear. She asked me breathlessly, "You know who we are? Franky and Johnnie? Song and dance act? Franky's my husband. We live off the Vauxhill Bridge Road. I walked all the way. Could you advance me ten shillings for his poor old bus fare, because he really does try so hard?"

"With pleasure, ma'am," I said, and did so out of Uncle Hugh's pocket. When her husband turned up, he was carrying a baby about eight months old. He was one of those blond, nervous, petulant, willowy men with an expression female novelists generally describe as "sensitive."

"What do you propose to do with the baby?" I asked.

Quick as a bird the woman said, "Oh, we'll only be on ten minutes. Perhaps somebody could hold him for me. Only ten minutes, sir, only ten minutes."

"What the devil is Billy Bax sending me?" I cried. "With Charing Cross Road crawling with talent out of work—"

"*Ssh!* You'll wake up Charley. Swear not to tell," she said, in her breathless way. "Franky was getting so discouraged he said he would end it all. And Mr. Bax . . . well, you know, he's a very passionate man. So, you know? But it doesn't mean anything really. There's no way of getting a foothold, unless . . ."

Thus, their baby was held, not by me but by a nursing mother who, as she said, "knew what it was." She was right in the front, in the fivepennies. Giving the child one of her breasts to chew on, she settled down to enjoy herself while Franky and Johnnie—as if I hadn't guessed—sang "Frankie and Johnny Were Lovers."

I was glad to get rid of them, but at the same time I swore the blood feud against Billy Bax. I swore to myself that when I met him he should have the rough edge of my tongue and the back of my hand right in the middle of his horrid face, which I visualized as flabby, sodden like wet blotting paper, its grayness relieved by the blood in his eye and the strawberry color of his blubbery lips. He would be about fifty-five years old. . . .

But one day there came into the vestibule a tall, slim man with a sly, ingratiating manner, dressed in a ten-guinea chalk-stripe suit not much the worse for wear and pointy tan shoes. His cuffs came down to his knuckles, and his collar was of the pattern popularized by the Prince of Wales, as he was then, before we stopped loving him. His hat was a homburg. You could have put the knot of his tie into a thimble. As for his face: it was an animated Rake's Progress. Under and over prominent watery brown eyes I saw a concentricity of black bags. Hard as he might try, he couldn't keep the muscles of his face in equilibrium. Knowing when these muscles were getting out of control, but unable to keep them in check, he occasionally let them go in a fireworks display of confidential winks and whimsical grimaces.

As my mother would have said, he didn't look a bit well. There was something about his posture that made me feel uneasy—he was too animated from the waist up and too deliberate from the hips down. Also, he punctuated his sentences with prefabricated laughter.

"Here's a list for Monday-Tuesday-Wednesday," he said, with a hearty laugh. "Jacob and the Angel, Eccentric Dancers, ha-ha-ha! Two single turns—The Tramp Juggler and Gritto, The Man Who Eats Bricks, ha-ha-ha! Well, as it happens, Gritto broke a tooth in Brixton, ha-ha-ha, so in order not to let Sam Yudenow down, I decided at the last moment to dub. Got it? I'm Billy Bax, Song and Dance—what's the odds so long as you're happy?—that's my line, ha-ha-ha! . . . Look here, let's have a pound on account, will you?"

I said, "Better ask Mr. Yudenow."

Billy Bax the Agent said, "I don't wanna do that. It's bad for prestige. Oh, for Christ's sake, look—ten per cent passes through my hands, and *I'm* taking the place of Gritto, ha-ha-ha! What's the odds, so long as you're happy? I been on the boards and better off 'em. I been on the boards and now I'm on the floor, ha-ha-ha! The show must go on—ask Sam Yudenow—so I need a quid at this very moment to keep my office open. Funny—isn't it? —ha-ha-ha! . . . Fix you up with a nice girl? I mean, free of charge? Ha-ha-ha!"

"I'll give you your pound," I said.

"And I'm much obliged, ha-ha-ha! As for the girls, remember there's a depression on. In the old days many a good ride I had for a sandwich, ha-ha-ha! But now you can bottle anybody for a threat or a promise. Only see what I'm reduced to, ha-ha-ha."

"Here's a pound, and sign a chit," I said. "And better make it good."

So Billy Bax came on that Monday night as a substitute for Gritto, the Stone Crusher. His was an odiously allusive style. The language, at its lowest, was not quite expressive enough for this debased man; he had to reinforce his double meanings with winks and leers. One of his songs was encored, the refrain of it being:

If you are a fat old hen
Then any old cock will do . . .

After that he went into what he called an "eccentric dance." When he came off I ran up to the dressing room, impelled by cold distaste, to tell him to moderate his act. There I saw him sitting on the edge of the bed, unnaturally rigid, ghastly in his make-up. As I came into the room he stood up stiffly, cried, "California, here I come!" and fell dead of heart failure. So perish all such.

This, I told Copper Baldwin, was heartache; but he upbraided me, saying, "Oh, be your bloody age! Your heart aches, does it? Then let it. What's a heart for? Gawd strike me blind, didn't anybody ever tell you that the heart is the most muscular organ in the body? Ever foot-slog forty miles a day? Then your knees ache and your hips ache—Gawd's sake, that's the way you get strong, you currant! You can believe me, cocko, it's a weak heart that never ached. And you're an unlicked pup as yet. You'll get hardened, you'll harden. Only it's a painful process. Everybody's got to carry 'is own pack until 'e drops, and the longer you carry it the heavier it gets. I'm not telling you a word of a lie. That is, of course, provided you don't live like a bleeding pig—on your Darby-and-Joan, for yourself. And you ain't a pig, are you, now? You're not, you know; otherwise why bother with poor old Miss Noel?"

I said, "Oh, that's neither here nor there—"

"Begging your pardon, son, it is both 'ere and there. What's she to you? It's a case of divine compassion; and you mark my words, cocko, when it comes your turn Gawd will pity you."

"I thought you didn't believe in God," I said.

He replied, "It's a manner of speaking. Always there is somethink close behind you. . . . Never mind Gawd. What's He to Hecuba? What's Noel to you?"

"The hell with Noel!" I cried.

"Leave 'er alone, poor gel, and she'll find 'er own hell. Found it, matter of fact. But what made you wash 'er, and dress 'er, and soak 'er in scent? Tell me that. And answer me this: what made you bring that gentleman, Sourbreast, up from town to gee the poor bitch up?"

"Sourbreast came here to pay *me* a visit," I said. "Although, if you must know, Copper, I first took Miss Noel to Sourbreast's place in Albany."

And well I remembered that incident. I took her in, subdued and decent. She seemed to inhale the flat while she was looking at it. The Sickert over the fireplace brought tears to her eyes, and when she caressed the spines of the old books there was something in her gestures that put me in mind of an aged bachelor caressing the head of someone else's newborn child. Then she saw the piano and asked, "May I try and play it?"

"Please do, my dear madam," said Sourbreast, uncovering the keyboard and lifting the great lid.

Then Miss Noel played, much as she had played that day when we washed her and changed her clothes.

Sourbreast cried, "No, really! Upon my heart and soul, this is talent, God bless me! I'll get you engagements, I'll be damned if I don't. Yes, upon my word of honor I'll get hold of Miller and hire you the Wigmore Hall." He was excited. "Leave it to me," he said. "I positively guarantee you fifty guineas. Seriously, this I categorically guarantee out of my own pocket! . . . Oh, please, no thanks!—we'll show a profit. But you'll need some kind of dark evening dress, and your hair done, and a manicure, and all that. Shoes, et cetera; I am not well up in these matters, you know. Could I, perhaps, advance you twenty pounds?"

"I really don't know what to say," said Miss Noel, weeping. "Nobody ever believed . . ."

But he took out of his wallet five five-pound notes (for he was of a generous nature) and thrust them into her hand. And he did, indeed, rent the Wigmore Hall, and poor Miss Noel was in her glory. She bought a long-sleeved black dress of some stuff they called "ring velvet" and had her hair trimmed and dyed dark brown, which, I suppose, was its original color. She had her nails attended to, also, and got herself a pair of black suède court shoes and a discreet little hat. I chipped in with a diamond clip from the Hi-Life Gem Company, which cost eleven shillings. Copper Baldwin came forward with a most ladylike row of artificial pearls—not too big, not too little—the largest one in the center was about the size of a marble. Miss Noel had already taken to washing. Now she developed a new manner and kept talking about her engagement at the Wigmore Hall. She gave me supercilious looks, ignored Copper Baldwin completely, and laughed in Sam Yudenow's face. There was no controlling her—she kept playing medleys and trying to perfect them.

Copper Baldwin and I throbbed with anticipation. We had clubbed together to hire a car to take her to Wigmore Street at six o'clock one Thursday evening. She had been closeted with Sam Yudenow, who had said, "I want to say a few words congratulations. A few words congratulations I want to say. You see? Stick by Sam Yudenow and he'll put a gold spoon right in your kisser. And you'll be buried in a silver casket miv trimmings!"

He came down wearing an expression of innocence and despair, saying, "Go on, fetch 'er. What do you want I should do, what? Carry her on my bended knees or something? I'm sorry to say the lady is, uxcuse me, pissed."

And so she was, with her forehead on the edge of the desk and her lap full of vomit. Near by stood a bottle and two glasses.

Doubling his fists, Copper Baldwin said to Sam Yudenow, "Now this time, you bastard, you *are* going to get it!"

"A moment, please, Copper—all I ask of life is you shouldn't do what you'll be sorry for later. Go into the ladies', put your head in the laventory, pull the plug, and cool off. Believe me, it's a godsend. . . . Lavenberg, don't look me no daggers. The poor girl can't 'elp it. Don't laugh; pity, rather. It's a dragedy."

I said, "How come a bottle of Johnny Walker?"

Sam Yudenow said, "Doctor's orders. Catarrh. But above all, I will not have my office polluted miv a sahr smell. Better put 'er down on the piano and work it off."

"What about the Wigmore Hall?" I asked helplessly, for Miss Noel was quite unconscious.

Sam Yudenow said easily, "Believe me, pianists are two a penny, as sure as I stand here. Wipe 'er down and spvay her with perfumed disinfectant. More I couldn't do for my own mother, God forbid!"

I said, "After this, Yudenow, I'm going to fix you."

He said absently, "Yes, I want you should do that. Good boy. Get on the job."

So Miss Noel went back to her tuneless piano, weeping as if her heart would break; and Copper Baldwin said to me, in a matter-of-fact voice, "In confidence, cocko, I've just made up my mind to murder Sam Yudenow."

And he expounded the cruelest plans for the liquidation of Yudenow that I ever heard of. Being a handy man with his mitts, said Copper Baldwin, he could rig up a gadget. Now if Sam Yudenow happened to be a bathing man, (a) he could drown him in a bathtub or (b) so arrange it that when he turned on the showerbath it would come out at boiling point. He had a working knowledge of electricity, he told me. "You know the bastard's got a weak bladder. A copper electrode in the carsey wired up to the generator—nothing conducts electricity like water. Stream o' pee is as good as a cable. Shape Sam's heart is in, one convulsion o' the bladder ought to bust 'im like a balloon—somebody done it to me once when I was working on the railways where we 'ad iron urinals. Yes sir, I went four feet into the air. I must 'ave 'ad a strong heart, because they wired me up to a live rail. . . . Somebody told me there was a poison you could make out of three ingredients anybody can buy for sixpence at any ironmonger's shop. Undetectable. You wouldn't 'appen by any chance to know the names of these ingredients, would you? If 'e was a drinking man I'd get 'im tight, I would, and give 'im a lovely great bubble of air in one of 'is fat old arteries. I'll bet you that would fix 'im. What's your opinion, Dan?"

I said, "Detectable—" entering into the spirit of the thing—"what about putting opium into his tea and then pouring molten lead down his throat through a funnel?"

"I could cut up a bit of water pipe. But wouldn't solder do?"

"I imagine so," I said, "only lead is heavier and holds the heat longer. I know a jujitsu blow—two, in fact—that are dead-sure killers, both with the edge of the hand. One is under the nose on the upper lip: you strike upwards. The other is on the bridge of the nose between the eyes, in which case you strike downwards. There is also, I believe, a jab of the thumb under the ear. I can't say I've practiced these things, but a Japanese told me so. His father made him strike a wet sandbag with the outer edges of his hands ten thousand times every day, so that they developed hard callouses sharp as glass. I do not think I have the time."

Copper Baldwin said, "Where's your tactics? I got hard hands."

Not without enthusiasm, I added, "I get it—stimulate a roughhouse when Yudenow is around and let him have it in the dark."

"That's the style!" cried Copper Baldwin. "You distract attention and leave the rest to me. But touching the matter of lead pipes . . ."

"I'm told that a woolen stocking full of wet pebbles is not at all a bad thing."

"I 'ave often contemplated a swift kick up the arse in the generator room," said Copper Baldwin, "or maybe an extra tablespoonful of copper sulphate in a Greenburger? Somebody else might get it, it's true, but it wouldn't be you or me—and the scandal would cost 'im plenty, which would be a fate worse than death for that stinker. Yes. Why swing? Better yet—let's cost the bastard. What say?"

"Cost him what? Cost him how?" I asked.

"You've got me there, cocko. If we burned 'is bloody show down, Yudenow would be only too delighted. It's insured to the hilt. It's insured; 'is wife is insured; 'is car is insured; 'e's insured. Kill the sod: you'll be doing 'im a favor. 'E's worth more dead than alive, the cowson bastard. But I want 'im punished. There's no use arguing, that man's got to suffer. Brute force and ignorance will get us nowhere. But what will? Get us anywhere, I mean. Can't we get 'im into trouble?"

I said, "Come now, Copper, there is always the question of integrity. Besides, I'll bet you anything you like that Yudenow could get you into more trouble than you could get him into."

"You're not far wrong there. The bastard would spend a pound to trace a farthing, just out of spite. Better think it over, son."

And then Cruikback turned up again in his Daimler. It was a limousine of 1911, such as only a gentleman would have dared to ride in, and the back of it was packed with those three-legged instruments that surveyors use, together with maps and parti-colored sticks, and tape measures the smallest of which was bigger than a Camembert cheese. He stamped into the vestibule in his huge cleated boots, shaking himself like a retriever, about eleven o'clock one night. I have never seen a muddier man. He was miry as a boar but the whiteness of his teeth looked elegant and cheerful in his dirty face. He was wearing the same old breeches but had slung about his shoulders a great pair of binoculars in a new leather case and had on a deerstalker cap.

"I stopped off," he said, "for a leak. Do you mind terribly, old thing, if I use your wee-wee place? . . . Ah, there, Mr. Baldwin! Gordon's Dry, wasn't it? Hadn't forgotten, you know—" and he took a sealed bottle out of his pocket and put it into Copper Baldwin's hands. Then he dashed into the nearest lavatory. It irritated me to see the joy with which Copper Baldwin received him, and I was doubly irritated when Cruikback came out with a dripping face, shaking water off his fingertips and saying, "No, really, young Laverock, that towel is unusable. Lend me a handkerchief or something, will you?"

Copper Baldwin offered him a red bandanna, upon which he dried himself, muttering, "I hope the dye doesn't come off. I mean, I hope this is a vegetable dye. I suppose you know that aniline is a coal-tar product, and there's one hell of a statistical correlation? I'll return this, of course, washed. What say we have a little bit of a drinkie?"

Copper Baldwin was already busy with his pocketknife at the capsule of the bottle. But now Cruikback took on a melancholy air, while he pocketed the handkerchief.

"A word with you, young Laverock," he said. "A matter of some seriousness." So I took him into the empty hall, and we sat side by side in two eightpenny seats.

Having borrowed a cigarette, Cruikback said, "Charming fellow that Baldwin."

"One of the best-read men I've ever met," I said.

"Uneducated, necessarily," said Cruikback.

"And what the hell do you mean by that?" I demanded, with some heat.

With his customary air of condescension, Cruikback said, "Old thing, you haven't got the correlation. You and I are educated—

you'll grant me that? But Baldwin has merely been subjected to academic exposure. Couldn't hold a candle. I suppose you know, of course, that given a thumb a chimpanzee can do it? No, common savvy and blood: these you can't deny. Anthropology. . . . But look here, old thing—I'm in a hole. Did I mention that I was married?"

I said, "I forget, Cruikback. All I know is you made my name mud—or something—that last time you came, and I'll be damned if you sleep in my room tonight. Cruikback, do you appreciate that you actually shat?"

"I thought that was all explained," he said stiffly. "It must have been bad gin. Laverock, for God's sake, what *are* you? Are you a Valetudinarian, or what are you? I know you were always a crank, you know, but sometimes I don't know whether to make head or tail of you! You might pay a little more attention. I told you just now that I was in a hole, didn't I? I mean, I'm married, and I've had a boy—or rather, my wife has. Now look here, young Laverock, man to man, I've got to get the poor little fellow out of pawn. Man to man, man—what would you do in such a case? Trouble with what the doctors call the prepuce—grew together, had to be circumcized like a bloody pawnbroker—and until I pay the bloody bill I can't get the kid out. Can you pause to imagine that? I don't believe you met his mother—my wife, I mean, of course. No family, I'm afraid, but a sweet gel. Now you know, Laverock, that a gentleman knows when to swallow his pride. Unfortunately, my wife doesn't. Her father is absolutely lousy with the stuff, but she'd got (it's her only fault) a sort of proletarian pride and absolutely refuses to raise the wind. I went to the old gentleman and told him I'd had the boy circumcized, but he was not impressed."

I said, "This is too bad."

"Now you and I, young Laverock, are Old Valetudinarians—men of education, such as it is, not subjected to academic exposure. I suppose you know, of course, that there is not merely a statistical correlation but a *justifiable* correlation of statistics between supply and demand? Incidentally, I ought to tell you that my wife is a Braddock. Then consider my position. Old thing, I hate to talk to you like this . . ."

I said, "Now look here, Cruikback, you know I'm broke or I wouldn't be here."

"I don't think you take me, young Laverock. I'm not on the cadge, you know; I'm trying to put a fortune in your hands. What do you think I'm surveying round Ullage?"

"I haven't the faintest idea," I said.

"Heard of the A.A.A.A.?" he asked.

"Why, that would be the Anglo-American Automobile Associates," I said.

"Right you are," said Cruikback. "And I'll give you the low-down, young Laverock. I suppose you know about the Ford Works that are going up at Dagenham? The Ford Works is making the town, I dare say you know. Dagenham used to be a stinking village in the swamp. Ford's made a rich suburb of it, with a branch line running out. And in, too, upon my honor! They cut roads, they electrified lines, and the value of real estate in Dagenham went up several hundred per cent, and is going up still. Why? The hoi-polloi have got to live on top of the job. Hence, lots, streets, buildings. Projects, Laverock, projects! Now who is Ford's greatest competitor in Europe?"

"A.A.A.A.?" I suggested.

"Right for once, young Laverock. Good show. What's going to happen is this: A.A.A.A. is buying land round Ullage for an enormous factory, and I'm doing the surveying. Now wait a minute, young Laverock—consider the implications, correlative and statistical! First of all, speaking purely mechanically, the railway absolutely must run a line out to Ullage—I mean, a passenger line, because now it becomes a Place. The land there automatically increases in value. Correct me if I'm wrong, of course. Village becomes town. Where there's a town, there's got to be a

High Street, or something of the sort, with shops and things. Well?"

I said, "Don't be silly."

"A cinema, even," he continued, with that old enthusiasm which had carried us all away a hundred years ago. "Simply hold the land, if you like, and let A.A.A.A. buy off you. Statistics prove that industry runs to a standstill without labor. Upon my word of honor, it's proved! A.A.A.A. pays well. Pay the working classes well, Laverock, and what's the first thing they do? Buy a bedroom suite and a piano. This I can give you on the best authority. And a pair of glasses, a haircut, drugs, et cetera. I speak to you as a Valetudinarian, Laverock. How many times did I beat you until the blood ran down? Buy a piece of Ullage. The factory site I can't offer, of course, but I can arrange it for you to get a nice piece of land northwest of the High Street for eight hundred pounds that is bound to be worth twelve thousand in eighteen months. I have documents to prove it. Only I want two hundred pounds for myself, to get my boy out of pawn. What do you say? As a Valetudinarian give me a plain yes or an honest no. Speak up, young Laverock, speak up!"

"Oh, Copper!" I shouted; and Baldwin, who had been eavesdropping on the whole conversation, came in with a rigid face, carrying the bottle and three glasses.

He served us as a butler serves his masters—in discreet measure. Then he served himself as a butler serves himself—three and a half fingers deep. "I say, look here, Cruikback, old thing," I said, "do you mind frightfully if we leave you the bottle for a few minutes, because I want a word with Mr. Baldwin?"

He said, "Oh, very well. I don't suppose you could manage to switch on a film or something, could you?"

"We got some magic-lantern slides," said Copper Baldwin. And so we had—left over from goodness knows when—of *The Pilgrim's Progress*. With these and the gin, Cruikback seemed to be comfortable. For my part I was glad to get Copper Baldwin up into the projection room, where I could tell him word for word all that Cruikback had said to me.

"As you say," he said—although I had said nothing of the sort—"it do seem like an act of Providence, don't it? But remember your arithmetic, cocko. What's eight hundred plus two? One thousand, by my calculations. . . . Hold hard, Danny boy—we're coming to that bit about 'Death where is thy sting, Grave where is thy victory?' Then 'e passed over, an' all the trumpets sounded for 'im on the Other Side. Gawd stone my Aunt Fanny, but if I 'ad a trumpet I'd 'ave a blow at it! Christ Almighty, Danno, can't you see where this leads to?"

I said, "Putting one across Sam Yudenow?" I said.

"And getting ourselves a lovely bit o' change, tell your mum. Only there's a formality, pally. A matter of a thousand nicker. I got a hundred and fifty. Would you 'appen to 'ave a matter of eight hundred and fifty quid on you?"

"No, but I think I could find something like it—" I began.

"Oh, bugger! I got 'Christian and Apollyon' upside-bloody-down! Damn that demented tinker—only you shook me. First of all, what's your strategy?"

"Beat Cruikback down," I said.

"You don't think that might be taking a mean advantage of a gentleman?" asked Copper Baldwin.

I said, "Certainly."

"Mind you, I want to see everything in writing," said Copper Baldwin.

"Better get this clear," said I, while he slipped into the machine that horrid Gustave Doré picture of the 'Trial of Faithful' while, pursing his lips, he imitated the sound of a trumpet and made a noise with his tomahawk upon the projector, managing at the same time to whisper, "Okay, cocko—when the film busts during a children's matinee, this never fails to wow the little bastards, specially if you put it in upsy-down. Repulsive, though, at the best of times, ain't it? . . . I suppose you know, Danny boy, this could mean a modest competence? And do Sam Smallpox down? Then we f - - - off. Get me? I got my papers: chips, which is the same as to say ship's carpenter—and for a ten-pun note I can get you a legitimate set too. I'm a pal o' 'Kicking Jack.' 'E runs the *Avocado*—unlicensed for passengers, but the idear is, 'Kicking Jack' signs you on as one o' the crew, and you give 'im a twenty-pound note. Ever been to Guatemala? I don't mind telling you, it's a hell of a lot different from Fowlers End. You take my word for it, son. I been. Oh, those laundresses—black as ink, white as milk, an' every one with 'er mouth full o' gold teeth! None o' your brassy, mind you—sweet as honey. What say? Eh? Don't believe what they say about cheese, and rancid butter, and all that. They're fresher than new-laid eggs. Oh, to hell with it all, Danny boy. Come on and let's go! Are you game? . . . Oh, now I got the 'Celestial City' arse upwards; but what's the odds? . . ."

His washed-out blue eyes grew dark with passionate reminiscence. He said, "I don't know what it is. It may be Sam Yudenow's Greenburgers that brings it to mind. But did you ever smell the hot breath of that jungle coming on a rotten wet breeze out of the mouth of the Rio Dolce by Puerto Barrios, and see the blacks under the naphtha flares, like in a fun fair, shouting, 'Fruit-ah, fruit-ah, fruit-ah!' It brings the blood to the surface, son. Okay, you'll get eaten alive: too many insects. Somewhere or other there's a statistical correlation—abolish insects, and where's your natural balance? . . . Believe me, you go past Cuba in a mist. Invariably a mist, in those parts; and the Caribbean's gray, gray-green. Unlike the Atlantic, which is dead dull gray; and the Mediterranean, which is blue. The Gulf of Mexico, though, is greeny-blue. All the same, off Cuba the flying fishes start to play. Porpoises, too. No, but I mean to say, they *play!* Make as many knots as you like, and there's your porpoise just an arm's length in front of you, kind o' laughing. Susceptible to music, too, Dan—not that I'm musical myself; but I swear to Gawd, with these two eyes I seen an old shantyman calling up the porpoises on a fiddle.

It's they what chase the flying fishes, boy, and there's the pathos on it—the poor bloody fish is geared for escape. But he can't escape, don't you see, because that's his destiny. 'E's got to get out o' the water, but 'e's got to get back in again. It makes you think. If 'e flies high enough, 'e'll land flapping on the deck of a steamer. If not, there's the old rollicking porpoise with about five hundred teeth smiling welcome. . . . And beyond Cuba the banana countries that everybody runs away to, where the coppers carry nickel-plated carbines. And don't believe what they tell you about the laundresses. They wash themselves ten times more often than Fowlers End, so help me Jesus, and if they smell at all it's like ripe coconuts. Oh, dear me!"

And all of a sudden I had a mad desire to go to these wonderful places with Copper Baldwin. "Hold hard," I said, "you've got a hundred and fifty pounds? Then leave the rest to me, and I'll arrange it."

So I went downstairs and talked to Cruikback, who had already got through about a third of the bottle.

He said, "Well, young Laverock? Thought it over?"

Shrewd now, I shook my head sadly and said, "Afraid so, old thing. Thought better of it."

He cried, "Why, what the hell do you mean, young Laverock? Thought better of what? No, really, I mean to say! *Qu'est-ce que c'est que ça?* No, if this isn't absolutely un-Valetudinarian, I give you my written permission to bugger me for a row of pins! Written and stamped, to boot! Take back your filthy gin," he said, swallowing about a tumblerful and afterward putting the bottle in his pocket. Then he was all concern. "You always were a strange one, you know," he said. "Hard up? In times like these, I can imagine. Why then, I'll tell you what you must do, young Laverock—you must take the bull by the horns, old thing, and borrow."

"Thanks—" I began.

"Not another word. Don't embarrass me."

I said, "I might be able to raise a few pounds from, for example, my Uncle Hugh—"

"Now that, young Laverock, is the very last thing I want you to do. I suppose you mean Hugh Laverock, of Laverock and Strype, in the City? God help you, young Laverock, you never were of what might be described as correlative intellect. When I have the time, I'll introduce you to a bloke I know, a comparative glandularist, and I'll bet you he'll find thymus. Yes, I'm sorry, but I'm afraid you've got glands. Of internal secretion, what's more. You don't happen to wet the bed by any chance, do you? But as I remember, you always were a backward boy. Go to the City, indeed! Can't you see that's exactly what I don't want? About three months from now, yes—which is why I want three and a half per cent of the stock in the Limited Company. I suppose you know you'll have to form one?"

"As I work it out, Cruikback," I said, "I don't see my way clear to raising a thousand pounds." I was being, I say, shrewd, swallowing insults like so many tonic pills and getting keener on them. "For this proposition—I mean to say, a bit of land in Ullage! —I could manage about three hundred pounds."

He said, with an air of finality, "Sorry, old thing—quite out of the question." Hereupon he became indignant, stood up, sat down, took a little gin, banged the cork back as if he were knocking down his worst enemy, and shouted, "No, this is the bloody limit! No, after all, I never thought I'd live to see it, but you hit—but I mean, hit—the precise correlation between caution and bankruptcy. Firstly, what about the two hundred pounds I need to get Henry out of pawn? I say nothing of his mother. As a man of the world, you know what women are; one has to provide them with this and that. Spectacles, medicine, vaginas, nail polish, hair, depilatories. Oh, no, damn it all! And then you come to me with an utterly mad proposition of going to your uncle in the City with my proposition *when the reason I am telling you of this is that I specifically want it kept out of the City!* Why, you little fool, don't you realize that if your uncle got wind he'd bust the issue? Or don't you? No, you don't—or do you?"

I said, "You confuse me a little, old thing, I admit."

"I dare say. You always were muddleheaded. You always lacked correlative control. Or shall I rather say uncorrelated imagination? Now look here, Laverock, before I go a step farther, answer me one question: In a nutshell, what do you know of high finance?"

I was compelled to say that, to come right down to the point, I knew about as much as would cover a silver threepenny piece. Nodding and smiling, Cruikback said, "As if I didn't know! I'll try and simplify the thing for you, old man. The nub of finance is, in fact, the boost of value. Even you understand as simple a proposition as this? It is to increase the value of a thing by playing on greedy people's avarice, and then cashing in and getting out. Now you know, I'm a very strong Socialist myself; only my Socialism takes a National form. Oh, don't imagine for one moment that I'm not a pretty strong Internationalist—but put it this way: a body must have a head. You'll grant me that? International Socialism under one flag—the color of this flag we'll work out eventually. It might be striped. Look at the Union Jack, bless it! If you were an industrial designer, would you dare to wrap soap in it? Or the Stars and Stripes? But perhaps I'm departing from my point. If you let your bloody uncle in on this, he's *bound* to let in half his fat friends in the City. They'll form a dummy company, try to snatch that land in advance of A.A.A.A.—and so good day to you and me. Oh, no, thank you. We have it and hold it with the titles screwed down, if you don't mind. This way, you must know we put a shield over our interests and deal a blow at the capitalist system, which is hand in glove with the bloody communists and making a mess accordingly."

"Work me that one out, old thing," I begged.

"Oh, now, I say, look here, this is no time for me to be teaching you economics! Managerial dialectics all in good time. You've heard of the inevitability of gradualness? It's a lot of hooey. Ever had a swift punch on the button? That's the inevitability of suddenness, and that's what counts. Look at Napoleon. We've got a *coup d'état* in hand—and you sit there picking your ears for wax! Now I'll tell you what I'll do. As confidential surveyor, I happen to know that A.A.A.A. is going to buy immense tracts of land northwest and southeast, in Ullage. Northwest come the workmen's houses, pubs, and so forth. If I were in your position, I'd get financing for a good dance hall. A.A.A.A., you know, will be employing people by the thousand. A good dance hall! Your greatest expense is an orchestra. Let's not go into detail now. As Napoleon said, there is time to worry about the Vistula after we have crossed the Rhine. I can get you that land on the northwest, but the factory must be southeast, where the railway line has got to run. I can get you a six-hundred-foot frontage there. It would cost A.A.A.A. four million to build round you—"

"But it's all mud," I protested.

"I know it is, my good ape. Otherwise, why would it cost A.A.A.A. four million to build around you? It'd be worth a hundred pounds a foot to them, can't you see? Yes, I'll get you that. . . . I dare say you wonder why I don't go to your proprietor, or somebody. Well, I'll tell you: he'd do me down, because I'm not a businessman. Furthermore, I've got to have a couple of hundred at once—and that's the kind of chicken feed a man like me simply can't ask for. So, say you raise five or six hundred and—honor of a gentleman—don't let a word leak out in the City until the gold rush comes and we make the killing. My cut, if you like, will be: Terms to Be Mutually Agreed. Gentleman's agreement . . . Happen, by any chance, to have a spare handkerchief?"

"You've got one there," I said.

"I know, but I mean a white one."

Out of the fullness of my heart I gave him a white handkerchief, which he used enthusiastically, whispering, "Other fellow means well, Laverock, but couldn't understand that one would rather use a snotty handkerchief from a gentleman than a clean one from the rabble. . . . I'm a raging Socialist myself. But I draw the line at colored handkerchiefs. *Verb sap*, what?"

"Not quite," I confessed.

"Better have a bit of gin, old thing. And try and pull yourself together. . . . How much do you think you can raise in about the next three days? No longer, young Laverock, because I'm not a gradual sort of man. You know me. Remember the time I thrashed the big Jew?"

"It was your nose that was bleeding," I reminded him.

With a light laugh he agreed: "Wasn't it, though? Too much blood; I always get a nose bleed when I'm excited. And the grass was slippery. How young we were then! . . . It would be far better, you know, if you could get hold of seven hundred."

"Do the best I can."

Grasping my hand, he said, "I knew I could count on you, Laverock. At a reasonable estimate we ought to have about a quarter of a million pounds' worth of property. Now, did I let you down? . . . Oh, look, I'm afraid I've drunk most of this gin. Had I better drive, do you think?"

"Look here, old thing," I said, "don't drive a man too far. You know what happened last time. If you want to sleep here tonight, Copper Baldwin will unscrew a few seats, and you can lie down in the generator room. I'm more or less responsible for what happened last time."

"The gin was bad," said Cruikback.

"But, according to you, my landlord's sister was not."

"Oh, no, did I? You should have stopped me. Is she clean? It doesn't matter in general, but my wife's a lady, you know, though a Braddock. Finishing school, and everything—"

"Her brother is looking for you with a carving knife," I said, lying, "and he has no fear of consequences."

At this he became grave. "You know me," he said. "I'm not afraid *ipso facto* of a knife, or of a dago per se; but a dago out for blood with a knife, *cum* 'no fear of consequences,' could be an infernal nuisance to a man in my position. That's the way of the world, young Laverock—it's the way things *are*. I'd be compelled to strike him (you haven't forgotten how I mowed down that gigantic great sheeney?) and there'd be a scandal, which I can't afford. I think I mentioned, I've got to get poor little Henry out of pawn. It's not that I mind so much as the fact that the poor little fellow has got to be circumcized. God damn it, Laverock, you must be aware, if you're a student of statistical correlation, that practically one hundred per cent of Jews are circumcized? And how do you like that? . . . No, but wait a minute. Let's get this clear. As I gather, the young lady thinks it's you. Oh, well—" he was full of confidence now—"these Mediterranean races are all wind, old thing. Just you call their bluff, young Laverock. Too much wine, and sleeping in the afternoon. It stands to reason, doesn't it? Where's the Roman Empire? Where's Byzantium? Where's Spain, Portugal, Carthage? I've never lied to you, have I? The Mediterranean races—not that I have any prejudices myself—statistically have no guts: dysentery—it's positively demonstrated—on account of green figs. If that dago comes up to you with a carving knife, you just take it away from him and give him a good talking-to. And if it comes to a roughhouse, don't forget the good old long straight left. Remember how I felled that immense Hebrew?"

"He felled you, and he wasn't immense," I said.

"You will have your little joke, young Laverock. But be advised by me—if it comes to rough-and-tumble, never bite a dago, because they have worms in the muscles, encysted. This is proved; it comes from goat's milk. . . . Since I see that I'm going to put you out, I think perhaps I'd better drive back. And, oh, I say, look here, better have that money in three days, or I'm afraid it's no go. Ta-ta! Thanks for the entertainment; I adored that bit with the blokes standing on their heads."

So he went away, and I went next door meaning to go to bed.

11

I ENTERED DISCREETLY, imagining that Costas and his sister had gone to bed, but I was surprised to hear activity in the kitchen. There was light under the door and, penetrating the stink of the Greenburgers, a piercing odor that seemed to go right through my head. As a smell it was not disgusting but positively painful: it made me want to rub my scalp and cry; it got on my nerves and made my heart beat too hard and too fast.

I thought, at first, that Sam Yudenow was getting them to try out a new recipe, so—I always was a light walker—I went to the kitchen and quietly opened the door. The stench became ten times stronger, but the air was clear, and I saw Costas, a mass of muscle in a sweat shirt, brooding over the gigantic copper steam boiler in which the Greenburgers were made. He was engrossed; no man ever looked more tense than Costas as he very gently stirred whatever he was cooking with a wooden spoon. On the floor near by stood three immense bottles. The back of one of them was turned to me, so I could only read the labels on the other two. One of them said: HNO_3; the other, GLYCERIN. Kyra, who was sitting at the table where they customarily prepared the vegetables, appeared to be harmlessly engrossed in mending a five-shilling alarm clock. And something must have gone wrong with the bell because, at her elbow, stood two dry electric batteries.

Happy in my new project and anxious to be friendly, I shouted, "What's cooking?"—whereat Costas started and splashed himself from chin to groin with his acrid mixture, and Kyra got a screwdriver under her thumbnail. The stuff must have been somewhere near boiling point, but he did not flinch. He pulled a long revolver out of his hip pocket and pointed it at me. I do not know exactly how stupid a man can get but, having always been something of a connoisseur of weapons and being a shortsighted and good-natured kind of fool, I thought he was simply showing it to me. So I approached, got hold of it by the barrel, took it out of his unresisting hand, and said, "Why, this is a rarity. Isn't this the so-called Russian Colt revolver? I mean, the one made by America for the Czar's army? One of the best-balanced pistols in the world. You don't see one of these every day. I'll give you a pound for it."

He said, with one eye on the boiler, "For Christ's sake, keep your finger off that trigger. It's loaded. For Jesus Christ's sake, don't even let it off in fun, not even at the floor!" Then the iron in this man seemed to melt. His eyes filled with tears; something snapped at the back of his voice, and he called to Kyra, "Darling, make him put it down!"

Then I saw a new Kyra. She had always been hard as nails; now she was hard and cold, and you could have shaved yourself on the edge of her voice as she said to him in French—which, I presume, she thought I could not understand—"Species of imbecile that thou art! Never draw a weapon you are not prepared to use, bollock-head! Oh, must it be, then, holy Mother of God? Take out the bullets, twot-head, and give him, the idiot, the fornicating gun!" Then she told him off in Italian, in what I dare to print only in the following terms: "Oh, penis! Oh, by the body of seven thousand bombs, by Bacchus, you private part, give the idiot the penising pistol, you anus!"

I pretended not to understand. Costas broke the revolver, unloaded it, and gave it to me, saying over his shoulder in Spanish, "Be silent, copulating cow, there is not wherefore. I double-defecate in your milk!"

"Feces!" she cried.

"Since your mouth is full of them, devour!" said he. "But, in the name of our Maker, get this vagina out of here, because this had better go in the icebox."

"Wait till your hands are steady, then, urine! Be calm, ear wax! This species of female organ of reproduction turned inside out and whitewashed still does not know his *derrière* from an excavation in the ground. I will take him upstairs, micturation of a camel—if there still is an upstairs by the time we get there—and you break up ice. Only do it outside, obscenity! *Spongocolarius*!"

All this was with machine-gun diction. As I must have said somewhere before, to the ignorant much is told—there is nothing like a good proverb—so I kept a straight face and pocketed the Russian Colt with one hand while I offered Costas a pound note with the other. But he said, "Please keep it, keep it. I have plenty more pistols."

She said to him in German, "You are a cretinous all-too-soon abortion of a harlot of the very lowest type. I suppose you know that, don't you? Dung-face!" To me, she said, "I forgot to make your bed. Let's go up. You see what I have to put up with. He keeps trying out new recipes. And look at the mess he's made of himself—soaked."

He said, "It is a kind of soup. Only it needs a filler to stabilize it. Otherwise—"

He was evidently one of those conspiratorial characters whose cryptic remarks so frequently turn out to be the death of them. Kyra said to him, in French, "Oh, in the name of God! Stand on your hands and whistle through your arse hole! Get the ice, defecatory swine; get the ice, cuckold! . . . Mr. Laverock, let me turn down your bed."

"No, let me," I said. "I beg you not to disturb yourself."

Costas said, "It is no trouble." Then, in Italian, "In the name of seven thousand penes, get that colonic irrigation out of this obscene kitchen, mother of dogs! . . . No, Mr. Laverock, it is a delight to have a gentleman in the house."

Then, as he made to light a candle, Kyra firmly took the matches out of his hand and, in a quiet, reasonable kind of voice, said to him in French, "Oh, you frightful son-of-a-bitch! Species of clitoris! My faith, you droppings that you are! What is it that it is that this is? Ah, no, but you enshit me! Enough is enough. The more it changes, the more it is the same thing. You are a turd with teeth, and there is nothing to be done about it. Pig, take the ice out into the garden, ten paces away, break it up fine, and bring it back in a tub. It is nothing to me—ah, my God then!—if Fowlers End goes up like . . ." She started to clap her hands but stopped herself before the palms met, keeping an anxious eye on the boiler. "Mr. Laverock, I am going to turn down your bed."

I said, "This pistol, Mr. Costas: it's the one with the extra grip for the second finger, like this—"

Knowing it to be empty, I pointed it at him in demonstration. God knows anything I aim at is safe unless I get to within three feet, but Costas did not know this. Also, he must have forgotten that he was still clutching the six big bullets in his sticky left hand, for he crossed himself right-to-left in the Greek style and said, "Fire if you will, sir, and let us die together!"

Losing patience, presumably, Kyra screamed at me, "Give me that f - - - ing gun!" I gave it to her, obediently, while Costas whispered, in French, "For the love of God, dearest, your voice vibrates! The soup is cooling, and I conjure you this is neither the time nor the place for vibration."

"Then get the ice," she said, calling him an odious name which coy ladies call by the diminutive of "cat" for fear of using a four-letter word.

Then, having given over that Russian Colt, I followed Kyra upstairs. Having closed the door on us, her manner changed. It was not merely that she wept—which she did—it was that she seemed to acquire a certain helpless dignity. It was as if everything was happening in spite of herself, and those large, lambent eyes were being opened with oyster knives, and those tears had been made, film upon film, the precious product of a generation or two of irritation. But for me she let them fall, in such a manner that I wanted to have them mounted or, at least, strung on catgut.

Soon she composed herself, dried her eyes on the backs of her hands, and asked me haughtily for a handkerchief. When I said that I was temporarily out of handkerchiefs she said, with dignity, that the tail of my shirt would do; and helped herself to it. Then she said, "Mr. Laverock, I don't know if you noticed what I have to put up with? If you want my opinion, I do not believe that Costas is altogether in his right mind. In spite of your appearance, Mr. Laverock, I believe you to be a gentleman. Could you swear on your word of honor to keep a confidence?"

Already under the impression that this lady believed I had robbed her of her honor, I kissed her hand—which tasted bitter and gave me a splitting headache almost instantaneously. She continued: "You see how he is. No, I beg you, don't pat my hand or it might go off. I must leave him, Mr. Laverock, or God knows what might happen to me. You remember, of course, that you have given me your word of honor as a gentleman? Then tell me something: are you going into town on Sunday?"

With all the courtesy in the world, I said, "For you, anything."

"I must get away," she said. "I must go to my aunt. But if he sees me leave the house with a suitcase, he will kill me. Will you do something for me? All I ask is that you take my suitcase to

Charing Cross Station and put it in the cloakroom. It will cost about sixpence. I'll give you the sixpence—"

"Oh, for goodness sake, don't let's discuss that," I said.

"And you will bring back the check?"

"Of course I will," I said. "But what *is* that stuff your brother's cooking?"

"It is an old-fashioned recipe," she said. "When it cools, you add to it one other ingredient and make something like marzipan. But let us forget that. You will take my suitcase Sunday? I can have faith in you?"

"Oh, absolutely," I said.

"In it there will be some heirlooms—Crown Derby china—so you must not drop it."

"Oh, I won't drop it," I assured her. "Incidentally, why don't you get Copper Baldwin to give you a hand with that clock? Honestly, Copper can do anything with a screwdriver."

"I only ask favors of people I love," said she. "Now let's work this out. You see how insanely jealous Costas is. Will you be catching the nine o'clock tram, darling? It is better that we know exactly. Only you must swear not to let me down."

"I've got to catch the nine o'clock tram," I said, "and I promise not to let you down."

"Then I will have my suitcase ready for you at precisely eight-thirty. Only you must swear to me to be careful with it. Simply take it to the cloakroom at Charing Cross and leave it there. Look, here is a shilling. You can keep the change if you like."

"That is quite all right," I said.

"I will send you a post card from my aunt's. Thank you. And now I had better go and help my crazy brother with his marzipan. . . . Do you, by any chance, happen to want me first?"

"Exactly at this moment—forgive me—my main desire is to take my shoes off and put my feet in cold water."

"Ah, you're lucky you are not a woman. . . . Thank you, thank you." She kissed me tenderly with bitter lips and tiptoed downstairs, where I heard her calling Costas all the permutations and combinations of the reproductive organs in four languages—not counting Greek, which I do not understand.

I should have had more sense, of course; but it was the Greenburgers that, literally, put me off the scent. And it never occurred to me to ask myself what she was doing with a broken clock at that hour of the night: Sam Yudenow's place was in a state of permanent debility and perpetual repair, and everybody had to turn his hand to everything and anything, no matter what time it was. Only a matter of two nights previous I had had to get up and eject from the cinema a stray dog which had secreted itself in the orchestra—attracted, it was assumed, by the odor of the violinist's feet—and had howled there, disappointed of carrion, far into the night. Was it for me, therefore, to raise an eyebrow at a restaurateur doing a bit of cooking while his sister tinkers with the works of an old clock? I have always been sympathetic to both occupations, cookery and clockwork. Without claiming to be good at either hobby, I insist that they do no harm to anyone but yourself provided you have not the pernicious habit of begging your friends to taste your latest version of a simple old dish. I nearly killed somebody once with a *rissole*. It was not that I put marjoram in it—it was that somehow or other it happened to contain the hairspring and several cogs of a Waterbury watch which I was playing about with.

But I could not get that bitter taste out of my mouth or that crumbly sensation out of my eyes. If this were not enough, my heart was going like a trip hammer and my skin in general reminded me of something I had read about a Mexican patriot named Zapata. His apologist, a German-Californian whose name I cannot recall, said that Zapata, like Villa, was not a cruel man; only if he killed you he liked you to know what was going on—for days, if possible. Otherwise, where was the point in killing you? Quite right, too; once you grasp mestizo psychology it is astonishing how clear and simple everything gets. It appears that this man Zapata used to peg people out on an ant heap and smear their eyes, armpits, and genitals with honey. A busy man, he could not wait to see the end, but my informant wrote that the victim remained conscious until he was practically a skeleton. He had some tricks, also, with telegraph wire that took you four days to die—but these do not apply here. Then again, he had an innovation of the thorn-bush game. There exists, in Mexico, a flowering bush full of formidable thorns, which grows at the rate of a couple of inches a day. The Mexicans are easygoing people, children of nature and lovers of music. So all Zapata needed to do was, tie you to one of those bushes while it was sprouting, sit down with a guitar and a bottle of mescal, sing "*La Cucaracha,*" and let natural history take its course. I began to understand what this felt like, that night. Similarly, I began to get the idea of Villa's trick with the bull hide. There is no cruelty involved; it is simply a way of thinking. Skin a steer. While the hide is still wet, sew somebody up in it very tight, and leave him in the sun; roll a cigarette and—preferably with a guitar—wait in the shade. As the hide dries, it contracts, squeezing its contents out from both ends. This takes only thirty-six hours.

So I felt, and I wondered why. And since I could not sleep, I wondered harder and harder. My mind went back to the kitchen and what I had seen there. Now, nervous and bewildered as I was, letters and figures started to dance behind my eyes. Nitric acid and glycerin? What kind of marzipan was this? . . . Then, suddenly, a formula clicked into place in my head. It may have been that my mind was running on figures, since I had been working on the return sheets that evening, and I never was good at figures. But this formula obsessed me like a half-forgotten tune:

$$C_3H_5(OH_3)_3 + 3HNO_3 = 3H_2O + C_3H_5(NO_3)_3$$

And it occurred to me, belatedly, that Costas was cooking nitroglycerin. My reaction was: *It would certainly be criminal to allow Kyra to stay in this house a moment longer than necessary. I must certainly get her luggage to the station first thing Sunday morning and go about my business afterward.* Then I sat up with what must have been a kind of yelp. I remembered that nitroglycerin is one of the unstable high explosives. There is no way of knowing how to take it: you may walk around with a pint of it in your pocket, and nothing will happen; or you may wave your finger at it, or cough in its presence, and up it goes. Three or four ounces of it will wreck at least one story of a house—any house, let alone this. According to my calculations, Costas had at least a gallon and a half of the stuff under steam in the kitchen.

But such was my character so many years ago that I said to myself, *It would serve Sam Yudenow right*—and went to sleep.

It seems that I forgot I was on the premises.

Kyra's suitcase was standing in the passage on Sunday morning. It was not so much a suitcase as half a trunk—one of those antproof things, lined with zinc, that people take to the tropics. It was of remarkably light weight for its size, so that I almost fell over when I lifted it. At this, Kyra clung to me, whispering, "You do not know your strength. Be careful, Mr. Laverock, be careful of the Crown Derby china, and for *my* sake don't fail to leave it at Charing Cross!" Then she gave me something like a running sheet: I was to catch the nine o'clock tram; change at such-and-such a place for the bus; and arrive at Charing Cross Station (give or take a few minutes) not a minute later than eleven-forty-five. And she gave me a shilling, which, not wishing to hurt her feelings, I dropped into the breast pocket where I generally keep a handkerchief for show. I have that shilling still.

"Hurry!" she whispered, and I promised that I would, saying that I had quite a bit of business of my own to attend to that day.

"And you're all dressed up too," I remarked, wishing to be amiable.

"Oh, go—go—go!" she said, in a hushed voice, between her teeth.

So I went, and she ran away to the kitchen. I was in no hurry; it was only a quarter past eight. I ambled rather than walked toward the tram terminal. Halfway there I met Copper Baldwin, who asked, "Shooting the moon, cocko? Doing a flit? . . . 'Old on a minute, cock, who's bag's that you got there? I bet you I've seen that one before."

I said, "It's the property of a lady, between ourselves, and if you must know I'm leaving it at Charing Cross Station for her."

"Oh, you are, are you? Charing Cross Station, is it? What's it got in it? Death-tick beetles or something?"

"Why death-tick beetles?" I asked.

"Bloody well sounds like it. Or clocks."

"I suppose a lady's personal property might contain a clock," I said.

"I suppose it might. Well, anyway, you got bags o' time. I'll walk you to the terminus and we'll 'ave a cuppa."

"Come along by all means, Copper, but I don't think I fancy a cup of tea."

"Oh, yes you do. 'Ere, let's 'ave that bag."

"Carry it if you like," I said, "only be careful. It's got some valuable Crown Derby china in it."

"I won't shake it," said Copper Baldwin. And so we strolled to the tram terminal, where there was a humble and unacceptable apology for a café, owned by a bald old lady whose tea was notorious the length of the tram line for its potency and astringent qualities. The drivers and conductors used to call her "Ma." For threepence she gave them a pint jug of her appalling brew; only they had to leave sixpence deposit on the jug—they might be transferred to another route, or elope, or emigrate, or fall dead. It was always a safe place to wait; the trams had to stop there, and the drivers had no objection to pausing for a little badinage while they steadied their hands after the jolting ride.

Copper Baldwin said, "Mine enemy's dog though it 'ad bit

me . . . No, I'd put the tea on the wound. But I've got a bit of gin in my pocket, and you can 'ave a bite if you like."

"Well, not that tea," I said.

"Is that a clock you got in 'ere, or a bloody woodpecker?"

"Come to think of it, it does tick a bit, doesn't it?"

"You spat a bootful, it ticks! Blind O'Reilly, I never 'eard such ticking since my father's aortic aneurism burst. Let's 'ave a dekko inside this 'ere case."

"Over my dead body!" I said. "I'm entrusted with this. It's a lady's property."

"Kyra's?"

"No discussion, if you don't mind, Copper."

In his moody, ruminative way he muttered, "People think that Greek is tough. But 'e's watered butter by the side o' that bitch. Piss against the edge of a knife."

I said, "Now that you mention it, Copper—never mind the knife, but . . ."

"You want a leak? Go back o' Ma's place. Avoid the lavatory even at two feet—tram drivers use it. Use the wall. Nobody looks except Ma and she's blasé. I'll mind this 'ere keyster for you while you're gorn."

"Thanks, Copper. But don't drop it—it's full of valuable Crown Derby china."

"I'll sit on it."

And, in fact, when I came back he was sitting on it, picking his teeth with one of his screwdrivers. The tram arrived and the driver and conductor bounded out for their jugs of tea and their few seconds of persiflage with Ma. I got Kyra's case aboard, and said to the conductor, "I'll hold this with me, if you don't mind —it's full of precious Crown Derby china."

He said, "My poor old mother had a china clock too—only it was French." And now that I came to think of it, the ticking inside that zinc-lined suitcase got louder and louder.

Since I was the only passenger, the conductor got cozier and cozier. He was a man to whom I took an instant dislike. He had a certain confidential air. "Been in long?" he asked.

I said, "I'm sorry, I'm afraid I don't know what you're referring to. In? In where?"

With an air of disgust, he said, "Oh, I get it. Raffles. Okay. . . . Now to come back to the matter of this 'ere Crawn Darby china, plus the clock: 'ow much a piece was you going to flog it for? Because, between men o' the world, for real Crawn Darby I could get you as much as sixpence a cup and saucer. Carm on, open it, and I might go as 'igh as eightpence."

"I do not know what the bloody hell you are talking about," I said, "but this case and its contents are somebody else's property."

He invoked the excrement of the bull and, not without reason, said, "Crawn Darby china from Fowlers End?—" Then, to paraphrase: "Innumerable gonads on that, for a copulating lark! See this jug? Black as ink, ain't it? Kind of a jam jar, ain't it? That's as near as *you*'ll get to Crawn-bloody-Darby round Fowlers End. Besides, what's it ticking for? Carm on, let's look-see."

I took hold of him where the arm joins the shoulders and shook him a little. To deal plainly, my nerves were getting a little frayed. But I was polite as I could be when I said to him, "Forgive me. It is not in my nature to talk in this tone of voice to gentlemen upon whom the public rely, but if you do not watch your step—so help me!—I will tear your bloody head off and stick it up your arse and call it fistula. You'll forgive my mentioning it, I hope."

He said, "Leggo my arm."

"That," I said, "if you don't mind my saying so, I would stuff down your throat. But first I would beat it digestible over the top of your head. Now, will you have the goodness to keep your hands off my property?"

Cowed, the conductor said, "Honest, guv, I never meant nothing by it. Only I thought if you was going to plong and wallop a bit o' stuff . . . Well, piss me, ain't *I* entitled to a bit o' the ting-a-ling? I mean, where's your buggerin' democracy? No, I mean, what 'ave we fought for? No need to go screwing a transport worker's arm orf, what the sod! Way I look at it, you're a bit of a tea-leaf. Well, Gord Almighty—I'm ideologically an atheist but use the term for convenience—way I look at it, spoil the Philistines bofe ways. You take it from the bourgeois, and a good job too. I take it orf you. It's the same as taking it orf the bourgeois. Ain't it? Only I give it back to the belly of the working class where it was took from. But is there any need, Comrade, to go twisting a fellow worker's arm orf?"

I intimated that I would twist off not only his arm but other vital portions of his anatomy if he did not leave me alone. The brutality of Fowlers End was getting me, I suppose.

The conductor withdrew and came back with a copy of the *Sunday Special,* turned back to a headline which said:

I.R.A. OUTRAGE AT WATERLOO

Suitcase of Dynamite Explodes

Time Bomb in Cloakroom Kills Three

The article went on to say that the cloakroom attendant had been alarmed by a loud ticking noise coming from a fiberoid suitcase that had been deposited there by a man in a black hat. He was not quite sure whether the depositor was wearing a mask but remembered the number of the slip. Rendered uneasy, by some sixth sense, he called the police, who, uncertain of the law pertaining to this matter and having no right to break the locks and look at the contents of the suitcase, banged on it with their fists; whereupon its contents exploded. A matron was taken to a near-by hospital to have a brass lock removed from one of her founts of motherhood, and two cloakroom attendants and a policeman were killed on the spot.

"And how is this supposed to concern me?" I asked.

He did not reply in words, but turned a page and pointed to another smaller item:

CYPRUS OUTRAGES

Desperate Measures Threatened
Cypriots to Demonstrate

As the story ran, there was a movement to give Cyprus back to Greece. Since Greece was hopelessly insolvent and Britain (those were the days!) was not, the Cypriots had nothing to gain and everything to lose by such a move. But someone had given them a slogan: ENOSIS—which, it appeared, caused confusion. ENOSIS, I gathered, meant something like "union." The much-traveled Cypriots—the waiters, the kitchen porters, and what not—who had scraped the trenchers of half a dozen languages and carried the spat-out leavings away under their celluloid shirt fronts, mistook the word for AMESSOS, which means "At your service." Somebody threw a dynamite bomb at the garrison; only, having been bought off a Syrian, it turned out to be nothing but five sticks of shaving soap. The detonator went off with a sharp crack; a hopeful prowling dog was splashed with soap. Then there had been a demonstration. After all, it was little enough they asked for, the Cypriots maintained: simply, in the name of independence, our strong point in the Mediterranean to give to Greece to sell to Russia. . . . In general, there was going to be hell to pay.

Tick-tick-tick-tick went Kyra's suitcase, while I handed the newspaper back to the tram conductor and told him, as politely as I could, to go to the devil. He did so—I mean, of course, to the devil of avarice and acquisitiveness that lived under his blue tunic—and I, idiot, hugged the suitcase, figuring while I listened to the heavy metallic *tick-tick-tick-tick* that came from inside it, amplified by its zinc lining. . . .

Nitroglycerin. Electric batteries. Clocks. . . . Kind of a questionable concatenation, I thought. Apply all this to the cloakroom at Charing Cross during a Cypriot demonstration after an open threat of violence, and there was something extraordinarily fishy about it. I began to sweat—not at the thought of a wrecked station echoing with the screams of mangled women and children, but at the idea of my Uncle Hugh identifying my remains and saying, "If only he had taken my advice . . ."

The tram stopped and I went to catch the bus. Looking back, I saw that tram conductor running. He stopped on one foot between a policeman and a telephone booth. It was possible almost to feel waves of cupidity emanating from him. Just as I caught the bus, I saw him make up his mind and plunge into the telephone booth: he was reasoning, of course, that there might be a reward out for me. Upon my word, I could almost see the workings of his vile mind in so many diagrams. . . . Very likely there was a reward for the apprehension of the likes of me and the prevention of the commission of such an act as he suspected me of. If not, the railway or the insurance company would certainly come down with something handsome. Then, judicially, a hat might be passed round among those who hadn't been hurt but could have been.

So he got on the phone. It was not that I disapproved of the conductor's action in this matter: his greed and his perfidy annoyed me, so I was determined at all costs to circumvent him. As I have said, I am curiously without fear; but I have nerves, like the next man. Kyra's suitcase seemed to get hot between my knees, and its ticking made its way into every joint in my body. Also, I have a social conscience, and there were about forty other people in the bus. Opposite me a nice old lady in a bonnet was soothing a little girl in plaits with peppermints. The child was weeping with an abandonment of grief such as I have seldom heard before or since. I gathered that she had a Teddy bear and one of its eyes had come out. Cross-examined, she confessed that, trying to put the Teddy bear's eye back, in moistening it with her tongue, she had swallowed it. . . . And, to my left, sat a hearty young woman carrying a lusty little boy with round eyes who could not be dissuaded from sucking his thumb. But she didn't mind—she was eating butterscotch, which, between her powerful teeth, sounded like breaking glass. There was a nice old gentleman, too—a clean old gentleman in a black coat and gray trousers—with that heart-rending air of meekness which decent old people cannot help assuming when they feel their age and have a tendency to ask, ten times a day, if they are a burden to you. And of course, they *are* a burden to you; children are a burden to you, you are a burden to yourself; what is the matter with a burden? "It makes muscle," as Copper Baldwin would say, adding, "provided it don't break your bloody heart."

And *tick-tick-tick-tick* went the suitcase.

I guessed that Kyra had timed her bomb according to the schedule she had drummed into my head; but I was afraid the bus might be late. I swear that in all the tortuous history of London transportation, there never were such intolerable delays as on that Sunday morning. Everybody wanted to go to town. The hearty young woman with the thumb-sucking son confided to me, "I'm taking the nipper to the zoo. You ever been to the zoo?"

"Now and again," I said.

"He wants to see the lions fed. You ever see the lions fed, young man?"

"When I was young," I said.

Then the old gentleman must pick on me and say out of the blue, "Ah, you might not believe it to look at me, but I got my wound at the Battle of Omdurman, yes I did! Winston Churchill was there, he was, not that I see him—"

"Oh, now, stop it, Grampa," the young woman said.

He stopped it, but said, "I don't want to poke my nose in where it's not wanted."

To the heartbroken little girl with the half-blind Teddy bear, I said, "I'll bet you you never saw a Teddy bear with a silver eye," and took out a sixpence. It fitted the furry orbit to perfection. She took a peppermint out of her mouth and gravely offered it to me. There was—because, perhaps, it wasn't raining—a prevalent holiday atmosphere. Even the bus conductor, pointing with a sour smile to a courting couple at the front of the bus, said, "Billing and cooing. Wait and see. The cooing's the woman's department; but wait till it comes to the bills."

It seemed to me that everybody was incredibly happy. I recognized myself, again, as one of the most stupid men that ever walked in the mud. "Stop the bus and let me off," I said abruptly.

"This is only Euston," said the conductor.

"That's fine."

I got off, with that suitcase, and looked for a policeman. There was none in sight. I looked at my watch. It said twenty past nine, and my heart leaped up—until I noticed, by the seconds hand, that the watch had stopped. A clock over a pawnshop said five to twelve. Another, outside a bakery, had stopped several years previous at twenty past nine. Desperate, I called a taxi and, in the melodramatic style, shouted, "Ten shillings if you will get me to the nearest police station in five minutes!"

The driver said, "Gimme fifteen bob if I get you there in one minute?"

"Yes, yes!"

" 'Op in. Put your trunk in front?"

"No, no!"

"Okay, guv, take it easy. We'll get you there, don't you worry." Then he simply turned his cab round and stopped, saying, " 'Ere you are then. Six tosheroons, I think you owe me. I mean, you *said* the *nearest* police station."

"But I was standing right outside it," I protested.

"That's right. And let me tell you, many another man would've taken you to the other end of town and back—"

There was no time to argue. "Have you change for a pound?" I asked.

"Now let me see," said he, unbuttoning two overcoats and a

waistcoat, scratching his head, undoing a cardigan, lifting a pullover, and slapping himself. "Fact is, guv, I come out today without a float. But if you like—"

"Keep the change!" I shouted. "Why, you didn't even put your flag down!"

"Werll, I mean to say, what for? That's the trouble wiv the present generation: no social sense. Are you aware of the fact that wear and tear of machinery is equivalent to working hours of manpower? So I should put my bleeding clock dahn? Let me explain—"

"Don't!" I said, and ran into the police station.

Now there is something about the atmosphere of an English police station that hardens the evildoer but strikes terror into the heart of the innocent. The man at the desk looked at me like the Angel of Death—he didn't want to do it but he had to—and the conversation went somewhat as follows:

"Yes, sir? Lost something, sir? Found something, sir? What's the trouble, sir?"

"I beg your pardon, Sergeant. . . . I hate to disturb you on a Sunday. . . . But this suitcase contains enough nitroglycerin to blow up half the city. And I'm sorry to say it's due to go off at any moment now."

"Your name, please?"

"Couldn't that wait till afterwards?"

"Address?"

"I'm warning you—"

"What's your occupation?"

At this moment the telephone rang and the Sergeant said, "No, sir . . . Yes, sir . . . By all means, yes, sir. Greek carrying a bag of dynamite. All right, sir. I'll make a note, sir. . . . Six foot one, stoops, talks good English. . . . I got that—"

"Yes, with a scarred face and a broken nose!" I cried.

"Scarred face and broken nose," repeated the officer at the desk. "How did I know? I thought you said so, sir."

"Fourth finger of left hand missing," I said.

"Don't worry, we'll find it. . . . Don't worry, sir, I'll post a sharp lookout. Good-by, sir." Then, to me, "What d'you want to beat about the bush for? Couldn't you say in the first place something was missing? Where'd you see it last? Speak up. On your left hand, I believe you said. A ring, was it? Description, please."

"If you do not take this thing off my hands," I said, "I will not be answerable for the consequences."

"Let me smell your breath."

Tick-tick-tick-tick went the suitcase. Almost weeping with vexation, I said, "This box has got a time bomb in it, due to go off at any moment. I warn you—"

"*I* warn *you*, none o' these larks. What d'you want? First, you've lost a ring. Now you've found this little trunk. Well then, why don't you take it to the Lost Property Office? Oh, well, all right, fill in this form. If it is not claimed within six months, et cetera—"

Then a jolly-looking old jailer came to my rescue, saying with wheezy good nature, "I think the gentleman's got it into his head that there's explosives in this case. Why not open it up and have a dekko?"

The Sergeant looked at me closely and said in a knowing manner, "And it seems to me this person, or persons, has got a broken nose, too." He shot a question at me: "*Parlez-vous* Greek?"

Hopping from one foot to the other, I replied, "*Non, mais cette* Goddamned trunk *est* stuffed miv $C_3H_5(NO_3)_3$. *Écoutez donc, comme elle* ticks, *pour* Christ's sake!"

"I thought so," said the Sergeant. "Repeat that, please, while I take it down."

The jolly jailer said, "Look, mister, save time and public money, and open it up."

"I haven't got the keys!"

The man at the desk said, "He's not here on a charge. No right to search him without his permission. Better fill up a form."

"I *do* detect a kind of ticking noise," said the jailer dubiously. And he produced from some recess in his clothes what might be described as a Brobdingnagian charm bracelet hung with a thousand little keys. He squinted at the locks on the case and found the right key at once, lifted the lid and stood back. All that came out was a stale smell.

Fascinated, tense in throat and stomach, I watched the Sergeant uncovering a knobbly object surrounded by old newspapers and covered with an old stained camisole. It was tamped in by a variety of old socks and a suit of woolen combinations worn into holes like a fishing net. At last were exposed a cheap alarm clock and two dry batteries in a tangle of wires with shiny, newly cut ends—nothing more. The hands of the clock stood at precisely twelve-thirty; I noticed this, because I didn't know where else to look—and, right on the dot, the alarm went off in a tintinnabulation that frightened me into a state bordering on idiocy, so that between that and relief I could not hold back a high peal of laughter.

Then the Sergeant let me have it. He had been a Lance-Sergeant in the Guards, in his time. It was not so much his vocabulary but his command of the most injurious phrases and epithets in the English language; and what he said to me I do not like to think about, let alone make public. He wanted to charge me with something—obstructing the police, for example—but, finding himself in a false position, decided to be merciful. It was hoaxers like me, he swore, that lost us half a million men at Passchendaele, and if he had his way he would take me into the cells and give me a bloody good hiding. Henceforward, he assured me, he would have his eye on me. If it were not for a corrupt administration, he would in any case squash me against the wall like a bedbug, drive me into the floor like a tintack—tough as I no doubt thought I was—belt me, scoff me, and in general make my life unbearable. When, about here, I asked if I might please have a glass of water, the jolly jailer intervened before the Sergeant fell dead of apoplexy and, citing some obscure law whereby they cannot apply the thumbscrew, crush to death a prisoner who refuses to plead, or refuse an accused man a drink of water, took me to the back of the police station and offered me, in the coziest of the cells, a mug of tea and a slice of cake.

He was a fatherly kind of fellow and gave me advice, namely: "You college boys are always up to larks. But don't you try that one here again, that's all I'm telling you, because there's about nine counts we could get you on. Drink your tea, grab your bag, and take your lucky."

So, burning with shame but faint with relief, I took Kyra's suitcase to Charing Cross Station, where I proposed to check it in the cloakroom.

The clerk said, "One moment, please," and disappeared. About half a minute later I found myself surrounded by big men in undistinguished clothes, one of whom said to me, with all possible politeness, "Excuse me, but would you happen to mind if I happened to have a little tiny look inside that case of yours—if you're sure it wouldn't be too much trouble to let me have the loan of the keys for just a moment?"

"Oh," I said, "look as much as you like. Only I haven't got any keys."

"That's funny, isn't it?"

Meanwhile, a crowd was gathering. I remember that a matron pointed at me, shouting, "Serve 'im right!" Then she asked her neighbor, "What's 'e done?" A space was cleared by the police. One of the cloakroom clerks fainted away while the polite detective opened Kyra's suitcase very easily with a hairpin and a penknife. Seeing that there was nothing inside it but old newspapers, dirty washing, two batteries and an alarm clock, he became annoyed. He, too, gave me a lecture, but only a mild one.

I stopped it by asking, "And is there any law which says that a gentleman may not carry such articles in a suitcase? Are we living in the Middle Ages?"

He said no, not exactly, but orders were orders. So I checked Kyra's suitcase. The clerk, who had been brought to with a dose of water, banged it down on a shelf and started the bell of the alarm clock ringing again; at which he fainted again. I couldn't blame him: they were hard times for cloakroom clerks—if it wasn't dynamite from the I.R.A., it was dead babies or portions of unidentifiable female torsos. Once some practical joker deposited a horse's liver in a tin trunk one summer's day and went away never to be heard of again.

It seems that I fell into this class because, although he said nothing more, the polite detective followed me with such a look that it seemed to go right through my back like two knitting needles.

It would appear that I was born to be misunderstood, and to misunderstand.

I had duties to perform, arduous and unpleasant ones, for which I never was spiritually equipped: I had money to borrow—and while I was convinced that on the Cruikback deal I could return my investors at least seven hundred per cent, I felt that I was on a begging errand. To keep up my strength, I went to a teashop and ordered poached eggs on mashed potatoes. By God knows what miracle of divided consciousness, I put my elbow into it.

12

June whistler was wearing, again, that preposterous gown; and she had been otherwise busy with needles and crochet hook. She had made five pairs of diminutive woolen boots and was working now on a cashmere layette, crooning in a clear sweet voice (but it only had one note) some kind of lullaby, of which I remember only these lines:

Good night, brother squirrel, to bed I must go,
I spend all my winters in sleeping, you know . . .

When I came in she cried, "Daddy!" and offered me a sedate embrace, almost at arm's length.

"You mustn't be too rough with me. I can distinctly feel kicking."

"What, already?" I asked.

"I'm awfully healthy, you know, and with some people the little baby develops quicker than in others. Thank God I come of good sound yeoman stock! Really, you know, it's quite unnecessary to gestate for nine months. It runs in my family. I was born at seven months, and even then they had to get me out with steel forceps. I come of a healthy breed. Oh, darling, I was so looking forward to seeing you! What a pity we can't make love."

After what I had been through that day, it would have been a great relief to go to bed with this charming girl with the manzanita hair. In fact, it seemed unreasonable not to. If she were indeed pregnant, by her own reckoning she couldn't be more than twelve days gone.

"At this stage," I said hopefully, "I'm sure it couldn't hurt." I could not help adding, with some irony, "Or are you afraid, perhaps, that I'll get kicked?"

She replied gravely, "No, it isn't that. I got *The Midwife's Handbook* out of the library, and at this stage the foetus is head downwards. So the kicking is upwards. And it looks like a dog, a little dog."

"Do you think it might bite me then?"

There was no stopping her, for the moment. She ran on: "The human foetus goes through all kinds of stages. Isn't it marvelous? You'd be surprised at the stages the human foetus goes through. In our family we skip a few of them, but generally you look like a tadpole, and then a fish, and then a dog—only instead of limbs you've got buds, little buds—" Evidently she was thinking of roses, or something. "And at last there is a real human being with a soul. And it doesn't hurt, really; and it needn't be expensive. I didn't hurt my mother a bit, only it cost thirty-five shillings for ether. . . . I beg your pardon, were you trying to be sarcastic just now?"

"Tadpoles, dogs!" I muttered. "I beg your pardon, sweetheart, only I've had a hard morning. Honestly, June, I'm prepared to take my chance of being bitten or kicked as the case may be. Really, I'm quite a strong man. I've already been kicked by pretty hefty fellows. And at twelve days, even if this foetus had teeth on it like a mastiff, isn't it so to speak imprisoned for the time being? I mean, be reasonable. It might look a bit like a dog, but it isn't, so to speak, kept on a chain to bite people. I cannot consider you, darling, as a kennel. As for its turning out a human being, you can believe me from current experience, the odds against that are about a hundred to one. It won't mind. Come on, June?"

"Oh, darling, if only it was yesterday!"

"And what was it yesterday? An amoeba, or something?"

"I'm trying to make you understand. It was the little birdies that go *tweet-tweet-tweet*," she said.

"This I do not understand."

"Well, if you want me to put it in plain English, I was squiffy, and twittered." And when I still failed to grasp her meaning, she said, "Wait a minute," and got out *What Every Girl Should Know*, turned the pages until she found the item she wanted, which she marked for me with a delicate pink thumbnail. Feminine euphemisms never fail to amuse and astonish me; women will employ the vilest vulgarisms and the most sickeningly allusive argot rather than the clean scientific term. June Whistler was simply menstruating.

There are certain situations in which all you can do is slap yourself violently on the forehead. This was one of them. I swallowed several times and then said, "Look here, June. After a delay of four days you start naming your future son—"

"Five days."

"Then you start knitting dozens of pairs of little woolen boots—"

"Only five pairs," she said, her eyes filling with tears.

"On top of that you menstruate—"

"Don't *use* such language in my house! I had the red flag out."

"Excuse me, I will not use any such sickening roundabout talk. Then you start making cashmere layettes. For God's sake!"

She said, "It's in *The Nurse's Vade Mecum*: often a girl can squiff up to the eighth month. And I think you're being absolutely beastly!" Her anger being aroused, she tore up the *Sunday Express*; relented, wept, wiped her eyes on one of the little white boots, and said, "Comfort me, Daniel—I did so want my little Belisarius."

I couldn't help it: this was the crowning absurdity of the day. "Little Belisarius!" I cried, and burst into helpless laughter. "Little Belisarius!"

She hurled the nurse's *Vade Mecum* at me, missed, but followed it up with an eccles cake, which, by good fortune, hit me on the chin. I say good fortune because, at the sight of this little round cake sticking to my face, her anger vanished and this best-hearted of women began to laugh. Then she contemplated the baby boots and the partly finished layette and said, "I can unravel them and make you a sweater."

"It would be better," I said, "to give them to Dr. Barnardo's Home."

This idea brightened her up considerably. "I'll finish the layette," she said, "only I'll stipulate, definitely, that the child they go to must be called Belisarius."

I said, "For God's sake, sweetheart, don't do it! They'll make his life a misery. Say you had a baby of that name. Would you address him as Belisarius? Certainly not. You'd call him Belly. That name would stick to him throughout his life. In any case, gifts of this kind ought to be unconditional." Mirth overtook me again, half hysterical. "Twittering!" I exclaimed, and she couldn't help laughing with me; she was relieved, too, only she didn't want to admit it.

Very tenderly she peeled the eccles cake off my face, scraped its filling off my cheek with a fruit knife, put it back where it belonged, and served it to me with a cup of tea. Then, as if struck with an inspiration, she said, "But perhaps you're hungry?" and produced a small paper packet. Her eyes filled with tears as she assured me, "Really, they're awfully nutritious. Honestly, they absorb twenty times their bulk, and it doesn't take five minutes.

Couldn't I make you a Greenburger—just a little one? Let me lick that eccles cake off your face and fry you a lovely Greenburger?"

I said, "No Greenburgers," and, taking the envelope out of her hand, opened the window, and threw the envelope into the street.

"But this is preposterous!" June Whistler said, in her great-lady manner.

"I dare say," I said, adding, "Twitterer!"

After a spell of helpless laughter she became grave—somewhat in the manner of a little girl who is arranging a cardboard-box funeral for a dead mouse—and said, "This is no laughing matter, you know."

Hardened, perhaps, by Fowlers End, I said, "To me this is a great laughing matter. Sit down, June, and let me talk to you."

She plucked disconsolately at the maternity garment which she expected, somehow, to fit tight in no time at all, brightened, and said briskly, "Of course, you know, I'm awfully frugal. I allowed for taking in. Really, I could turn this into a summer frock under your eyes. . . . Dan Laverock, I won't be laughed at!"

"Shut up and sit down," I said, with a peculiar lisp because the eccles cake I had tried to swallow was still clinging to the roof of my mouth.

"I love it when you talk to me like that. Call me a bitch. Oh, please call me a bitch!"

"I'll see you in hell first!" I cried. "You are nothing of the sort."

"Would you like to bite me?"

"Certainly not," I said, with indignation.

"Not even pinch my breasts?"

"You know perfectly well that I don't go in for such things," I said, "only I want to do something worse to you."

She cried, "Oh, do it, do it! But not where I'm twittering. . . . Will you mark me all over with your talons?"

"I will do nothing of the sort. I was simply trying to say that I wanted to borrow some money off you."

June Whistler said wistfully, "Are you sure you wouldn't prefer to thrash me within an inch of my life?"

"Definitely."

She became pensive then but said in a little voice, "Then will you let me give you my all?"

I said, "Your all, no. Certainly not. On no account your all."

"Why are you so cruel to me?"

"Oh, for Christ's sake, don't be such a bleeding idiot!" I shouted.

"There is no need," said she, with sudden dignity, "I say there is no need to throw a lady's condition into her face. Take my all!"

"Well, what's your all?"

"Seven hundred and eighty-four pounds, eighteen shillings, and fourpence."

"Well," I said, "let me have two hundred and fifty, and I think I can guarantee you five hundred."

"I'd rather you took my all, so long as I get it back."

"This is an investment," I said.

"It would have been so much easier to discuss it yesterday," said she, discontented. "You can hit me if you like, where it doesn't show. Oh, well," she added, upon an enlivening afterthought, "perhaps this is some new, subtle way to hurt me. Have another eccles cake?"

Ignoring this last question, I said, "Do you want to invest two hundred and fifty pounds or do you not?"

"Yes," she said, and went for her checkbook.

"Without guaranteeing the time, I promise you that you'll have five hundred back for it."

Tucking the check into my breast pocket, June Whistler whispered, "I'm sorry there won't be any little Belisarius. I'm oogly-googly-guggly-wug. I mean—" her eyes refilled with tears—"it's not my fault. Don't blame me if I have the snorts. Really, it's in the Bible, somewhere. But you shall have your little Belisarius, believe me. Only, you know, you've got to plant your seed within me, or somewhere. . . . Are you sure that check's enough? Won't you at least take half of my all? . . . Oh, how unkind nature can be! Couldn't I persuade you, for example, to burn me with a lighted cigarette and pretend to strangle me with a silk stocking? I think I've got a cigarette somewhere, and I'm sure I have stockings . . ."

"Perhaps some other time," I said. "Meanwhile—" I tapped the check—"you'll get this back, and with a vengeance."

"I hate to twitter, but it's in the Book of Deuteronomy. Or some Book. I shall wiggle like the devil until I've stopped blooping. Lover, come back to me—oh, damn this squiff!"

So we parted. I felt, somehow, that in taking leave of June Whistler I was taking leave of our senses.

In the street I saw a policeman and four or five Sunday loiterers staring intently at a puddle, so I could not help taking a look over the policeman's shoulder. Something appeared to be festering on the tarmac. As I looked, it grew. It was fascinating to observe how this object was absorbing the puddle. It looked like an unearthly kind of green fungoid porridge. A man touched it with the ferrule of his umbrella, at which it collapsed—only to rise again, while little puffs of escaping vapor made craters in its repulsive surface. The policeman said, "I have been on the force thirty-two years, but I admit that this has got me baffled—" he wrote in his notebook—"this might be important."

An excitable little fellow in a blue shirt and a black hat, probably a minor poet—they often live near the zoo—said, "It's got a smell of decay, but it's growing!"

Observing that the entire packet of June's Greenburger had fallen into a comparatively small body of water, I went away quietly but quickly; because if it was going to go on at this rate, I felt, it might block the street.

Then I went to see my mother. Perhaps she was getting old

and tired: she had stopped being particular in her premonitions and was foretelling everything. She said, "Something seemed to tell me you were coming." Ignoring my protest that I had promised a week before to visit her this Sunday afternoon, she went on, "So I got in extra crumpets and made you a surprise."

"Not meringues?" I asked.

"Eccles cake. You always did adore eccles cake."

Heavily, no doubt, I said, "I did. True, I did." Then I said, "Listen. Do you remember telling me you had a few hundred pounds? Three hundred, I think you said?"

"Actually," she said, "it's more like five or six. I had a feeling—"

"If you lend me some of it, I'll give it back double."

"Oh, my darling Daniel, I've been saving it for you, and I don't want it back double or single, truly I don't. Only I want you to promise me one thing: *Not a word to your Uncle Hugh!*"

"I promise," I said, and, to please her, took another eccles cake, while she went to an old Sheraton cabinet that my father used to love and took out an antique tea caddy, carefully locked, but with the key still in it. From this she dragged a roll of bank notes big enough to choke a horse, saying, "Take it, Daniel, my dear boy, take it."

"Why are you carrying so much loose cash in the house?"

"In case of burglars," she said.

"Couldn't you put it in the bank?"

"I can't, in case of your Uncle Hugh. Oh, do please take it away. Only nobody must know. *Not a word to your Uncle Hugh.*"

I said, "He's not such a bad sort. But I promise you I'll pay you back with a hundred per cent interest."

"If you do, I'll give it straight back to you," my mother said, "but first of all I'll show it to your Uncle Hugh—"

"Oh, damn my Uncle Hugh!"

"Invest it wisely, is all I ask," said she, beginning to cry. "Have another eccles cake—just a little teeny one?"

"I have a long journey ahead of me. Could I take it with me to eat on the way?"

She packed me twelve, and so I went away with a total of six hundred and fifty pounds, eighteen shillings, and sixpence in my pocket over and above what I'd had to start with. The odd sixpence, my mother's, was a Canadian one with a hole in it; I put it in my pocket for luck, and there it rests to this day. Did it bring me luck? I don't know. It is true that I am still alive to tell the tale, but is this luck? I cannot answer this question.

Before going back to Fowlers End, which I had come to regard as home, I went to a coffee shop and had what was ambiguously called a "pie," with boiled potatoes. These nourishing tubers had all the qualities of unscented soap, except that they did not lather. God knows what was in that pie: if you offered it to me now I would hurl it right in your face—but then I enjoyed it.

To my astonishment, when I got back to Fowlers End, Sam Yudenow was there, in a state of rage bordering on the frenetic. Only he had it under control for the time being and was standing like Napoleon on the *Bellerophon* (but he was smoking a cigar and wearing a homburg hat) uttering almost Napoleonic phrases. I have read, somewhere, that Napoleon Bonaparte had a shrill voice. So, today, had Sam Yudenow. But instead of brandishing his fists in my face and calling me *Coglione*, Sam Yudenow said, "The little I ask of life, the minute I turn my back! The Gveek has abdicated. Put that in your pipe and stick it up your arse!"

I asked, "What's up with you?"

"Costas has abdicated," said he, "miv his contortionist of a sister, so-called. Sister! They were living in horrible sin, the no-goodniks! In horrible sin they were living; and that's what happens when Gveek meets Gveek. Uxcuse me, I'm upset. After all I done for this enemy of society, off he goes miv this contortionist! All right, all right, so I always suspected—so? She resisted the advances of the yobbos. This, in itself, was suspicious. Even me, when I tried to touch her a little bit—even me she resisted. Praps, I said to myself, she's got syphorrhea and wouldn't like to unfect me, knowing I got a family, a piano, responsibilities? No. When Gveek meets Gveek, first thing they do they take their clothes off. It's on record. Leverage, did you ever go to the Bvitish Museum? If not, do so—it's got a seating capacity I haven't yet worked out—but that'll teach you Gveeks and Romans. You'd be surprised, Lavitoff, you'd be surprised.

"Some of them went about miv wings dressed like cows: Assyrians, which was a kind of Cypriot. My heart is too full, but the Romans had no bodies. My worst enemies should go bust like those fellows miv their carryings-on! But the Gveeks were the worst lot of bastards of the whole bloody lot. No exaggeration. Look, I've been around—specially in Fowlers End—but the Gveeks I do not know how to describe. I'm sorry, it's not my fault—the men ran around stark bollock naked, except for a helmet, a randy shield, miv a shiv. *Miv* their things hanging out! Believe me, when you were twelve you had such a thing—in marble, yet. And the women? Twenty times worse. What's a Gveek idea of beauty? Confidentially, I'll tell you: to take their arms off above the elbows so they can't defend themselves and then, the crook of the arm in the thvoat, and off miv their drawers. Believe me! Otherwise, would there be so many Gveeks?

"And what do they come to this country for? To make trouble miv the police. *Putric acid* I got in the kitchen; a batch of Greenburgers ruined so they smell like cabbage; and the bloody Gveeks abrogated. I knew it all along; I felt it in my heart. And on top of it, the coppers are here—this is all I'm short of—accusing me of androcity miv putric acid! This reminds me: Mrs. Grue was sick in the aisle, and there's enough acid in that carpet to burn a hole in your stumminck. On this I want you should get cracking. . . . Gveek women: their face is all in one straight line, and they got no holes—I seen it, in museums I seen it. Malnutrition. Give the layabouts a shiv and a shield, and that's all they want, the uncivilized bastards. And putric acid—I suppose they drank it all up, the bloody foreigners! Oh, give me civilization or I don't know what! No, Lavatory, there is a limit to the lucrid. I'm ruined." Then he said, in a different voice, "Would you cook me up a few Greenburgers?"

"No," I said.

I think he meant to quote a play he must have seen in some penny gaff before the turn of the century, saying, "*Et tu, Brute?* Then fall, Caesar!" It came out as: "Ertcher, Brute—I got Scissors—" and pretended to faint. There being no Pompey's statue, he fell into the ladies' lavatory, out of which I hauled him by the lapels of his coat. He moaned, "Cut out that lark, ruffian—this suit cost me seven and a half guineas. Oh, ungratitude!"

He got up, and his lips were trembling now, as he said, "The bogeys ask me, 'So? How come putric acid in the kitchen?' What can I say? I can only say, 'Ask the Gveeks; don't ask me. If you want my opinion, Booligan has got something to do miv this.' I offered them twenty complimentary tickets. They wouldn't take 'em. There was traces mytroglycerin in the Greenburger boiler. I'm a married man—already I'm astigmatized as a blow-off. I count on you."

"What for?" I asked.

That stumped him. He shouted, "I don't want you should ask idiotic questions! I'm counting on you, I told you—isn't that enough?"

"Buy an abacus," I said, "and count on that."

Sam Yudenow rose to the occasion. "What's an abacus?"

"Something you can count on, made of wire and beads."

"Oh," he said, relieved, "we got plenty wire in the genevator room, and a lot of pearl beads. Tell Copper to knock one together. So I'll count on it. In the meantime, what am I going to do about my Greenburgers?"

"Pack 'em dry," I said.

Sam Yudenow said, "I must think—" clutching his forehead

and taking a green pencil out of his pocket—"I must think, Lavenduck. You don't know what a comfort you are to me after those Gveeks. Believe me, you don't know what they are. But Gord will punish them. Look at Socrates—he poisoned himself. Don't think I'm ignorant just because I don't know nothing. One of them went about in a tub miv a lamp: Diogenes. Alexander the Gveat died from alcoholic poisoning after he knifed his best friend. There's show biz for you. Oh, the Gveeks, the Gveeks! Some of them were blind (but that was a poet, so what do you expect?) and mark my words—" he tapped my chest with an impressive forefinger—"they're all dead. If they're so tough, why aren't they still alive? . . . Gveeks!"

"You'll die, too," I told him.

Loftily he said to me, "This is a subject I prefer not to discuss."

"*I* will die."

"Well," said Sam Yudenow philosophically, "I suppose we must make exceptions?"

"But not you? Upon my word, Mr. Yudenow, you shall decay—die and decay, and your flesh shall be eaten by worms. You can take it from me, the worms are waiting . . ."

"Worms I bar."

"Worms you cannot bar, unless you get yourself cremated to ashes."

"Ashes I don't like. Play a game cards—so what you got in the ash trays? Ashes. And they smell. Boy, did you ever get up in the morning and smell an ash tray full of ashes? And where there's ashes there's smoke. No, did you ever come down miv bare feet to ashes, dust, and the curtains full of smoke?"

"No," I said. "I only know the smell of dead smoke. I mean, the smell of live cigar smoke is the soul going upwards. When it is cold and clings, it is rotten—"

"I don't like this kind of talk," said Sam Yudenow. "There is a Gveekishness in it. So cut it out."

Then he left, thoroughly depressed. Before he got into his

big car, he shouted, "And I hate the thought of bloody worms. Get that for a start!"

But I saw in his eyes an anguish, an appeal. He yelled, "What's more, I don't like your altitude!" Then he was driven away.

Copper Baldwin came out of the shadows, smiling his up-and-down smile, and said, with quiet relish, "Scared the balls off him, eh? You should 'ave seen poor old Sam when the Greeks buggered off in a taxi—livid, definitely livid. Then the ice-cream machine broke down, a batch o' Greenburgers got burnt, and when the police came in and a bogey tapped 'im on the shoulder 'e 'ad a kind of convulsion and lost 'is truss. No, I mean it was a scream. Well, this truss sort o' slipped—it was out o' nervousness—and clipped itself onto 'is organs o' reproduction. It's in the Bible, you know, in the Song of Solomon: 'My love put 'is 'and into a hole in the door and my belly shrank at the touch.' Oh boy, did his old bastard of a belly shrink at the touch! You should 'ave 'eard 'im yell, 'Copper! For Christ's sake, Copper!' Plainclothesman says, 'You've got one, Mr. Yudenow: I'm one. And I'd like the favor of a word.' But poor old Sam keeps on yelling, 'A file! Bring a small trilingular file, and get me out o' this!' Naturally, they make a note o' that. Well, I came along, I surveyed the situation, and got 'im out of bondage with an oil can and a tack hammer. Laugh? It's a shame you wasn't 'ere, you would 'ave died."

I asked, "What was the cause of all this?"

"Oh, Costas' trousis exploded. You know, they was cooking soup—I mean, home-made, and that's tricky stuff. He was wearing overalls—I mean, a bib-and-brace—and it seems he must 'ave upset some o' the stuff over 'imself. So when 'e changed to scram, 'e left this bib-and-brace behind 'im. Old Sam comes in, in a rage, to find out why the café ain't open, sees these trousis, and goes berserk. 'E chucks 'em out o' the window, right across the road. They blew down a wall. Somebody 'ad dropped the word, anyway, that there was a dynamite outrage being planned on the premises. So, by sheer chance, the busies got 'ere just when the trousis went bang."

I told him that I, too, had been suspected of an attempt with a time bomb on Charing Cross Station; and that I had had a fine time of it.

He replied, "I shouldn't be a bit surstonished; you bloody near was. Lucky for you, I got at the keyster with my little pair o' pliers while you was out at the back. I disconnected that one." He took down a fire bucket and pointed out twenty-three things that looked like exaggerated sticks of shaving soap. " 'Ome-made dynamite, tell your mum, and by the smell of it about eighty-five per cent nitroglycerin. Before we do another thing, let's get rid of it. If it was anything else, I'd say, 'Chuck it into Godbolt's.' But there's a risk implied 'ere. Lately that vicious bastard 'as been taking to reprisals. I found three dead cats in the vestibule this morning, and one of 'em I distinctly recognized—a drowned tabby we gave 'im three days ago. That bloody boy Tommy 'as been bought over. It's sabotage. What a little *agent provocateur* 'e turned out to be! . . . No, if this was something 'armless, like shit or something, 'e'd be welcome to it. But—and I was in the Engineers, and I know—this 'ere dynamite is unstable. I never did trust that Greek's cooking. What we got to do is, get it out o' the way."

"How?" I asked.

"We could send it to the War Office. Then it goes off, and that's a hanging matter—twenty-odd sticks o' dynamite in Whitehall, and the least you can do is blow the arse off somebody round the Admiralty. Maybe we better bury it."

"Where?"

"I would suggest somewhere round Ullage, in the swamp. Point is, to get it there—I wouldn't trust myself with this stuff on a bicycle, on these roads. Better put it in a shopping bag and walk it."

We did this thing and buried the dynamite in an inaccessible slough. Copper Baldwin comforted me, saying, "It's bound to deteriorate. Sometimes it takes twenty years to go off. But the way we planted it, I think it will just be washed away."

"But say it goes off?" I asked.

"There won't half be a shower of mud," said Copper Baldwin, "but you and me'll be well out o' range, and the cry will be 'Poor old Ullage, serves it bloody well right!' Did you get the bees-and-honey?"

"The money? Yes, I got it," I said.

"Then, after tomorrow, cocko, we are company directors," said he.

"I was one, once," I said.

"I thought there was a peculiar kind o' look about you," he said.

Swallowing this insult, I asked, "Incidentally, Copper, how did the police get the wire on Costas? Who gave them the word?"

Copper Baldwin was lighting a cigarette while I spoke. Before the match flame went out on a puff of smoke, I saw him wink and heard him say, "Ask no questions and you will be told no lies. *Verb sap.*"

13

I ALWAYS CONSIDER the following day, Monday, as the eventful one. This, no doubt, is the quality of youth which takes its history in sips and has no memory.

First of all, I was made into a limited company. Copper Baldwin came in with two hundred pounds, and I produced out of thin air (as it must have seemed) the five hundred pounds I had promised. Misgivings were already getting hold of me, so I kept the remainder next to my skin. This was a most sickening day. It got at my stomach and spoiled my appetite. I felt as I believe Ivar Kreuger felt in the small hours before he did away with himself. The weight of the guilt of the whole world was on my shoulders, and there was a Horatius' Bridge between my gullet and my diaphragm where those behind cried *Forward* and those in front cried *Back*, making a clattering great lump there—a broken formation of myself. As for my heart, it seemed to me that it retrenched. First, it shrank to the size of a marble and made a piteous noise against my ribs; then it got to be, by sheer self-inflation, the size of a lung; but, deflating, got so heavy that I was afraid to take my left boot off. I knew that what was hurting my heel was a nail but—the way I felt that day—I couldn't be sure.

We worked all night getting ready for Monday, the "Change Day," pasting up posters. I was already so nervous that I got myself involved in the sticky side of a twenty-four sheet and slapped down the various parts of a forty-eight sheet upside down and in reverse—which turned out to be the best bit of publicity the Pantheon had ever had. That evening, trying to make head or tail of it and failing in the attempt, Sam Yudenow said to me, "Now this I call nishertive. You're learning, Daniels, you're a comer. Good boy, get the buggers guessing. You and me, we're thinkers, we read. But rahnd Fowlers End, give the sods puzzles. This is originality, and you can regard your wages raised as from any moment now. . . . Between ourselves, confidentially, what *is* this forty-eight sheet?"

I said, "I'm afraid I was a little upset. That forty-eight sheet advertises three different pictures," and waited for the outburst.

But he said, "Quite right. When I get a anspiration, I could show Sam Katz something yet! Grauman? Let 'im keep his Chinamen. Lavendrop, take a pair scissors and get cracking on the eight sheets and the double crowns! . . . Oh, Jesus, will nobody never understand that nobody never understands nothing but what they don't understand—specially rahnd Fowlers End? A yobbo looks at a forty-eight sheet. It says, say, 'Norma Talmadge.' What does that name mean to him? All he can think of, the layabout, is to say, 'So what's Norma Talmadge?' Anyway, as you know, rahnd Fowlers End they only go to the pictures to eat miv one hand a sausage and miv the other to have a feel in the dark sequences. This way, son, you 'ave aroused the public imagination. The public says, 'What the f - - - is this?' And it comes twice. . . . Ah, when Yudenow meets Katz, hire an evening suit!"

I remember, vaguely, that I had put together—thinking they were parts of the same poster—Maria Korda in *Lady of the Pavements*, *The Four Feathers*, and Gloria Swanson in *Sadie Thomp-*

son. People did, indeed, suck their thumbs as they looked. But this was by no surrealistic design of mine: I was so emotionally disturbed on account of impending legal business that once I fell off the ladder and hit Copper Baldwin in the face with the paste brush. He, too, was in a state of exaltation. Having sat down in a paste bucket, he got up and said in a shamefaced manner, "Nothing like this 'as 'appened to me for forty years." Then he went away, convinced that he was drunk, and pasted up double crowns at such extraordinary angles that medical opinion in Fowlers End attributes to this the fact that the old-age pensioners to this day hold their heads on one side. Truly, we had had a hard time of it becoming executives.

First, there was a little argument concerning the name of the company we were going to float. As I reasoned, my mother, June Whistler, Copper Baldwin, and I were shareholders. I counted myself in on more or less metaphysical grounds: it was *my* mother's money, after all, and *my* June Whistler's. My mother's maiden name was Morgan, and June's middle name, as she reluctantly divulged, was Puddingberry. Legitimately combining names, I argued, why not call ourselves "J. P. Morgan"?

Copper Baldwin said, "Cocko, don't carry a good thing too far. But I'll tell you what. My father's name was Baldwin but my mother's name was Steel. What about 'Baldwin Steel'?"

I said, not without irony, "No Rockefellers in your family, by any chance?"

"Thank Gawd we never 'ad no Dutchmen, but there was a Ford—"

"No, wait a minute; a motor company is going to buy our land," I said. "Best not annoy them, perhaps?"

"Could put us in a better bargaining position."

"Oh, don't be silly, Copper—they'd be on the wire in half a second. . . . Look, your nickname is Copper and my Christian name is Daniel—"

"Then, for Christ's sake, call it Daniels Copper Enterprises!

It sounds like metal, and it looks like a five-to-two. I mean, a Jew. Most of the *bourgeoisie* are Gawd's chosen people, and a Biblical name makes their 'air curl."

"So be it," said I heavily.

"Daniels Copper," said Baldwin, with glum satisfaction. "That'll do. Daniels Copper Limited."

It was he who led me to the offices of a firm of attorneys in Chicken Lane, Threadneedle Street, uncomfortably close to my Uncle Hugh. I kept looking over my shoulder, half expecting to see him grinning at my heels and smelling of mixed grill out of Pimm's. Threadneedle Street is formidable, but Chicken Lane is terrifying: it is the ghost of a street. The Great Fire of 1666 skipped it, and the more's the pity. Men digging to lay drains constantly find human bones—victims of the Great Plague of 1665. You can smell them still, if you try. Even on a busy day, when it is full of people coming or going—for nobody seems to have any real business there—it preserves an atmosphere of senile decay. If you want to explore it, go there between Saturday evening and Monday morning, during which period the City lies like a dog in the shade.

We went on a business day. Near the top of Chicken Lane was one of the last of the old cook shops, as we used to call them; one of those places into which one used to walk and ask for a pint of soup and a pennyworth of bread—threepence. There, in the good old days of the depression, they sold meat by the ounce—you could, for example, order four ounces of roast beef, pease pudding, and cabbage, put down a shilling, and get threepence change. I believe it was the forerunner of the cafeteria: you grabbed knife, fork and plate, waited in line, and gave your order to the carver, who justly weighed it out. There were no tables; you ate standing at a shelf, and very good it was, too. . . . I am letting nostalgia get at me again, forgetting that if I had kept the appetite I had in the old times I should by now have sunk into the ground by sheer dead weight. Still, perversely, my mouth waters at the memory of how it used to water at the sight of that bubbly-looking beef and those sizzling sausages. The aroma of the onions permeated the lane. I say nothing of the pork, which, with its glazed surface, was far more beautiful to me than old mahogany to a connoisseur.

Copper Baldwin dragged me past a bookshop, saying, "Yes, I know all about that. Romance. Chuck your life away for 'alf a volume o' Macaulay's *History of England* out o' the penny tub, and go wivout your lunch. It's a bloody mug's game. There's public libraries, aren't there? What was Carnegie for? . . . This is what I love about the capitalist system—they got to take it but they got to give it back. 'Ospitals, the works o' Sir Walter Scott, slum clearance, the League o' Nations, shit-houses, Zionism, the Salvation Army, and pie in the sky—" Getting cantankerous, he argued with himself. "And what's the matter wiv pie in the sky? At least that's one promise you're certain not to live to see unfulfilled."

I said, "For Christ's sake, Copper, shut up. You're making me nervous."

"Then don't be, cocko. You are going to meet Mr. Payne of—" he repeated the name of the firm with relish—"Payne, Payne, Payne, Payne, Rackham, Rackham and Payne."

These old City lawyers—the more names they paint up and the dirtier they get, the more respectable they become. I had a cousin once by the name of Everingsley who qualified and set up in business as a solicitor near Hatton Garden. People shunned him like a leper. But when, acting on the advice of my Uncle Hugh, he called himself Everingsley, Everingsley, Son and Everingsley, he made a go of it.

I believe there was only one Payne, but he looked like a concentration of several generations of them as he sat, making a pyramid of his bony hands and swaying his head like a snake in a stiff collar. I do not know why, but his office made me feel cold through and through. Three of its walls were covered with black-framed certificates of incorporation printed in red; but on the wall over where he sat hung a stuffed trout and a photograph of an old lady who might have been himself in disguise. He kept in a kind of cubbyhole a little woman of an age that I could not determine; but by the odor she gave off I thought he must have kept her there for at least thirty years. And I could just imagine him putting her out at night for five minutes and then locking her up with a saucer of milk while he wriggled away about his nocturnal business. Or flapped, for he wore a morning coat with long tails much too big for him.

My first impulse was to run away, but Copper Baldwin had a nerve grip on me just above the elbow, and his fingers were like steel. So what could I do but bow politely? "Meet Mr. Laverock," said Copper Baldwin, quick as a mongoose.

I behaved like an idiot, pointed to the name of the firm on the glass door, and said, "Mr. Payne? Or Mr. Payne?"

Then June Whistler came in, dressed all in black and wearing a little golden cross on her breast. She must have thought that she was going to be asked to swear to something, because she was carrying a prayer book, brand new. Evidently she had stopped to buy it on the way, at that benevolent place near Cheapside where they sell Bibles and stuff in various languages. As it transpired, June's prayer book was in Swahili, but we didn't need it anyway. Goodness knows what I signed: I only know that I became Managing Director of Daniels Copper Limited. Secretary: J. Puddingberry Whistler. Directors: Percival Clarence Baldwin (I never saw him blush before) and Ezra Payne.

I left my mother out of it: Uncle Hugh would have got to hear of it, and I wanted no discussion with that man. It was not that I didn't love him, only he had no faith in my acumen as a man of business, thereby wounding me in my tenderest sensibilities. Tit for tat, I had long prophesied the collapse of Uncle Hugh and his system—which, by some prestidigitation or trick of catching a point of balance, was still there. But I did not want him to know that I was speculating in real estate; he would only have asked me irritating, unanswerable questions about what had happened to my principles and so forth. . . . And so a hearty laugh, and lunch at Tozer's, a real City man's lunch—a Dover sole; steak-and-kidney pie made with mushrooms, oysters and skylarks; a piece of very ripe Stilton cheese; a glass of port—disgusting! But thinking of it I had a mad desire to excuse myself for ten minutes, rush out to that cook shop, and devour a plate of boiled beef and carrots, simply to clarify my intellect.

We got the business over and done with in no time at all. When we were out of that malodorous office and back in Chicken Lane, I said to June Whistler, "Well, now you are a director of a Limited Company, eh?"

"Hold up, lady!" cried Copper Baldwin, as she fainted in his arms. "It's all right, so am I. . . . If you ask me, the lady wants a drop o' brandy."

She came to in a few seconds and, still clutching her prayer book in Swahili, allowed herself to be led into the private bar of the Wat Tyler, which was almost exactly opposite the cook shop: one of those extraordinary pubs that look forlorn and forgotten but in which big business is done in the City. Coming into a place like Chicken Lane and pushing open the sticky red door of the Wat Tyler, you find to your astonishment well-dressed men, all whispering. This was before the Wat Tyler got a direct hit with an eight-hundred-pound bomb in 1941. It was in all the papers: there were fourteen corpses and seven hundred skeletons—the bomb had turned up another old plague pit under the foundations. That was the night brave London burned, and St. Paul's, marvelously untouched, stood nobly against the flames.

Well, there is no more Wat Tyler now, but there was then and a charming place it was. When I called for brandy, the landlady produced a hundred-year-old bottle of very young liquor which she poured as if it were molten gold, and charged for it likewise. Baldwin and I had ale. At the first sip of brandy, June Whistler, who could not take her eyes off the bottle, revived. "It really is remarkable when you think that Napoleon himself might have drunk this very same brandy," she said.

"Ain't it?" said Copper Baldwin. "Or Stanley Baldwin, or Winston Churchill. Marvelous. You drink it all up, ma'am, and we'll get a bite."

It was impossible not to smell the cook shop, and I could see his Adam's apple working as he swallowed something that was not his pint of ale, which he had finished at a gulp. I said, "Let's go across the road—" my mouth was watering, too—"Let's have boiled ham and pease pudding."

"I'd love that!" said June Whistler.

But Copper Baldwin, with jaunty disdain, said, "That place is for pen-pushers—in celluloid collars. You stand up and eat like a bloody—excuse me, ma'am—like a confounded 'orse at a bloody manger. No, we'll go to Tozer's, where the directors go. They make a special kind o' pie—steak and kidney, oysters and mushrooms, and skylarks."

Dreading to meet my Uncle Hugh, I said, "Come on, Copper, we've got to get back."

June said, "Did you ever read 'Ode to a Skylark'?"

" 'Hail to thee, blithe spirit, Bird thou never wert . . .' " said Copper Baldwin, "and something about 'profuse strains of unpremeditated art.' But economically valueless. One nest o' skylarks will devastate an acre, in season—"

"I couldn't eat a skylark," said June Whistler, her eyes filling with tears, "but I'd like to taste one. . . ."

So we went to Tozer's, where grave and hearty men used to sit in booths and eat themselves half insensible at lunchtime. My appetite had left me. As soon as he set foot in this ancient and somber restaurant, Copper Baldwin showed signs of a desire to flee. All over the place men in stiff collars who were built like cubes were talking millions and writing on the tablecloths.

The waiters alone were worth the money—Tozer made them wear frock coats, and the youngest of them was over sixty. God knows where he found them: they all had the air of scions of some great house, begotten on the wrong side of a monogrammed blanket, who had been kept in the scullery for half a century or so to nurse a terrible grievance. Our waiter was the spitting image of Austen Chamberlain. Frustrated though I was in the matter of the boiled ham and pease pudding, I enjoyed Copper Baldwin's discomfiture. But June Whistler was having a good time.

As if attached to an invisible thread, the little finger of her right hand went up in the air. With this finger she adjusted an errant wisp of hair, while she said to the waiter in a languid voice, "Really, I think I could eat a skylark."

"The pie, ma'am?"

Becoming irritated, I said, "Presumably the lady doesn't want a skylark in a cage!"

"One pie. . . . Gentlemen?"

"Three pies," I said.

"Cocktails?"

"Champagne cocktails," said Copper Baldwin aggressively. "And make 'em double."

The waiter called a wine waiter who looked like Prosper Mérimée, "The Man Nobody Could Love." He took the order with such an air of disgust that I wished I were dead; June Whistler thought him distinguished. There was a busboy, too, who resembled Chopin in the last stages of consumption, and a headwaiter who put me in mind of President Wilson. The proprietor had once been mistaken, in Smithfield Market, for King Edward VII when he was Prince of Wales.

I said to Copper Baldwin, "And what would have been the matter with boiled ham and pease pudding?"

"Better order wine," said he, putting down his empty glass with a grimace.

"Beer," I said.

"What, can you order wallop from that bloke wiv the silver chain round 'is neck?"

"I can and I will," I said. Then the food came, under silver covers. It was common or garden steak and kidney, with foreign bodies in it. I said, "They buy only two or three skylarks in the summer and keep on using the bones—"

But June Whistler did not hear; she was engrossed. While tears trickled down her face, she was saying between substantial mouthfuls, " 'Bird thou never wert' . . . Oh, the cruelty of men! To cut off his melodious pipes . . ."

Copper Baldwin was eating sourly; he knew he was in the wrong. Assured now that my Uncle Hugh was not likely to be in today, I got my appetite back and, having emptied my plate, called for dessert and cheese. I tried to revive the spirits of Copper Baldwin. I made June Whistler keep a skylark bone for luck. The meal had put heart into me. We all felt better. I told preposterous anecdotes about my Uncle Hugh, whom I represented as a species of bloated clown—at the top of my voice, too.

I called for port, I called for brandy and liqueurs, but when I called for the bill—in spite of Copper Baldwin's protests—an assistant headwaiter, who could have stood in for Henry James, said respectfully but very distinctly, "It is *paid*, sir, thank you."

"Paid? By whom?"

"Mr. Hugh Laverock, sir, the gentleman in the booth immediately behind you. Thank you, sir."

Feeling as if every bead of the perspiration that sprang out all over me was a small pin, I leaped to my feet. Oh, indeed, separated from me by about an inch of oak sat my Uncle Hugh, who had been eating chateaubriand and drinking burgundy with a pair of rollicking stockbrokers. As I looked, the wine waiter, with an entirely different aspect from that which he had presented to me, came up with a bottle of unquestionable port.

"Have a nice lunch, Dan?" asked Uncle Hugh.

I could only say, "Thank you, but–"

"Didn't want to barge in on your conference, old boy, but you don't mind if your silly old uncle picks up the bill, I hope? Oh, by the bye–George Chowder, Bill Saulte–my nephew, Daniel Laverock. Introduce your friends?"

There was nothing for it but to do so. Copper Baldwin shook hands in his dour way. But June Whistler, comforted with skylarks and stayed with chartreuse, decided to be amusing. I was tormented by the fear that she might tell my Uncle Hugh about our big deal and tried to drag her away. But she wouldn't come. They made room in the booth and offered B-and-B. There was nothing to do but accept–I was indebted again to that man.

Having swallowed a thimbleful of brandy-and-benedictine, I said, "Must get back on the job, I'm afraid. Look here, Uncle Hugh. This lunch. You mustn't. I mean. No, honestly. After all's said and done."

"Well, all's said and done, my boy, and that's that. But shall I give you a tip? There's an improved sound system coming out, and a new photoelectric cell. Talking pictures are in."

"A mere fad," I said. "A novelty. Are you ready, Copper?"

Ill at ease in such company, Copper Baldwin was very ready indeed; but June Whistler was not. She said, with hauteur, "Really, I can't gulp. It's awfully bad for one. Besides, I got the day off, so I'm a lady of leisure."

So I shook hands with her and my Uncle Hugh, bowed politely to his friends, and left the restaurant with Copper Baldwin, seething with humiliation. I was sure that my Uncle Hugh had overheard every word I had said about him; and the annoying part of it was that he not only took it in good part, he seemed to find it funny.

When we got back to Fowlers End, Sam Yudenow was waiting in the vestibule, looking–with writhing lips and twitching nostrils–at a pitch-black Burma cheroot of the cheapest and vilest kind, which he was holding between thumb and forefinger. "Fire that rewinding boy!" he shouted. "Back to the reformatovy school miv him! Like a millionaire already, so he comes up to me and sticks this in my mouf, and says, ''Ave a cigar!' Is this discipline? Is it right? Laveridge, go and give 'im a bloody good hiding. I would've done it myself, only I was taken off guard. Take this cigar away; put it on Godbolt's doorstep—he'll think it was a dog. It tastes exactly like it. . . .

"What a morning I've 'ad! What a booking I made! I tell you an experience. A veritable *Covered Wagon*, that trade show! And a lovely title: *Sinners Beware!* We all owe a debt to society. This is it. Honest to Gord, it'll frighten the piss out o' the layabouts. And 'ere's the secret of show biz—let me not see a dry seat in the house—give 'em the horrors, the dirty rotten yobbos! *Sinners Beware!* It's all about venereable disease—pox, to you—spine-chilling, frank, revealing. That'll put a stop to all this so-called sexual intercourse! Not that I give a flying bugger if the whole lot of 'em catch black syphogonic cholera so their heads fall off, so long they pay for their seats, the scum. But I'm a funny fellow—I like to be unspirational, the layabouts. So wait till you see this picture, Daniels. You'll never drink another cup o' tea so long as you live without you first boil yourself. And before you touch a woman, paint 'er miv iodine, soak 'er in permanganate of potash. Then run for your life.

"Oh, it's marvelous, it's terrible, it's breath-taking! Draft me some streamers, double crowns, eight sheets, twelve sheets, twenty-four sheets, forty-eight sheets. Never since the *Covered Wagon* 'ave I wished there was such a thing as a ninety-six sheet! *Sinners Beware!* It's clean as a whistle, but we play up the sex angle, get it? It's scientific. It's German. It's all about pox and clap and 'ow to get it—as if the layabouts don't know. Rahnd Fowlers End anybody who 'asn't got clap 'as got pox; the rest are consumptive. So let 'em learn a lesson, the stinkpots! Lavendrock, tell me like a father—*'ave you been drinking tea out of a cup lately?*"

"Well, what am I supposed to drink tea out of? A jam jar?"

"Did I say that?" asked Sam Yudenow. "At home it's different. I got a set from Hacker the Breaker, miv scalloped cups, and my wife is clean as a whistle. Did I say a whistle? As a gentleman I withdraw that statement. What is filthier than a whistle? Everybody breathes into it, and it 'as to be shook out. Spittle comes. When Booligan was 'ere, the police whistle was going day and night. Ever smell the inside of a trombone from the wrong end? Mauseating. Gord forbid that my wife's tea set should be clean as a whistle. Tea we drink, in my house, not gob. . . . But this picture: it's unfantic, it's gryadammatic, it's credible, it's unbelievable! Laveridge, pox is like a snake. They done it like *Mutt and Jeff*. You go into a teashop, so you say, miv a mysterious smile, 'Tea and a Bath bun.' And very nice too. But believe me—I'm telling you for your own good—in the wim o' this cup is a chip, and in your lip is a crack, so magnifried objects come out. Result, geneval paralysis. . . . There was also a sequence. In a park a bloody policeman kisses—miv a mustache yet—a nursemaid miv a pram. Nursemaid kisses contents of pram. Result? The baby's face falls off. It's marvelous!"

He was overcome with emotion for a moment but went on earnestly, "Tell me one thing—*do you wear a belt?*"

"Yes, I do," I said.

With tremendous vehemence Sam Yudenow cried, "Get rid of it!"

"Then my trousers will fall down," I said.

"Thvough belts comes pyorrhea. You'll see. Thank Gord I wear braces. In *Sinners Beware!* you'll see a sequence, a sadder and wiser man it should make you, you! Jesus Christ, so there's somebody like a postman miv a sword. A blonde gives 'im a mysterious smile in a room where there's a brass bed miv knobs on. So he takes off his belt, he takes off his boots, he takes off his jacket, he takes off his trousers. The boy is well brought up—he takes off his cap. Two seconds later, so this nice boy is bald, miv a thing on his head like a volcano—ain't nature marvelous?—and his wife is paralyzed, and his son is blind, and his daughter is mad miv Hutchingson's teeth, and there's a whole hospital full o' babies miv sores and not a nose between 'em. A shundder ran up and down my back—it was just like Fowlers End, only there were clean sheets. No more belts, no more teacups. Let the layabouts drink octupuses out o' chips. Buy yourself a new teacup. Your face falls off, and I'm the sufferer. Miv no nose, Sam Yudenow don't want a manager. It looks bad, kind o' style. In my vestibule it gets people groggy. Next time you get a chance to undress, and I want my managers should change their shirt at least once a week, look out for a rash on the chest. And lay off the tea. If you go to a restaurant, carry miv you a few crystals permanganate o' potash: put 'em in the coffee, sprinkle on the chops, make a solution in a glass water—a glass water costs nothing—and give a good soak to the cutlery. And *never use toilent paper somebody 'as used before*. . . .

"But there is hope, thank Gord! A couple poor boys made it incurable, miv mercury and arsenic. You seen mercury? Believe me, it's fascinating, like germs—you can't put your finger on it. It's too fast. It's faster than germs; it runs after them and crushes them. Arsenic is a deadly poison; it gives them such a deadly poisoning your worst enemies should have such a deadly poisoning. Only your teeth fall out. Believe me, teeth are a source of infection, 'better out than in,' as the duchess said when she blew off. Venereable disease was invented by a Yisher fellow called Ehrlich. That's what *they* say. But the originator o' pox was Wassermann—another one, miv an assistant, some Gveek called Reaction. . . . No, Lavendrock, the time comes when you don't want to be commercial. You want to do good. I want to spread venereable disease over the country. And put a stop to any intercourse whatsoever. I booked *Sinners Beware!* for a whole week, miv an option. It should gross more than *The Four Feathers*. It shook me. Boil me a glass o' water."

14

THEN THIS PASTICHE OF a man started to tell me about a man he met at the trade show:

"When I came out from *Sinners Beware!*, Lowbridge, my eyes were dim miv tears. Thanks to Ehrlich, Reaction and Wassermann, the baby gets its face back. It shook me. So I go into the vestibule for a smoke. No jokes, my heart was actually beating. So I see another bloke wiping his eyes—a nice man, dvessed like a gentleman in an Amevican hat miv a brim. First look at a man's hat, then look at his shoes; draw an average, and you can't go wrong. So I go up to him and say, miv tears in my eyes, 'A good show, no?' He says, in a proper Amevican accent, 'Yes, sir, it sure conveyed its message. It shows you, you can't be too careful of restaurants.' I say, 'That bit where the old woman went mad and set herself alight—' He says, 'After her husband went to that restaurant. No, sir, there's nothing like a home-cooked meal. Have a cigar.' And he gave me one; it comes all the way from Philadelphia. It was delicious—everybody turned rahnd to look at me when I lit it, and a blonde miv a pair pumpkins on 'er waved 'er hand at me. So I ask him what 'e is. . . . Who is he? Guess. No, don't try. Why don't you ask me?"

"Well, who was he?" I asked.

"Don't ask. But 'e tells me: 'I come from Los Angeles and my name is Lasky.' So I nearly 'ave a heart attack, but miv a mysterious smile I tell 'im: 'By a strange coincidence, Mr. Lasky, as it 'appens, I'm in the show business too.' Well, this Mr. Lasky gets me by the 'and in a grip—Booligan should've 'ad such a grip—and says, 'Glad to meet you, proud to know you, Sam! I'm here in England to study lasts. I'd like to see your latest lines.' Well, Daniels, you know me; I wear my heart up my sleeve. A man like Lasky to bring to Fowlers End? It ain't good stragedy. And a person like Lasky could be influential—more, he could be fluential.

"So I stops at Freybourg and Treyer as we walk along and I buy two triple Corona-Coronas. I take him to Oddenino's for a drink. I talk Yank: 'How's about a snort?' I spit all the way. Lasky is Lasky, that you can't deny. I buy chewing gum. I know 'ow to behave myself, believe me. What will 'e have? So he says, 'A Manhattan.' He was a proper Amevican all right. He cricketized the cigar because it came from Cuba, and some relative of 'is got killed miv the Rough Riders fighting the wild Indians there. Then 'e says, 'I sure appreciate this, Mr. Yudenow, and if there's any way I can help you in our mutual concern, you have only to call on Lasky. I've been looking over the works in Northampton.' I tell 'im I got a couple places in the Midlands, but money is tight. Meanwhile, whereas, miv a mysterious smile I send a waiter to the Plaza to buy two of the best tickets. So I say, 'Come and 'ave a look at my show,' and take 'im across the road. He sits through twenty minutes of it—sound-on-disk, and they got one of 'em out o' place—and then says, 'I really do appreciate this, Sam, but I have a conference.' I tell him, 'Mr. Lasky, your will is law.'

"So out we go. 'The new trend, I observe, is pointed,' he says, 'and at our last Rotarian, Sam, I made a crack. I said, "Let us get to the *point,* boys." Still, Sam, don't you find a tendency to the colorful?' I said, 'Well, of course colorful! What then colorful, Mr. Lasky?' He says, 'It can't last.' I tell 'im, 'Believe me, Mr. Lasky, too much labor cost is involved. All the bloody layabouts want, I mean the public, is a bit of comfort, Mr. Lasky.' So he says, 'The old-fashioned style, I say—cut 'em blunt and square.' 'Quite right. Be blunt and treat 'em square,' I tell 'im, 'only stand for no bloody nonsense. It would be a good thing,' I say, 'if you and me went into production. Oh, give me production, and we'll show the yobbos! Out of ice-cream and monkey-nut concessions alone is an honest living.'

"So then this fellow says, 'Sam, I think we are talking at cross-purposes—' what's a cross-purpose? —'I'm here buying English leather and English lasts. I aim to make a high-grade English gentleman's shoe at a popular price.' Then it comes up in me like acid, and I lose, praps, my temper a bit. I tell 'im, 'What is all this about leather? Trickster, you said you were in show biz!' So he says, 'I'll thank you to mind your language, mister. I never said I was in the show business or ever associated with it. My name is Charlie Lasky, and I am in the shoe business. It was nice to have known you. . . .' Can you imagine my feelings?"

I could not help laughing. But Sam Yudenow wouldn't say die. "Believe me," he said, "that was the real McLasky smelling out boiling-hot prospects. It's all right. I feel it in my heart."

Copper Baldwin said, "I dare say 'e's after that bit o' property up the road."

"But the hu-bloody-miliation of it!" said Sam Yudenow. "What property up the road? What do you mean, property up the road?"

Copper Baldwin said, yawning elaborately, "I thought you knew. A.A.A.A. is going to start a new factory at Ullage, the land being cheap. Running in a branch o' the railway line, they tell me. Matter o' ten thousand families. Didn't you know? I thought you knew. Well, I never!"

Sam Yudenow screamed like a horse in a fire, then calmed himself and said, with an attempt at dignity, "Everybody is fired—as from the week before last. . . . No, wait a minute, come back, deal miv poor old Sam Yudenow like a friend, and your wages will be raised as from my earliest convenience. Where did you pick up this crap?"

I said, "It's not crap. You see, I happen to have been at school with one of the leading surveyors, and I got it from him. There's going to be a factory like Ford's at Dagenham, and a great housing project, of course."

"All secret stuff," said Copper Baldwin, "but I should worry—eh, Mr. Laverock? *I* got no money to buy up land. 'Ave I, Mr. Laverock? Nor 'ave you, or you wouldn't be working for old Smallpox, would you?"

I said nothing, but Sam Yudenow flew into a rage. "Let there be no more reference to pox in connection with me!" he shouted. "Pox, pox, pox, pox—all day long I had it drummed into my head! Laventory seats, teacups, belts, caps, pevambulators—wherever you turn is pox, pox, pox, pox, pox! Or clap, clap, clap, clap, clap! Soft chancre, hard chancre, leave me alone! I wear braces, don't I? I eat at home, don't I? Bring me a contortionist to get the taste o' this out o' my mind! . . . Tell me more."

"You 'ad it," said Copper Baldwin. "I got nothing more to say." He added cryptically, "Only I wish I 'ad a few thousand pound, that's all."

"What would you do, Copper? Copper, what would you do?"

"Oh, nothing. Nothing at all. Buy a bit o' frontage on the souf-east side, could be, and a few lots to the norf. I'm only pissballing, but I'd get meself a nice bit o' land round Ullage, because I mean to say, after all, in the first place the A.A.A.A. would 'ave to buy me out on the frontage; and in the second place where there's ten thousand families there's got to be entertainment. Fruit machines, amusement arcades, a *palais de danse* . . . Skip it. Forget it. Only a daydream."

Sam Yudenow said, "A block o' flats."

"Foundations wouldn't take it," said Copper Baldwin, shaking his head. "Whole thing would keel over in a month."

"What are insurance companies for?" asked Yudenow.

"No, guv, I'd think on the long-range plan. Little 'ouses—they'd stand up five years—down payment, and weekly by the book. Make an arrangement wiv a wholesale furniture company: twenty pounds' worth on the Never-Never system for a hundred and twenty pounds, twenty-five pounds down. A.A.A.A. pay good, and you know what the working classes are. Also, a tally-man—I beg your pardon, I mean ladies' and gentlemen's clothing on the easy-payment system. Jewelry too. Come to think of it, while I was about it, if I was a man in your position, I'd get a pawnbroker's license, and make an arrangement with a good bookie to set up shop. Be a squire, that's what I'd do, if I 'ad a few thousand nicker. Wouldn't you, Mr. Laverock?"

My conscience compelled me to say, "No."

"That's because you are young and inexperienced. Well, the population increases. You finance a few doctors on a percentage basis—the dance hall will take care o' *that*—let alone this and that. A good watchmaker, a dentist, a barker, and a ladies' coiffeuse you can't go without. Similarly, an undertaker. An optician, too, because in those plants these clumsy bastards at the lathes are always getting bits o' steel in their eyes. It's a gold mine, cocko, if only I 'ad a few thousand to lay out on a bit o' land up Ullage way. . . .

"Then there's pianos; as soon as the proletariat gets their 'ands on a few quid, it's pianos—pianos and motorbikes. Set up a piano teacher on a fifty-fifty basis. Naturally, there must be a bleeding lawyer. They're laying about Soho two a penny. Buy one of 'em a new suit—black jacket and striped trousers—make 'im wash, and be 'is sleeping partner. Yes, the way to take over a town is to put exactly what you want into it. Fish and chips—the working classes can't exist without fish and chips—and a cook shop—" here he gave me a sidelong look out of his washed-out eyes —"as soon as your old man is earning a living wage, do you cook dinner? What's the matter wiv boiled ham and pease pudding?

"Or a lovely cut off the joint? Put a butcher in business, touching the matter of joints, because the Sunday dinner keeps the family together. The bitches will be too idle to cook it, so their delinquent progeny will take it to the baker's shop to put in the oven. You finance, of course, a baker's shop. Then—you know what thumb-fingered sods they are—they're always breaking cups and saucers. A crockery shop wiv vases, genuine Ming for eighteenpence, and a two-hundred-piece tea set for next to nothing. Get me?"

Sam Yudenow said, "An off-license? Beer, wines, and spirits to be consumed off the premises?"

"Certainly. And sweets, tobacco, and newspapers. Comics, bags o' comics. Stationery—I mean, rent books and smutty postcards. That sort o' concern you can start on a fifty-pound note. And a snob—that's a cobbler. I could lay my 'ands on a dozen army snobs that'd give anything to get a last between their poor old knees. Army men, nothing fancy, but good enough for the bleeding proletraiat. . . . Well, pretty well owning the town, in two shakes I'd 'ave a town hall, an urban district council; the councilors by the balls or otherwise according to sex; and me as mayor. In no time at all, it would be Sir Copper Baldwin—if only I 'ad a few thousand pounds."

He paused for breath, tipping me a wink. I felt I had to say, "You are talking a lot of bloody rubbish."

Sam Yudenow said, "Illegitimate cricketism I will grant you, but don't be constructive. . . . Say they make you a 'Sir.' What's your wife?"

Copper said, "Oh, she'd be Lady Baldwin. . . . If only I 'ad a few thousand pounds."

Sam Yudenow came out of a kind of daydream and snapped, "Get stuck into the job, loafers—I got to go to the West End."

I watched him through the glass as he got into his car. He was driven in the direction of Ullage.

Now when Sam Yudenow got to Ullage, the first thing he saw was a wooden standard for a poster which was being put up in the mire by five sweating men superintended by a foreman in a red muffler and a bowler hat of antique pattern, who kept shouting, "Now then, now then! I got my eye on *you*! Forward now—a bit backward! Sideways, Gord 'elp us, the *other* side! Steady, steady—plant it steady, you twots! Blind O'Reilly, you got the effing banner bollocksed! 'Old it now, Stan—'old it there, Stewart—git ready wiv 'at maul, Steptoe. Right? Drive! . . . Hm, the bastard sunk up to the hilt, didn't 'e? Pretty bloody wizened, this 'ere soil, if you want my opinion. 'Emmingway, git some stones. Faulkner, pull the bitch out straight. 'Old on, Dannay—lend 'im a 'and, what's-yer-name. Yes, you I mean, Doyle . . ."

Sam Yudenow watched while a hoarding went up. It was something like a circus banner—canvas on a frame, flapping in the notorious Ullage breeze—so that Sam Yudenow could not read it. It was, considering all he had heard, a commercial strip-tease. So he waited while the foreman in the bowler hat shouted, "Anybody like the sack? Well then, watch them props, 'old them stays! . . . Ea-say, easy now; that's about it! Make all solid and knock orf for a smoke."

Sam Yudenow saw, "as if it was miv my own eyes," as he put it, the erection of a hoarding such as he had never seen before. It was about sixty feet long and thirty feet high, and upon it were painted in huge red letters the cryptic words:

A.A.A.A. SITE—DANIELS COPPER LTD.
Chicken Lane, Threadneedle St.

Clutching at his heart, Sam Yudenow went to the Ullage Hippodrome, where the proprietor, who had his worries, received him without enthusiasm, saying, "What the bloody hell do you bloody well want? Do me a favor—say it in a pig's whisper and bugger off. Do you mind? Failing which, I'll kick your arse off the premises, and chance it. Now then."

Sam Yudenow became charming. "This," he said, "I am afraid I do not understand, old boy. So what's the matter? Things ain't going so good? There's show biz for you. Miv me, believe me, also things is up the spout. Now in a case like this, what do you do? In America they got two alternatives—staticians worked 'em out—expand or contract! Me, I got nothing to expand. My balls got chewed off. So let's contract. Let's make a contract. What'll you take for the hall?"

"I ain't selling."

"What does 'e mean, 'e ain't selling?" cried Sam Yudenow to the murky sky. "Listen, darling, everybody's selling. Is Lasky nobody? Lasky's selling. Sell; then buy; make mortgages; put it in your wife's name—"

"I haven't got a wife."

"Don't worry, I'll get you one. . . . And after all, what is there in Ullage? Yobbos, swamps. . . . Expand or contract! You make a contract, I expand—it's a rule of nature. Later on, miv economics you expand, and I contract. Give a little, take a little."

"Look, you, I'm not in a good mood today, and I give you fair warning: do you see this fist?"

"And very nice too. I wouldn't like a punch in the nose miv a fist like that. For goodness' sake put it in your pocket, because it frightens the life out o' me. Whereas the business of this show. Later show me your fist, I'd like a photograph of it. What would you call a price for such a show?"

The proprietor of the Hippodrome, which had always been a losing proposition, who would have been glad to get out with a clear thousand pounds, said, "I'd start considering at eight thousand."

Sam Yudenow pulled out a handkerchief, clapped it over his mouth, and cried out in pain. "Uxcuse me," he said humbly, "it's my lip. You mustn't make me laugh, I forgot to tell you. I got chapped lips. It can also crack the corners of the mouth. What d'you mean, eight hundred pounds? What is it, a *Covered Wagon*? A gusher? A gold mine? Don't be silly, eight hundred pounds!"

"I said eight thousand."

"Oh," said Sam Yudenow, slapping him on the shoulder and laughing heartily, "you want to be facetious? Okay, old Sam can take a joke. . . . Eight thousand *what*? To be frank miv you, it would cost me more than that to wire your charming hall for sound. No, I'd strip it to the bone. Out miv the seats. A new floor would cost me a pretty penny. I want to turn it into a skating rink. I'll tell you what—we're all in show biz together—I'll make it eight hundred and fifty pounds, spot cash. Take it or leave it."

"I leave it."

Now, presumably, the bargainers came to grips. Sam Yudenow said, "Good-by. It's nice knowing you," and put back in his pocket a checkbook he had been waving.

The other man said, "Wait a minute. We'll settle for twenty-five hundred, and I'll take my lucky."

"Two hundred and fifty ain't enough," said Sam Yudenow firmly. "I won't let you do it. You'd be robbing yourself. You made a slip o' the tongue—you meant eight hundred and fifty."

"I said twenty-five hundred."

"You been miv any dirty women lately?"

"Any of your business?"

"No, but it's unsymptomatic—people sell St. Paul's Cathedval, they start 'otels, distilleries, goodness knows what, all for twenty-five pounds. Play the man, for Christ's sake, play the *man!* What'll you do miv twenty-five pounds? Look, I want to be a good neighbor. Eight hundred and fifty, take it or leave it, and I'm not asking your gross. A hundred and fifty pounds o' this I want you should spend on a sea voyage."

"Don't talk wet!"

"I'm like that. I want you should take eight hundred and fifty pounds. Quit show biz, start a nice little restaurant—I know a man who can supply you especially miv Greenburgers, the latest thing."

Before they parted, the proprietor of the Hippodrome had a check for eight hundred and fifty pounds, and Sam Yudenow had in his pocket a holograph deed, fully witnessed, which made him proprietor of the Ullage Hippodrome, which, twenty-four hours earlier, he would not have taken as a gift.

Then, as I subsequently learned, he called Daniels Copper Ltd., in Chicken Lane, Threadneedle Street, and said something like what follows:

"Chickens? Par'me. Daniels Copper Limited? . . . Then this is Sam Yudenow. Call me a pal and I'm your pal. Call me a hog and I can turn out to be a proper pig. Let's get down to cases. The time has come but it's so. Forgi'me, please?"

A voice replied, "This is Payne, Payne, Payne, Payne, Rackham, Rackham and Payne. To what are you referring, sir?"

Somewhat out of countenance, Sam Yudenow said, "Daniels Copper Limited, if you don't mind."

"We are their attorneys. Yes?"

"Well, look. It works out like this: as it 'appens, as a matter o' fact, between us, to tell you the truth, I own the 'Ippodrome in Ullage. Not to tell you a lie, between friends, I could do miv a few lots o' land. Believe me, it grips me right in the bowels. All these poor people, I can't stand it. I'm sorry, Mr. Bowel, I can't stand it—I'm a funny man—it gives me a pain. Ever 'ad it? A subtraction in the arse, and digestion goes backwards. It makes acid. Acid I don't want; I got it already. Later, Gord knows what, to take the Name in vain. . . . So what's giving miv Daniels Copper? So what are they digging for? How comes copper rahnd Ullage? Answer me only this."

The lawyer replied, "I understand, sir, that Daniels Copper is a concern with wide interests. I am not at liberty to speak of them at present."

"Look, I'm not trying to take a liberty. Wide interests: so if I'm interested? And believe me, Sam Yudenow is wide. Oh, believe me! Wide as a carpet. They used to call me 'Sam Wide' in Billingsgate. You know that, you must know that, mustn't you? And believe me, I'm open—wide open—I gape like . . . Uxcuse me. To conclude, let me continue. A yes or a no; to who belongs lots in Ullage?"

The lawyer said, "Mr. Yudenow, you are asking for information which I am at present not at liberty to divulge—"

"Divulge!" cried Sam Yudenow.

"I'm sorry I can't do that but—"

"Never mind the 'sorry,' give me the 'but'!"

Then the solicitor told Sam Yudenow that, as far as he knew, this land around Ullage was, according to his information, being bought (always provided his information were correct) by some firm, as he was informed, of motorcar manufacturers who proposed to deal with it accordingly. "Accordingly miv what?" shouted Sam Yudenow, and the lawyer replied, "Accordingly."

Sam Yudenow said, "What is a copper company doing miv Ullage?"

The solicitor said gravely, "I have not the faintest idea. But, as you know, there are ramifications."

Sam Yudenow muttered, "Ramifications. Hm! So that's what they're up to. So long as we know. I don't want no ramifications. Piss-hounds!"

"What was that?"

"Nothing. Let's get together, just you and me."

"I'm free tomorrow, if you wish to consult me."

"Not for the world! All I want to do is consult you and praps buy you a little smoked salmon in Bootle's. Who is trying to insult you? Gord forbid. All I want is to make a deal, so you want to kick up a row? A person wants a few lots in Ullage, so you should be civil. . . . Civil, be! You get it? The angle is, you ought to be civil. Not to be a wild Indian miv stomach'awks, only civil. Go on, scowp me. Better not. I don't care if you're Norman Birkett and Marshall Hall, I'll prove to you there's a law in this land! So where do you think you are? Russia? The Czar's dead, believe me. I read it in the newspapers. And the Cossacks are unbanded. Who do you think you are?" Sam Yudenow shrieked, carried away," the Preobrazhensky Regiment, or what? Give me a yes or a no. Get off the line before I cut you off. Wait a minute, I'll cut you off. Bollocks to you, pisspot!" Then he sang, "*Bollocks, and the same to you—Bollocks, they make a bloody fine stew* . . . Got it? Only be civil. Is this too much to ask? I want a few lots rahnd Ullage. So what are you in business for? . . . Confidentially, between us, I am an untimate friend o' the Lord Mayor London. We went to school together and we are like brothers."

"What's his name?"

"Aha! If I told you, you would be as wise as I am. Look it up in the dictionary, in the dictionary look it up. I gave 'im 'is first cat, and if you don't believe me ring 'im up and ask 'im. But uxcuse me, I get carried away. A civil question demands a civil answer. My middle name is Show Biz. I am proprietor of all sorts o' property all over the place, let alone Ullage, where I own the skating rink—beg pardon, the 'Ippodrome—and I am a freeholder, a lease holder, a copyholder, et cetera. Also, a British subject, which entitles me to liberty o' conscience. So say something, or has the cat got your tongue?"

"Well, I must, as you understand, pass the matter on to Daniels Copper, Mr. . . . What did you say your name was? Biz?"

"Yudenow!"

"That is why I asked you," the solicitor said; so Sam Yudenow spelled it out, adding, "Listen. I'm a rich man and I can make it worth your while. I want a few lots in Ullage. I'll retain you. I'm a poor man, but you know. A fiddle 'ere, a fiddle there. Look at

Booligan. Believe me, I can put my 'and in my pocket. What comes out, that all depends. So is it so much to ask, a few lots in that smomp at Ullage? Ullage! Where *is* Ullage? *What* is Ullage? What do you think, I'm going to dig for copper there? Ullage? . . . No jokes, a few lots, how much?"

"I must consult my principals."

"Mr. Ullage, listen to me: in business you don't want no principles. Ethics, by all means. Morals, yes. Principles, no. They lead you to the work 'ouse. If we are to do business, let me unstipulate—*no principles*!"

"Mr. Yudenow, you must understand that I am only a servant of the company, Daniels Copper Limited."

"I'd make it worth your while," Sam Yudenow insinuated.

"I'm sorry, Mr. Yudenow, but that's quite out of the question."

"Servant o' the company—believe me, I know servants. I got one. She comes from Dublin, whereas evidently they don't 'ave laventories, if you will uxcuse the expression. So she leaves a turd shaped like a triangle, like Egypt—a veritable pyramid—and runs away miv an Irish Guardsman who deserted, yet. Miv my best overcoat. What did 'e want to do miv it, I ask you? Make a weskit of it? Go argue miv servants. . . . But uxcuse me, Mr. Ullage, 'ow comes the servant problem? Uxcuse me, please, I ask only to be informed. That's Gveek, for your information. Gveeks! Your worst enemies, believe me, Mr. Thingummybob, should 'ave Gveeks! I 'ad one, and what a layabout 'e turned out to be! Let alone never mind. So this Gveek—the other one, thank Gord, poisoned 'imself miv 'emlock. In a bowl, yet—never trust a Gveek miv a bowl. And sex. 'Is last words—I got it out of a magazine—was. 'I owe a cock to Esculapenheim.' . . . You take me off my point. A few lots, Mr. Cox?"

The lawyer said, "I'm afraid you don't grasp the situation, Mr. Yudenow. You own, you say, the Ullage Hippodrome? Then I dare say you have heard that the Anglo-American Automobile Associates—in other words, A.A.A.A.—have bought up considerable properties in Ullage. I have it on the authority of a respected client that the railway is going to run a branch line out there. Solely for the purposes of transport, sir, solely for the purposes of transport. Daniels Copper has considerable interests in Ullage, as I have indicated. I don't imagine they propose to mine for copper, but there is such a thing as building speculation—what our transatlantic cousins call 'real estate.' It is quite romantic, really. What was once a village will become a thriving industrial town. Something like San Francisco on a smaller scale. When you ask for a lot in Ullage at present, you are asking—if you will pardon the pun—for quite a lot."

"Are you in business or are you not? Give me a simple 'yes.' "

"Daniels Copper has holdings, some of which might be available. Let me see, just a moment; why, yes, I believe there is some land on the southeast, unless I am very much mistaken. And bless my soul—it must be an appalling oversight on the part of A.A.A.A. —according to the map there would appear to be a piece of frontage. But this seems too good to be true: I can't see a concern like A.A.A.A. leaving vacant frontage where they are bound to build."

Philosophically, Sam Yudenow shrugged into the telephone and said, "So we all make mistakes. I ain't much to look at, but I'm funny that way myself. Did you ever see a picture called *Russian Duel*? A couple loafers put one bullet in a gun and spin the barrel. In turn (they toss a sixpence for who goes first) each one puts the muzzle to 'is head and pulls the trigger. The villain goes first. *Click!*—and the glycerin is dropping down 'is face. Then the 'ero goes next. *Click!*—'e makes miv a mysterious smile. Believe me, now the villain 'as got a proper sweat on, trembling like an aspirin. Like Booligan. *Click!*—and gives the gun back to the 'ero. *Click!*—so there's only one bullet left; who's got to get it? The villain. So 'e goes yellow, puts the gun down and gives up the girl. Later, the 'ero opens 'is hand and there's the bullet. It was never in the gun. Believe me, I'm like that. I'll gamble my life away. So what is Daniels Copper asking for lots—because, in any case, I can't afford it? Only I'm curious. The *Covered Wagon* spirit I got; I'm a pioneer myself. Well?"

Mr. Payne said, "It is difficult to make head or tail of you."

"What do you mean, 'ead or tail? You think you can toss me like a coin? Tails! A dog am I? I ask a civil question. You give me tails. Forever hold your peace—speak up!"

Mr. Payne recounted this telephone conversation later, with a kind of mystified amazement. He said that there was something about Yudenow that made one want him to go on and on. He added that he wished he could write books. Anyway, Yudenow came to the office and did an under-the-counter deal in landed property around Ullage. He got half the housing project on the northwest, and on the southeast a third of the factory frontage (Mr. Payne would not let him have more) for seven thousand pounds. He must have been extraordinarily voluble, because even Mr. Payne, with his snaky memory, could not recall the whole of the conversation, or discussion, which lasted three and a half hours by the clock. We wouldn't take a check; the deal had to be settled by banker's draft, in return for which the solicitor drew up a deed of unbelievable magnitude. With the name of Daniels Copper fixed firmly in his head, Sam Yudenow wanted mineral rights, these to include oil. He also claimed the right to open a clay-pipe factory, a smithy, and a fried-fish shop. He slipped in a clause that entitled him to set up a brickyard and a lime kiln. He was leaving nothing to chance.

He got back to the Pantheon at about six in the evening, just when I was undertaking what is to me the almost impossible task of throwing out an old lady. She was considerably less than sober, so I ran over to the Load of Mischief, bought a glass of "Red Lizzie," and lured her with it. It must have looked ridiculous—me walking backward, holding this glass, and making caressing noises like squeaky kisses such as you make to a cat; she following, hypnotized. Having got her into the street, I gave her the glass, which she drained at a gulp, then fell on my neck and cried.

Sam Yudenow would choose this moment to arrive in his big Renault. He nodded in a most unpleasant way and said, "The place for this is the genevator room. Do anything, only I don't want a bad name." He looked pale but happy.

Copper Baldwin came down from the projection room: one of the machines had started to run backward. "Poxy Sam," he said, "what 'ave you been up to?"

"Up to what? Up to where? Who, me?" said Sam Yudenow.

"You been doing something wicked," said Copper Baldwin.

"Don't make me laugh, please, I got a cvacked lip. It pains. But listen, I want your advice, yours too, Laveridge. For a name for a dance 'all, what's the matter miv the 'Covered Wagon'? Temporary, under a tent, like a covered wagon. Shafts—'Acker the Breaker could find me old telegraph poles; 'orses 'e's got from the roundabouts. A good name, the 'Covered Wagon,' no? I'm thinking o' starting a little company: Yudenow Developments Limited. I'm only pissballing and I don't want you should give it another thought. Only kind o' think it over, sort o' style.... 'Ow's the house?"

"About five hundred and fifty," I said.

Instead of urging me to rush into the street and drag in a few more, to my astonishment he said, "Nicely, nicely."

Just then there came the reverberation of a shocking explosion. It shook the Pantheon. The projectionist had a heart attack and had to be smacked in the face while young Headlong took over—and what that boy did with *Sinners Beware!* should not happen to a dog. He ran it too fast, he ran it too slow; it was all one to him if two frames appeared at once on the screen; and, having developed a weakness for the woman who shows one of her legs when the soldier takes his belt off, he managed to rerun that reel for the rest of the night. Nobody noticed; they thought she must be somebody else.

Sam Yudenow said, "Did you 'ear that 'orrible bang?"

Copper Baldwin said, "Didn't you?"

"Don't answer a question miv a question! Was it Gveeks?"

"Don't talk like a berk. Where 'ave you been all your life? That's dynamite; they must be blasting for foundations round Ullage."

Impulsively, Sam Yudenow said, "By me this is music!"

"Why, what's Ullage to you?"

"It means so little to me I'm delighted it should be blasted," said Sam Yudenow.

Later Copper Baldwin took a walk up the road, and came back laughing. As soon as he caught his breath, he said to me, "Ever 'ear about Deucalion? Aquarius? The Water Carrier? Stone me blind, I never trusted Greek cooking. That bloody stuff went orf, and there ain't a window left in Ullage. Nor a square inch uncovered with mud. The 'Ippodrome 'as got a crack in it you could lay three fingers in. No casualties, except one old woman—but they'll 'ave to wipe 'er orf before they can tell. The cream o' this jest, cocko, is that this 'ere stuff blasted down to an underground spring, and Ullage is knee-deep, more or less. I never laughed so much since Father died. Fancy a bit o' gin? This calls for a celebration. Laugh? You would 'ave pee'd yourself. The War Memorial fell onto the roof o' the chapel, which, unfortunately, was empty at the time. Nothing left but a stump. Oh, it's lovely. This almost makes me believe in Gawd. 'Ave a bit o' gin, do 'ave a bit o' gin!"

I asked, "What's so funny?"

He said, "Sam Yudenow bought the 'Ippodrome orf Johnny Wills, and the insurance policy ain't been renewed. What is more, I got news for you: I called that man in Chicken Lane. That bastard Yudenow nipped up to the City and bought a portion of our 'oldings in Ullage for seven thousand quid. 'Ow d'you like that?"

I said, "I never was very good at figures, Copper. Let's work out the percentages. Seven hundred produces seven thousand—"

"Ah, money breeds money."

I said, "I don't believe in money. What I was trying to work out was the percentage due."

"I'm against vested interests myself," said Copper Baldwin, "therefore, I say, bugger off and give the bastards an object lesson in the capitalist system. Thirty-five hundred for you, thirty-five hundred for me, and Bob's your uncle. What say?"

"Nothing of the sort," I said. "My mother is an investor, a lady in whom I am interested is an investor . . . Damn it all, Copper, let us be equitable. I hate greed—"

"But we chewed Sam's bollocks off, didn't we?"

"Keep them, and much good may they do you," I said. "But what this takes is an accountant. Take it first and last, Copper: everybody gets it on a percentage basis, and quick! My mother first of all, then Miss Whistler. Deduct Mr. Cruikback's percentage—"

"I love that man," said Copper Baldwin. "I'd like to make 'im managing director. Three and a half per cent? I'm surprised at you. Mr. Cruikback? Three and a half per cent? Now look 'e gets two hundred smackers—let 'im plow it back and give 'im ten per cent. Where's your bloody acumen?"

"This seven thousand pounds is to be divided among the shareholders in this company," I said, "of which you are the least."

"It ain't business," said Copper Baldwin, in protest.

"And a good job too," said I. "What's the matter with you? You've got ten times your investment. For goodness' sake, what more do you want? And I may tell you," I added severely, "there's not many jobbing mechanics in times like these that can put their hands on a couple of hundred pounds. Better be grateful."

"Grateful. To this I 'ave one word to say," said Copper Baldwin; and he moistened his lips, filled his lungs, and blew out a disgusting noise. "For beer money, et cetera, I am compelled to rely on extracurricular activities. Jesus, I want to show you the coast of Cuba coming up like a thread o' fog! Let alone the porpoises. No, really and truly, they *play*. I caught one once by accident, and you'd be surprised the difficulty I 'ad trying to chuck 'im back. 'E went to chew my foot orf, but that was only a love bite. Fixed 'im with a fire ax and served 'im for a stew off Venezuela. Surprising amount o' oil. But there was a Nicaraguan boy liked the liver. Man's best friend is the porpoise—I cut 'is jaws out, dried them out, and mounted them on a board. Sold 'em for a pound. What about this drink? I'll grant you your principles, so come on now!"

So we went to the Load of Mischief. Copper Baldwin was in such a state of exaltation that he could not stand on one foot for more than a few seconds at a time. He shouted, "Drinks on me!" And, in the murmurous, respectful half-silence that followed—drunk with triumph—he said, "Anybody mind if I oblige with a little song?"

Nobody minded. Clearing his face of all traces of cheerfulness and emptying his glass, he turned up an imaginary collar and proceeded to sing. But before he did so he warned the company: "Okay. This'll cheer you up, you grizzling lot o' miseries. Bleeding juveniles. You never 'eard the like o' this before, and you'll never 'ear the like o' this again, you bastards, you!"

A heavy-set man with a fixed expression of melancholy, but with a polite air, shrugged himself into a half-upright position and said, "Excuse me, but did you apply that remark to me?"

"You're drinking wiv me," said Copper Baldwin, "that's unanswerable, ain't it, wage slave? . . . I will now give you a ditty."

Then, to a combination of tunes, he sang as follows:

My poor mince pies are full o' tears,
My raspberry tart is jelly,
My daisies I bullock'd for two pig's ears
To warm my Auntie Nelly.

A tosser on a Wilkie Bard,
A lord on a Charing Cross,
Is 'ow I fell, and it's bread-'n-lard
To bear my milkman's 'orse.

No titfer to my loaf-o'-bread,
No strike-me-dead to eat,
No place to go for an Uncle Ned,
Or boots to my plates-o'-meat.

On the Johnny Horner I must stand
In this land of the yet-to-be,
'Olding out my Martin's-le-Grand
For the price of a Rosie Lee.

Without 'eavens above or china plate
I know I can never be missed,
So I shake in the chivvy of 'orrible Fate
My trembling Oliver Twist.

I must die for the want o' Johnny Rann,
No Little Nell shall be rung for
This Pope-o'-Romeless pot-'n-pan
My ding-dong has been sung for . . .

When we went back across the road, deafened by applause, the Inspector was waiting in the vestibule. "Copper, where were you last night?" he asked.

"Naturally, on the premises."

"Whose?"

"Whose what? Premises? Generator trouble, Inspector. You want to see our generator? Come and put your 'and on it. Only first of all make a chain 'and to 'and, you and the boys. Try it and see. Doctors say it's good for the nerves. They can always identify you by your teeth, anyway. 'Ave a go?"

"None of your sauce. There was a burglary in Thurd Street,

Pickles Road. House of a gentleman in the legal profession. Thief took only cash out of a safe, but the skivvy recognized him, you know."

"Good girl!" exclaimed Copper Baldwin.

"Was this man with you last night, sir?" the Inspector asked me.

"Oh, definitely," I said.

"An alibi, eh?" the Inspector said, looking daggers. Then he went away.

After he was halfway down the street, I asked Copper Baldwin, "Where *were* you last night?"

"Cocko, don't talk shop. And if you do, don't go too deep."

15

TOO MUCH MONEY is too good to be true. It ceases to be real. Call yourself a treasurer and you can simply print the stuff. Whether you can roll purchasing power of bread and meat off the presses after you have eaten the wheat and the cattle is a problem for the economists, and I know nothing of economics. But you can get drunk on them. And, you know, drunkard breeds drunkard. Hence, inflations. Now that I come to think of it, I was a one-man inflation; and I am sick at the thought of it.

As I worked it out, every investor had, already, in hard cash nearly a thousand per cent of his or her original investment. With deductions, call it a mere eight hundred per cent or so. I apportioned everything, according to capital investments minus outgoings. By this token June Whistler had two thousand, five hundred pounds to come, Copper Baldwin had two thousand and my mother had three thousand, five hundred pounds—the odd eighteen shillings, since I was bad at arithmetic, I put aside for "Entertainment." And I had a hundred and fifty pounds under my belt, and was still a company director holding massive projects in Ullage worth heaven knows what when A.A.A.A. moved in and started negotiations. I saw myself as somebody a shade more important than Uncle Hugh—one of A.A.A.A.'s stockholders, what they call a "comer." If he thought I would let him in on the ground floor, I decided, Uncle Hugh would never have made a bigger mistake in his life. No doubt he would cringe for the handling of the remaining stock. Then my horse's laugh would be something worth hearing.

I'd take him, say, to Claridge's for lunch, and lecture him on imagination in business. Money, I would indicate, was a product of the higher imagination. If it came from produce, merely, we'd all be shoving wheelbarrows and shouting in cracked voices, "Coconuts!" or "Apples-a-pound-pears!" or "Who will buy my blooming lavender?" As it was, henceforward he had better be careful. Economics, that was the word; and let him look it up in a dictionary. While I was willing to concede that Stafford Cripps, Montague Norman, and other such dilettantes had a smattering, it was a case of Youth at the helm. And his face would be red—it was never otherwise, but it would now be redder—and he would be sorry for having entertained the idea that I was not cut out for big business.

I indulged myself in the most delicious fantasies. I blazed with thought-forms of jewelry while my feet tingled with imaginary kisses. A ballerina bit my ear and I smiled indulgently until I discovered that it was a Fowlers End flea, striking at which—in blind rage at being nibbled out of my dream—I hit myself on the side of the head. I never knew I packed such a punch.

I was intoxicated, in the manner of some decent fellow who, never having had more than sixpence, finds himself with a five-pound note. Money really does burn a hole in your pocket if you are not acquisitive. Well, it had better burn a hole in your pocket than in your heart, I suppose.

I went, first, to June Whistler's place. There a chill descended upon me as in the science-fiction stories; out of a clear summer sky comes a Something. Your bones turn to water. In this case, it was draped in mauve.

I had not time to open my mouth before June Whistler cried, "Daniel Laverock, really, I think you have behaved abominably! Oh, I know I have been a fool. But does this confer on you the right to be detestable? Parasite!"

I said, "This I don't quite understand, my dear."

"I beg your pardon," she said, with indescribable *hauteur*, curling her back hair with two fingers of her left hand, "I'm not your dear."

"If it comes to parasite," I said, deeply offended, pulling out of my pocket an envelope full of money, "I promised you a return on your investment. Here's about eight hundred per cent. Take it. Furthermore, you are a shareholder. I don't suppose you meant it, but you have hurt my feelings. If you were a man I would punch you right on top of the nose—" I had already picked up Fowlers End usage —"Being a woman, you deserve a smack in the face and a good kick up the arse!" Then the Old Valetudinarian spirit came upon me as, opening the envelope, she saw the money and her eyes filled with tears. Relenting, I said, "You might at least say thank you."

June Whistler said, in a most plaintive manner, "I don't deserve this. I don't want it. Take it back. Oh, Dan, I'm sorry to say I took a man out of the gutter and he ravished me like a mad beast—"

"Why didn't you tell me this before?"

"Then I met an honorable man, a decent one. He offered me security. And then . . ."

In a white rage I asked, "And precisely who was this bastard who ravished you like a wild animal, or whatever it was you said? I'll kill the bastard!"

"No, darling, you mustn't!"

"Oh, I see," I said, "you still love him, is that it?"

"Very dearly. You mustn't hurt him. He ravished me like a gorilla. No, really, he raped me like a buffalo."

"Point him out!" I shouted. "And I'll ravish him. I'll show him buffaloes and gorillas!"

With a solemn and mysterious look, June Whistler opened her handbag and took out a powder compact, which she opened, and held the mirrored lid under my nose, saying, "It was you, but I forgive you."

When I lose my temper I do it in reverse. When I am almost at my worst, I whisper; before the berserker, I become dumb. Now I whispered, with the extraordinary deliberation that comes over me at such times, "Pardon me. You will excuse me. But what, precisely, is this act in aid of?"

"Go!" June Whistler cried.

I said, "I never hit a woman in my life, but I am strongly tempted."

"Yes," she said, nodding in perfect agreement, "knock me down and lay me out, ravish me like a mad dog, roll me over and do it again, and let us part friends. . . . Would you like a meringue?"

"No," I said, "no meringues. I still don't get this lay."

June Whistler became severe. She said, "I have yet to see the situation that is improved by beastly vulgarity. But you always were a dirty stinking crap-hound, weren't you? Corrupt filth! Who picked you literally out of the gutter, you and your tin of herrings? Bah!"

"Look, if you want the economy of it, you've got back a couple of thousand pounds and your tin of herrings," I said. "And now good-by forever."

June Whistler said, "Wait a minute—" and went into the kitchen. She returned with that ill-fated tin of herrings which she handed to me with a grand air. I nearly told her what to do with them in the language of Fowlers End, but remembered myself and said that she should keep them in memory of me; whereupon she wept.

"I have treated you like a dog!" she said.

"Think no more of it," I said.

Then, with genuine tenderness, she offered me the packet of bank notes and said, "I'm sorry we must part like this—" crying her eyes out —"but take this. Please take it. I don't need it, and I won't need it. I'm going to get married. Please take it, do!"

Now I do not know how the mind works, but an irrational irritation took possession of me at that moment. *What right had she to get married to anybody?* At the same time, I was somehow relieved; but, ashamed of itself, this same relief exacerbated the irritation. Knocking the envelope out of her hand, I said, "Good-by!"

Before I got to the door, she was after me, holding out a meringue and saying, "At least take this . . ."

So I took it and put it in my pocket while I kissed her good-by out of sheer pity. She made circular movements and said, "Just one last time to remember me by?"

But my back was up. I said, "No. The surgeon's knife, I say. If you sever, sever forever. Good-by."

By the time I had got to the middle of the street I had a sudden yearning for her: I was prepared to propose marriage. I went back to the house and, quite diffidently, knocked at the door. June Whistler opened it about six inches and said, "Go away."

"I have decided that I love you," I said.

"You know that I have always loved you," said she. "But just let's be tender memories. Scram."

Shoving my hands in my pockets and clenching my fists I went downstairs again and walked a hundred yards before I discovered that my left hand was full of crushed meringue of the most sticky nature. I thought, *She had made it for me*. Licking it off my palm, I mixed it with my tears and felt that loneliness was creeping in upon me.

But why shouldn't a girl better herself? I asked myself.

Finding no answer to this, I abandoned the question, squared my shoulders, and went on to my mother's house. The dear old lady was delighted to see me. She said, "I knew you would come; something seemed to tell me. Daniel, dear, how haggard you look. Have you been fretting?"

I ought to say that "fretting" was, in my time, an enemy of education: every week all the Sunday newspapers were full of cases of "fretting"—boys of twelve who were found stark and cold, hanging by the neck on their braces, with notes pinned to their bosoms saying that it was because they did not know enough trigonometry to get through an examination. The whole country was full of swinging boys with their tongues hanging out and unthumbed books of logarithms at their feet. They had "fretted."

I even considered it myself, once, on the eve of an examination when I did not see my way clear to get through algebra. Only there must have been in me a love of life—I could not bring myself to repeat the act after my braces broke and I fell to the floor of my bedroom with a terrible bang, which I had to explain away. I said I had fallen out of bed. My father sized up the situation, with his usual perspicacity, when he saw me with half my braces inexpertly knotted about my neck and noticed the other half, freshly torn, dangling from the ceiling. He was a man of law, bless his heart, and so got a swift juridical view of the situation. He said, "Daniel! If you go on this way, I give you my solemn warning you will live to be hanged."

But my mother insisted that I had been "fretting," and put the book of logarithms into the kitchen stove—where, no doubt, they helped to cook me a better dinner than if I had attempted otherwise to digest them. My argument was: *Who wants to know the height of a tree by measuring its shadow? A shadow,* I reasoned, *is neither here nor there; and for that matter neither is a tree here or there.* I was in the metaphysical stage. *Man born of woman,* I decided, *was neither here nor there. Nothing was anywhere. . . .*

Only I liked my four square meals a day, having abolished God. . . . That was then.

Now, my mother said, "You mustn't fret. Something seemed to tell me, so I made some meringues. And I'll tell you something, Daniel—I held back a few pounds, which, God knows, you're welcome to. Only promise, no bookshops?"

I said, "You've got hold of the wrong end of the stick," and tugged out of my pocket an immense roll of money, which I handed to her with a sardonic bow, saying, "Enough to choke a horse, if a horse were fool enough to eat it. Eh?"

At this she cried, "It was because he fell off the roof into the cucumber frame," and fainted away in sheer horror. But she came to in a little while, and I told her that I had made a deal, and here were three thousand, five hundred pounds—all for her. "Your poor father always predicted it would come to this!" she said.

My temper was frayed. "What the hell do you mean?" I asked. "Come to what? Eight hundred per cent and your money back?"

"Oh, I don't know where to turn. Oh, Daniel, Daniel, why did you do it to me? How am I going to explain this to your Uncle Hugh? Where shall I put it, because I'm sure you'll need it again?"

I said, "Put it in the bank. Need it again? Why 'again'? It's your money. Put it in the bank, Mother, put it in the bank!"

"Your Uncle Hugh would find out," she said.

"The bank's business is secret, confidential," I cried.

"Daniel, you know I hate to be secretive with your Uncle Hugh—"

"Oh, God damn and blast my Uncle Hugh!"

"My poor boy, you're overwrought and blasphemous. Have a

meringue and I'll get you a glass of brandy. Only I beg you, don't drink it."

"Then why offer it?"

"That's only nice. . . . Your Uncle Hugh, my dear, is a fine man. Don't speak so hardly of your Uncle Hugh. He meant you nothing but good, and he has a good heart."

Something in her tone put my teeth on edge; there was an excessive sweetness in it. I said, "I have an appointment. I'll see you later."

"Dear Daniel, just to please your old mother, your silly old mother, do take a teeny little sip of brandy?"

"No, thanks."

"I'm so glad!"

Then I went out for a drink, all on my own, to the Prince of Wales, by the Common. This vilest of all hostelries was put up shortly after Queen Victoria's legitimate successor was decorated for dancing a Highland fling at a tender age. It still has a prefabricated look, a halfhearted look, a jerry-built look. It should not be there. It should not be anywhere. But it has pretensions to gentility in that it has a saloon bar patronized by spies from the Inland Revenue. They mingle with the vacuum-cleaner salesmen and such rabble, and are always to be distinguished by the fact that they give or take nothing for fear of counter-spies by whom they might later be accused. Buy a double in that place and some insect of a man will scurry up and ask if you are someone else. Naïvely you correct him, saying that you are not someone else but So-and-so. Begging your pardon, he scratches his way out. Two years later the bureaucrats, after an enfilading fire of cross-examination about your expenditure, take careful aim and shoot one last deadly question at you: *Weren't you having doubles in the Prince of Wales—two years, three months, and nine days ago?* Then, out of the wall crawls Judas all in black, and you are done for.

In those days it was a nondescript, dull, middle-class place on the Common, and you could find your way to it simply by watching men in black coats taking their dogs out after sunset—they always looked north, south, east, and west in an abstracted way while the dog pee'd—and then they scuttled like beetles to the Prince of Wales, where they hastily gulped fourpennyworth of bitter. Beyond the Common lay some scrubby, useless land studded with silver birches, called Samshott Heath. Perhaps you have seen, in some side street, a mattress thrown out for the dustmen as unfit to use even by the poorest of the poor? So was Samshott Heath thrown out by God.

I went into the saloon bar, which was somber enough to strike terror into the boldest. Not into the timidest: into the boldest. It did not encourage boldness. Clearly on display was a frame such as they put obituaries in, enclosing a document in microscopic print pertaining to the licensing laws. I paused to read it while the proprietor, an ex-civil servant, looked at me like a proper little Godbolt. Disliking his manner, I went up to him and asked, "Got accommodation for an elephant?"

He said, "Don't know what you're talking about."

"Oh, you don't, don't you? It says that you are bound to provide 'Accommodation, et cetera, *for Man or Beast*. . . .' I am a man, you will concede? I happen to have a beast, an elephant."

This civil servant of a publican, instead of laughing in a jolly way, offering me a drink on the house and (taking me aside to whisper a confidence) beating me up outside the public bar as the good old publicans used to do, said sharply, "Get out of my house!"

"I won't," said I.

"I reserve the right—"

"On what grounds do you reserve what right?"

"You're drunk."

"Aha! Libel—slander—defamation—accusation of obnoxious habits—and loss of business," I said, with a knowing smile, taking out an old envelope and a pencil. "I demand the names and addresses of everybody within earshot. I insist that you call the police. Categorically, I want a surgeon to smell my breath. Slander, eh? False arrest, is that the idea? Then Payne, Payne, Payne, Payne, Rackham, Rackham and Payne shall know the reason why! Give me a double whisky and soda. And if I wish to bring an elephant into this hostelry, I am by law so entitled. Also, cheese and pickled onions, and a crust of bread and butter. You are bound to provide me with refreshment, and my beast. I know the law. I own an African elephant, two camels and a mule. By God, sir, I'll have your license! Well?"

The landlord said no more, but hastily poured me my drink of whisky. Various emotions were chasing themselves around the shallow dome of his shadowy skull now. He was hoist by his own petard, this unfrocked *tchinovnick*: he had broken the law in several places. He had refused "entertainment" to my beast, an elephant, and considering me drunk (although I had not touched a drop all day), had said so in a loud, reedy voice. But having pronounced me drunk, which was defamatory, he had gone and served me. This was almost a hanging matter.

There was nearly a riot in the public bar, from where several men had a clear view and listen of the altercation. One shouted, "Carm on, Steve!" Two or three others begged me in various terms to kick off his private parts, knock his bloody eyes out, show him who was who, and have his liver for the bloody cat. I had aroused the beast in the mob. An Irish navvy cried, "Up the rebels!" A man with a mustache gravely emptied his pint pot, dried himself on his sleeve, said, "God save the King!" and struck the Irish laborer on the head. Then I demanded, "Landlord, call the police!"

"No, no, for heaven's sake, no! Here's your change." He pushed toward me eighteen shillings and eightpence.

"And what's this for," I asked, "considering I haven't paid you yet?" And I flung down one-and-fourpence.

The man was out of countenance. He looked from the money to me, and back to the money, and asked, "What's this?"

Seeing what he was, I said, "Coin of the realm. Would you like me to put down nine hundred and sixty farthings and ask for a pound note? I may, you know. Somebody call a policeman! . . . Or do you question that I have nine hundred and sixty farthings? Defamation, eh? Good! You'll hear more of this."

While I gave him a mysterious smile he begged me to pick up my change—what time a Hogarthian, gap-toothed, hairy-handed gathering in the public bar were geeing me up, as the carters used to say, urging me to take the landlord's tripes home for supper, to tenderize his kidneys before stewing them, and please to let them have a marrow bone. They liked the look of me. Pointing to the change to which I was not entitled, I said to the landlord, "Drinks all round for my friends in the public bar." There was a deafening cheer, and they ordered extravagantly, while a lady old enough to be my grandmother, exhibiting underwear which I hesitate to describe as she executed a Cockney cancan, sang "Knees Up, Mother Brown."

I sat down with my drink and my pickled onions. At least I had got back at somebody. I drew a deep breath, took a sip, and prepared to relax when I heard—as in a nightmare—an odious voice saying, "Look here, my friend. Look at this tie. If one is a little muddy, why, what the devil's a bit of honest dirt? Eh? The noblest work of God, what?"

A solemn, heavy voice replied, "The rank is but the guinea's stamp—the man's the gold for a' that."

"My very words," said this detestable voice, which I associated with lying rumors and stolen soda pop, with braggings and bullyings and bashings. "Now, I'm a good Socialist, and I'll give you the general line. Why should A.A.A.A. cut in on Samshott Heath? Where's your statistical correlation? Answer me that. You can't, can you?"

"Am not prepared to say I can," said the heavy voice.

"But the working man, statistically, has his rights, you'll grant?"

After a pause, the man with the heavy voice said, "Booger the working man, the idle sod! But statistics I grant you. Now then!"

"But what about correlation?"

"Oh ay, I dare say there's something to be said for correlation. But booger labor. Let's get this right, Mr. Cruikback. Listen to me. I've worked amoong bloody laborers and, if you will excuse the expression, to put it delicately, they are not fit to shovel shit. Don't blame me, it's the way they're made. I'm sorry to say it joost happens they're no bloody good."

"But what about A.A.A.A.?" Cruikback asked.

"They're joost as bad," said the man with the heavy voice, "and mark my words, the time will come . . ." His tone changed. "Yes, I'm nobbut a common old builder," he said, while I could almost feel him nod. "Come on now, you're a surveyor. Gi' me. Anglo-American Automobile Associates, is it? A.A.A.A., is that it? I'm only a common old working man, so let's have it, and I wouldn't say no to a fifty-pound note."

"Oh, I say, look here!"

"Look wheer?"

"You see, of course, my wife is going to have a miscarriage."

"I'm only a common old builder. Yes, I'll allow I can lay my hands on two or three hoondred thousand pound; but call that loock. I'm a working man. When my good lady had to have a miss, we used to do it with a bottle of gin, and parsley boiled in Epsom salts. When it begins to work, pretend to trip, like, at head of stairs; this failing, sit on her hard—it might surprise you, with all your education, to know the strength of a buttock. Gi' the lass a sack o' potatoes to lift, make her roon oop and down stairs, kick her in belly and feed her smutty wheat. Frighten the lady: go 'boo' in the middle of the night, and catch her around unexpected corners. Yes ay, mister, and when she faints carry her to bedroom, off wi' t' drawers, and an enema or douche of strong Epsom salts. Or parsley—starvation diet—then chuck lass downstairs again. Fall on her accidental, like, with the elbow over the lower bone. That ought to work. If it doesn't, I'll gi' ye an address; only the woman charges two guineas. If, however, you use a knitting needle, be sure to sterilize it first. Heat knitting needle red hot, but spit on it first to cool it—poor little boogers, they got their own troobles without knitting needle being red hot—or pass water on it. That'll case-harden knitting needle and disinfect and cool at same time. . . . Is she a bleeder?"

"I don't know what the bloody hell you are talking about," said Cruikback, in an offended tone.

"Tha' doesn't? Eeh well, lad, let's drop matter. . . . About Samshott Heath. Business is business. Let's have t' dope, and here's a fifty-pound note for 'ee."

Then I got up, filled with a great anger and a sense of shocking destruction; also of maddening bewilderment. But anger was predominant. My awe of Cruikback went away like a mist in a high wind. I confronted him and said, "You bloody little crook!"

"Remember Snellgrove-in-the-Vale!" he cried.

"So I do—" and let him have it right between the eyes.

Coming out of a brief unconsciousness, he said, "I'll let you get away with it this time, Laverock," and passed out again, bleeding as if I had cut his throat.

The builder from the north said to me, "To tell 'ee the truth I never did like the look of that booger. Has he been trying it on? Wi' me, I mean? Because if so, I'll show him a bit o' Lancasheer. Ay, will I!"

I said, "Pray do so without further delay," and left the bar, dreaming of the "bit o' Lancasheer" Cruikback was bound to get. The Liverpool Kiss, as elaborated by Sam Yudenow, is merely the hors d'oeuvre to a "bit o' Lancasheer"; and poor Cruikback had a theodolite with him. The man from the north would have got hold of that by all three legs. His feet being tired, he would undoubtedly use this scientific instrument as a bundle of rods—

oak rods—and, having beaten the part you look through into splinters on Cruikback's head, would do his best to break the sticks in a bundle on his back. And I had not the slightest doubt that this man, who was built cubically, would give Cruikback something to remember him by, by way of the shins, the coccyx, the insteps, and the genitals. Perhaps, I thought happily, Cruikback will lose an eye or two?

I got out before the police came, and started to make my way to the station, in order to reach which I had to pass my mother's house. I didn't want to, because I knew that she would be looking out of one window or another, so I went to the other side of the street. And there my Uncle Hugh was waiting for me.

"Skulker!" he cried. "What the hell are you cringing about this locality, sponging off—"

"Hold hard, Uncle Hugh," I said, "where do you get that 'skulk', that 'cringe'? I don't like it. Take it back, or—"

"Or what, you unmitigated cad?"

I said, "In consideration of the respect with which I regard you, the fact that I believe you to be a nice man; in consideration, I say, of the fact that my mother has a high regard for you, and so had my father; in consideration of all these things, let us, as the poet says, kiss and part."

This seemed to exacerbate his irritation, this "kiss and part." The very idea of kissing me was sickening to him; the parting part, suddenly, he did not mind a bit, although he used to like me. He said to me, "Now look here, Daniel. You were a born idiot. That I don't mind. With those bookshops of yours, you made an unmentionable fool of yourself. Well, we are all allowed one mistake. In your show business career, you have been behaving like such an ape that I could tear out the little hair I have left. Write that off as youthful enthusiasm. You went into bucket-shop-keeping—it's in the *London Gazette*—but this, considering your ignorance, I can find an excuse for, if not condone. I always knew . . . Never mind. I repeat, I never knew that you would turn out to be what you have turned out to be. Thank God your father is dead!"

I cried, "You leave my old man out of this!"

"The sweetest girl that ever walked!" he said.

I asked, "*Who* ever walked? What sweetest girl? What's up?"

He said, "Anything but a thief. I promised—"

"To hell with your promises!" I told him. "What the devil do you mean by 'thief'?"

He continued, "And under pressure of circumstances, even this I can overlook. But, you dirty dog, what the devil do you mean by seducing one of the noblest works of God? What do you mean by it, eh?"

I said, "I have seduced no work of God. To whom, or to what, do you refer?"

"Miss Whistler," said he. "Do you deny it?"

"Categorically, I do."

Uncle Hugh shouted, "You swine, you seduced that girl! You took advantage of her!"

"She took advantage of me," I said.

He replied, "You dissipated pig, how dare you speak like that about the lady I am going to marry, you lecherous beast!" and struck me in the face.

He should have placed the blow lower; as it was, I was merely startled, and asked, in the terms of a then-popular song, "How long has this been going on?"

He already regretted having struck me and said, "I'm sorry, Dan, my boy—we're only young once. Being young, we are foolish—we don't know what we have got—we don't know what we ought to be thankful for. It's a question of appreciating your values. Shake hands with me, my boy, and forgive my having beaten you just now. I didn't really mean it, only my back was up."

My first impulse was to tell him that he could not knock the skin off a rice pudding, or fight his way out of a paper bag—a wet paper bag—only, to satisfy his vanity, I said, "I don't think you broke bone. A deep bruise is all. You have a terrible punch, though, but I rode with it. That's why I'm not in an ambulance now."

He said, "Ah, my boy, you ought to feel my right!"

"I'm not so stupid," I said. "But may I ask what all this is in aid of? What's June Whistler to you?"

"I'll tell you frankly, Dan. Man was not meant to live alone. Reciprocity, I say, in life as in business. She needs somebody to look after her. So do I. She's a young lady you can take anywhere. My friends are mad about her. Good yeoman stock, too. She was indiscreet with you, perhaps? . . . Well, I know what it is to be a young dog on the rampage. I didn't mean it when I called you a cad—I'm sure you aren't, really. Only be a good fellow; try not to see June again, will you? She told me, for your information, that she didn't care if she ever saw you again as long as she lived. We are going to be man and wife. . . . God knows what your poor mother will say. . . . I have an option on a little property near Chobham in Surrey. I think I'll build there. June wants a terraced garden and dogs. I know a man whose setter has littered. I'll get her a pair of pups. And she has a sound head for business and a wonderful eye for clothes. Makes 'em all herself. Appreciates good wine. The only girl in the world. Don't laugh," said he, giggling, "but she said that I was the only boy. Come to think of it, my boy, I was very much in the wrong to wallop hell out of you like I did just now; because actually I stole her away from you. I couldn't help it. How are you fixed?" Out came his wallet. "Have a fifty?"

"Got one."

"Have a cigar—quadruple Partagas—take the lot, keep the case! Come up the road and have a brandy?"

I said, "I don't like the look of that pub. There seems to be an ambulance outside."

"Well, better not, perhaps. Now I've got to see your mother.

But never think of me as anything but your old friend. Unwittingly, perhaps, you changed my life."

In spite of a peculiar melancholy that had come over me, I slapped him on the back and cried, "God give you joy! Be happy, old friend!" and went my way into the rain.

There never was a more appalling desolation than Fowlers End when I got back there in the early evening. The twilight was never more sulphurous, the inhabitants never more depraved. But Copper Baldwin was waiting for me in a state of almost uncontrollable excitement. "'Ave a bit o' gin," he said. "I got news for you. Come on in."

It being Sunday, the Pantheon was closed and empty, and the generator was still. A cat, driven to it by the rain, had found its way in, presumably through the office window, and was curled up on one of the eightpenny seats, cleaning its face of traces of a recent drink of milk. Copper Baldwin and the cat had been treating themselves to a little refreshment, only he did not smell of milk. Also, for the first time, I saw him in his best clothes, and he was wearing a hat.

He offered me the bottle: it was not gin but slivovitz. "And where the devil did you get this?" I asked.

"I give an Estonian stoker five bob for it."

I asked, "And where did you meet an Estonian stoker?"

"Round the docks, cocko, round the docks. And I brought you a present. It cost me a ten-pun' note, but cheap at the price." And he took out of his pocket a greasy envelope and said, "Papers, Mr. Laverock—first-class seaman's papers. I got mine. So we can sail as soon as the *Avocado* does, in three days. She's sailing in ballast, boy, for bananas—all the way to Guatemala, son—and what do you think o' that?"

I looked at the papers, which were thick with the grime of years and about as dog-eared as papers can get. "But these," I cried, "are made out in the name of Frank Mudd and signed with a cross! God damn it to hell, Copper—what do you take me for? *Mudd!* No, I mean to say, for Christ's sake, there's a limit to everything! A man can take so much! Mudd!"

"That was the name of the geezer I bought 'em orf. And that's your name for the time being, son. What's in a name? I tell you, it's all fixed. Captain John Williams will take you on nominally —purely nominally, mind—as a member o' the crew for a twenty-pound note. That pays your passage. I'm 'chips,' which means to say carpenter. A rose by any other name would smell as sweet. And mark my words, an *X* is a bloody sight easier to forge than a signature. You can take that from me. I got a bit o' capital now, and for certain private reasons I think I'd better be moving. Oh, and incidentally, so 'ad you. Because O'Toole is out and raising a mob. Out on good behavior, and this I don't like, because my knowledge o' mankind tells me that if a sod like O'Toole behaves 'imself before 'is time is up, 'e's brooding. 'E's itching to get at somebody. That means us. And there are other factors. I 'ave reason to believe the 'busies' are trying to frame me; this I don't like. So what if you call yourself Mudd? A sea voyage is what we need after the stink o' Fowlers End. Read your John Masefield! There we go, and the porpoises playing, with Cuba—"

"You told me all about Cuba before," I said, pretending to be annoyed. But I pocketed the papers, thinking of the "dolphin-torn, the gong-tormented sea" and of the landfall of Guatemala, where the Rio Dolce rolls sluggishly into the gray Caribbean under a burning sky, smelling mysteriously of the inland jungle . . . while the washerwomen in spotless white shout from the shore, and in the evening by the weird light of naphtha flares the loaders pass green stems of bananas, shouting, "*Fruta, fruta, fruta*!"

. . . *So let my name be Frank Mudd*, I thought.

Nevertheless, having had what I assumed to be my revenge upon Sam Yudenow, I felt guilty. I wondered how I could look him in the face. All of a sudden I discovered in him a number of desirable traits: what these were I cannot remember; let us say that I found in myself a lot that was undesirable.

Pig breeds pig and crook begets crook. It is better to be swindled than to swindle. My sense of guilt was excruciating. But what was I to do? I had already involved, as I thought, innocent parties. Was I to demand the return of their profits? I mentioned my state of mind to Copper Baldwin, who, laughing heartily, said that I was the private parts of a female. And when I asked, "What about Sam Yudenow?" he called down such appalling curses on the head of that exhibitor that even I blenched. The Great Curse in the Book of Deuteronomy is chicken feed compared with what Copper Baldwin wished on Sam Yudenow. It was horrible to listen to him. . . . He had drifted back to South America, and to that thin fish with backward-set spines which, attracted by human urine, rushes into the urethra and cannot be dislodged except by means of a jackknife, when Sam Yudenow came in.

I did not know where to hide, I felt so guilty; but he came up to me and held me at arm's length and said, "Above all things give me loyalty. Lavender, let me kiss you!"

I said, "Certainly not."

"Just a little kiss?"

"What's the big idea?"

Then Sam Yudenow made a species of apostrophe, in his fishmonger's voice, which might have been heard a quarter of a mile away, and attracted half the loafers of the neighborhood. Slapping me as if he had me on a slab and shouting as if he were selling me, he bellowed: "Look at this boy! Oh, Jesus, look at this bloody boy! Did I say boy? Back every word I take. I meant man —man, I meant! You know a codfish has seven million cods at one go? Laventory has got more balls than a codfish. A haddock, even. Copper, correct me if I'm wrong, but I could climb all over him.Yipes, but am I wowed! Does Sam pick wrong? Does he, arse holes! No, give me loyalty or buggery, and the hell with it! Lavenjuice, stick by Sam Yudenow and Sam Yudenow will stick by you. Regard your salary—what I mean to say, raised as from a certain date. Believe me, I'll work it out. Don't bother to thank me! You done me a good turn. . . . So can't you even say thank you?"

Copper Baldwin said, "Have you been and done this bastard a good turn? Because if so—"

"I swear I haven't!" I said.

Sam Yudenow said, "Oh, concerning good turns, O'Toole is out miv good behavior and blood in 'is eye. Take the advice of an old fool: get *bofe* elbows around the thvoat, put 'im on the floor face down, get bofe knees in the small o' the back, and tug; when you hear a heavy crack, let go. Okay? You got your instructions? Okay. But in dealing miv this layabout, above all wait for that crack. You'll recognize it; it's like plucking a flower miv a stalk, only louder. Blood comes out o' the nose. . . . Oh, boy, I could kiss you! But I'll come to that in a minute. First inform O'Toole that Sam Yudenow is thus-and-so. Then take measures."

"I'll buy a ruler," said I, attempting irony.

"Copper's got a steel tape. Are you made of money? . . . I want to embrace you. Copper, you too I want to embrace."

"Just try it and see," said Copper Baldwin. But curiosity got the better of him, as it was getting the better of me, and he said reluctantly, "Come clean, piss-face—what's up?"

"I want you should regard your wages as increased. Fair enough?"

"What have I done?" I cried.

"A certain little something that the others 'aven't done," said Sam Yudenow.

"Speak!" said Copper Baldwin, taking out his tomahawk.

"One thing I don't like in the Pantheon, and that's violence. Put that chopper away. You talk to your boss, no choppers—it makes a bad impression, kind o' style. Got that clear? So put it away, I don't like it. You could hurt somebody miv a thing like that. Go on, split my head open; see who's the sufferer! . . . To continue, gentlemen, I could kiss you!"

Copper Baldwin cried to high heaven, "My Gawd, what am I going to do with this bastard?" The Almighty gave no answer, but Yudenow continued:

"One other stroke, I mean of luck, like this I can remember. Bless you! And that was this: some Indian rahamajah wants caviar. We're at war miv Russia—go and get caviar! What's caviar? The roe of a fish: fish eggs. Now there's roe and roe. Herring roe couldn't pass for caviar, neither could cods' roe—the tenxture is too fine—but salmon roe, yes; also lobsters' eggs. The female lobster, all over 'er belly she's got eggs. Later comes the cock lobster and you know what they are. All right, so it's human nature. So long it shouldn't happen in the genevator room. So what do I do? I scrape off a few lobsters, pack the eggs in ice—and a guinea an ounce to Krassin at the Soviet Embassy. I was unspired.

"Also, they ask me for a fish they call an eel pout. Okay, so I give the bastards a conger what I pump up miv a bicycle pump in the bladder. A shilling's worth conger eel—three and a half guineas. Sturgeon I couldn't raise; only I said I had fillets—I gave 'em mackerel out o' season miv a mysterious smile. A guinea a pound, and they should know the difference! It was a veritable *coup d'état*, believe me. Wrapped in seaweed—that was the showman's touch—and delivered in a basket on somebody's head. That shook 'em. This stinkpot, so he comes back miv the empty basket and says to me, 'Jesus Christ!' So I say, joking, 'Mistaken identity. What's up?' So he says, 'When those bloody foreigners saw me coming in miv a basket on my head they called me comrade. That f - - - ing mackerel, they said, was full o' the Craspian Sea. They give me a glass o' methylated spirits and a pound note and called me comrade. It was the seaweed what done it, Mr. Sam—you are a genius!' And so I am."

In something like hopeless desperation, Copper Baldwin said, "I'm sorry, for Christ's sake, but there's only one thing to do with this twot!"

"Before we have discussions," said Sam Yudenow, "I beg you, please, as a gentleman to put dahn that hatchet. Copper, I'm sorry, but I'm made that way. Rahnd Fowlers End they wouldn't mind, but I was brought up under circumstances, and one o' these circumstances was: *Before civilized discussion, do me a favor and put dahn that bloody chopper!* Copper, bury that hatchet. But not in me. . . . I thank you, and a very nice combination tool it is, too—" Sam Yudenow took the tomahawk out of Copper Baldwin's nerveless hand —"good Sheffield steel. Trust you, Copper, to pick a good tool. Why, God save the King, you could *thvow* a job like this! Thus—" and he threw it underhand, so that the sharp head of it buried itself in the lintel of the door. Then he went on: "Do me a favor, don't run for a ladder. A lick o' paint and a bit o' lettering, it could be an off-angle ad for *Dr. Fu Manchu.* You're good boys, you asstimulate my think-box: what the doctors call the 'Kotex.' But enough!"

"The point, come to the bleeding point!" Copper Baldwin shouted.

"Points are dangerous," said Sam Yudenow. "That bastard Booligan put a tack on my chair. Thank Gord I missed it, but if I 'ad got that point—I am a light man—puss would have walloped. And I loathe cats. So I'm a fool? Take advice from a fool, please. Cats are fow. The fowness of cats you 'ave to live to see. Only one kind cat is worse than a male, and that's a female. To change the subject: ever try to get rid (Godbolt aside) of a dead cat? In civilized society, you thvow the cat into Godbolt's. But where will you find society? And what is society? I ask only to be informed. Charleston, black bottom, waltzes—society! But the most classical kind o' cats 'as got blue eyes. Ever see a blue-eyed cat? Simonese, two colors. Copper, believe me, a Simonese—so it roars like a proper little lion; therefore, beware!"

"If you do not come to the point—" Copper Baldwin began.

Sam Yudenow said, "What's he talking about, point? What does the man mean, point? I beg your pardon, Copper, so which were you referring to what point? . . . Okay, to please you I'll come to it. But before I come to this point everybody's wages is practically doubled as from a period to be mutually agreed. Can I say fairer?"

I said, "Talk sense."

Then Sam Yudenow said, "It was wonderful, it was so wonderful! I got that piss-bag by the bloody bladder. Simple enough? You know who I mean: I mean Godbolt. He outsmarted me, he thought, ha-ha! Sure, he chewed my balls off, et cetera, oh yes? Not on your life! . . . Gentlemen, before anything I want you should read the Holy Books. I thank you. So what is the whole philosophy? *Do unto others!* Go on then, do—but let it be 'unto others.' So I'll tell you about 'unto others' as it should be unto you, mind you! Across the road that shitpot, Godbolt, got wind. So what of, did he get wind? Of the property deal at Ullage. Naturally that twicer wants to get in on it, this property deal. That dirty rotten bastard wanted to cut in on me, because Godbolt 'ad his filthy suspicions. So why cut in on me? This I ask you. . . . So, instead o' coming to me like a *Covered Wagon* and offering his hand, what does this crap-hound do? You would scarcely believe this, Lavender, being a gentleman, but this cowson son-of-a-bitch makes inquiries as to whom the Ullage property belongs to. So it turns out, this particular part o' the property belongs to Hacker and Hacker. What this implies you know, eh?"

"Which Hacker?" I asked.

Copper Baldwin said, "What 'Acker?"

"Which, what, who, where, why? Next thing we'll get et ceteras. I will take the *which*. I refer to Hacker the Breaker. As it 'appens, 'e is my wife's brother. Any shame in that? If so, step outside. . . . Now, you are my dear and loyal friends and 'ave stood by me as such. My dear and loyal friends didn't take old

Sammy for a mug: miv one eye open, Sam Yudenow sleeps, if at all. Sam Yudenow is a helpless party; therefore his spies must be everywhere. Believe me, gentlemen, I'm not a strong man. At any minute I could drop. Therefore, in your wife's name put it and make a separate Limited Company. It's the only way to live."

"And what 'ave you been up to now with this Limited Company, you sod?" asked Copper Baldwin.

"Who, me? What's all this? What d'you want? What d'you mean? What're you saying? What d'you know? . . . I'll reply: The answer is, literally, it makes nothing. But you boys 'ave done me a turn, and it is my will that 'enceforward your wages should be increased substantial."

Copper Baldwin said, "The detail, Smallpox, let's 'ave the detail, will you?"

"For you, anything. . . . Well, it seems A.A.A.A. is going to build rahnd Ullage. I told you—"

"*I* told *you*!" cried Copper Baldwin.

"Let us be calm," Sam Yudenow said. "You told me, I told you; no arguments. To continue—I told you A.A.A.A. was setting up in Ullage. If you'd saved your money instead o' plundering it, you could've bought a bit. Never mind. By Sam Yudenow, what is past is past. From the gutter you 'ave come, to the gutter you will go. Whereas, meanwhile, who should get wind of it but that twicer, Godbolt? And what does 'e do, this swine? Like a snake he creeps until he finds the representatives o' Hacker and Hacker. You know 'is style—like Lord Bacon said, 'Some men are born shits, some achieve shitness, and others have it thrust upon them.' Godbolt is all thvee. Behind my back he went to buy me out. And so he did, the rotter, for twelve thousand pounds. And 'ow d'you like that? Miv, mind you, the lease on the Hippodrome at Ullage for eleven thousand pounds! The lengths to which a certain class people will go! As for the depths, don't ask. Lavendrop, it's kind o' disgusting, kind o' style, no?"

"What is?" I asked.

"That people should take other people for fools, that's what I mean. You done a lovely stroke, and believe me, Sam Yudenow won't forget it. . . . But that crab-louse at Ullage, Johnny Wills, to play such tricks with me! Confidentially, between us, d'you know what he actually did? 'E made a bid for the Pantheon—*my* Pantheon! Can human discrepancy rise to lower depths? So all of a sudden Wills is a duke or something? To offer to buy my Pantheon!"

"What did you say to him?" I asked.

"Have I no integrity? What did I say to him! . . . 'Yes,' of course! But it only goes to show. . . . Well, now you got the whole picture. Oh, give me a little profit and a quick return! Go put money into Ullage: no good. And I hate these shady deals; they make bad feelings. . . . Who's got the rest o' the stock?"

"Some firm," I said.

"Daniels, find out. And I'll make it worth your while. I'll substantially raise you. Can a man say more?"

"Not much more," I said.

Sam Yudenow said to Copper Baldwin, "And what are you laughing at like a monkey?"

"Thoughts."

"Mend seats. Think in your spare time."

16

SAM YUDENOW RODE AWAY in his big car but came back before six o'clock with ferocity written in every line of him. Brandishing his fist in my face, he shouted, "Twicer! What is this, a new deal? Fascist! Communist! Anti! F - - - ed pig!"

I said, "Of course, if you want to be offensive . . ."

"To be offensive? Do *I* want? May you drop down dead! I wish you no harm, layabout, only I want you should 'ave black cholera and worms should eat you; nothing more. I'm a reasonable man. . . . What's wrong miv a banker's draft? Why not buy a few shares Daniels Copper? They say, 'No!' So why no—whereas before, meantime, it was yes? Only because suddenly there is mixed in, already, a City firm stockbrokers which they control the majority shares. So who's Whistler? Also Morgan? Whistler and Morgan, answer me that! And who's—? Never mind. . . . What's the point, Laventory and Strype not selling, what, I want to know?"

I said, "Don't ask me."

"And what did you mean, may I ask, by playing a double-

double game miv me and Godbolt? Shut up! A civil question demands a bloody civil answer. Talk, and talk fast. Look me straight in the eyes. Only never let me see the sight o' your face again. Go on. Shut up!" Yudenow was frantic. I found Copper Baldwin's bottle of gin and poured him a glass, which he drank, saying, "Take this muck away!—" handing me the empty glass —"There's too much goings-on around my circuit. Give me a drop more, I ploppitate. After all I've done for mankind! . . . Kind o' style, I mean to say." Gradually, it came out that in the City, he had also stopped at the offices of Anglo-American Automobile Associates; but the latest proprietor of the Ullage Hippodrome, acting on his first and last inspiration (he was never to need another) had been there before him and got to see one of the high executives. Here occurred one of those incidents that make business history: in effect, it was to real estate something like what the interchangeable part was to industry.

The managing director of A.A.A.A., a man named Roper, said he didn't know what Godbolt was talking about. Then he considered the matter—Henry Ford had gone to Dagenham in Essex, A.A.A.A. in secret was investigating various hitherto unusable properties, and Ullage, if added to the list, would appear to involve few landowners, primarily Mr. Godbolt and a Limited Company. As it happened, Ullage he calculated would come out at half the price of the other sites and need no more than two miles of railway line.

God knows what happened thereafter in the City. I was in no mood to inquire of my Uncle Hugh. But even I, in Fowlers End, could not help knowing that Godbolt was dealing for what was to him a fortune, but it was a sum that A.A.A.A. regarded as next door to nothing. Fifty-seven thousand pounds—it was as simple as that: Godbolt had brought Ullage to Roper's attention. For Sam Yudenow the crowning humiliation came several days later when Godbolt called upon him and offered him an immense cigar, which Roper had given him, saying, "Take this. I always knew the Lord would put you on the path of Righteousness." Then Yudenow again had a species of hysterics—but these were nothing, I imagine, to what he had when he heard the outcome of the deal.

I am quite sure that it was Yudenow who, out of sheer spite, fomented what happened next at the Pantheon. It was no longer his property, but he could not keep away from it. I see this as a kind of *crime passionel* with retroactive jealousy at work, saying, *I don't want you any more, but nobody else is going to enjoy you.* Fowlers End will not soon forget that Saturday night. There was something in the air; we knew that the enemy was coming.

Copper Baldwin removed from the pockets of his overalls that hammer-tomahawk-jemmy and went away to hide it, saying in his axiomatic way, "Carry one o' these, and who knows who might take it orf of you? Now *you* wouldn't use a chopper on O'Toole, but O'Toole would use a chopper on you. . . . Mrs. Edwards, get out the jar!"

Trembling from head to foot, Mrs. Edwards fumbled for and found one of those screw-top jars in which fruit is preserved. She poured into it the contents of the till, silver first, screwed the lid down tight, and gave it to Copper Baldwin, who said, "As Sam Smallpox would say, 'Drop it in the laventry system.' I could show 'im a trick worth two of that. But believe me, Dan—while a few of 'em keep us occupied, the others go for the cashbox. . . . Mrs. Edwards, Mr. Laverock says lock up and go 'ome. Where's that bloody little skiver, Johnny Headlong? Just when you want these little bastards, they are never around!"

But at this moment Johnny Headlong crept in from behind with the air of a Red Indian about him, war-painted with excitement, and said in a breathless whisper, "Mr. Laverock—O'Toole's mob is gathering. I counted fourteen, drunk as lords. Pute 'as got an iron bar, the Bull Squires 'as 'is kicking boots on, the Brick Foster—'e's got knuckle-dusters. The rest 'ave all got something, like razors and fings. But O'Toole, '*e*'s relying on 'is mitts and 'is boots." The boy was frantic with excitement. "They been on the beer, guv, so belly-punch. When they leans forward to spew, use your 'ands. Don't worry, I'll stand by you. 'Ave a cigar." And he offered me one of those miniature cheroots that used to sell at six for tenpence.

I said, "Before you go back to the projection room, young Headlong, tell me one thing: where's this mob now?"

He replied, "Like I told you, guv'nor, beering up in the Load o' Mischief."

"Scram," said I. Then, to Copper Baldwin, "Tactically speaking, Copper, I think our best bet is to carry the battle into the enemy's camp. He hits twice who hits first. After all, there's only fourteen or so of them to our two. I'll bet you anything you like that if I take O'Toole and you take another simultaneously, they'll cut and run. Let's try it and see?"

"What, in a confined space?"

"Certainly," I said. "All the better. Look at Horatius, look at Thermopylae—"

"Look at the Load o' Mischief, with three back entrances. Who defends the rear? And where's your lines o' communication? Don't give me no bloody Greeks—Spartans, I beg your pardon—because this is Fowlers End. Besides which, you got a crowded house here, and those bastards mean mischief. That sod O'Toole, 'e's looking for a bull-and-a-cow to end all rows, a proper bundle. . . . Oh, blimey, if only I 'ad five picked men from my squad . . ."

"I say, attack!" I said.

"And I say, defend!" said Copper Baldwin. "Again—but if I 'ad my way I'd turn the lights up, play 'God Save the King,' and give everybody a complimentary ticket for another show. Shut the gaff for tonight."

"*If* you had your way," I said. "If you had your way, you would submit to tyranny, would you?"

"Within reason." We were becoming heated.

"You will admit that this mob violence is bad?" I asked.

"Well, I mean to say, the French Revolution was better than Louis the Sixteenth, and all that. Besides, they'll wreck the joint, that mob. And poor old Sam—"

"Hold hard, Copper, since when was he 'poor old Sam'?"

"You can't 'elp—" he began, and then stopped himself. "Oh, for Christ's sake, this is Wills's 'ouse now! Ain't it funny?" he added, with a sort of wistfulness. "It feels like nothing will ever be the same again. I fell in hate with that man."

I said to him, "Look here, Copper, I'll have no discussion. If I lock the panic bolts, and somebody yells 'Fire!' where are we? If I play 'God Save the King,' and empty the house, where are we? I'll fight them, by God I will, and you'll stand by!" I was really worked up into a state of exaltation now. "And if you think I'm afraid of your Darby O'Kelly O'Toole, so help me God I'll step across the road and haul him out with these two hands!"

Copper Baldwin sighed and said, "Don't waste your time, cocko. 'Ere they come."

Indeed, O'Toole and his friends were advancing upon us in a mob. I had barely time to say, angrily, "This is what comes of talking tactics," when they were at the foot of the steps. With ineffable dignity, I said, "Hello, O'Toole. Glad you brought your friends. Only I'm sorry to say we are full up. Come again another evening, won't you?" Thereupon, Darby O'Kelly O'Toole laughed, and when he laughed he became indescribably sinister.

He had a wide mouth, gaps in his teeth, and a protuberant jaw. His eyes, which were of a strangely pale color, seemed to expand and bulge, while the immense tendons of his short, thick neck were like vibrant strings played upon by the talons of his predatory passions. Laughter in O'Toole produced a chain reaction (as we were later to call it) that seemed to run all over him. I don't know the anatomical terms, but between the lobes of his ears and his eyebrows he threw up a new set of arteries, and between the angle of his jaw and the place where his collar might have been, along corded muscles, appeared something like pale blue worms.

At the same time he conveyed the impression of swelling.

His clothes became too tight for him, his veins got too small for all that his Irish heart was pumping through them; he had more breath in his powerful body than it could conveniently hold and had to let it out in something between a snarl and a glottal stop. While he did this he eased his shoulders, squared his elbows, sniffed, spat, and beckoned. Then Pute stood at his left hand and the Bull Squires at his right, and the Brick Foster brought up in his immediate rear. Behind him were grouped, haphazard, the rest of O'Toole's gang.

(I wish it to be put on record that I believe my first suggestion to Copper Baldwin would have worked; but I was compelled to face the fact that while I was the better strategist, O'Toole was the tactician. There is not the slightest doubt that if, in the time we took to discuss the matter, Baldwin and I had rushed across the street and laid out the ringleaders, nothing would have come of this attack. It is one of the little "ifs" of history; and I am convinced that I am not far wrong in my conjecture that O'Toole would have adjusted his tactics to mine and come back again in double force and twice as angry when I was least expecting him.)

Anyway, there he was, backed by as appalling a group of desperate thugs as I have ever seen in my life—and I have seen quite a few. He came into the vestibule smiling and deliberate. Copper Baldwin spat on the palms of his hands and flexed his knuckles while he made a curious shrugging circular movement with his neck and shoulders, and—there is no other word for it—pawed the floor with the balls of his feet. His eyes were more than half closed, and I could see his melancholy nostrils twitching, if you can call a slow expansion and contraction a twitch. For the sake of his wind he was saturating his lungs with what passed in Fowlers End for air.

As for myself, I remember that a strange tingling chill came over me, and into my mouth crept a taste of bitterness and of blood. To Copper Baldwin, who was beginning to shuffle and dance, I said, "Oh, cut it out, and stand shoulder to shoulder!"—what time I stood like a monolith. Brilliant in theory but inexperienced in action, I couldn't find it in my heart to make the first move. And, savage Liverpool Irish as he was, there seemed to be some psychic plug stopping up O'Toole's temper. Yet he had to loose it; the others were waiting for his first move. Call it a constipation of the temper.

For, contrary to general belief, the Irish are not a fierce fighting people but a cringing and obsequious people—essentially a nation of tradesmen and politicians. They are no more fighters than they are poets, as they claim to be. I suppose that the most formidable of Irish fighters was Daniel O'Connell, who did it under protection in the House of Commons, and the most notable of their poets and singers was Thomas Moore, who made his reputation in London drawing rooms with such stuff as "Oh, Believe Me, If All Those Endearing Young Charms." . . . In battle with an Irishman, watch your shoulder blades. The only really dangerous Irish are, by origin, Anglo-Saxon, Scot, Spanish, and French—and the very Mayor of Dublin, as I write, turns out to be a Jew. And look at De Valera; he had scarcely an Irish corpuscle in his veins. For the rest, the Irish who know how to fight are Scandinavians.

But they have a tradition of wildness they feel they must live up to, although their national weapon is not the shillelagh but the Blarney stone. They cannot even box until they have been at least two generations in America. Before they fight, it is necessary for them to stamp and champ themselves into that state of maniac desperation which they call "getting their Irish up." They can be pacified, I believe, when sober with a little of their own line of talk. Only, when they are sober they seldom want to fight. The Irish are all right: all they lack is another fifty thousand years of evolution to erase the mark of the beast.

I said to the leader of this mob, "Why, I think you must be Mr.

Darby O'Kelly O'Toole." For the sake of atmosphere, I added, "Why, surely now—well, then, Mr. O'Toole, you must be related to the O'Kellys who have a right to call themselves 'kings' in Ireland, and to the famous 'Darby Kelly' they made the song about."

"What of it?"

"Why, then, I should be happy to shake you by the hand and offer you a little something to drink. I am proud to meet the descendants of the O'Kellys and the O'Tooles. Now where is it the O'Tooles come from?" I asked, talking smooth and fast. "Will it be County Clare?"

He was nonplused, but I could sense a certain softening in his attitude. It was that incorrigible boy Johnny Headlong who provided O'Toole with a catharsis for the constipation of his temper by coming between us and, poking him in the face with one of his execrable six-for-tenpence cheroots, shouted in the manner of the early Mickey Rooney, "'Ave a cigar, cock!" O'Toole started out of a dream of peace and knocked the boy out of the way with a backhand blow that might have stunned a donkey.

Copper Baldwin said, "Leave the kid alone, Liverpool!"

"And phwat was that ye called me?" asked O'Toole.

Then the fight started.

I know that when you fight a Liverpool Irishman on the rampage it is best, tactically, to keep your distance, just as you would in the case of a capstan running wild with whirling bars. But consider my predicament: being shortsighted it was essential for me to in-fight. When I boxed at Snellgrove-in-the-Vale I developed what the sportswriters call a "style": I had to see what I was hitting, so I got in close, disturbed my opponent with my right arm, and then brought my left over in a swishing arc. If it landed, there was the end of him; if it did not, there was the end of me. It was all in fun, then; I had no face to spoil, only it was regarded as somewhat *outré*, because we had been instructed in that old English style with the "long left" which has made the

American boxer the master of the world since it is so easy to counter.

I could not walk into the windmill of an O'Toole, so I tried my luck from a longer range than I was accustomed to—and hit Pute, who, as I learned later, had been creeping up behind me.

When I saw him fall and heard his iron bar clanging on the stones of the vestibule behind him, the Spirit of the Lord came upon me. Observing that O'Toole was winding himself up for a roundhouse punch calculated to go through an oak plank, I stepped in and did the same again. I landed—I had aimed at the point of his jaw but hit just under his ear.

I was going to follow with a right uppercut, but he was down, and I grazed the chin of the man immediately behind him, who, because he wore glasses, was nicknamed "Goggles." He at once shouted, " 'Norn 'it me wiv me glasses orn—it's a criminal f- - - ing offense!"

This unmanly protest from a fellow who was carrying eighteen inches of gas pipe so annoyed me that I snatched off his glasses, dashed them to the floor, and punched him on the nose, crying, "Take that, you little wretch!" I believe I remember adding, "You cannot get more out of this life than you put into it."

Copper Baldwin, meanwhile, was engaged with the Bull Squires, and I knew now why Jolly Jumbo's crowd nicknamed him "The Little Ghost" when he fought, bless his heart, for Old Maunder's rent. It was next door but one to impossible to hit him. He was wily as the Peddler Palmer with his box of tricks and tricky as Jimmy Wilde, whom they call "The Ghost with the Hammer in His Hand." Copper Baldwin's blows landed, not hard but frequently.

"Keep close, Copper, for Christ's sake, keep close!" I cried, as the Brick Foster advanced with his knuckle-dusters, and I felt my left arm go numb as one blow caught the point of the shoulder.

Copper Baldwin had picked up Pute's iron bar, with which—

always cautious—he was striking, quick as a snake, not at heads but at chins and collarbones; while I, thanking God that I could still feel my left hand, was doing my best with my right and praying for the police. For Darby O'Kelly O'Toole was getting up, and his face was terrible to see. If ever Irish was up, his was.

But young Headlong came down breathless, shouting, "Phone out of order!" and, with a shrill snarl of rage, threw himself upon O'Toole and (there's Fowlers End for you) bit him in the bridge of the nose and held on like a Staffordshire bull terrier. O'Toole bellowed with anger and pain but could not shake him off.

"Git to the phone box by the pub," said Copper Baldwin, "Call 'Emergency' and git the 'bogeys.' Me an' the kid'll 'old them—on your way back, take the bastards from the rear. You got the weight to bust through, Dan. Remember Gideon!"

I said, "Oh, bugger Gideon. Hadn't I better nip out the back way?"

"Where's your tactics? Don't you know a panic bolt can only be shut from the inside? You ain't opening *my* rear to any f - - - ing assault."

"Tactically speaking—" I began, when a juvenile delinquent struck me on the head with a bicycle chain. Half stunned, I said, "Oh, no, I mean to say, look here!"

Then there came into my mind something I had read somewhere—something to do with Davy Crockett or Abraham Lincoln, or both—and I kicked O'Toole in the belly and gave Pute my heel in the face for luck, confronted the mob and made a noise like a wolf, howling, "Wa-*hooo!* My name is Mister Laverock, but they call me Poison! I chew nails and spit rust! *Yow-eee!* I'm meaner than a rattlesnake and chaw the living buffalo! I hold the spotted painter by the tail and stare out the lynx! *Yip-eee!* Step right up and lay right down—you unutterable cads—because I've got claws like a silver-tip bear! I can run backwards faster than a deer can run forwards, and when I'm mad I'm a one-man wave of destruction! Step right up, gentlemen; bite, bollock, or gouge; come one, come all, single or collective, in the name of democracy!"

Since nobody stepped up for the moment (I think they rather liked this form of address) I elbowed my way through and, in about half a dozen strides, got across the street to the telephone booth near the Load of Mischief, where they were pulling the old wall down. More tactics: I couldn't have them panicking my full hall, so I was heading them off—this brilliant stroke occurred to me, it is true, several days after it happened, but it wasn't bad, really.

The phone booth was one of those old-fashioned ones made of wood on three sides, but with a plate-glass door. This was before the days of dials: you had to lift the receiver, wait for the operator to answer, give your number, insert two pennies, and twist a knob. In case of emergency, you were supposed to say "Fire!" or "Police!" as the case might be, and simply wait.

After what seemed to be an hour, a voice asked, "What number, please?"

"Emergency—police station," I said.

"Please insert two pennies."

"Damn it, I want the police!"

"I have yet to see the situation that is improved by the use of filthy language," said the voice.

"Quick, get me the bloody police!"

"Kindly modify your shitty language and insert two pennies, please." I was fumbling in my pockets. There were florins, half crowns, little silver threepenny bits, halfpennies, and a pound note—but no pennies.

I shouted, "Look, I haven't got any pennies. This is an emergency. This is a matter of life and death. For Christ's sake—I'll fold up a pound note and put it in the slot, only get me the police!"

The voice said severely, "All right, young man, just for taking the Lord's name in vain and using bad language, you can fold up your pound note and stick it up your arse." There was no time to argue the point, because I heard an ominous scraping noise outside.

Darby O'Kelly O'Toole, assisted by the Brick Foster, had lifted a sort of pudding stone, a great lump of old brick and mortar weighing about a hundred and fifty pounds, and together they were poising it in their four horny hands to throw it at me through the plate-glass door. It stood to reason there was nothing for it but to open the door—it opened outward—and fight my way back to the Pantheon. The door of the booth being hinged on the right, I pushed it with my left hand while I lunged with the other. I felt an electric shock; and everything went black and at the same time I heard a rending noise.

They have killed me, I thought. . . .

But then I felt a dragging weight on my right arm. I had forgotten to replace the receiver before hitting O'Toole. All the power of my body must have been behind that punch, because the instrument and pay box, the screws of which must have been rotted already by the stinking winds of Fowlers End, had come out of the wall.

As for what that chipped telephone receiver did to the Irishman's eye, thank God for the darkness that fell, or I might not have had stomach for the rest of the fight. As it was, he fell senseless, letting go that mass of brick and mortar, which fell on the instep of Foster; and he howled to the sky like a coyote.

Behind this pair stood Pute and half a dozen others. I still had the mechanical part of the telephone box in my hand, gripping it by the receiver. My heart beat high. I swung it like a medieval *morgenstern*, bellowing at the top of my voice, and knocked one of the louts into the rubble.

Twirling this interesting weapon around and around, I fell upon the demoralized rear of O'Toole's force, utterly defeating them. The last man I hit, as I remember, was a weasel-faced man in a beret named Jonathan Bible; and he may think himself lucky that I did not land fair and square, or he would not be alive to boast of it.

There was a ricochet off his miserable shoulders and onto the back of his head; whereupon the cord parted and the box went through Godbolt's window in a shower of pennies. The noise of these coins falling on the pavement—not the sound of broken glass, for Fowlers End was used to that—conjured up a host of ectoplasmic creatures, materializations of twilight. They rushed into the jagged breach, looking for loot. Who they were and where they came from I do not know; and nobody knows where they went with whatever they could lay their hands on, because only one was later arrested in the swamp, clutching to his bosom an old-fashioned wire-and-canvas dressmaker's dummy clothed in a coarse chemise. He was a half-wit whose name nobody knew: he didn't know it himself.

Meanwhile, Mrs. Godbolt, who kept saucepans and kettles of water boiling on the stove, emptied them out of the first-floor window on the heads of the mob, while her husband, brandishing a pair of scissors, exhorted them to repent before it was too late. It was something like *The Hunchback of Notre Dame.*

Most of the boiling water fell upon the helmet of a policeman, Inspector Dench, who had arrived just then at the instance of the General Post Office to see who had been mucking about with the telephones; and he assured me later that there is nothing more agonizing to wear than a policeman's helmet soaked in boiling water. He roared like a lion and tore his helmet off.

Then, I suppose, he remembered the years that immediately followed the end of World War I, when dogs had to be muzzled on account of an outbreak of rabies. Policemen were instructed, if they saw a foaming dog with its tail between its legs, to take off their helmets, thrust them out for the dog to bite, and then, having warned the dog, use their batons.

He took off his helmet with a loud cry, thrust it into the face of one of the looters—who, it transpired, was a pregnant servant girl looking for diapers—and hit her on the shoulder with his truncheon. Later, before he was relegated to duty in some even more deserted place, he swore by the Almighty God that there was froth on her lips and she had a tail.

I got back to the Pantheon twirling nothing but the telephone receiver on the end of a bit of flex; and there was Sam Yudenow, embattled. He was fighting like a fishmonger, and for what he shouted I must refer you to one of those "Dictionaries of Unconventional Language."

". . . Take away my sodding living?" he cried. "So what'll become of my wife and children, loafers? Go make the salt-o'-the-earth fat on the dole, the scum! Don't be working-classes, shitpots—find a job! Come on, you poxy pigs, come on! . . ."

It was to be noted that while Sam Yudenow was hurling all the invective and doing a species of belligerent tap dance, Copper Baldwin was throwing most of the punches. Then, when I attacked from the rear with what was left of the telephone, Miss Noel came out—something to haunt your dreams—crying drunk and swinging that three-legged piano stool that was raised and lowered by means of a wooden screw.

At this, we all fell back, friends and enemies alike; and Inspector Dench came in, followed by a sergeant and four constables. "Any trouble here?" he asked.

Sam Yudenow said, with irony, "Tvouble? Don't make me laugh, I got a cvacked lip. This ain't tvouble, it's a rehearsal. Tvouble! Tickle me under the arms, I want to giggle."

"Isn't that blood I see on the floor?" asked Inspector Dench.

Sam Yudenow started to say "Sherlock Holmes—" but Copper Baldwin interposed, "What the 'ell would blood be doing on the floor? Tomato ketchup!"

The Inspector asked, "And what would tomato ketchup be doing on the floor of the lobby?"

"Vestibule!" said Sam Yudenow.

"Taste it and see," I said.

Frowning at me, Sam Yudenow said, "I'm serving a high-class brand nourishing snack—Greenburgers! So they need a bit tomato sauce? A crime? Try one; see! Lavendorpf, half a dozen special Greenburgers, *miv*! . . . What d'you mean, miv *what*? Miv a slice ham, miv a slice cheese, miv tomato sauce. . . . Copper, wipe up. . . . Where's that bloody boy?"

He was referring to Johnny Headlong, who had disappeared. Copper Baldwin looked sad. His expression said, *I did not think young Johnny would have turned yellow. . . .*

Inspector Dench said to me, "Your mouth's bleeding. So are your knuckles. What's the cause of that?"

I said, hastily improvising, "I've got what they call 'The Blood Disease.' "

He said, keenly, "It doesn't, by any chance, get caused by a beetle? Does it attack potatoes?"

"The Bourbons and the ruling houses of Spain and Russia have it," I said.

"Paint it with iodine. What are you doing with that telephone receiver?"

"It came loose in my hand."

"Under what circumstances?"

"Something must have been wrong with the line."

"Isn't that blood I see on your cuff?"

Copper Baldwin rushed out, scooped up a fingerful of it, which he held under the Inspector's nose, saying, "Tomato—taste it." When the Inspector declined, Copper Baldwin seemed to lick it himself—that is to say, he offered himself the forefinger but sucked the third finger—and said, "Lovely, tell your mum."

Now Godbolt came in, struggling for breath, crying, "Police! Inspector! I'm a leaseholder, a freeholder, and a copyholder; I'm a ratepayer and a taxpayer; and I demand—"

"Now I'll tell you what," said the Inspector. "Better be careful how you interrupt an investigation: I've got my eye on *you!*"

Then there was brought in a tray of Greenburgers. Reinforced with everything that could be found to put in them, they were more than doubly repulsive. The Inspector took a bite, and said, "Not bad at all."

He took another bite. "Might go better with a mustard pickle."

"Thank you for this advice," said Yudenow. "This I got to remember.... Laveridge, make a note—mustard pickle! ... Maybe, Inspector, a bit chuntney?"

Everything was going well, but then that boy Headlong had to choose this moment to dash into the vestibule, hard put to it to breathe, gasping, "Okay, Mr. Laverock. I run to Ullage. The Ullage mob's on the way, and oh Jesus, will we do 'em! Jack Palmtree's got a Woolworth's chopper an' 'e swore on 'is muvver's grave 'e'd chop O'Toole's—" Then he saw the Inspector and said, in an unnaturally casual voice, "Ahem. Just thought I'd warn you, Mr. Laverock. Better get up to the rewinding room now. ... 'Ave a cigar, Inspector?"

Inspector Dench said, "No."

Headlong had to explain in a rasping whisper: "I'm sorry if I done somethink wrong, Mr. Laverock. But if you play one side orf against the other, ain't there a rule o' war?"

Sam Yudenow said to him, "Upstairs!" Then, to the Inspector, obsequiously, "Another Greenburger, just a little one? ... Copper, get mustard pickles...."

So it came to pass that just as the ambulance came to pick up O'Toole and one or two of his friends, the Ullage boys turned up with war whoops, armed to the teeth with homemade weapons, and found themselves confronted by Inspector Dench, a sergeant, and four constables, all smelling strongly of Greenburgers.

The invaders were dragged away with imprecations. Then "Laid in Lavender" came to an end; and we played "God Save the King."

"It's me for the high seas," said Copper Baldwin.

"Me, too," said I.

Epilogue

"Well, cheer up, cocko," Copper Baldwin said. "You got your passage and you got your papers. Now work it out this way: for a lousy twenty-pound note you travel like a gentleman; and for a dirty ten-pound note you got your papers. We all got our money back, and to spare. Cheer up, young 'un, cheer up."

But I kept looking one way and another, mostly at the receding coast line, which, I believed, I should never see again. Before me lay the great gray sea. I put my forehead on the rail and wept.

I did not know why, because we had given up love of country in those years—love of anything. But it was as if I saw before me something like homesickness in perspective.

Copper Baldwin said, almost in a whisper, "I know 'ow it is, son, but you've got to face it. Face it, 'old on to your cash. Only face it. And now I *must* get below."

In a broken voice I said, "But my papers. They're in a silly name."

"What's in a name? I got to get below. See you."

I settled myself to look at the wake that fanned out in foam to the coast of England, with which, in spite of all it had done to me, I found myself in love. Now I wanted to go back, to starve for her if need be. But somebody took me by the shoulder and spun me round.

He was a gigantic man with a fiery face and icy eyes: John Williams, Master, better known as "Kicking Jack" Williams. "Admiring the scenery?" he asked.

"Kind of pretty," I said.

He shouted, "Keep your bloody mouth shut when you speak to me! Get below, you little bastard!"

"I paid my passage," I said.

"Passage? What passage? I've got your papers. What d'ye mean, passage? You're one of my crew, and your name is Frank Mudd. Bugger off before I flatten you."

"You took twenty pounds off me—" I began.

"This," he said, "I have never heard of. Your papers say Frank Mudd, trimmer. Got it? Trim coal, or tough as you think you are—" and he hit me with a right hook to the jaw, knocking me down.

I saw his right foot describe a little circle, poising itself; then he let it down lightly and shrugged gently as if to say, *Where's the sense in smashing up a hand?*

"Get up," he said wearily. "Off your arse, you, and this is the last time I'll be lenient with you. Get below!" I struck him with all my force on the side of the head, and hurt my hand.

He said, "Be sensible. I could stand a week of playing patty-hands. Now will you get below, or shall I put you there?"

There must have been some trace of sympathy in his nature because, seeing me cast a last glance at the land, he said, "Gets you like that at first. Pity."

And then he kicked me—scientifically, not to maim me—so that I sprawled six feet away.

So I went below.

ABOUT THE AUTHOR

GERALD KERSH *wrote his first book at the age of seven and published it privately in a limited edition of one copy, bound in his father's brocade waistcoat. He tore up his second and third literary efforts but, at twenty-three, found a publisher for his fourth, a novel. Unhappily, he was sued by four uncles and a cousin who had seen the manuscript, and the book was withdrawn. But Mr. Kersh persevered, to the tune of five thousand magazine articles, three thousand short stories, and twenty-three books, including the best-selling* Night and the City, *which was made into a film, and* Fowlers End, *his latest. He is also the author of the famous World War II poem "A Soldier: His Prayer," an excerpt of which can be found in* Bartlett's Quotations, *woundingly attributed to Anonymous.*

Mr. Kersh was born in 1909, in Teddington-on-Thames. He was, he says, a morose and tearful child but uncommonly hardy. He first gave evidence of his iron constitution at the age of four, when, after being declared dead of lung congestion, he sat up in his coffin. During the London blitz, he was bombed. Later, serving as a war correspondent attached to SHAEF, he was buried alive three times without ill effect.

He has lived in England, France, South America, the Barbados, and Italy. He is married and now a resident of New York City, where his military bearing (a token of service with Her Majesty's Coldstream Guards), his sartorial splendor (waistcoat, walking stick, and fedora), his powerful frame (he was once a professional wrestler), his compelling voice (he is a raconteur in the spellbinder tradition), and his handsome beard (he will not discuss it) make him an extravagant delight to his friends and an astonishment to strangers.